THE VALKYRIE COVENANT

VALKYRIE COVENANT DUOLOGY
BOOK ONE

J. A. TOWNSEND

ISBN-13:
979-8-9911503-1-6

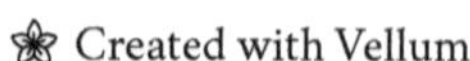 Created with Vellum

Idirhalla

THE GREAT HALL
NORTH DISTRICT
WEST DISTRICT
CAPITAL ISLAND
ROMAN DISTRICT
SOUTH DISTRICT

OLUNDY

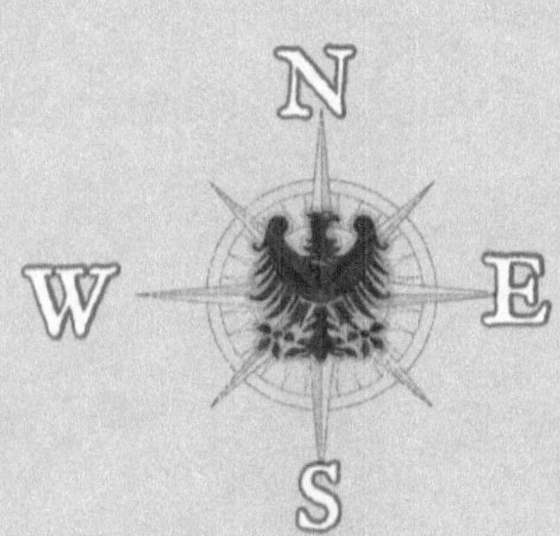

N
W
E
S

To Justin, for a lifetime of support, and my friends for their unwavering confidence.

CHAPTER
ONE

There is a bird trapped in the chimney.

As if today hasn't been a chaotic mess already, now I have to save a bird. Its frightened flapping and the scraping of its talons across the stones elicit throbbing in my temples. But when I hear the muffled cawing, my heart plummets into my stomach.

Badb.

The goddess associated with crows and ravens, harbinger of doom and death. My unusual upbringing is not ideal for situations such as these. The terror of what the omen could mean cuts through the usual dull ache of my grief.

Unfortunately, this isn't even the first disaster of the day.

No, the chaos began bright and early, trying to coax Gran into eating her breakfast.

Breakfast that was subsequently thrown across the dining room. The puddle of oatmeal now staining the blue and cream rug. That was followed by her brandishing her pillow as a shield and a candlestick as a sword when I tried to get her dressed.

But rather than tackle the trapped bird alone, I concede defeat and decided to enlist our groundskeeper, Torin, into my bird-saving crusade. Torin's family has served as the groundskeepers since the construction of Branch Hall some 500 years ago. However, we affectionately call the estate *"The Hall."*

A plume of ash and soot rains down into the fireplace grate, and my anxiety for the life of the bird ramps up. If the poor creature dies before I have even attempted to save it, Badb will make sure the rest of my days are cursed. I cast my eyes towards Gran, who is settled in her favorite wingback chair, a floral shawl tucked tightly over her narrow shoulders. Her long silver hair is braided firmly up into her signature coronet to avoid obscuring her slightly unfocused, sky-blue eyes. She reaches out a steady hand and plucks a piece of her puzzle up before placing it in its rightful place. And that is all I can account for my small victories today: *she's dressed and calm.*

Since her diagnosis, I haven't felt comfortable leaving her side for too long when it's only us two home. The fear of her wandering off and becoming lost or, worse, injuring herself, plagues my every thought. Lizzie, Gran's live-in nurse, has today off, and with no therapies scheduled for today, I won't have anyone coming to help soon. So, I'll be taking a bit of a risk leaving her unattended for any length of time, but this might be a life-or-death situation for the poor creature and, of course, a curse on my future.

The sounds of the trapped bird grow louder, and Gran flicks her eyes toward the fireplace. "Guards used the door in my day," she mutters under her breath, before returning to the puzzle. *Shit,* she's noticed the bird.

Deciding it's worth the risk, I back slowly from her chair before turning and sprinting down the main hallway, one of my favorites in the house. The high ceiling has large timber beams spanning across the width. The wood was milled from trees on our own grounds, according to Torin. Portraits of my ancestors spanning centuries and gorgeous landscapes of the estate's gardens flash by as I run. The expansiveness and wealth of the

Hall still amaze me, and the oak staircase I race by is one of its most remarkable features. It boasts intricately carved poppies, ravens, ivy, and various symbols reminiscent of Viking runes.

I slow my pace into a jog to make the right turn into the servant's area that makes up the back entrance. But as I burst through the back door, the beauty of the garden causes me to stop in my tracks.

Do I really need to sprint the whole way there?

It's only a modest trek through the southern garden, past the curving stone wall, and through a small wooded area to where Torin's cottage is located. So I could sprint the whole way there, but it's really not that far. Besides, it's not like the Gods can take any more from me, right? My parents are already dead. It's also a rare clear day, and the smell of freshly tilled soil and early blooming flowers gives off the illusion of new possibilities. Inhaling slowly to calm my already burning lungs, I decide to continue on to Torin's at a much slower jog to enjoy the surrounding scenery.

The rapid beating of my heart draws forward a story my parents used to tell me of a magical land far away, surrounded by towering mountains and majestic waterfalls that cast rainbows around the entire realm. I push the memory aside and pick up the pace, not wanting to be away from Gran for too long and not really wanting to deal with my grief any further.

But details of the story burst through my mind again: winged women soaring in the sky, guarding a city made entirely for warriors.

I wish I could fly far from here.

The magic of the story is overshadowed by the cloud of my sorrow hovering at the forefront of my mind. My parents were so full of life and vitality that it still seems incomprehensible to me that they're no longer here. They seemed so utterly invincible to me, almost otherworldly. Naturally, I never pictured a moment without them in my life.

I try my best to keep my grief tightly bottled up, but it's been challenging to hold it together. When Gran has rare moments of lucidity and mentions how my eyes are the same dark blue color as my mom's, I feel myself breaking. What hurts even more than the comparison, though, is when she's having uncontrollable outbursts during her denser memory fog, and she calls me Bryn, my mom's name.

The pain of those moments spears through the dull ache of their loss.

A white daffodil peeking through the grass catches my eye as I jog by. The beauty of it reminds me that not every moment here has been full of heartache. I'm so absorbed in my own little world that I almost miss the dark green Land Rover parked outside Torin's cottage.

It's the very loud, gravelly caw from a nearby bird that brings my attention up from the path and around to my current surroundings. The caw sounds like a raven, but I haven't seen any ravens since I've been here. I scan the nearby trees, trying to locate the bird. A weird prickling sensation washes over my skin.

I'm being watched.

When I finally spot the surprisingly large raven, it's perched right above the cottage and is, in fact, watching me.

My stomach churns with dread. If the bird in the chimney is also a raven and not a crow, that would mean it's a sign from the Father, *Odin*. His two ravens symbolize thought and memory as if I haven't been struggling with that.

Hopefully, it's not this raven's friend currently stuck in our chimney, but it does appear to be judging my slow pace for help.

Shrugging off my thoughts of watchful gods and judgmental birds, I carry on. I've almost reached the oak door of the gray stone cottage when it swings open, and Torin steps out into the dappled sunlight. Although he's pushing his mid-sixties, he's still a formidable man with broad shoulders, a tall stature, and tanned skin from the hours he spends tending the Hall's garden. He settles his flat cap over his cropped chestnut hair, and his honey-brown eyes settle onto me. A hint of worry creeps into them, and his shoulders slightly tense as he addresses me.

"Ah! Miss Helena, is everything okay with Miss Adi?"

The raven makes a deep clicking squaw that interrupts my reply. Torin quickly cuts his eyes to the beast that's now perched on the low branch of the birch tree, its ample weight causing the branch to sag.

I clear my throat, trying to reign in the scold I want to give the creature. "Hi, no, Gran's fine, but I seem to have a visitor trapped in my chimney and our friend up there." I gesture to the bird. "Wishes to inform you that I didn't run fast enough down here to ask for you to join my bird-saving crusade."

Torin chuckles a bit, his shoulders sagging in relief, but his eyes flick to the raven again. "Ye wouldn't believe how often that happens. Let me get my net, and I'll be happy to get that squared away for ye, Miss Helena."

A slight noise of disapproval slips from my lips before I can stop it, and Torin chuckles. He knows I hate being called Helena, and I've reminded him several times since I've been back that it's Lena now.

But before I can correct him, he smiles softly at me. "Lena," he corrects, and I smile gratefully in return.

"Thank you so much for your help! I'd hate for the poor thing to die up there." I add on the last bit a little loudly, hoping the nosey raven hears that I am trying my best.

During one of my mom's many lectures on birds, she taught me that ravens are notoriously intelligent creatures and can memorize faces. I'm hoping he, or maybe she, can tell I'm making an effort here. The last thing I need right now is a bird with a vendetta or a watchful God.

Torin ducks inside to get his net, and I stand at his threshold, peering in.

"Is Lachlan here?" I call loudly.

My stomach is a riot of butterflies as I hope for even a glimpse of the gorgeous man Torin's adopted son has grown into. Peeking around the stone cottage, I observe the distinctly masculine decor. The mismatched furniture and animal heads haven't changed at all since I was a child. But Lachlan has; he looks nothing like the scrawny kid I remember from my youth, except for his eyes. They're still the same gorgeous green that evokes images of an evergreen forest, but somehow more magical, like a forest from a fairytale.

"Nae, he's not here," Torin calls as he shuffles back to the front door.

I sag a bit with defeat and take a step back, allowing him to walk through and close the door behind him. I've only seen Lachlan a handful of times since being back here. There was a hint of attraction thrumming between us. *Or maybe just from me.* But that's nothing new. I've always had a crush on him. Only now it had almost begun to seem like he was beginning to see me as something more, too.

"Oh, I saw his truck and thought he was here." I flick my thumb at the truck parked in the driveway.

Torin leans around me, surprise lighting his eyes when he spots the truck. "Huh, well, he's not inside. He must've ridden with one of his crew members to town."

I purse my lips, disappointment washing through me. Lachlan is a contractor and is in very high demand, managing many of the historic manors between here and Orkney, where he now lives.

We walk side by side, our pace quick, on the way to the Hall, and I fill him in on Gran's fits that have occurred today. Torin grunts his disapproval when I finish telling him all about my exhausting day so far.

As we make our way back up to the southern wall and enter the garden, a light breeze ruffles the lavender petals of the wisteria blooms, that twine up the gate, their lovely flowery fragrance filling my nose.

The birds chattering in the trees add an ambiance of tranquility as Torin opens the back door for me and we make our way inside. When mumbling reaches our ears, we share a look of confusion.

A few words carry down the hall as Gran whispers, "You're too big for the chimney now, my dearie."

But that's all I am able to hear before we round the corner into the room. I spy the bird I thought was stuck in the chimney, now settled on Gran's right shoulder.

The image before me takes a moment to register in my mind before I sputter out, "Gran! What is—are you ok?!"

My hands clench into fists at my sides and my eyes widen as I take in the absurdity before me. This raven isn't nearly as large as the one by Torin's house, but it's still a sizable creature resting on Gran's small shoulder. Fear floods my body and I'm torn between running away screaming or throwing something at the bird to get it away from her.

But a quick glance over at Torin, to see him trying very hard to master his face and conceal a grin, has my panic stalling. I guess this isn't a dire situation after all, but a humorous one. How many times does one see a wild bird perched on someone's shoulder? All I can imagine is grisly bird attacks, with talons and beaks, damaging eyeballs.

Gran slowly turns her head my way, annoyance simmering in her eyes. "I'm just talking to a friend. Can't you see he's excellent company?"

The raven turns in my direction and tilts its head. *Is it agreeing with her?* My lips slowly part, and my eyes bulge.

Realization slams into me, two ravens. I'm in for a world of trouble. Torin begins chuckling, and I whip my head back towards him in utter disbelief.

"Looks like I won't be needing this after all," he says and

leans the net against the wall. "Miss Adi, would ye and your new friend,"—he points to the raven—"like to take a walk about your favorite garden?"

Gran gracefully stands from her chair, a queen rising from her throne, and takes Torin's offered arm. She soothingly dotes on the raven as they pass me. The state of the room now lays bare before me. I don't even try to stifle my groan.

Ash and soot rained all over the hand-scraped wood floors and antique furniture. A splattering of what I assume to be Gran's tea is flung about the cream-plastered walls, the puzzle on the table, and various spots on the sage green damask curtains. My left eye begins twitching with each calamity. I know it could have been much worse; there could be bird poop everywhere or a dead bird on the rug, cementing my cursed future from Badb or the Father, now that I know there are two ravens.

But still, this was the cherry on top of an already challenging day.

The sinking feeling conjured by vengeful gods is slowly beginning to dissipate, leaving way for the anxiety that slithers its way up from the pit of my stomach as I take in the amount of cleaning that has just landed in my lap. Perhaps I've overreacted, and it wasn't an omen after all, and it was just typical bad luck.

I wasn't always this way; I didn't use to have such crippling anxiety and fear. But in the last few weeks, Gran's disease has become chaotic, and her outbursts more violent. I don't really have the nerves to handle the conflict this disease brings, and that's all I've been doing lately. Most of my life before my parent's deaths was uncommonly peaceful. So, I didn't develop the necessary skill set for battle.

Gran, however, is a formidable opponent, an extremely battle-hardened woman. She should be running a country or coordinating war strategies, not wasting away from vascular dementia.

The mundane task of cleaning begins to soothe away any lingering anxiety. But the state of all this almost ruined priceless antique furniture makes my heart ache. I rub a hand across my chest and take slow breaths. I didn't grow up wealthy. Although my parents and I were supported by a trust fund, thanks to Gran, we lived very meagerly. Only kept what we could easily pack as we flitted from place to place. There was no limit to our travels, as my parents often combined my schooling with whatever adventure we were currently experiencing.

This is actually the longest time I've ever stayed in one place. I could have continued our way of life and traveled wherever I wanted, but it felt unbearable on my own. Besides Lachlan, I've never had any friends. When you live in a very religious-dominated country, as a pagan, people find you strange and don't really want their children around you. Because of that, when I did reach adulthood, I had a really hard time connecting with anyone else my age.

The loneliness eventually became debilitating, and seeing as the only people I have left live here, it was a natural next step. The last five months have begun to give me the purpose I so desperately needed while drowning in the abyss of my grief.

My legs burn as I bend down to plug in the vacuum cleaner to finish tidying up the mess. My jog to Torin was the most physical activity I've done in some time, and my poor muscles have begun withering away from the lack of use. I used to climb mountains and spar with my parents, and now I can barely jog the quarter mile to Torin's. *Pathetic.*

The light ringing of the doorbell breaks through the sound of the vacuum, and I tip my head back, groaning loudly.

When I swing the door open, I see none other than my saving grace standing on the worn flagstone steps—Lachlan. My breath catches in my throat and my heart begins to beat erratically. He's so tall, he's nearly eye level with me from where he stands, three stairs down on the stoop. The light breeze ruffles his longer, dark, unkempt hair, and my fingers flex against the door frame, aching to reach out and touch the silken tresses.

"Key," he breathes, his eyes dancing as he takes me in. "Are ye alright?"

The familiar cadence of his Scottish accent causes my blood to heat, but more than that, my heart swells at his use of my childhood nickname.

Gran took to calling us Lach and Key, partially because we were always attached to each other and partially because my naturally sunny disposition always brought Lach out of his surly one. My eyes line with silver at his obvious concern, and I quickly usher him inside and into the parlor.

"Not really, it's been a day," I complain, trying to hold myself together. "Gran's having a rough time. She's been yelling and throwing things; not wanting to bathe this morning or eat, and of course, she did not want to get dressed. It was a battle to get anything done, and then I finally got her settled in the parlor with one of her puzzles, and I heard a poor bird trapped in the chimney—"

"A bird?" He asks, his eyebrow arching.

The motion causes my eyes to lock onto his, the familiar pools of green wreaking havoc on my already overworked heart.

But I nod and forge on. "I had to go get your dad for help, and the whole time, I'm worried about leaving Gran in the house alone, and then when we got back to the manor, the bird was on Gran's shoulder! She was talking to it, but all I could think about was it attacking her!"

His eyes crinkle at the corners, his smile carving through his granite-hewn bone structure as he chuckles at my hysterics. It makes my entire body tingle when he looks at me like that.

"Looks like I got here just in time to be the hero then; what do ye need?"

I motion to the drawing room. "It's fine now. I got it all cleaned. It's just been an emotional day."

Lachlan nods as he takes in the state of the room and stoops down to pick up a black feather I must've missed. The motion has his muscles flexing through his long-sleeved shirt, and I stifle a sigh. But a dull ringing begins building in my ears, and I wonder if I'm going to have a panic attack from the stress of the day so far or from the attraction I feel towards him.

As he stands upright, he turns slightly towards me and I glimpse an emerald-colored jewelry box in his other hand. The annoyance of the ringing climbs higher now, bordering on a piercing shrill. My eyes zero in on the box in his hand as he holds it out to me. I look up at his face to see his lips moving, but his voice doesn't permeate the shrill sound. I'm doing my best to act normal, but the ringing isn't lessening; my breathing shifts into quick pants as my panic rises.

"Did you say something?" I ask.

But I must have yelled because I see Lachlan's face break into a smile and then his shoulders shudder in what I assume is laughter. I tug an earlobe, hoping to ease some of the pressure, and it works as the ringing begins to subside. When the sound abruptly cuts off, I heave a sigh of relief.

Lachlan repeats, "I said I got ye a present. It's from the antique shop in town." He scrubs the back of his neck with his other hand and shrugs. "I ken ye like the old stuff, and I wanted to get ye a homecoming present. Well, belated homecoming present." He holds the box out closer to me, and I take it in both hands, beaming at him.

"You didn't have to do that," I gush.

But secretly, I'm thrilled he's bought me a gift and remembered my love of antiques. I gently lift the lid off the box and stifle a gasp. Nestled inside is the most stunning, ancient-looking gold medallion attached to a thin gold chain. The medallion is about the size of a coin, with etched runes swirling around a poppy. My mouth drops open, and it takes a moment for me to be able to speak.

"Lachlan, I can't—I can't accept this. It must've cost a fortune," I breathe, looking up at him. His eyes are full of an emotion I can't quite place.

"I insist, Key."

I shake my head in disagreement, but my eyes are locked back onto the enchanting necklace. Lachlan slips the necklace from the box in my hands and unclasps the chain, holding it open in front of me.

"Allow me," he murmurs.

I blink up at him in shock, my mouth slowly parting. Amusement dances in his eyes before he steps around me. The movement has brought him close enough that his familiar scent wraps around me. Storm clouds and cedar fill my nose and chase away my lingering doubts as I breathe him in.

In a trance, I slowly drag my golden brown hair to one side and drape it over my shoulder, out of the way, so that Lachlan can settle the necklace around my throat. The medallion doesn't look heavy, but as soon as it's clasped around my neck, a small weight presses upon me, like a cloak has been wrapped around me. Grasping my shoulders in his large hands, I feel a light, comforting squeeze before he leans down to press a chaste kiss to the side of my head.

Lachlan whispers into my ear, "Welcome home, Key."

I delicately stroke the medallion resting on my chest and turn my head to gaze up at him. Our cheeks nearly touch at the closeness, and I lean back, pressing against him.

Something flickers in Lachlan's eyes, but I'm drawn to his lips, the curiosity of what they would feel like against mine burning through me. When I search his eyes again for even a hint that he's thinking the same thing, I'm a bit saddened not to find my feelings wholly reflected in them. Slowly, I withdraw, bringing the walls that had kept me safe every time we had to leave another town firmly back into place. I'm a fool. He's my oldest friend, my only friend, and I shouldn't put us in situations like this, no matter how much I want to.

"Well, if ye dinna need me here, I better get back to the crew," he mutters quickly. "But I'll see ye at dinner on Sunday, right?"

My smile is hesitant and my cheeks burn with embarrassment, but I nod. "Of course, it's your turn to cook."

He smiles broadly at that, his eyes warming and the corners of them crinkling again. As soon as he's out the front door, I replay the incident and how completely stupid it was over and over. Lachlan didn't lean into the almost kiss, but he didn't pull away either. *Could it be possible for him to feel the same?*

We didn't stay in close contact, but there was always a shared connection when we were together. No matter the distance or the time we spent apart, we always found ourselves right back where we had left off. It has always been so easy being together. I don't know how I feel about jeopardizing a friendship like that.

But the attraction.

I long to have a partner like what my parents found in each other. To be loved, cherished, and understood. It wouldn't hurt for him to be tall, dark-haired, and gorgeous. I roll my eyes at the thought.

When I finally track Gran and Torin down in the kitchen, they're putting the kettle on to refill their cups.

Gran glances up when she hears me approaching and smiles broadly at me. "Hello, dearie."

I'm surprised by her mood change since I've been gone, but I don't let on. A large part of me is relieved she's not calling me Bryn.

"Hello, Lachlan stopped by," I respond to her and Torin, who's studying me with a perplexed expression.

I toy with the medallion around my neck, and Gran's face

turns white as a ghost's. She lurches out of her chair, her teacup sloshing tea as it smacks against the granite countertop.

"Where did you get that?" Each word is pronounced sharply as she points at my necklace. I flinch at her commanding tone. It's a voice I've never heard from her before.

"Uhhh…Lachlan just gave it to me as a welcome home present. He bought it from an antique shop," I answer, shifting between my feet. The tension in the room is thick; Gran's features haven't softened, and her eyes bore into me like I have more to tell.

"Heirloom," she whispers.

"Gran…is everything alright?"

Her mouth parts as if she's going to reply, but she quickly shuts it.

"Did you say heirloom? Do you know where this came from?" I press, pulling the necklace higher so she can see it more clearly. She takes a small step back, and like a wave receding, the small amount of clarity in her eyes vanishes.

Her disgruntled expression slips away, leaving behind only a subdued, bland smile. "My dear," she trills and pats my cheek as she walks past me and out of the kitchen.

Torin and I are left staring at each other for a moment.

"What was that?" I ask, trying to grapple with what transpired.

Torin shakes his head before grumbling and leaving the kitchen as well. The moment is set aside as I track down Gran. Then it's a constant battle to keep her settled for the rest of the day.

CHAPTER
TWO

The reoccurring nightmare that has haunted me for the last 5 months is still lingering when I struggle to get out of bed the next morning. It always plays out exactly how it had in real life: a police cruiser turning onto the gravel lane of the cabin we had rented for winter. Two officers approach the front door, their heavy boots thudding loudly against the front porch, announcing their arrival long before they knock on the door.

I see it happening as if I'm floating above my body. The heavier set officer removed his cap, head hanging, the younger slender officer stuttering out the words I never expected to hear. The scene flashes forward to me standing in a cold morgue between the two sheet-covered bodies of my parents.

It's weird, but I remember initially being relieved they were beside each other, even here.

In my dream, I don't relive seeing them uncovered, thankfully. The bruised and nearly unrecognizable faces of the people who meant everything to me are enough to make my stomach churn even now. The coroner mutters something about an autopsy, but explains that this was the most gruesome motor-cycle accident he's ever been called to.

I shake my head, shock numbing my tongue. The cold of the morgue burrows down into the marrow of my bones. My dad had incredible reflexes and rode with the utmost care, especially with my mom.

How could this happen?

My chest is a hollow gaping hole.

Luckily, Lizzie is on duty as I creep from the Hall. My feet lead me down a narrow path that takes me to the stream on the south end of the property. I need to be close to my parents today. My mood is reflected in the weather. The clouds are a thick gray, blotting out the sun and casting a chill in the air.

I tighten my robe around me and meander along the path.

My childhood memories seem to be the only thing I cling to for solace lately, which is why they have led me here to the ancient pine tree that stands close to the water's edge.

When I was little, my mom told me it was a fairy tree and that if you left an offering for the fairies, they would offer you favor. I pull a scrap of pale blue ribbon from my robe pocket and tie it into a bow before placing it at the base of the tree.

I stand there a moment, closing my eyes, and send up a prayer to whichever God may be listening.

"I'm lost," I cry. "I have no purpose and no dreams, and I miss them so much." A tear slips down my cheek. "Show me the way," I whisper.

The wind carries my words away.

The sun breaks through the dark morning clouds, bathing the land around me in its glow. The sun's warmth attempts to burn away my gloom as well, but I don't allow it.

Turning on my heel, I hurry back to the house, not paying attention to the ribbon that has vanished.

My room is on the second floor and overlooks the front entrance to the Hall. It's a spacious, cozy room decorated in shades of purple. The wisteria and clematis that climb the front door stoop reach right under my leaded window, and the fragrant breeze floats in from where it's open.

The breeze ruffles the sheer violet curtains, and something lightly clatters to the floor. Passing the antique bed, I make my way over to the window to see a twig with an attached clematis bloom on the mauve rug.

That's curious.

I peek out the window to the long pebbled driveway and the circular courtyard that encompasses the bubbling fountain, but I don't see anything out of place. Shrugging it off, I deposit the flower onto my nightstand before flinging open the oak armoire to grab some jeans and a light sweater for the day.

As I head into the bathroom, I debate what I should do with my tangled, wavy hair before I see myself in the mirror.

It was definitely a rough night.

Bruised shadows bloom under my eyes. The contrast of the violet on my pale skin makes my slate eyes look hollow.

A combination of my parent's faces stare back at me in the mirror. My mom's cheekbones and my dad's full lips.

The resemblance makes the hole in my chest grow. The matter of my hair gets set aside as I pull out my small cosmetic bag and begin to revive my appearance.

A moment later, a much fresher face stares back at me. I brush my long hair back and contemplate what to do with it. I loosen a breath and settle on a braid while wondering about the small offering that was left on the window seal. *Are birds leaving me offerings now?* I chuckle and push the thought aside while I plan out my day.

I don't want to be alone, and with Gran's busy schedule, I decide to hang out with Torin. Spring is fighting to make its presence known; the early spring flowers bloom brightly, and buds cling to the branches of the bare trees.

My hands are warm in the pockets of my jacket as I meander

down a path that will take me to the stables. Torin often likes to start his day off by tending to the horses.

Thundering hoofbeats reach my ears, and I spy Torin, with a proud seat, upon the inky black stallion my Gran gifted me when I first arrived. We named him Sleipnir, after Odin's eight-legged horse. I'm relieved to see someone giving him the attention he deserves.

If I'm being honest, he always felt like too much horse for me. My parents were excellent riders and often said horses respond to your emotions. I firmly believe that. I'm naturally anxious, so it makes sense for horses to react to my undercurrent of fear when I ride them. It usually wasn't a good time for either of us.

Torin notices me watching from the fence and guides Sleipnir my way.

"It's a wee bit early for ye, isn't it?"

"Just a bit," I respond, pretending to yawn as I play into his joke.

Torin leans over to pat the horse's strong neck. "I hope ye dinna mind; I've been taking Sleipnir out in the morning. A strong beast like this must be ridden often, or they'll go mad."

I know it was not his intention to make me feel guilty, but it still manages to creep over me. I shift on my feet.

"No, of course. I'm glad you've been spending time with him. I need to do better at getting down here."

My response is weak and timid.

"If you're afraid, I dinna mind holding the reins until ye get comfortable in your own seat," he offers as he analyzes my expression.

I guess I wasn't as covert as I thought in hiding my fear.

Truth be told, I took a nasty tumble off a horse when I was younger, and I don't think I ever really got over it.

I had always liked to throw my arms out wide and pretend I

was flying. But the falling snatched the dream from me and the fear has persisted.

I clear my throat. "Once I have more free time, I would really appreciate that."

He smiles down at me. "Well, it looks like we have a bit of time right now, don't we?"

I purse my lips, annoyed that he picked up on that, and slowly nodded my agreement.

"Meet me at the stable and I'll lead ye around."

Torin races off on Sleipnir before I can make another excuse. A deep sigh works out of my chest, but does nothing to calm my fears.

The stable isn't original to the manor and was added on quite recently; the old one had fallen into complete disrepair. Lachlan did an amazing job of blending it into the other structures on our estate. The stone, clay tiles, and oak doors are a perfect match to the Hall.

But inside, you can tell it's completely modern. Stained concrete floors and large glass and iron lanterns illuminate the entire building, showcasing the detailed wrought iron stall gates.

Of the six stalls, only two are occupied, Sleipnir's and Rosie's, my Gran's silver mare. Honestly, Rosie is much more my speed. She has a sweet temperament and isn't in a hurry to go anywhere.

Torin has Sleipnir tied to one of the hitching poles by the stalls and grins at me when I walk through the door.

"I ken you're nervous, but ye must learn to master your fears. Ye never know when you'll be faced with something you'll need to master," he says, patting Sleipnir. "There's strength in controlling a beast larger than ye and garnering its respect."

He's right, but I don't know how that relates to my current life or even my empty plans for the future. After quickly switching out my flats for my riding boots in the tack room, Torin holds his hand out for me to mount Sleipnir.

Luckily, my long legs have retained a bit of their muscular form from my life before, and I easily swing astride the giant horse. I grip the reins tightly in my fist and squeeze my thighs lightly, adding the slightest amount of pressure to his sides to get him to move forward.

Nothing happens.

After several more tries and my growing frustration, Torin clears his throat.

"He canna move forward, my lady, when you're pulling him to a stop."

He points to my hands, firmly holding the reins up to my chest, in a halt position. I grimace, realizing my fumble, and relax my grip.

"Ease up, lass, I'm right here," Torin says and gently takes the reins from me.

He leads Sleipnir to the dirt warm-up ring attached to the stable yard. My knuckles are turning white from the tightness of which I'm gripping the saddle horn, my heart thudding forcefully with each step we take.

Why is this so difficult for me?

I've ridden horses most of my life. I need to get over this useless fear. We reach the practice ring, and Torin looks up at me. My jaw clenched with unease; he shakes his head lightly.

"Have ye ever tried mindfulness?" His tone is a bit hesitant like he's afraid to offend me.

"Is that like meditation?"

"That's resting your mind. Mindfulness is listening to your mind and the emotions you are feeling and learning how to control them," he answers.

I shake my head, having only ever meditated before.

Torin's smile is comforting, bringing me back to the present. "I want ye to try it with me."

"Uhhh, ok, what do I do?"

"Close your eyes and open up your other senses to your surroundings," he begins, his voice taking on a tranquil quality. "Focus on what ye hear, what ye smell, and what ye feel physically."

"I hear —"

"Nae, dinna tell me, lass, just think about it." He chuckles softly.

"Oh, sorry," I grumble. I feel like a giant idiot, sitting atop Sleipnir in the middle of the ring with my eyes closed, trying to hear and smell things.

But Torin continues without missing a beat. "Nae problem, ok, we're finding our place, our senses are open, and we're going to open our mind to what we feel on the inside." He pauses. "Listen to whatever your mind is feeling, whether you're tired, hungry, scared, things of that nature. Now, you're gonna hold it, metaphorically, in the palm of your hand while taking a deep breath to the count of four."

He waits, allowing me time to inhale. "Now hold your breath for the count of four, and then exhale for the count of four, and hold that emptiness for a count of four."

Again, he gives me time to follow his instructions, and do what he's instructed. I begin to feel the effects.

My pulse begins to slow, and my mind stops spinning.

"Now you're gonna tell yourself: I feel this, but I'm gonna put it down and you're gonna put what ye ha' in your hand down while ye continue doing another sixteen-count breath."

My thoughts, once screamed through my mind, are now only whispers. The weight on my chest eases away.

I peek open my eyes and see Torin smiling broadly up at me. "Did it help?"

My smile is answer enough. "Where did you learn that?"

He shrugs off my excitement. "Ach, when you're my age, ye

pick up a thing or two, lass. Now let's see if we can fix your seat, too."

Torin leads me around the ring once and then makes me do another round of mindfulness before he leads me around again, but this time at a trot, and follows it up with a sixteen-second breath.

On and on that goes until I get the hang of it and feel more in sync with Sleipnir's gait. Torin hands me the reins and nods at me to give it a go on my own. I ease Sleipnir into a canter, and my nerves, which usually roil under the surface, do not reappear.

I've never felt so sure of myself, especially while on the back of a horse. My cheeks are burning from the tooth-bearing grin I have plastered on my face.

A shooting star of a thought whizzes by.

I wish my dad could see this.

All too quickly, my happiness dissipates, and my smile falters before completely dropping. I pull Sleipnir to a stop in front of Torin and quickly dismount.

"Thank you for the lesson, but I'm sure Gran's therapy is almost through, and I should head back," I mumble, holding the reins to him.

Torin pauses, sensing my discomfort, before he takes the reins from my outstretched hands. I came down here not to be alone, but now that my emotional walls are crumbling, I only want to be alone. The amazing feeling of riding without fear is overshadowed by the heartache of my dad never seeing it.

On the way back to the house, quieter than the songs of the birds, and the wind rustling through the evergreens, is the very distant gravelly caw of a raven. I look up from the path, but don't see any ravens. Chalking it up to my imagination and hoping it's not another omen, I keep heading for the house.

The soft notes of a piano echo down the hall and gently tug me toward the formal living room. When I peer through the door, I see Maggie, Gran's music therapist, squeezed onto the bench beside her. Maggie is a sweet soul and dutifully nods along to Gran's playing.

The song is soft and whimsical, flowing like a gentle river.

But there's something about it that pulls on my memory. I begin humming along, knowing in my heart what the next note will be.

Without looking up, Gran calls over the music. "This was the lullaby I used to sing your mother."

Instantly, happy memories flood my mind, chasing away the sorrow that had begun to grow after thinking of my parents.

My grief has become such an emotional roller coaster.

The lullaby I remember now is about the north winds, the Mother, and the sea.

The melody calms something deep within me as Gran finishes playing. Maggie excuses herself and slips off the bench and out of the room. I take her place beside Gran. Resting my head on her shoulder, she gently removes her hands from the keys to place one on top of mine while the other cradles my cheek.

"I'm so glad you're here, Lena. There's so much I want to tell you, but there's so much I don't remember. Just know that I love you, and I am so sorry." Her eyes aren't completely clear, and the glassiness of the memory fog is battling against the sparkling blue. She won't be here for long.

The lump in my throat keeps me from responding, and it isn't until the tears trickle their way down my cheeks that it eases enough that I can respond.

"I miss you so much when you're gone, and them, too." My voice cracks. "So much, every day."

She strokes my cheek and begins wiping away my tears. "I'm afraid things won't be getting any easier, dearie; you must become stronger."

I want to argue.

I want to scream that all of this is so unfair, and I didn't do anything to warrant all this pain and suffering.

But instead, I swallow the frustration and grief down. We sit together for a moment longer before her eyes turn glassy; *she's gone again.*

She quickly moves her hands back to the piano keys and slides away from me. My chest aches. But before I move from the bench, she glances sidelong at me, her eyes more cloudy than I've ever seen them.

"The necklace has answers," she whispers.

Maggie clears her throat from the entryway, catching me off guard, and we trade places on the bench. Gran keeps playing, but my mouth hangs open in shock. A strong pull from questions unanswered that her comment triggered has me desperate to find the answers.

My necklace is warm against my skin, and the faint humming sound of a note held too long begins ringing in my ears. I have so many questions, like a puzzle without all the pieces and I want it solved; purpose begins burning in my veins.

Where do I find answers?

The office may have some. There are many books, family diaries, and photo albums in there. I'm probably losing my mind, but the ringing and strange interactions with Gran are really starting to drive me mad.

My steps are quick as I march down the hall and through the office's double doors. It's really more of a library with its walls of bookshelves lined with books, knickknacks, artifacts from the grounds, and photo albums.

The albums are probably the best place to start. That way I don't have to read through pages of an ancestor's diary. I grab the first album off the lowest shelf and haul it to the writing desk right in front of the floor-to-ceiling leaded windows that make an entire wall.

The view from the windows is like a picture out of a storybook, rolling hills dotted with mature trees stretch on for as far as the eye can see. The aroma of old camera film and mint floats up from the pages that are thick and yellowed with age.

I flip through the pages slowly to keep them from ripping. Briefly scanning each picture of faces and places, not recognizing anything, before I finish the first album and exchange it for the next one.

The first picture on the next album causes a gasp to escape me.

This task will be infinitely more difficult than I initially thought. A tear escapes and slips down my cheek before dropping onto the plastic-covered photo.

My parents gaze up at me from sprawled on a picnic blanket under a large tree. Far in the background of the image, barely visible over the tree line, is a pitching roofline with battlements.

I lovingly trace my father's face. He was always handsome, but seeing him in his youth is remarkable. My finger begins tracing my mom, her long hair blowing in the breeze.

My tracing halts.

Peeking out from the neckline of her white billowy dress is the unmistakable medallion that's currently clasped around my neck. This was my mom's necklace? Is that what Gran meant by heirloom?

Even more questions whirl through my mind, and I quickly flip through the rest of the album, looking for another glimpse of the necklace, but there is none. It's as if it vanishes after this day.

I flip back to the picture of them under the tree and pull it out gently from under the plastic sheet, checking the date on the back. The date tickles something in my memory; it's the day before they left for the States.

This picture was taken the day they found out they were pregnant with me.

Closing my eyes and taking a deep breath, I whisper, "What does this mean, Mom?"

This feels important, but I couldn't even begin to imagine what it could be. We didn't keep any secrets from each other. Only one topic ever felt off-limits: my dad's family. Everything else could always be discussed freely.

A sinking feeling begins to creep over me when I realize maybe they weren't always honest with me. I drop the picture onto the desk and exchange the photo album for another one, beginning the process again.

But my search is fruitless; frustration rises when Maggie walks in.

"I'm about to head out; Lizzie is with Adi," she trills, slinging her long chestnut braid over her thin shoulder.

"Oh great, I'll walk you out," I mumble, looking up from the album. "Let me put this back right quick."

"What is that?" she asks, her hazel eyes lighting with curiosity.

"Photo albums; I'm trying to find anything about this neck-lace,"—I flash her my medallion—"without asking Gran. She's had some strange reactions to it."

I walk over to the shelf and slip the album between the others.

"Have you seen her sketch?" Maggie asks.

"What sketch?"

I brush the dust off my cardigan.

"The one from this morning looks just like that. But the strangeness is normal; it's probably the disease twisting her thoughts," she mutters.

Gran is mumbling about feathers everywhere when we get within earshot of the chair she's relaxed in. I glance around, half expecting to see a busted pillow somewhere before I realize her eyes are closed. Lizzie sits quietly across from her, laying the puzzle pieces on the low-lying table. She was exactly what we needed when Gran's illness became unmanageable. I was so relieved when she and Gran instantly clicked, and she promptly settled into life here at the Hall.

"Gran, Lizzie, do either of you need anything?" I offer.

Lizzie shakes her head, and her curly auburn tresses bob up and down with the movement. Gran's eyes flash open, and she smiles.

I move to kneel in front of her but get distracted by her sketchbook lying face-up on the floor beside her chair. With painstaking detail, she managed to recreate the medallion. Every slash and curve of the ancient-looking runes sprawled in a spiraling circle has been sketched onto the parchment by memory alone. *How on earth did she draw this after only seeing it twice?* And briefly at that.

Maggie clears her throat from the doorway, and I look up, still grappling with the sketch before me.

She waves and mouths, "See you later."

But I can barely manage to nod back.

"Bryn, dearie, did you have a nice time in Olundy?"

I flinch when Gran's voice echoes through the quiet room.

The name slices at my heart.

"Gran, I'm Lena, Bryn's daughter…"

Her face twists with agitation.

"NO, no. Bryn. You're my Bryn. Stop it. No, Lena!" Her voice raises with each word.

"Oh dear," Lizzie mutters, coming to stand behind me. She places a tiny hand on my shoulder, offering support.

"You're right, I'm sorry, I'm sorry, Mum," I reply, trying to calm her down.

Her frown eases, and she starts to stroke my hair, murmuring, "Bryn, dearie."

Lizzie squeezes my shoulder gently. Her hand is so small it

amazes me that she manages to carry the immensely heavy load her job requires.

Family medallions are the last thing on my mind for the rest of the evening as Lizzie and I walk on eggshells to keep Gran calm while trying to get her fed and down for the night.

CHAPTER

THREE

Lizzie nearly tackles me when I leave my bedroom the following morning.

"Lena! She's lucid, really, really lucid!" she squeals.

My breath gets caught in my throat, and I can only manage a nod before Lizzie dashes off down the hall again. Excitement brims in my veins; hopefully, I can get answers from her now.

I grab the picture of my parents out of my room before tracking Gran down in the drawing room. She's seated in her favorite wingback chair before the windows, sipping her tea. She glances up at me; her blue eyes are clear, she's still lucid.

I haven't missed her this time.

Relief lightens each step as I walk towards her and kneel at her side.

"Good morning, Gran."

She tracks my every moment and pats my cheek. Her expression is solemn.

"How long was I gone this time, Lena?"

"You were in and out for a bit," I answer. "But you're here now."

I hope my smile is comforting enough to ease her worries.

Gran's smile is tinged with sorrow; she sees right through my foolhardy attempt. "Was it bad?"

"Nothing I couldn't handle; it's okay, I promise." The lie comes easily.

I pull the picture out. I don't really want to ask right this second, but I don't know how much time we have before she's gone again.

"Gran, does this look familiar?" I ask, holding the photo out to her.

Taking the picture from my hand, she rolls her eyes. "That's your mother and father; of course, it looks familiar."

"Obviously," I tease back. "But look at her necklace."

I point to the medallion perched on my mom's chest. As she studies the picture, I pull out the necklace that I tucked behind my charcoal sweater.

Gran's eyes flit up to me, noticing the necklace. She gasps. "Where did you get that?" Her head whips back and forth between the photograph and my necklace.

"Lachlan gifted it to me, but he bought it at an antique shop. How did it get there? Did she give it away?" My questions ramble together.

That's the only thing I could think of happening. Maybe it's only a piece of junk my mom donated because she didn't want it. But why am I so drawn to it? Even now, I can feel a slight pulsing from the medallion, like it's emitting a dull electric current.

"No, she wouldn't have done that." She looks back down at the picture of my mom. "But I can't say any more about it," she finishes, abruptly.

I stare at her quizzically, my mouth slowly parting in surprise, but she begins staring at the necklace clasped around my neck. Gran reaches out to touch the medallion, but drops her hand, clasping her fingers together in her lap.

"I wouldn't lose it, though, if I were you," Gran mumbles, nodding to herself.

"That's a bit ominous," I trail off. "Do you know more about it and won't tell me? Or do you not remember at all?"

Her brows pinch together momentarily. "It's like my mind went blank. I know it's important, but I can't tell you more."

"Ahh, I see."

My shoulders slump in defeat.

She suddenly changes the subject. "So what did I miss?" A smile brightens her tired face.

I begin filling her in on the last couple of days, starting with the birds, and she laughs loudly at my story.

"It was really on my shoulder? Like a pirate?" she asks through her giggles.

"Yes! You scared the hell out of me, talking to it and everything!"

She chuckles, and her eyes sparkle. "If there were two, then it was just Odin, dearie."

Gran has always had a healthy respect for the Gods. But at times, she talks as if they're old friends.

We spend the rest of the day connected at the hip, giving Lizzie the day off. We take walks through the grounds, hand in hand, while I fill her in on everything else I can think of, including my growing affection for Lachlan.

The day is a haze of tea, laughter, and cherished moments. The peace has reinvigorated my mind. Time rushes past, even though I do my best to absorb each new memory we make and hold on to it tightly. I hope tonight goes just as well. Gran glances at the clock on the mantle in the parlor before not so suddenly eyeing my casual attire.

I roll my eyes before saying, "Yes, yes, I should probably get changed. I hear you."

I fake a frown.

Gran trills from the parlor. "Wear something pretty."

"Alright, you can give it a rest," I call over my shoulder as I trudge up the stairs.

Alone in my room, though, I begin to pace as the anxiety slowly starts slithering into my chest. Something has shifted for me with Lach, and now nothing in my wardrobe seems suitable for the occasion. I want to impress him, for him to look at me with the same wanton expression I struggle to hide from him.

I open the window to allow some fresh air into the room before I slump onto the floor; my head rests against the settee's cushions. I do a round of mindfulness to pull myself together. It really has been the most useful of tricks for dealing with my anxiety.

I need to properly thank Torin for finding an easy solution.

Closing my eyes and opening up my senses, I focus on the rustle of the breeze through the vines below my open window and the distant chattering of the birds. Taking a deep breath, I inhale the scent of the clematis and wisteria spring blossoms floating in my room. My pulse begins to slow, and I do another round of breathing and mindfulness before I'm finally calm enough to pick myself up off the floor.

My mind is clear, and my confidence is back in place. I grab the only dress I have, a black tea-length cotton dress with straps that tie into little bows on the shoulders. But right as I'm shutting the bathroom door, the faint whisper of wings can be heard over the sound of the door clicking shut.

With my dress on, hair curled, and face painted lightly with rose blush to match the gloss I applied to my lips, I descend the stairs. Each step is carefully placed as I grow accustomed to the small kitten heels I wear instead of my usual flats.

The doorbell rings, and I loudly call, "I got it!"

But the door swings open before I can grasp the handle, and I'm met by the most staggeringly handsome man.

Lachlan is dressed fashionably in a black sweater with a white collar peeking up from beneath it, charcoal-tailored pants, and black wingtip boots. I take a moment to eye him up and down, appreciating the graceful elegance he's exuding.

My eyes slowly make their way back up to his face, and I notice the surprise lighting his eyes. His partially parted lips kick up into a breathtaking smile.

"Ye are stunning," he breathes.

His eyes simmer with something unreadable. I grin while twirling in place so he can get the full effect of the dress. He chuckles, jostling the load I hadn't even realized was in his arms.

"Thank you!" I beam before reaching out to him. "Here, let me help you with those."

But he breezes past me. "Nae, I got these," he responds, heading towards the kitchen.

The bag is unceremoniously dumped onto the kitchen island, and Lachlan begins unloading them. Arugula, olive oil, balsamic glaze, bushels of grapes, a lemon, prosciutto, burrata, and basil leaves are unloaded onto the island.

"Are we having a fancy salad?"

He waves a large loaf of ciabatta bread that he pulls from the paper bag. "We're having fancy sandwiches."

His sarcasm causes me to giggle.

"If you can't cook, we could've just ordered something," I tease.

"Ach, I ken how to cook, but I dinna ken if ye were still a picky eater. Besides, everyone loves sandwiches."

I roll my eyes. "I haven't been a picky eater since we were kids!" I huff.

But he crosses his arms. "Ye took the tomatoes off the pasta last time."

I grumble to myself about nosey busybodies. Gran walks in on Torin's elbow. Her eyes are brightened by the sage green pantsuit she's wearing, the gold buttons gleaming from the kitchen lights.

Torin's tanned skin glows, complemented by his dark green

sweater and khaki trousers. They're both dressed rather nicely and almost matching, in a way. Lachlan and I look to have coordinated on purpose with our black ensembles.

Torin brings a bouquet of wildflowers out from behind his back, where he had hidden them, and extends them to me.

"These are for ye."

The bouquet is a dainty mix of creamy white primrose and rich purple violets. Taking the flowers in both hands, I bring them up to my nose and inhale their delicate fragrance.

"Oh, these are lovely; thank you so much."

My eyes sting with unshed tears as I track down a vase to place them in.

Memories of my parents flood my mind. My dad would often pick wildflowers, and my mom would weave them into a flower crown for me.

Lachlan breaks through my sadness, though, with a jab at his dad. "Way to upstage me, old man."

"Dearie, the boys put together a bit of a surprise." Gran gestures to the two men. "Torin, would you like to show us?"

Gran's mischievous smile thoroughly strokes my curiosity, and I follow them. When we walk out onto the terrace, my eyes widen.

Oh Gods.

Thousands of twinkly lights are wrapped around the trees near the house and stretched to the roof. The entire terrace is illuminated with thousands of tiny lights, like walking through the stars.

"How?" I ask, spinning around to absorb the display of the magical lights against the darkening sky.

"Apparently, we took our time getting ready, and Lach's crew managed to throw it together while we were distracted," she answers, standing beside me.

The backdoor creaks open, and Lachlan comes swaggering our way, holding four glasses of white wine in his hands.

"This is incredible." I smile broadly at him as he hands off glasses to Gran and Torin before facing me.

"I ken ye had a hard week, so I wanted it to be special." He shrugs and hands me a glass of wine, clinking the top of his glass to mine.

"If ye two would ha' a seat. We'll be right back with your meal," he says to Torin and Gran, nodding to the outdoor table and chairs, which have been moved directly under the criss-crossing lights.

"Key, can ye give me a hand?"

Butterflies swarm in my stomach, but I follow him inside.

"What did you need help with?" I perch myself on the stool in front of the island.

"Nothing, I just wanted your company," he answers while laying lemons on the cutting board. I cough into my wine glass, the sip I was taking stuck in my throat. "What's your favorite memory from this place?"

My smile falters, and silence stretches between us. My grief overwhelms my ability to answer. Lachlan glances up from where he's slicing a lemon at my lingering silence.

"Key, I am so sorry, I dinna even think...." he trails off as he comes around to stand beside me, the knife and lemons forgotten on the counter.

"No, it's okay, it just, um, it sneaks up on me sometimes, ya know?" I respond while tightly hugging myself to keep from breaking apart.

"I ken it does," he says as he wraps his strong arms around me.

He squeezes me tightly, holding all of my pieces together. His familiar cedar and rain scent envelops me. I lay my head against his chest and focus on the rhythm of his steady heart-beat against my ear. Lachlan rests his chin atop my head, rubbing a hand up and down my spine.

He murmurs, "When I lost my parents, granted, I was very

young, but that loss did stay with me. It does get easier, but it's always there, lingering."

His confession is heartfelt. I appreciate the genuine sympathy he's sharing with me. His parents were not a topic we ever discussed growing up, but his surliness was always apparent as he struggled with his sorrow.

"I feel a bit guilty now," I mumble against his chest.

"Why is that?" he asks.

I tilt my head back to gaze into his eyes. "I was lucky enough to have twenty-one years with my parents, and you didn't even get a fraction of that with yours."

His smile is sad, but he says, "Ah, the age-old question: Is it better to ha' loved and lost than never to ha' loved at all?" He lightly kisses the top of my head before slowly pulling away, taking his warmth with him.

Circling back to the island, he picks up the other half of the lemon and the knife before resuming his slicing.

I joke to lighten the heaviness clouding the room. "Handsome contractor and philosopher, eh?"

He smiles, not taking his eyes off the lemons before him.

I blush into my wine glass while wrinkling my nose in embarrassment. But then I notice the slight reddening of his ears. Perhaps my attempt at flirting wasn't too terrible after all. With each sip of wine, I feel like I'm finally stepping back into my body. My confidence begins simmering right below the surface of my skin, and a spark of light blooms in my chest.

"How's business?" I ask.

"Business is booming; it's hard to imagine I only just started this company." His eyes stay on the cutting board before him, but he's a million miles away.

"Do you miss traveling?" I ask him, assuming the distance in his eyes is because he misses his wanderer's lifestyle that he traded in for his busy day job.

He chuckles. "Am I that obvious?"

I grin. "Of course, I never would've pictured you in one place. You were always jealous of our nomadic life."

He nods his head in agreement. While I always wanted to stay here at the Hall with him, he would always beg to join us in the States.

Lachlan begins washing the arugula in the sink. "Ye always did want to stay still."

His eyes fall upon me, and I feel the weight of his stare on my skin.

"I wouldn't say I wanted to stay still; I just wanted a normal life. With friends and relationships. I wanted to belong to somewhere or someone," I murmur.

His eyes meet mine, and my skin flushes at his attention. I want to shove the words back into my mouth.

Lachlan shakes his head and turns off the sink. "Ye led a life of adventure and wanted a mundane one instead?" His voice is light and teasing, but something about his tone when he says 'mundane' makes me sit up straighter.

"I didn't say mundane, just average." I roll my eyes.

Lachlan shakes the arugula, sending drops of water flying across the kitchen. I squeal when splattered with several, and he laughs at my shocked expression.

"You did that on purpose!"

His eyes dance, taking in the droplets splattering my face. "See, there's no fun in normal, Key."

I grin, dabbing the water off my face with the towel he hands me.

Naturally, our conversation flows back and forth as Lachlan finishes putting together our dinner and places the four sandwiches on two serving trays.

"Do ye think ye could grab the sides?"

I give a mock salute. "Aye, captain," I tease.

His eyes flare. "It's chef."

I grab the fruit and crisps that he brought for our sides and follow him out. I'm still simmering with happiness as we make our way back to the terrace.

Gran and Torin turned on an outdoor speaker, and the soft strings of classical music faintly play underneath their conversation. They have known each other for most of their lives, perhaps even longer, and appear now to be just two old friends walking through years of memories.

That thought suddenly has me realizing that Torin is exactly the person I should be asking about my mom's mysteriously appearing necklace.

We set down the food, and Lachlan proudly proclaims, "Dinner is served!"

Gran chuckles, studying the sandwich in front of her. "And what do we have here?"

Lachlan grins. "While I was traveling, I came across this little hole-in-the-wall place that served these delicious sandwiches, so I convinced the owner to give me the recipe. And here it is: fresh bread, spread with melted burrata cheese, topped with arugula, prosciutto, basil, a squeeze of lemon, and a generous amount of balsamic glaze." He glances around the table as we all make skeptical faces at the food on our plates. "I promise it's good."

I close my eyes and give silent thanks to the Father and Mother for our many blessings before taking the first bite. Gran and Torin stare quizzically at me. I politely smile behind my hand as I swallow.

"Okay, he's not lying; that's really good." I take a sip of wine to wash it down before I dive back in to devour the rest of the sandwich.

Everyone follows my lead, and what follows is a chorus of murmuring agreement. It's not exactly a five-star meal, but it is surprisingly delicious.

My necklace rests just underneath the neckline of my dress, and the bronze begins to warm against my skin. The warmth startles me enough that I interrupt the current conversation.

"Torin, you were here at the Hall when my parents left to go to the States, right?" I try to make the question sound conversational. However, my sudden burst of enthusiasm sparks curious looks from Gran and Lachlan.

"Aye, why?" He studies my face closely.

"I found a picture of my mom wearing this necklace." I pull the medallion up from where it currently rests under my dress. "But Lachlan found it at an antique shop." I glance sidelong at Lachlan. His face is strangely neutral. "I was wondering if you knew anything about it?"

The question is met with silence that stretches on a beat too long.

When I look away from Lachlan and back to Torin, he whips his face back to mine. His angry expression is quickly replaced with a neutral one. Was he just glaring at Lachlan? I search Lachlan's face for any hint of discord, but he ignores me, swirling the wine in his glass.

"Am I missing something?" I ask, glancing around the table.

Torin ignores my last question and answers the first. "Nae, lass, I dinna ha' any answers for ye, unfortunately."

Gran's head swivels back and forth as she follows the conversation. Her shoulders slump at Torin's reply.

"Oh, okay." My voice is full of defeat.

"But if it's answers you're after, your mum left a bunch of things behind, and I put it all in the attic. I'd start there," he adds, his face softening.

Hope sparks in my chest, a new path to answers. "Thank you."

Lachlan stretches an arm out behind my chair and leans towards me. His movement distracts me from the thoughts of my necklace.

"Do ye ha' anything planned while you're here?" He asks in between sips of his wine.

"Not really, just caring for Gran and enjoying her good days."

Gran looks over at me and smiles sadly. "You need some excitement, Lena, a purpose other than watching me die." Her stark honesty has my stomach bottoming out.

Torin's fork screeches against the porcelain plate. "Adi," he admonishes. "Dinna talk that way."

She rolls her eyes at him before flicking her gaze at me. "There is so much more to life, Lena, and you need to start living yours. You are important, my love."

My cheeks bloom with color at her loving words. "Says the grandmother to her only grandchild," I mumble under my breath.

But she shakes her head, frustration creasing her brow. "No, I mean it. There's a whole other world out there that needs you."

Torin coughs and pats a hand on the back of Gran's, where it rests on the table. "I ken what your Gran is trying to say is, ha' ye given any thoughts on your future? Do ye plan to go to university or travel?"

Gran glares at him. "Well, of course, she's going to travel."

The direction this conversation is headed makes me shift in my chair.

To be honest, I haven't given any thought to my future. I've been barely managing to survive one day to the next. Lachlan grazes his thumb over the top of my shoulder. My eyes drift sideways to see him drawing circles on my exposed skin. The sounds of Gran and Torin's bickering fade into the background.

Lachlan leans in. "Dinna let them gang up on ye like that," he murmurs in my ear.

Goosebumps erupt down my arms, and I shiver before turning back toward Gran and Torin. The rest of dinner continues without a hitch and is full of laughter and stories.

Lachlan clears our plates after we finish our meal, and while he's in the house, Torin turns the music up and leads Gran into a stunning waltz. I smile, watching them twirl around the terrace.

Lachlan comes up behind me and whispers, "Care to join them?"

My body goes hot and cold simultaneously, and I turn towards him. He stretches out a hand in offering. Biting my bottom lip, I nod and take his hand. My pulse races and my skin flushes with heat at the contact.

But he freezes, his eyes locked onto the lip I have trapped under my teeth. His gaze darkens for just a brief moment before he sighs, sweeping me up into his arms and we float around the terrace.

I'm sad to see Lachlan and Torin go a few hours later, but I'm surprised at how quickly time has passed. As I help Gran get up the stairs, she pauses at the top of the landing.

"That was such a lovely time, dearie. I haven't had that much fun in ages!" Her smile lights up the hallway.

"Me too. My cheeks hurt from smiling so hard."

The ghost of Lachlan's arms are still embracing me.

"You and Lachlan looked smitten," she adds, with a tilt of her head.

She watches me with an uncanny stillness. A predator locked onto prey. Times like these make me realize what a force she must have been in her youth.

"It does seem like that sometimes."

Her smile only grows as she kisses my cheek. "Sweet dreams, dearie."

Relieved she didn't launch a full-scale operation for more details, I mumble, "Night Gran."

As I turn to head to my room, Gran calls, "Lena."

I turn around and see her standing at her door, her eyes full of emotion. "Yes, Gran?"

"You are much stronger than you know and meant for so much more than our life here," she breathes.

Her kindness warms my heart, and I nod. "Thank you."

FOUR

An abrupt tap, tap, tap, sounds from my bedroom window. The noise breaks through my slumber. I blink my eyes open, looking around the room for the sound. Rain is splattering onto the floor from the window I carelessly left open. I rub the sleep from my eyes as I make my way to it. The effects of the very deep sleep have me stumbling. Thunder crashes loudly and I begin pulling it closed quickly.

My feet slip against the wet floor as movement catches my eye.

Down on the driveway, Torin races by heading towards the main road. His shoulders are rigid as he screams Gran's name over the sound of the rain. Fear slices through me, and I fly from the window, hurriedly throwing on clothes. I tie my hair up as I take the stairs two out at a time, flinging myself out the front door.

Torin's voice manages to carry down the driveway from where it connects to the main road. My pulse races, and every fear I've ever had about Gran being lost or hurt since her diagnosis whirls through my mind. She must've woken up in a fog and left the Hall without telling anyone.

Terror begins gnawing on my chest.

Not again. Please, I can't lose anyone else.

It's too soon, we still had time.

My clothes are entirely soaked through from the pouring rain, and I use my hand to shield my eyes from the downpour. The repetitive, gravelly caw of a raven in the wooded area has me whirling around. *Not now.* The sound is unusual like—a cry for help.

The wind causes the limbs of the trees to sway, and like a mirage, Gran materializes between them. She steps out behind a large oak tree, still dressed in her pale pink nightgown that clings to her frail body.

"Gran!" I call loudly while waving frantically.

She briefly looks my way before turning to walk between the field and the wooded area, not at all perturbed by the storm. I yell at Torin, and he turns towards me. I throw my arms over my head and begin pointing to where Gran is.

Luckily, he catches my meaning and begins to jog my way, but I'm already moving towards her. My footsteps kick up water and mud as I race across the driveway.

She's covered head to toe in splattered mud, and her eyes whirl around wildly. I approach her slowly, as one would approach a cornered animal.

"Gran, it's me, Lena."

Her wild gaze finds my face. "Bryn! They're gone!"

"Gran... Bryn isn't here right now; I'm Lena, your grand-daughter." I reply hesitantly, not wanting to trigger her and hoping it will calm her down.

Her body trembles. Her nightgown ill-equipped for the rain. I need to get her inside. Who knows how long she's been out here?

"You must go. She has to stop them. Bryn!" She raises her voice louder and begins throwing her arms around in weird movements, like she's drawing something in the air.

Slowly, I take another step closer as Torin reaches my side.

"Gran it's alright, you're safe here. Come with us to the house. We'll get you cleaned up," I speak slowly and softly.

Gran flicks her gaze to Torin, and relief floods her features. "Oh, Torin, she has to be safe."

Gran cries and flings herself into his arms.

Torin wraps his arms around her and rubs a soothing hand down her back. He murmurs, "Aye, Adi, we're all safe. Let's get ye dry and cleaned up, shall we?"

They turn together and make their way back to the house. Torin wraps an arm around her shoulders, shielding her from the rain, and she nuzzles into his side. My knees find their way to the soggy grass, and my arms wrap around my chest, trying to hold the pieces of myself together, but a sob escapes. The adrenaline rush begins waning, and the emotions I've worked so hard to hold at bay are now breaking to the surface.

I bury my face in my hands and let the grief, fear, and shame flow. The rain mixes with my tears and I let myself grieve for all that I've lost.

This is all my fault.

I should've been up earlier, and this wouldn't have happened. A breath hiccups out of me, and it's an effort to inhale normally again. Where is Lizzie? What if she had been hurt? What if we couldn't find her? She's all I have left now. I exhale and try to push all the negative feelings out.

Trying to calm myself down, I take slow, measured breaths, letting the rain wash everything away.

Just as I'm beginning to piece myself back together, a truck door slams, breaking my concentration. A very worried-looking Lachlan rushes towards me, holding the collar of his coat above his head.

"Did ye find her?" he calls, jogging towards me. I can only manage a nod in confirmation. He wraps me up in his arms. The strength in them warms my trembling body. "Are ye okay?"

Trying with all my might to keep my voice from breaking, I mutter, "It's all my fault."

The dam breaks again, and another sob escapes.

Lachlan soothingly shushes me as he strokes a hand down my back, much like Torin did for Gran. We stay locked together for a long time while my sobs finally subside, my tears drying up.

"It's just a bad day; tomorrow will be better," he whispers onto the top of my head.

I'm still lost in the darkness of my despair. "And if it's not?"

He pauses and pulls back to look me in the eye. His face, the picture of strength, and his eyes brimming with an emotion I don't recognize.

"Then say it again."

Those four words spark a delicate, tiny flame of hope in my chest. I inhale slowly, fully, finally feeling like I can breathe again. Squeezing me tightly once more, he kisses the top of my head before letting go, interlocking our fingers, and pulling me back to the house. The intimacy warms my bones and chases away the lingering chill of the rain. It doesn't feel foreign, but almost as if we've done this a thousand times before.

We're halfway back to the house before I remember the raven that essentially saved Gran, and I turn to search for it. The tug on Lachlan's hand has him stopping with me.

He turns to me and asks, "Forget something?"

"There was a raven..." I trail off, realizing how incredibly stupid it would sound to tell him a bird helped me find Gran. He raises his eyebrow, waiting for me to finish.

"Never mind. Thank you again for being here."

I reach for his hand and he smiles, taking my hand and leading me back to the house. The rain eases into a light drizzle as we make our way inside. I slip my boots off by the door and tread carefully. My wet clothes and hair leave droplets in my wake.

Inside, we find Torin sitting at the bottom of the stairs, a comforting arm draped over Lizzie. My terror returns, rising from the gloom, but Torin blurts out, "She's just upstairs. She went to shower and change."

I sigh deeply.

Lizzie murmurs, "She's lucid, not completely, but enough that I thought she could handle showering on her own without getting hurt. I'm so sorry, Lena, I didn't even hear her wake up this morning." Her hazel eyes are lined with silver, her slight frame trembling with the effort of holding back tears. Lizzie has never missed one of Gran's wake-ups since coming to live with us.

I try my hardest to keep my own emotions in check, but I am not quite ready to reassure her.

Trudging upstairs, I find Gran's door is ajar, and she is nestled under her cerulean sheets and floral quilts. Her room is the mirror image of mine, but where mine is shades of purple, hers is shades of blue. She lies on her side, facing me, and holds out a hand when I enter. Her clean pink nightgown slides up her thin arm at the motion. I'm relieved that she managed to shower and put on a clean set of clothes. I sink onto the floor in front of her bed, grasping her outstretched hand between both of mine.

"I'm sorry I gave you a fright this morning..." she trails off. I realize it's because she doesn't remember my name.

"That's alright, Gran, how're you feeling?" I ask, hoping my use of 'Gran' will put her at ease.

"Exhausted. I'm afraid my fire has gone out, and I need sleep."

"I'm so sorry. I'll cancel your therapies today," I whisper, leaning forward to brush a light kiss on her forehead. A final phrase slips through her lips. "You need to go home, Lena."

Before I can ask, she's already breathing deeply.

Lizzie is standing in the hallway, right outside the door. Her sweater-clad arms hugging herself while her head hangs limply; she's really beating herself up. I pat her shoulder as I brush by. She bites her lip and slips into Gran's room.

My footfalls are nearly silent as I pad down the hall towards the stairs. The faint sounds of Torin and Lachlan's voice carry up to the second floor. They're in a tense conversation by the tone of their voices, and only bits of their words reach my ears. I quietly move closer to see if I can hear any more.

The only words I can make out are "dangerous son," from Torin and, "job," from Lachlan.

A loud creak sounds from under my foot. Stupid old wooden floors. I hold my breath. But it's obvious they heard me when their conversation ceased. Not wanting to seem like I was totally just eavesdropping, I call down to them, taking the steps quickly.

"Well, she's out and doesn't want to do any therapies today, so Lachlan, you don't have to stay. I think I can manage while she's out."

Torin simply nods his head and walks out the front door.

But Lachlan turns to me and says, "Nae, we can hang out. Just the two of us while she rests."

His smile causes my pulse to race for a different, happy reason, and my feet stumble on the stairs. I want to rush to him, but I catch myself and slow down on the last few steps. I come to a halt right before I reach the bottom. "Well, we can't do much; I don't want to leave the house so I can listen for her."

He thinks for a moment before asking, "Want to check out the attic?"

"This is going to take way longer than I assumed." I cough. We stand in a crowded, very dusty attic. Even with it being the entire top floor of the Hall, it is crammed full of boxes, old furniture, and junk.

"Whoa." Lachlan peers around the cluttered mess. "Your family dinna get rid of anything, do they?"

He's not wrong. Floor to ceiling, wall to wall, it's completely covered.

"We don't even know what we're looking for. This is going to take forever," I whine.

"It won't be too bad. What if we find treasure?" Lachlan raises his eyebrow and rubs his hands together.

His question makes me giggle. When we were little, we would scour the creek bed next to the faerie tree for shards of glass we pretended to be gemstones. It didn't matter how often we looked, we always found treasure there.

I exhale. "Ugh, I hope you're right. How do you want to do this? You take the left, I take the right, or I start here and you go to the other side and we meet in the middle?"

Lachlan shrugs. "I guess I'll take the left, and ye can take the right; that way, I'm close by if ye need some muscle." He flexes his arms, and I giggle again while rolling my eyes.

He's trying his hardest to keep the mood light, and I really appreciate his effort. It used to be the opposite between us; he was the gloomy one, and I would go out of my way to cheer him up. Now the tables have turned and I don't take for granted having him by my side.

The time passes quickly, and we each stick to our sides, opening and browsing boxes before coming up empty-handed and closing them back up. Periodically, we'd find something interesting that warranted walking to the other side and showing off our treasure. Lachlan ends up finding more interesting things, but we spend the entire time talking and laughing. Adoration settles deeper into the marrow of my bones.

I try to pay attention to the boxes before me, but occasionally, Lach will catch my eye, and I'll admire the way his muscles flex through his long-sleeved shirt or the way his hair falls forward when he moves certain ways; it frames his strong jaw.

He's so beautiful it's hard not to stare. My fascination with him is not new. I feel like I searched for him in all the boys I had casual dalliances with. But no one ever compared to the one I had stuck on a pedestal. Lachlan had a few romances throughout the years, and it did sting. But I didn't ever have a claim on him. We saw each other sporadically throughout our lives, and even though we were as thick as thieves when we were together, we were apart for much longer.

At the back of my mind, though, I had always hoped we would end up together.

Images of a future with him begin to build as I daydream about a life, together, at the Hall where we share so many memories. Lachlan would be closer to the estates he manages, and with my trust fund, maybe I could go to a university. I've always been fascinated by history. Some of my favorite memories are listening to my parents talk about the great lives of historical figures like Cleopatra or Sappho. Or maybe we could travel together. One of Lachlan's great loves was traveling, and it would be wonderful to experience that with him. I wouldn't mind having a nomadic lifestyle again if it was with him.

But if I'm being honest, I've always been too afraid to put myself out there.

Especially with Lachlan.

That's a rejection that would cut deeper than any other relationship ever has. Not that I even have a ton of experiences with relationships, but what little I do have has always felt like I was bidding my time for something bigger, *for him.*

Lachlan catches me staring and quirks his head to the side. "Where'd ye go?"

My blush crawls up my cheeks, and I wipe my forehead with the back of my hand.

"Do you — never mind." I shake my head and bend down to rifle through the box at my feet.

"Oh no, ye don't." He grins broadly. "What?"

I stare down at the box in front of me, not really seeing the contents, and trying to work up the courage to ask him out. But I fail miserably; my confidence is sorely lacking. "Do you ever go to any of the pubs around here?"

Lachlan chuckles. "Of course, I go out with the crew and some friends all the time. Why? Do ye want to come with us?"

I roll my eyes. Of course, he would have no shortage of friends. He has roots here and is the charismatic one out of the two of us now.

I pull out an ancient leather sandal that has long straps before tossing it back in the box.

"I don't want to invite myself out with you guys," I mumble.

"Key," he drawls, his voice causing my blood to heat. "You're welcome to go with me anywhere, anytime. I've actually got to run up to Orkney next Friday, and I'll be gone for the weekend." Lachlan casually throws my way.

My stomach sinks, but I try to play it off. "Oh? What for?" I ask, trying to make my tone nonchalant.

"Well, I've been living out of a suitcase for the past month and need to switch some things out and check on my place," he responds, sliding a box that has a large 'B,' on the side in front of him.

"Try living your whole life out of a suitcase," I mumble.

He whips his head towards me and chuckles. "Are ye upset with me?"

My feigned, uncaring mask falls away. He can read me like a book. I don't know why I'm so surprised; my mom always told me I was an open book, freely showing my emotions like a picture on a page.

"No, sorry." I grimace. "I'll just miss you, is all."

Lachlan freezes when he glances into the open box. "I think ye should come take a look at this."

I shuffle along the walkway until I make it to the other side of the box he has opened. Placed right on top is a gaudy necklace of braided metal with three sizable spaced-out blue rectangles that are made to resemble sapphires.

"Woah, that's heavier than I thought it would be," I mutter, passing it off to Lachlan.

The next items are long, almost sheer, flowing skirts in different shades of white and cream. They're thicker than chiffon but as light and silken in my hand; it's a fabric I can't quite place. Below the skirts, I find an even bigger swathe of the same fabric and hold it up to my chest.

"This looks just like something my mom would wear," I whisper.

Lachlan eyes me warily. No doubt waiting for my mood to shift into something darker. But the sleeveless gown is beautiful. The neckline cuts straight across the collarbones, and ruching is sewn across the bodice in three different places. It's very regal and totally my mother.

I move to drape the dress across the boxes next to us and reach back in for the piles of leather at the bottom. But a piece of folded parchment falls to the floor when I pull out the pile of leather straps that have become entangled. Lachlan stoops to pick up the folded parchment that had clattered to the floor, and he carefully unfolds it.

A light floral fragrance wafts from the paper. Something about the scent tugs at my memory, and I instantly forget about the tangled leather and drop it back into the box as I study the faded ink on the parchment.

It's hard to make it out completely, but it looks like a map of an island.

The island is drawn out in black ink, but there are several depictions on the island drawn in gold ink. Some of the gold-colored drawings are of curved mounds with small openings; they resemble burial sites. The other drawing is of small vertical lines, twelve of them in a circle.

But what caught my eye was the drawing of my medallion shimmering in the top right corner of the map.

"Lachlan, that's my medallion in the corner. Look!"

The elation at finally finding something related to the necklace has me jumping up and down. A cheer flies from my lips, and I quickly smother it behind my hands to avoid waking Gran. He chuckles at my exuberance, but then his brows furrows in concentration. Relief flows through me; as if a heavy load has been lifted.

Lachlan gently lays the map out on top of the box and leans in closer to study the gold drawings. Realization flickers across his features, and he digs his phone out of his pocket. A couple of swipes later, he holds his phone out to me, excitement brimming in his smile.

"Look!" His phone is pulled up on a map of the Orkney Islands; it's a perfect copy of the map in front of us.

"It's Orkney!" I gasp.

Lachlan is still glancing back and forth between his phone and the map. "The gold drawings here line up with the Ring of Brodgar, and look, that mound is where the Maeshowe chambered cairn is." He grins broadly at me. "Would ye care to join me now?"

I've never been to Orkney, but from the way he describes it, I think it sounds like a place I would love to see. But leaving Gran for the weekend when we don't know how many good days she has left really worries me. My mind is spinning with the connections and the possibilities this could mean, though. I bet if I asked Maggie to stay with Lizzie, I could manage a weekend trip. That and Gran's last words, 'You need to go,' push me.

"Can I really come with you this weekend? There might be something there that would have answers, and I—"

Lachlan cuts me off. "I would love to ha' ye come with me, Key."

Satisfied that he seemed genuine and wasn't just placating me, I smile back at him, saying, "I can't believe we actually found something."

Lachlan still seems to be locked onto the map, tracing the outline of the medallion. I don't know if it's the excitement fueling my newfound courage or just his unnaturally handsome face, but I quietly say, "I'm excited about our first adventure together; we make a great team."

Lachlan's eyes quickly flash from the map to mine, and he smiles. "We do make a great team." His eyes are bright, spurring me on.

"We kind of belong together." I hold my breath, waiting for his reply.

His eyes dim. "Of course we do; you're the Key to my Lach."

His smile is comforting, but his words are not.

It really doesn't answer my romantically charged questions, but if all I can ever have from him is friendship, I'll take it. I'll take whatever he can give me as long as he always stays around.

"So what does one wear in Orkney?" I tap my finger on my chin, contemplating what to pack, and he chuckles.

CHAPTER

FIVE

Birds fly overhead through the gloomy clouds, the weather looking grim and unhappy. But I've never felt more alive as we ride the ferry from Aberdeen to Orkney. My smile hasn't faded once in our journey here and is currently smashed against our window as I admire the North Sea. The glass is cool against my cheek, but my excitement is warm throughout my entire body.

Lachlan chuckles as he glances at my delight. "It's a 6-hour ferry ride. Ye might want to catch up on some rest."

I gawk at him like he's grown two heads. "And miss all this!" I fling my thumb to the view out the window.

"Aye, it is beautiful, isn't it?" He agrees, but his eyes are on me and not the sea.

Lachlan's hair is disheveled from the wind, and his dark green eyes are sparkling like emeralds in the sunlight that burst through one of many clouds and stream through our window. I can't help myself as I reach out and smooth his hair back from where it's fallen over his eyes. His hair is as silky as I imagined it would be, and I savor the way it glides through my fingers.

"Thank you for letting me tag along. It's been a while since I've been on an adventure."

Lachlan clears his throat, avoiding my eyes. "The pleasure is all mine."

He leaned in when I stroked his hair, and my pulse cranked up higher. Perhaps there is a bit more to this friendship, after all. Lachlan continues reading his book about Leif Erikson's adventures while I admire the color of the sea and the birds flying by. My guilt rears its ugly head and my smile fades.

"Are ye alright?" Lachlan eyes me from above the pages of his book.

I clear my throat. "Just worried about Gran."

He smiles kindly, his teeth flashing brightly against his tan skin and trim beard. "We'll be back soon."

I sigh, knowing he's right. I'm beyond grateful that Maggie agreed to stay with Lizzie and help with Gran in my absence. I didn't realize how much her disease had begun to twist my every thought into a giant ball of anxiety. Immense masses of land begin to rise out of the sea before us, and my guilt vanishes.

I suddenly feel as if I'm headed toward home.

When we disembark, my anticipation has only increased, my body practically vibrating with my excitement. Lachlan runs me through our itinerary again.

"Alright, I ha' to go check in on my place and drop a few things off. We can grab a bite to eat first though, and then… which site did ye want to check out first?"

"Hmm, I've got a few thoughts about that. Our map," — I wiggle the folded-up parchment in the air—"has twelve stones drawn, but you said there's actually only nine at the Ring of Brodgar, right?"

Lachlan nods his head in confirmation. "Aye, originally there were twelve standing stones, but a few ha' fallen or become damaged, and now there's only nine still standing."

"If our map is old enough that it was drawn with twelve,

then maybe we need to see a complete site for answers, because what if one of the fallen stones had the answers but now it's gone, so we wouldn't know? Does that make sense?"

Lachlan's brows furrow as he thinks over my logic and turns the truck on. "Aye, that makes some sense. Where did ye want to eat?"

"Oh no, this is your home you get to pick." I tease.

Lachlan rolls his eyes and pulls off the ferry. "Street food it is. How does smash burgers sound?"

I purse my lips. "You do remember I was raised in the States, right?"

"Oh, I forgot you're practically American, so burgers are a staple, right?" He mimics my accent and chuckles.

I cross my arms and push out my bottom lip. "I don't like the way you said American."

There's no bite in my words, and he reaches across the console to tug one of the braids I have framing my face. "Nae of that sass, or I won't be feeding you."

I stick my tongue out at him when he looks back at the road, but he catches me anyway, and we break out into laughter. It's so easy to be myself with him. The gray stone buildings are cozy in the light rain outside my window as I face away from him to hide my ridiculously large smile.

We devour our meals quickly, but the sun is already sinking low on the horizon.

"Should we wait until the morning to go?" I ask.

"Nae, let's go by the cairn before we head to my place. There should be lights at the site, and we can use the torch I keep in the truck," he replies.

But I'm not too sure how comfortable it makes me to explore an ancient burial site in the dark. That's a bit creepy. But the possibility of finally getting answers on this mysterious family relic looms over my head and tips the scales in that direction.

Briefly, I close my eyes to try some mindfulness, wrestling with the anxiety and a feeling I can't quite grasp but is steadily building. Guilt floods me, and I realize just how much I miss Gran. I do my best to recognize the emotion and imagine setting it down, figuratively, in my mind. I breathe in, hold it, and exhale on a four-count to try to ease the feeling.

Lachlan reaches over and caresses my arm. "Ye alright, Key?"

The use of my nickname releases some of my tension, and a smile breaks my concentration. "I'm just a bit nervous for some reason."

"Ach, no need to be nervous. If we dinna find answers, we keep looking, okay?" he replies, misreading my worries.

I don't correct him. "Sounds good, Lach."

The sun has set, darkness seeping over the land as Lachlan pulls over in front of a nondescript cattle gate. The burial mound is a shadow barely visible past the wire fences in the middle of a pasture.

"Um, don't we need to go to the tourist center and get tickets?" I ask, pointing to the visitor's center signs up the road from us.

Lachlan unbuckles and opens his door. He rolls his eyes. "That's such a tourist thing to say, Key, just get out. Ye can hop a fence, right?"

My eyes widen, and my jaw drops in shock as I sputter, "This is an archeological site!" I inhale sharply. "This is breaking so many laws! There are literally Viking runes carved in there!"

Lachlan merely laughs as he shuts the door and walks up to the gate, smoothly hopping over it and offering me a hand over the gate.

Grumbling, I exit the truck, but my ears begin that familiar ringing. It's the same sound as before when I first spied the necklace. The memory spurs me on, and I clamber, not nearly as gracefully, over the fence and grasp Lach's hand.

The ground squelches underneath our feet; luckily, the rain

has finally stopped, and I'm glad I went with my boots this morning. We make our way down the little path next to the fence that intersects the pasture. An eerie sensation washes over me, and the hair on my arms is beginning to rise, not just from the chill. I pause to glance around, and Lachlan comes to a stop right in front of me.

"Ye alright?" I can feel his eyes on me as he tries to read my expression in the dark.

"It's kind of creepy out here. Like we're being watched," I reply. Thankfully, the ringing is still a dull hum. Goosebumps begin spreading along my arms.

Lachlan turns in a semi-circle in front of me. "It's just a cow pasture, ach I forgot the torch. Wait right here."

He rushes past me and back the way we came before I can tell him that I'd rather go with him. The gravelly caw of a raven causes me to shriek, and I whirl around to look for the beast.

The light is completely gone, and darkness swallows the path.

Yeah, this is not a good idea.

"Lachlan!" I call out, fear drenching me, but there's no response.

He couldn't have gone too far already, but I can't see or hear him at all. I'm so close to the cairn and figure there's bound to be a light near the entrance. I stumble forward along the path to the mound and away from the sound of the raven. A twig snaps behind me, blocking my path back to the truck, and I freeze.

"Lach if you're playing games, it's so not funny!"

A flap of wings by my head startles me, but there's a loud thud on the ground, like footsteps, that frightens me into action. Throwing caution to the wind, I sprint to the mound.

My heart pounds with each strike of my feet on the grass. The ringing becomes more shrill. I'm so tense with fear that it's difficult to stay upright, and I stumble along the uneven path.

A misstep has me careening into the fence, and the wire rips through my sweater.

It stings, sharpening my terror, but I keep moving forward.

At best, it could just be a cow that's about to run me over. At worst, my mind conjures up murderous men with axes or demons. My pace increases with each frightful image.

At last, I see the glint of a metal gate in the moonlight and hurl myself over it.

It looks like I've made it to the entrance of the burial mound. As my luck would have it, there's no light here. My ears strain to hear over the high-pitched ringing and my rapid panting for any sound of what was chasing me, but there's nothing.

Unfortunately, the path took me around the mound, so there is no way to see where we parked or the direction from which Lachlan would be approaching.

I lean over to put my hands on my knees, trying to catch my breath. A loud screech breaks through the ringing of my ears, and I look up just in time to see a large black shadow swooping down at me. Moonlight shimmers off iridescent black feathers and sharp talons that are coming directly for my face.

A scream erupts out of my mouth, and I stumble backward through the entrance of the burial mound.

Somehow, I managed to stay on my feet, but the world is tilting off its axis. The ground rises up, and my hands move to shield my face, but not quickly enough; an explosion of golden light, as bright as the sun, scorches my eyes. Blinded and faintly dizzy, I squeeze them shut.

The flapping of wings slowly fades away.

I massage my burning eyes with my fingertips, and the ground beneath my feet rocks a little before becoming still.

A light breeze cools my skin and ruffles my hair. The air feels different than before. Lilac and jasmine wrap around me on another gentle breeze, and strangely enough, the warmth of sunshine upon my skin.

A golden light illuminates through my closed eyes. The sudden change in temperature and floral fragrance has me pausing.

Shock locks my body into place.

A few feet away, someone clears their throat, and a male voice whispers, "That doesn't look like Bryn."

The sound of my mom's name has me snapping my eyes open.

I scream.

SIX

This is certainly not the underground cairn I was just tumbling into.

I'm standing in the middle of the largest, whitest marble room I've ever seen. It is easily five stories high and constructed entirely in glittering white marble. Sunlight streams through various open-air vents on the ceiling. Towering pillars create four giant doorways, two on each side of the rectangle-shaped room. But the room is too small a word to describe this place; it's a palace.

Did I hit my head and die? Is this the afterlife?

My attention falls on the crowd gathered around me. I whirl around, my boots squeaking on the marble floor. "What the hell just happened?" I shriek.

A beautiful woman with slate-blue eyes approaches me. She's dressed in the same costume dress I found in that box of my mom's belongings, the pale blue color so light it's almost white. My brow furrows, and such a familiar feeling washes through me. The dress is a mere sheath for her outrageously toned body. Her bone structure is similar to my mother's, but sharper and unlined with age. Her golden skin is bathed in the spear of sunlight she's standing in. A gentle breeze ruffles her onyx hair, which rests just above her shoulders.

She takes another step towards me, her palms up, in a consoling gesture, as she reaches towards me.

"Hello." I'm grateful she speaks English, but her accent hints at something foreign, northern. "My name is Odessa." She places a hand on her chest. The many rings she's wearing sparkle in the sunlight before she reaches towards me again. "What is your name?"

A golden circlet rests above her brow and catches the light as she tilts her head. With a crown like that, she must be the one in charge.

"Am I dreaming? Is this like a coma dream, or did I die??" I ask, ignoring her question.

Odessa presses on. "Can you tell me your name, girl?"

Squeezing my eyes shut, I inhale slowly while mentally checking my body; nothing feels broken. Opening my eyes, I pat my head, checking for lumps, and rub my hands down my arms. My sweater is ripped open on my arm from the fence, but there's nothing where there should be torn skin. I cut my arm while running, so why isn't there a mark?

It's because I'm dead, right?

Putting that aside for the moment, I study my surroundings and notice that the woman in front of me, Odessa, has large opalescent white wings peaking over her shoulders. Their ends barely hovering above the ground.

Swallowing the lump in my throat, I choke out again, "Is this the afterlife?"

Odessa gives me a sympathetic smile, the movement causing her slate-blue eyes to soften. "No, girl, this is Idirhalla. Can you please tell me your name so I might be able to give you some answers?"

The name Idirhalla tickles something in my memory.

"My name is Helena—Lena, my name is Lena," I stutter.

A sting of pain has me glancing down to see the little crescent moons I managed to gouge into my palms. I felt pain, so this is real.

Realization flickers in Odessa's eyes as I meet her stare, and she softly asks, "Is your mother called Bryn?"

Tears well up at the surge of emotion her name invokes and spill over, rolling down my cheeks. "That was my mom's name," I whisper, choking on the sorrow that bubbles up. "She died."

Odessa covers her mouth with a delicate hand. "My sister."

Sister?

"I'm sorry, I think you have the wrong person; my mom didn't have a sister."

Odessa shakes her head and points to where my necklace hangs from my neck. "That was hers."

My body trembles and my mind struggles to make sense of her words.

Did she say my mom is her sister?

My silence stretches on, and the small group murmurs amongst themselves. Their faces blend together as my eyes spin around the room. Odessa looks at me expectantly; her face is kind. I force my eyes to focus solely on her.

Clearing my throat, I forge on. "Look, I don't know what's going on or where I am, but I need to go back. My friend is probably freaking out looking for me, and my Gran is sick, and she needs me. I need to get back, so can you send me back?"

Odessa studies my necklace briefly before looking me in the eye. "We can't send you back." Her expression is replaced with a teeth-bearing grimace.

My breathing quickens, the terror swelling, and I clutch my necklace to my chest. She responds to my rising panic and quickly says, "Well, we're not sure." She waves a hand to include the people around her. "The power, our magic, in this realm is fading." I inhale sharply through my nose. "We were hoping when we heard your mother's charm." She points to my neck-lace. "That it was her coming back to save us."

I force myself to inhale slowly, trying to master my panic, and observe the surrounding people; they're a mix of stoic-faced men with eye-boggling muscles dressed in linen or leather outfits. The few women that are gathered are a variety of shapes and sizes and are stunningly gorgeous. Two men shift slightly on either side of Odessa, looking much younger than the other gathered men.

But out of the two, only the red-haired man I am comfort-able looking at. His face is even more kind than Odessa's, and there are raven-black wings rising behind his shoulders. My knees begin to wobble as her words catch up to me.

Meeting Odessa's eyes, I say, "I'm sorry, did you just say magic? Where am I? And how do you know my mother?"

My pulse is still racing, and now my stomach twists into knots. I'm going to be sick; my mouth fills with saliva, and I swallow hard. My face turns a sickly green shade.

Odessa reaches one hand out to me while pointing the other one at the doorway behind her. "Why don't we step outside for some fresh air, and I can show you?"

My mother's eyes peer at me from Odessa's face, urging me to take her hand. She places my hand in the crook of her elbow and pats it. "I guess if your mother is my sister, that makes me your aunt."

Her smile is comforting, but I don't return it. The nausea is steadily building, and my legs continue trembling. Odessa feels my shaky movements and gently strokes my hand as she leads me through a giant doorway that opens to a sprawling terrace. She spreads her arm out as soon as we step outside.

"This is Idirhalla, which translates to the Between Hall." She gestures behind her to the colossal room we left. "And that is the Great Hall, your mother's former palace."

My breath catches as I take in the world around us.

From the vantage point of the terrace, I can see far into the distance. Below lies a small city on what appears to be an island, encircled by towering mountains that slice through the surrounding ocean. A glittering river winds its way through the middle of the city.

My chest aches.

I recognize this place. Even without seeing every detail, I know that the river that winds through the city is crossed by four arched bridges, that the same city boasts colorful buildings, and that there are farms way up in the mountains.

Because this is the land my parents told me stories of when I was a child.

I close my eyes, remembering their stories about the waterfalls that cascade down from several mountains and how they create dazzling rainbows. I open my eyes and look at the mountains. My thoughts are confirmed when I see the rainbows glowing in the sunlight.

Odessa's last few words echo in my mind, and I whip my head to her.

"Did you say my mother's former palace?" The pieces finally click together.

The costumes, the stories, the lectures, and the strange otherworldliness.

My mother was from here. My heart cracks with the revelation.

Odessa addresses the people that have gathered by the doorway. "I need a moment alone with Helena." She addresses the blonde-headed man standing in front of the others. "Julius, can you begin the council meeting? I will be there as soon as I get her settled."

Julius had been the other man flanking her in the throne room. His height overshadows the men next to him; he's slimmer, though, a swimmer's physique compared to most of the men's brute muscles. As he nods to Odessa, I study his features.

Short, sun-kissed blonde hair and dark golden eyes, the color almost black except for their strange glint in the sun, make him fairly attractive, but a slight sneer spoils his good qualities.

"Of course, my dear," he murmurs.

His voice makes me want to recoil, but he throws me a small smile before herding the remaining audience with him.

Odessa waits until the footsteps have faded before she speaks.

"Your mother was Queen Bryn."

Her words halt my breathing altogether. My mother was a queen here.

I blink hard, trying to wake myself up, but it's futile. This is all real.

"I have heard of this place, but only through the stories my parents told me as a child."

She leads me further out onto the terrace, and I can see that part of it overlooks a small garden, with vibrant colors contrasting against the terrace's white stone. To the left of the garden is a cobblestone walkway that leads down to some long wooden buildings and spacious, flat grounds. But beyond the garden is the breathtaking view of the city that stretches out before us. We take a seat on a cool marble bench, and Odessa sighs.

"Well, I'm glad they mentioned this place to you, but I'm sorry you didn't know the truth before you arrived." I nod, agreeing. "I assume you don't know really anything about this place, though, do you?"

It's hard to peel my eyes off the city as I take in the buildings separated by roads and trees.

"They told me of a place." I take a calming breath, still trying to adjust to my surroundings. "A place that was a paradise for the chosen warriors to come live and train for the Father's armies." My parents' loving faces appear in my mind before I push on. "They described a massive hall like the one we were just in, a land that looked identical to this one, and people with wings." I turn towards her. "I just thought it was their attempt at explaining an afterlife. I didn't think it was real."

Odessa pats my leg. "It is very real, and that does sum it up quite nicely, but things have changed since your mother was the Queen here."

"Like how?"

"Well, originally, we would travel back and forth between the human realm and this one, bringing the warriors Odin had chosen for his army, but we don't do that anymore. I mentioned earlier that we heard your mother's charm and assumed it was her. That necklace you're wearing opens the bridges between worlds, but we haven't been able to travel since the magic started to fade. I'm really not sure how you managed to reach us at all." Her gaze goes distant momentarily before her eyes sharpen, and she clears her throat. "But it's changed in more ways than that. Odin, the Father, has returned to the God's Realm. There is no war coming, so there's nothing to 'train' for. We live as we wish." She scrunches her nose. "Well, we did, but with the power in Idirhalla weakening since your mother left, terrible disasters have been occurring. It has brought about some unique challenges."

I clear my throat. "How is this tied to my mother?"

Odessa stares out at the city before us. "The power is tied to the royal bloodline through your mother in a covenant between her line and Odin. I've been the reigning queen in your mother's absence, but we only share a father and not the maternal blood-line through which power is linked."

I nod, but it's difficult to wrap my mind around the fact that I'm the daughter of a queen in a realm that has, or had magic, and is currently crumbling because of her absence.

"I have a few questions," I say, my brow furrowing.

Odessa smirks, her eyes flash playfully. "I'd be concerned if you didn't."

"First, not to be rude, but what are you? Like, why do you have wings? Second, what kind of magic is this power-fading thing? What does it do?" The questions tumble out of me so quickly I'm worried I might've lost her.

Still, she tilts her head. "It's not rude at all. I'm a Valkyrie, like you and your mother; that's why we have white wings. You will see others with black wings, but they are not Valkyrie, just guards." Her wings rustle in the breeze. I open my mouth, but she raises a hand to stop me from cutting her off. "We call it magic or power, but it's a blessing we get from the Father, and it's different for each person. Some of us have specific powers that are beneficial for battle, like creating invisible shields or moving things without touching them. But we all have a nearly immortal life span and quick healing capabilities."

My body sways on the bench; I feel like I'm on the verge of passing out as every new revelation pelts me like stones. I jolt off the bench. "I need a moment."

Odessa's eyes fill with understanding as she murmurs, "Take your time. I know it's a lot."

The ground is solid underneath my boots as I pace back and forth by the stone and filigree metal railing that separates the terrace from the garden, a small drop below.

I halt beneath the branches of a broad, blossoming tree.

The light pink petals dance in the breeze. The fragrance of the blossoms is heavenly as it washes over me. Overcome with the magnitude of emotions coursing through my body, my eyes close, and I attempt a round of mindfulness, but the massive amount of emotions to pick through and set aside is daunting. Instead, I sink to my knees and focus on the feeling of the ground beneath me.

But thoughts swarm me.

This world is in jeopardy because of my mother? Guilt

consumes me, and my stomach roils. The next question stings. How could she ever let that happen? I squeeze my hands into fists. I'm trapped here. This is too much. My palms become sweaty.

I can't be trapped here; I've got to get home.

I force my mind to quiet with a few rounds of counted breathing; I pick myself back up and walk back over to the bench—to my aunt.

I've spent my whole life without family other than my parents and Gran, but now I have an aunt. That's a small silver lining, I suppose. She pats the space I vacated in welcome before I sit beside her.

"Okay, so how do I get back? Because as happy as I am to meet you, as I said, I have people back home who need me and are probably worried about me."

She ponders my request for a moment before she replies, "I believe you'll need your own power to manifest, and you might be able to travel back, but if I'm being honest, I would like you to stay here. You are your mother's daughter and the rightful heir to the throne."

I swallow audibly; the daunting responsibility she's placed on my shoulders threatens to undo me.

"But if I don't want to stay, then what happens?" I whisper, glancing up at her circlet.

Odessa clasps my hand with hers. "I won't say that I won't let you return if we find a way. I want you to stay because I think you are the only person who could save us. Magic would be restored if you stayed. But if you leave, then magic will begin to fade again and with it, our realm will cease to exist."

I tense at the meaning of her words, the weight of all that responsibility pushing heavily on my shoulders.

She smiles, sadly. "But if you do not wish to stay, I will not force you."

My shoulders sag a bit in relief and she studies the change in my expression.

"You have more questions."

I bite my lip. "Yes. You said I have wings, but I don't. And my mother definitely didn't. And maternal line? Does that mean my Gran is from here?"

Odessa's wings flare a bit as she rolls her shoulders, preparing to answer all of my questions, and it's mesmerizing; the light sends rainbows reflecting from each glossy feather. I definitely would've remembered if my mother had those. I've dreamed of being able to fly my whole life, and a small part of me hopes she doesn't have the wrong person.

"Since you weren't born here, your wings never developed; there's little to no magic in the human realm. There's just enough for the smaller creatures and some shifters. As for your mother, she was a very powerful Valkyrie and, like me, had the ability to vanish her wings." Odessa's wings vanish, and my face twists in utter disbelief. Odessa chuckles at my expression. "And if your Gran is your mother's mother, then yes, that would make her Queen Skadi."

The thought of my Gran ruling as queen here makes perfect sense; she always seemed more suited for a throne than her favorite wingback chair at the Hall.

"My Gran is really sick; that's why I need to go home," I mumble.

Odessa pats my thigh consolingly. "There's not enough magic in the human realm to sustain her immortal body, so she would have begun to age and fall victim to many human ailments. I'm sorry, Helena."

A question begins forming in my mind, but the more I focus on it, the more it slips through my fingers.

Odessa stands and pulls me up with her, interlocking our elbows. "You can ask me more questions on the way, but let me show you to your room so you can rest and come to terms with all this. I need to fill everyone in on your presence here." My nod is barely noticeable and doesn't seem satisfactory enough for her. "Unless you don't want to be alone?"

Remembering she told the man from before, Julius, she'd be late to the council meeting, and that she is the Queen after all, I reply, "No, it's fine, I'll be okay to sort through this on my own for a bit."

"Okay, good. I'll be right back after the meeting, and we'll get you a proper dinner. I'll have someone bring up some refreshments in the meantime, though; there's no telling how long this meeting will last." She rolls her eyes as she finishes. The action is so normal and endearing I find myself leaning into her, hoping to absorb some of her strength.

We walk arm in arm into the Great Hall, the entire palace sparkling white marble from floor to ceiling. The place I materialized from is marked with a gold rune, consisting of a long main vertical line bisected by a short line at a slanted horizontal angle and a small triangle on its side of the beginning of the main line. Odessa glides us over the rune that's positioned in front of a large glittering chair surrounded by peaks of glass; a pale green light radiates from within the hazy clear stone that resembles quartz.

The chair is large enough to seat four grown men, and my jaw drops. She notices my stare and shocked expression and nods towards it.

"My throne." She smirks.

But we keep walking across the room and down one of the open-air hallways.

"The Great Hall consists of a single throne room with four entrances, two on each side; the hallway we're in now is on the north side of the Great Hall; it has two levels of sleeping quarters, bathrooms, private entertaining chambers, and a library. If you had taken the hallway to the right of this one, it would have led you to the dining hall, kitchen, and meeting chambers for councilors. The entrances on the south side of the Great Hall are the ones we just came from that connect to the gardens and the training ground. While the other passageway on the south side has a stairway that leads down to the capital." Odessa explains as she leads me down the hall.

The soaring ceiling has large gaps throughout, allowing sunlight to shine through and reflect off the polished marble floors. Our feet echo as we continue walking past open stone doors. I catch glimpses of large rooms with couches in neat rows and floor pillows strewn about haphazardly, and they look cozy and inviting. There are smaller wooden doors along the hallway, each with intricate carvings of knots framing them; most are shut, but the open ones reveal bedrooms with towering windows overlooking spectacular views, canopy beds covered in various rich earth-toned colors, and plush-looking rugs.

This place really is a paradise.

A question forms in my mind, and I clear my throat. "You said the magic was fading; how do you know?"

She tilts her head to the side, thinking. "It was a slow progression at first, but our powers began to decrease noticeably. Our gifts lessened in might, and then our healing capabilities began to slow. There were several unfortunate accidents until we realized what was happening." Sadness dims her eyes, and my stomach sinks, recognizing the grief that mirrors my own. "Then the weather became volatile. Devastating winds have ripped through the city, damaging buildings and trees. The usually mild winter in the mountain regions has lasted three years now and decimated many crops. By the second year, we had begun relocating many farmers to the southern parts of the mountain so that it wouldn't continue to impact our food supply."

My mouth drops open; that sounds terrible.

She takes in my expression and pats my hand. "Not to worry, you're here now, and it should all return to normal."

I grimace at her assumption; I need to get back home.

We stop at a door at the very end of the hall. There's a poppy carved into the wood parallel to my eye line. That'll help me remember which room is mine. We passed more than a dozen rooms on our walk here, and I was so busy thinking everything through that I hadn't even bothered to count the doors. She pushes open the door, and I'm speechless by the wondrous room in front of me.

Floor-to-ceiling windows make up the adjacent wall, but there's no glass separating the room from the outside; only gauzy curtains fluttering in the breeze. The bed is like the others I glimpsed on the way here, a large carved wood four poster with a white canopy stretched across the top. The bed is draped in many varying shades of white and cream with plush-looking pillows. A circular rug depicting mountains, birds, flowers, and grassy hills lays beneath the bed and stretches out into the middle of the room.

Odessa walks to an armoire across from the bed and opens it up. "The climate stays mild here in the Capital, so you might want to change into something cooler." She nods at my jeans and ripped sweater. She pulls out a long skirt and matching top and places them on the bed. "There's also a bathing room attached if you need to use the toilet or splash water on your face." She points to the doorway I didn't notice was on the other side of the armoire.

I'm frozen at the threshold, trying to keep up with her instructions.

Odessa walks to me but hesitates. "I'll be right back, and I'll have some refreshments sent up, okay?" I nod at her. She gazes into my eyes as she cups my cheek. "I know you're probably in shock, but I am really happy you're here. Eat something, and I'll return as soon as I can."

She walks past me and pulls the door closed behind her, leaving me alone facing the room.

CHAPTER

SEVEN

My head tilts back while I attempt to take a deep breath, but it cuts off as a sob rips out of my chest. Sinking to the floor, I wrap my arms around my knees and bawl. The fear, shock, and anger pour out of me with each tear that falls. Lachlan must be terrified, and I'm sure he's tried to tell Gran.

But who knows if she was even lucid enough to know who I am and the magnitude of what it means that I'm missing?

What if she thinks I left her like my mother did?

My stomach roils, my mouth filling with saliva, and I surge up to find the bathroom.

Hidden on the other side of the sizable armoire is the doorway to the bathing room. There's a short wall around the corner from the door concealing the toilet, and I'm so grateful for the modern comfort as I retch.

Once my stomach is empty, the effects of the shock subside, and I lean against the wall. The bathroom is as elegant as the bedroom. Everything is crafted from the same pale blue marble with dark veins of charcoal running throughout it. A wide rectangular sink is carved into the wall. Right above it hangs an oval mirror that seems to glow from the natural light that's pouring in from the skylight overhead and the towering windows making up an entire wall. A sunken tub, spacious enough for five adults, is tucked in the corner.

Despite the abundance of light and cold stone, there is a comforting warmth instead of a chill. Flames flicker from sconces hung around the room, but their light is overtaken by the sunlight. I pad lightly to the sink and rinse my mouth out. The water is crisp and frigid, invigorating my senses.

A knock echoes through the room, and I freeze before I remember. Odessa said she'd have refreshments sent up. I wipe droplets of water off my chin with my sweater sleeve and pad over to the bedroom door.

I crack the door open hesitantly, but no one is there.

A tray of food sits on the ground with a small glass of water. I glance down the hall before I push the door open further and bend down to pick up the tray. I'm not really hungry; shock still numbing my limbs. My mind is still spinning.

I place the tray on the bedside table and sink onto the side of the bed. But when I see the splattered mud on my jeans and boots, I lurch off of it. I eye the sheer curtains over the windows for prying eyes before I slip out of my muddy clothes and into the clothes Odessa laid out for me. The fabric is divine against my skin, and the breeze is able to cool my heated skin from my warm sweater.

A breeze flutters the skirt around me like the curtains by the windows. It's cream-colored and flows down to right above my ankles. While the matching tank top is sleeveless with a square neckline and four ruching lines cut across the bodice, similar to the dress I found in the attic. It's lovely and comfortable, and my mind appreciates one less thing to worry about.

The bed is like a cloud as I collapse onto it and try to grapple with my current situation. I lay the pieces out in front of me, so all the stories my parents told me were real, I somehow traveled to another realm, and I'm stuck here until, hopefully, my magic manifests because I am supposedly the only person who can restore magic to this realm.

No big deal. I can figure this out. *Right?*

The smell of the food permeates the room, and my empty stomach growls. The shock must be ebbing, finally. It's roast pork, some cheese, and what looks like raspberries. Some food might help me think clearly, so I sit up and dig in.

I've never, in my life, ever had food as delicious as this, and I wind up devouring the entire plate. With a full belly and the effects of the adrenaline rush, I slip into a deep sleep.

I'm awoken by a gentle knocking on my door and Odessa calling my name. My head leaves the pillow so swiftly it has the room spinning. I stumble my way to the door, pulling it open. She breezes past me and inside the room.

"I'm so sorry that took much longer than expected. I had to have several discussions about your sudden appearance and who you are." Odessa sits regally on the corner of my bed, her dress fanning out around her. "Have you had enough time to adjust? How're you feeling?"

I lean my back against the door. "I feel a bit better after eating and napping, but it's definitely an adjustment."

"Hm, well, how about a tour? Or is that too much for you?" Her tone is still gentle, but there's a hint of a challenge in her eyes that makes me bristle.

"A tour is fine, but are there certain shoes I'm supposed to wear? I don't know the customs here," I reply, looking down at my bare feet.

Odessa glances down at my bare feet as well and then heads to the armoire. She shuffles things around and reaches to the very back to pull out a pair of leather sandals with many straps.

"We're not stuffy with customs; these should fit you." She tosses them to me, and I catch them with a small oomph.

Apparently, I passed that test; she beams when I don't drop them. I lace them up and follow her out the door.

"If you start to feel overwhelmed or tired at all, let me know and we'll come right back here, ok?" she calls over her shoulder.

I feel a huge sense of gratitude for her compassion.

She must be a very beloved queen.

I nod and continue following her, but I slow down as her wings reappear. The feathers are a mix of lengths, but the longest ones make up the end of her wings. They resemble a swan wing, delicate but also mighty. They're astonishingly white and the light refracts off of them in rainbows.

Odessa's steps are confident, and her arms swing slightly, her muscles tense with the movement. She is incredibly toned. Her body looks like it's carved from the marble we're currently walking on.

Our steps echoing off the floor are the only sounds, and I feel the need to break the silence. "It's really quiet; do many people live here?"

"Not anymore." She sighs. "Now it's just a few of the remaining Valkyries." She ticks off her fingers. "Their mates, if they're mated, and a few servants. Then there are the guards, but they live in the barracks attached to the training grounds."

Mates.

My parents told me about that concept, too. Love that goes beyond the normal balances of the world and fate. Hearts bound together that nothing could ever separate.

I always thought they were only talking about themselves.

We halt in front of the throne. "Do you have a mate?"

Her grin slips into something mischievous as she replies, "Yes, Julius."

I want to recoil at her words.

Julius? The sneering blond guy from earlier? *Gross.*

But not wanting to offend the only person I know in this realm, I just smile and ask, "How did you know?"

"When you find your mate,"—she scrunches her nose as she works to phrase it in a way I might comprehend it—"well, there's no escape. When you know, you know, and that's it."

Her words elicit images of Lachlan. Gods, I hope he's ok.

I wonder if he's told Gran yet? I don't know if I want her to be lucid or not. If she is, would she explain to him what happened to me? Would he even believe her, though? Or would he chalk it up to a crazy old lady with dementia? Would it be easier if she didn't remember me at all?

My thoughts of Gran cause more questions.

"Why did my family leave here?"

Odessa frowns at my words and looks up at the throne. "Queen Skadi abdicated her throne when Bryn became more powerful than her. At the time, the strongest Valkyrie of the royal line ruled. Skadi abdicated peacefully, and to keep from interfering with your mother's rule, left for the human realm; it's not uncommon."

"Oh, but why did my mother leave?"

Odessa inhales through her nose and keeps her eyes directly ahead. "No one knows why exactly, but there were rumors," she trails off.

A non-answer, a politician's answer. She seems annoyed with this line of questioning, and I get the feeling it's not something she would like to discuss further. But the questions plague me. Could I be in danger here? Is that why they never told me? Did they leave because they wanted to, or did they flee?

Odessa must sense my unease because she quickly adds, "I think it was because your mother wanted to live a normal life with your father. He wasn't from here, and an outsider is frowned upon. She left roughly a century ago." She waves her hand in a circle.

Her explanation doesn't make sense, though. Yes, my mother loved my father greatly, but she wouldn't have ever abandoned her duties. Her stories of this place dance through my mind;

there was always an undercurrent of honor and gallantry. There's no way she would have walked away.

Odessa cuts through my train of thought. "Did you want to look at the dining hall and library, or did you want to check out the training ground?"

There's a sparkle in her eye when she says the 'training ground,' so I opt for the latter.

Her pace is quicker than it was before, and even though we are equal in height, I struggle to keep pace with her. We're just reaching the opening between the throne room and the terrace when she begins speaking again.

"As I mentioned earlier, this realm was a training ground for Odin's chosen warriors. He wanted to raise a large army for the Great War that was foretold to take place between the realms." We walk through the passageway and across the terrace, towards the stairs. "But as time went on and no war came, training for it seemed less vital, and enjoying life as we wished became more desirable. Most of the Valkyries still train daily as a way to observe the old ways and use their magic, what little they have left, but it's a choice for them. Most of our citizens have no problem adapting to the new ways, especially once injuries took longer to heal."

"What are the new ways?"

She says that phrase as if it's a different way of life. My mother raised me in the old ways. I wonder if my upbringing was similar to that of the children here.

"We've managed to shift our way of life from focusing on the gods and their archaic traditions to a new world without stuffy customs. We live how we want and appreciate the life we have without offerings or praises."

"Oh, I guess that makes sense. What are the citizens like here?"

"Our citizens here aren't just men; women can be warriors too, obviously,"—she grins—"and so inevitably partnerships happened between them, and children came along, so the realm has slowly evolved into what it is now."

We pause at level ground, standing on the path between the terrace and the training grounds, which are now beginning to peek out behind a grove of ash trees. The land here is lush with tall, vibrant green grasses that dance in the gentle breeze. Bright red poppies are scattered among the field with a smaller star-shaped, white flower I don't recognize. The sun is high overhead, its warmth kissing my face.

"What is it now?"

"It's a paradise for the chosen, a world between gods and mortals," she breathes.

CHAPTER

EIGHT

The clang of metal reaches us well before we reach the training grounds. Excitement quickens my pace as we walk towards the sound. The path we've taken looks to be meticulously laid cobblestones, but it's been trodden so many times the stones are worn smooth. Some of Odessa's smaller feathers flutter in the breeze and our skirts billow about our ankles. The breeze isn't cold, only cool enough to diminish the sun's burn.

Odessa pauses at a wooden archway that marks the barrier between the grounds and the training area. The horizontal beam that makes up the top of the archway has carved letters in a language I don't recognize, but seems familiar.

"What does that say?" I ask, pointing at the letters.

She snorts. "A relic from the past,"—she rolls her eyes—"it says: Those who live without discipline will die without honor."

The breeze halts as if the very land has stilled to hear the words. The brief pause is interrupted by the reverberation of metal on metal and the grunts of warriors. Odessa steps to the side, my view now unhindered to the handful of warriors in various activities.

My eyes are drawn to the tallest man and woman I've ever seen. They are sparring with swords and wooden shields. The man leans quickly to the right as a sword nearly grazes his long, braided black hair. He rightens himself, and his shirtless abs flex with the motion before being concealed by the shield he hoists into place. Blocking the next blow, the woman throws at him with her sword.

I don't know which is more impressive, the speed at which the man is moving his large body or the strength she is putting behind each of her assaults. She moves like an asp, but the sound of her sword crashing against his shield cracks as loud as thunder.

Odessa nods at the couple I'm staring at. "That's Tane and Mathilda. Tane is the only warrior willing to spar with her." She eyes them. "Mathilda is a Valkyrie known for her strength; it's her blessed power from the Father."

I nod, not taking my eyes off the scene before me.

Mathilda's honey-colored hair is pulled away from her face in two braids that are gathered at the top of her head in a high pony; they whip side to side like thick ropes with each lunge. Sweat is glinting off her tanned skin even though she's dressed in what I assume is training gear.

The complexity of the woven leather gives me the impression it was made specifically to keep the warriors cool and comfortable during their physical activities. Flashes of her tanned skin peek out from the crisscrossing gaps in the leather across her chest, which end right above her navel. The crisscrossing leather has gaps in the back that accommodate her wings, which flare wide with each lunge and tuck tightly when she shields.

The leather of her pants looks like they've been sewn onto her muscular legs. When she lunges at Tane, they flex with her movements and her wings slightly spread to counterbalance her bracing stance.

It's like an ancient depiction of battle.

Tane tries to retreat a step from her lunge, but she's too quick, and the shield he's holding is blocking part of his view. She slips a booted foot behind his retreating leg and yanks toward her. In one swift motion, he sprawls onto his back while he reaches out and takes her with him. Mathilda throws her weapon and shield out to the side as she lands on top of his chest, her wings tucked tightly to her body.

They burst into laughter. The affection they exude has me clutching my necklace. My chest aches with memories of Lachlan. Mathilda's wings flare as she stands and reaches down to pull Tane up easily. He retrieves her weapon and shield before he hands them to her and they walk to the refreshments table in the shaded corner of the training grounds.

"How come Tane doesn't have wings?" I ask, eyeing them as they rest together.

"He's only a warrior," she replies dismissively.

The only other people on the grounds are at the opposite end, near a long, metal-roofed, wooden building. The man is the red-headed man from the group earlier, the one with the raven black wings. I study him as he draws back a bow. His copper-red hair glistens in the sunlight while his wings seem to absorb the light.

Odessa turns with me and points at him. "That's Evander; he's one of the royal guards."

"His wings are beautiful," I mumble. His muscles flex from drawing the bow taught.

"The men who have been selected as guards for the royal family were either the male children of Valkyries or children of warriors who made the cut for selection. Once chosen, they were gifted with raven black wings by Odin," she replies.

Evander's wings vanish right after he fires the arrow that sinks into the center of the bullseye. I gasp as tattoos now ripple across his arms.

My face twists in shock. "What just happened?"

Odessa chuckles. "Part of their gift is also shape-shifting. He can shift the wings into tattoos upon his arms." She points at the wing-like black outline inked over his shoulders and down his entire arms, stopping at his wrists. "See."

With his wings now gone, I catch a glimpse of the tiny female at his side. She whips her chestnut brown hair from her eyes, and it sways right below her chin, the ends curling delicately. Her training top outlines her petite frame, but instead of the leather pants, she's paired it with a flowing skirt. She's handing Evander another arrow before I realize her hands are resting on her hips.

A small gasp escapes me, and Odessa sighs through her nose.

"And that's Wilhelmina; as you can see, her blessed power is moving things with her thoughts. Before magic faded, she could easily toss boulders, and now she's reduced to that."

"Is she a Valkyrie too?" I ask, not seeing any wings.

"Yes, she is. But Wilhelmina is...*different*. You won't see her with her wings out very often." Odessa is barely masking the signs of displeasure before she turns and grins at me. "Let's get you introduced, shall we?"

Her feet crunch against the soil of the grounds as she takes a few steps onto the grounds and then halts abruptly. Everyone turns to stare at us; I shift uncomfortably on my feet as Odessa stays rooted on the spot, causing them to come to us.

Once they're all gathered around, she steps back beside me. "Tane, Mathilda, Wilhelmina, and Evander, this is my niece, Helena." Her pause and head tilt my way, a clear indication she wants me to speak now.

I give an awkward little wave. "Hi, I'm Helena, but please call me Lena." My words are met with silence. "Uh, you guys all looked really cool out there."

They all continue to stare at me expectantly, and I grimace at the unwanted attention.

Luckily, Mathilda jumps in. "Are you adjusting well so far?"

Tane speaks before I can. "Did you really ask her that? She's only been here for a few hours." His accent indicates he's a New Zealander; I smile at the unexpectedness of it.

"Well, what else was I supposed to say? You're just standing there staring at her," Mathilda snaps back, but there's no bite to her words. Tane knocks her hip with his.

Wilhelmina breaks up their bantering with her soft, lilting voice. "Lena, such a pretty name."

"Thank you. Yours is pretty too, Wilhelmina, right?" She makes a face, her freckles scrunching on her nose. "Just Mina."

I immediately feel a kinship towards her.

Nodding, I say, "Mina."

She grins, pleased that I honored her request.

Evander juts his hand out. "Nice to meet you, Your Majesty." His eyes blaze with kindness.

I take his hand and give a small but firm shake, but I look over at Odessa for confirmation.

"He is… correct… you're the daughter of the Queen and the rightful heir to the throne." She sounds as if she's thinking it through as she says it.

"Thank you, Evander, but please, no titles, just Lena."

His cheeks redden, but he dips his head in confirmation.

A door slams loudly from the long building, and Julius struts towards us, flanked by two Valkyries. The Valkyrie on his right is as dainty as Mina, but that is where the similarities end. Her soft, rounded face is framed with wavy, strawberry-blonde hair that reaches her hips and complements her enchanting blue eyes.

The female on his left reminds me of a moonbeam. Her hair is as white as moonlight flowing down to her hips, as well. She's tall and wraith thin, her dark brown leathers standing out starkly against her pale skin. There's something vacant about her expression, though her pale green eyes, almost silver, look around dully.

As they reach us, Odessa gestures with her hand to the female that resembles a moonbeam. "Luna." Then to the smaller, soft-faced female. "Elowen."

They both nod in greeting.

Julius steps forward abruptly and into my personal space. "What do you think of everything so far, Helena?"

I'm assuming this is his best attempt at pleasantry. I don't step back, so I have to stare up into his eyes. "It's been a bit overwhelming, but it's so beautiful here, and please call me Lena," I reply with a smile.

]

He gives me a grunt of acknowledgment before angling between me and Odessa. "I need to speak to you, love."

Odessa glances around him at me. "I'll be just a moment."

They walk away, pausing under the archway. The others begin talking amongst themselves, and I glance at the two newcomers. Luna is studying her nails while Elowen is studying me.

"Umm, hi, Elowen, right?" I ask her.

She cocks her head to the side, the motion predatory, but her gaze is distant. "Helena, is it?"

Every time I hear my full name, I think of Shakespeare. Helena, from *A Midsummer Night's Dream*, with her lovesick plight and low self-esteem, is not a character I ever want to feel aligned with.

"It's just Lena."

I have to work to think past the memories of my parents. Luckily, she seems lost in her own world and doesn't even notice my struggle. Elowen smiles faintly, her eyes still unfocused.

"Unusual that your name, Hel-len-a,"—she pronounces each

syllable—"sounds like Hella, the queen of Helheim, and one of our enemies. Have you come to destroy us all?"

My smile is forced as I grit my teeth. "Unusual, *yes,* but Helena means light in Greek."

Elowen flinches at my response, her eyes sharpening into focus. "I see," she replies, her voice a shade softer.

Mathilda's laughter breaks through our conversation, and Tane smiles fondly at her; they must be mates. When I turn back to speak more with Elowen, she's slipped away and is speaking quietly to Evander and Mina, leaving me alone with Luna. I open my mouth to address her, but she sighs, still looking at her nails, and walks away.

Mathilda notices me awkwardly standing outside the group and makes an effort to draw me in. "Did you do a lot of training in the human realm?"

"Uh, not really. My Dad gave me a training sword when I was a child, but I lived under the assumption this place only existed in fairytales," I reply, and my answer silences everyone as they gawk at me.

Images of the wooden sword he gifted me for Yule flit through my mind. I spent hours outside with him, teaching me how to stand, parry, lunge, and strike correctly. It always seemed unconventional at the time, but standing here now it all makes sense. He was preparing me for this. For them.

Pity reflects in Mathilda's eyes, and she responds, "If you ever want to train, we,"—she gestures to the group—"would love to have you."

"That's very kind of you, but I don't know how long I'll be here for."

I need to get home.

Footsteps crunch against the dirt as Odessa and Julius rejoin the group.

"It might be a while." Odessa grimaces. "Julius was just speaking with the councilors and they say the only way to manifest your powers is to learn our ways. With you here, magic should begin to restore, hopefully, and the pathways between realms should open."

"How long will that take?" My voice rises alongside my panic.

"Well,"—Julius smirks—"it took a while for magic to fade, so it will probably take some time Helena."

Lena, I want to shout at him. My frustration is growing. I cannot stay here for a long time; I have to get back. Gran needs me.

Elowen places a comforting hand on my shoulder. "I can feel your magic," she whispers, her eyes glassy again. "It's an ancient magic." Her face scrunches up before she slowly lets go of me.

Odessa glances sidelong at Julius before looking back at me. "Elowen has the gift of sight. But it's been erratic as of late." She links her arm through mine and steers me away from the group. "Come, let's eat, and we can talk more."

The rest of the group goes back to training while Odessa and I walk arm-in-arm to the terrace, Julius following a step behind.

The hair on the back of my neck is standing on end, and I catch myself frequently checking behind me as we walk back to the Great Hall. His face remains passive each time, either staring directly ahead or scanning the surrounding area. My necklace presses against my chest, feeling like ice against my skin, even with the sun beating down on us as it sets.

Back in the Great Hall, we meander to the dining hall for dinner; Odessa seats us at the high table, the only table that runs horizontally at the front of the dining hall; the rest of the tables run vertically. She gestures to the chair on her right, the top rail of the chair intricately carved with ravens, identical to the chair she sits in. The rest of our table is also surrounded by beautifully carved chairs featuring different animals, wolves, swans, elk, and a fox. Julius takes the fox chair on her other side and drums his fingers against the sturdy wooden table top.

A young female, probably in her late teens, places a plate full of delicious-smelling food in front of me, and I smile as I thank her. She quickly looks down and backs away. Two other young girls are also placing plates of food in front of Odessa and Julius, but they don't acknowledge their presence. I wait patiently for the blessing, but Odessa looks at me expectantly.

"Aren't you hungry?"

"Yes, I just didn't know if there were any customs or anything?"

I pick up the silver fork.

Shouldn't we be thanking the gods for our meal?

She chuckles. "Not anymore; just eat as much as you want. Tonight, we're having roasted lamb, fingerling potatoes, and cabbage."

I silently say my thanks to the Gods for our meal and their many blessings before I pile my fork full of roasted lamb and a portion of the potatoes and moan at the incredible flavors. Paradise indeed; this is the most delectable food I've ever had in my entire life. The flavors meld perfectly in a way that no other food has before.

Odessa pauses her eating to watch me take my first bite. "Good?"

Forgoing all my manners and answering with my mouth full, I mumble behind my hands, "Oh my gods."

She chuckles and resumes eating.

How strange that they literally live in a realm hand-crafted by Odin, and they didn't even thank him for the meal?

Julius begins speaking with her, and I tune him out. Lost in thought about Gran, Lachlan, and Torin. They've been constantly lingering at the back of my mind all day. I've been missing for a few hours now, and I can't even imagine what they must be feeling. If Gran is lucid, would she think that I found my way here? Guilt plagues my thoughts, and I push away my half-eaten plate. The plate scrapes lightly upon the table, drawing Odessa's attention.

"You're finished already? You need to eat more so you won't burn out too swiftly tomorrow."

"What's tomorrow?"

Julius rolls his eyes, but Odessa answers. "You didn't hear us? Julius has offered to train you. We hope it will manifest your power quickly. But that's after I give you a small tour of the capital in the morning."

A slight frown mars my face. "Oh, okay."

'Learn our ways' echoes in my mind. The sooner I do this, the sooner I can get back home.

Julius chimes in. "Did you expect to lounge around all day, and your power would just come to you?"

Odessa clears her throat and gives him a stern look. "I'm sure she didn't understand how it would work. Don't be unpleasant."

He shrugs off her reprimand and goes back to his meal.

She turns back to me. "You can head back to your room if you're finished, and I'll have someone fetch you in the morning. You're going to need plenty of rest."

I nod and push away from the table.

The effects of the most bizarre day of my entire life weigh heavily on my limbs, and I trudge back to my room. Mercifully, the Great Hall isn't too difficult to navigate, and I easily find my way back to my room.

The door shuts behind me, and I fight with what little energy I have left not to slump to the ground. Collapsing onto the bed, the rest of my energy depleted, but when the smell of cedar and rain fills my nose, I lurch out of the bed. The breeze ruffles the curtains, blowing the scent away, and my heart sinks. For a brief moment, I thought this all had been a dream after all, and I was waking up.

I walk to the window, pull a panel of the curtains aside, and lean against the edge of the stone. Mountains rise in the distance, and the smell of fresh, clean air fills my lungs.

How is this possible? And why wouldn't anyone tell me?

I clench my hands into fists. Fury rages through me.

How could they keep this life-altering secret from me?

I spend a long time at the window pondering every story my parents have ever told me. My emotions flip from astonishment to irritation. Every story they had ever told and led me to believe were fairytales had been true all along.

I want to go home. *I need to get home.*

It takes a while, but soon my anger begins to dissipate as I work through rounds of mindfulness.

Acceptance is still a long way off, but I'm able to think clearly and a plan begins to take shape. I am stuck here, for now, and if I want to get home, I'll have to practice their ways so that magic will restore and, hopefully, open the bridge back home — to Gran and Lachlan.

The thought makes my stomach hurt. I miss them and my life there. And the life I had begun to imagine having with him.

But resolve settles into my bones; I can do this. I can make it back home.

Tomorrow will be the first day of a very long journey.

CHAPTER

NINE

My eyes blink open. A loud banging rattles the entire door and sends shockwaves into my brain. Before I can even call out, Mathilda barges into my room.

"Woah, I didn't realize you were still sleeping. Are you ok?" She pauses just beyond the threshold; her pale green skirt and matching top cause her tan skin to glow as if lit from within. Slowly, I pull my body into a sitting position, the movement difficult as my head feels like it's going to explode. My hair is damp and clings to my neck. I push a palm to my temple.

"My head is pounding. What time is it?" My words come out raspy, my throat dry from sleeping all night with my mouth open.

"It's just past nine. Let me grab you some juice while you get dressed. Everyone is already waiting for you in the throne room. I'll be right back." But she halts, her hand on the door. "Wear one of the dresses. You're meeting your people today." Her smile is bright, kindness radiates from her eyes, and she slips out the door, her long skirt trailing after and her wings nowhere to be found.

Stumbling my way to the bathroom, my vision doubles and blurs. My limbs feel heavy. I splash water on my face and glance at myself in the mirror. Gods, my skin is smooth and glowing like Mathilda's, and my eye color has changed. They're no longer a slate blue but a startling turquoise, like the sun reflecting off the ocean. My body appears different too, my limbs feel longer, and a newfound strength glimmers in the lines of muscle definition.

I take a deep, calming breath and close my eyes, willing strength into my mind as well. My lungs fill effortlessly like the very air here was made for me. My mind stops spinning and immediately the low-level anxiety that I feel constantly vanishes like smoke in the wind. Well, that's a positive change, at least. My necklace feels lighter around my neck and not like the small weight I've grown accustomed to. It shimmers in the light pouring through the window.

My hair isn't quite as wild as I was expecting from a hard night's sleep, but my clothes cling to me in places where my skin is still damp from sweat. I braid my hair back into a single Dutch braid, pulling out the tightness of the plait to make the braid appear thicker.

The armoire is now fully stocked with a ton of dresses, skirts, tops, and training leathers. Odessa must've had more items sent up yesterday when she was giving me the tour. I smile at her thoughtfulness. She truly thought of everything.

I select the same dress that resembles the one I found in my mother's box of belongings and slip it on. The light blue dress is a twin to the one Odessa wore yesterday. Thoughts of home plague me as they climb to the forefront of my mind.

I've been gone a day now if time even works the same here; I really hope everyone is ok.

I'm lacing up the leather sandals when there is a knock at my door.

"Come in!" I call. The door cracks open, and Mathilda's kind face peeks around.

"Brought you some juice. Are you all ready?" She holds out the glass; the orange juice inside sloshes around but doesn't spill. I nod and stand from the bed, walking her way.

She gasps. "Woah, you look like—a Valkyrie! Did your eyes change colors?"

We begin walking side by side down the hallway towards the Great Hall and with my longer limbs, I manage to keep pace with her effortlessly.

"I think they did. Is that normal?" I can barely keep my voice steady.

"That's incredible,"—she studies my face—"it must be your body reacting to the magic in our realm, but we'll ask Odessa; she's still waiting for us." Mathilda's slight grimace makes me worry that it's not a good thing.

I take a sip of juice to soothe my dry throat. "Holy Gods," I mutter. Mathilda giggles.

"Is all the food and drinks here this incredible?" I ask.

She beams and her eyes seem to glow. "Of course."

We're crossing the threshold into the throne room when Odessa's voice rings out. "There you are!"

She's surrounded by a small group of people. I recognize Julius, Evander, and Mina, but the rest are a collection of surly or impassive male and female warriors. Odessa appears slightly agitated, her fingers plucking at the pleats of her ice blue gown, the bodice structured formally than the one I chose. It's more fitted with boning like a corset.

But Julius isn't hiding his annoyance at all, his arms crossed tightly over his leather-clad chest, a scowl on his face. What is his problem? I didn't take that long, did I?

Evander is grinning broadly at me, though, bringing me some comfort. He nods in greeting. His raven-black wings perfectly framing his long copper hair.

Mina smooths down the front of her lilac gown, identical to the one I'm wearing. She glances up at our approach and smiles, a twinkle in her eyes.

"Sorry!" I reply, taking a few steps closer. "I slept really hard and then had some difficulties when I woke up."

A servant approaches and takes the glass from my hand. I thank her, and she smiles before bowing and ducking away.

Mathilda steps beside me, the movement clearly meant to offer support. She grins, tilting her head towards me. "Look at her."

To my complete horror, the gathered assembly eyes me up and down. Like a bug under a microscope, the attention of all those eyes feels like hands raking down my body. Odessa, in utter shock, covers her mouth with her hand and retreats a step. Julius drops the scowl, his arms going lax and falling to his sides as he studies my unexpected changes. Something passes between Evander and Mina before they turn to smile at me.

"Is this, uh, normal?" I ask, as I tug on the end of my braid nervously.

Odessa nods. "Yes. It is common to have a few changes as one adjusts to the magic here, but not this quick." She glances sidelong at Julius, an unreadable look passing between them. The moment passes swiftly, though, and she plasters on a smile, addressing me again, "But don't fret, you're beautiful, darling."

I drop my braid as I smile at her compliment. "How does it happen, though?"

I still don't understand how less than twenty-four hours can bring such visible changes already.

Odessa clears her throat and smirks as she explains, "The realm was created by Odin. The very land, air, and water all contain magical properties. Every breath you've taken, every bite of food or drink you've ingested has supplied you with magic." She eyes me closely. "But it shouldn't have happened so quickly, not with the small amount we have left in the realm."

Her smile still doesn't reach her eyes. The slate-blue color looking more gray today. "Well, let's get on with it. Evander, are the guards ready for the procession?"

Evander clears his throat and dutifully bows his head. "Yes, my queen. We have guards along the parade route. I will take up the lead position with you and Lena."

Odessa merely nods and extends her elbow to me. I reach for it, but a sharp pain erupts from between my shoulder blades, causing me to flinch.

"Are you alright?" she asks, concern lighting her expression.

"Yes, I must've just slept weird." I roll my shoulders back, trying to soothe the pain, before taking her arm in mine.

Odessa studies me for a moment, her eyes narrowing with suspicion. "Then smile. You're going to meet the people."

We take the steps, all four hundred and eighteen of them, down to the city below. Yesterday, my legs would've protested, but today, they keep up with the others easily. My body is brimming with new strength and my muscles pulse with it.

The capital enfolds us as we take the steps down, and my eyes bulge. There is so much to see between the people, the buildings, and the homes dotted along the streets. So much life effuses from the city my blood seems to sing in answer.

All my life, I've been searching for a home, struggling to make places fit, like squeezing my feet into shoes too small. But nothing has ever come close to the excitement building in my chest when I take in the city before me.

Odessa gestures around us. "The mountains to the west are the Badb mountains, the ones to the east are the mountains of Edda, and that river you see cutting through the city is the Ayele."

My heart swells with emotion, almost bursting with it, and a laugh bubbles out of my chest.

Mina is on my other side, her eyes shining as she asks, "It's beautiful, isn't it?"

My mouth has fallen open, gaping at everything around me. "It's the most beautiful city I've ever seen."

Her smile is full of pride as she gazes around her home. The breeze brings the smell of spices, like cinnamon, rosemary, and thyme, and I inhale deeply. The cobblestone street is lined with trees, separating cottage-style houses adorned with vibrant flowers from the charmingly colorful art nouveau-inspired buildings. The buildings boast picturesque windows that offer glimpses into the various unique shops.

The sun blazes off the clay roofs, adding an extra sparkle to an already magical place.

Clusters of people line the sidewalks on either side of the wide street, congregating under the shade from the mature trees. Small children are perched upon their parent's shoulders or hanging from the tree branches. They smile and cheer at our passing entourage. Their joy is contagious, and I smile from ear to ear and wave back excitedly.

Men in the crowd are clad in leathers or muted linen tunics and trousers, their polished knee-high leather boots gleaming in the sunlight. The women wear a combination of flowing dresses or skirts in a delightful array of colors.

Mina leans in to whisper, "Try to figure out who came from which war it makes boring public events much more fun."

I really enjoy getting to see the people, and I am not the least bit bored, but I ask, "Which wars?"

She rolls her eyes playfully and scoffs at me. "The time span for the recruitment period was quite large. I'd say anything from Egypt's first dynasty, so 1250 BCE to"—she taps her chin—"to the Battle of Hingakaka in 1810."

I halt, gawking at her. "You mean to tell me that you were recruiting warriors for this tiny island for almost 5000 years?"

Her grin is wicked. "I'm not that old," she huffs, and her short hair floats up and around her in the breeze, making her already young face appear even younger.

"How old are you, exactly?" I study her expression and she flicks a stray hair away from her face.

"I'm one of the youngest. I just celebrated my 116th birthday. Mathilda is 200 something. I think. I don't really remember. We don't usually keep track."

My mouth pops open in shock. "I thought you were my age," I splutter out.

She shrugs. "It's kind of the same, really. We don't age here as you did in the human realm. I'm still considered a youth. Which is why I never recruited anyone. Odessa did a lot of recruiting, but she's much, much older than we are."

"There must be millions of people here," I breathe, looking around at all the different faces. There is no way there are that many people here; this island looks so small from the terrace's vantage point.

Confusion flickers across her face. "This isn't the only island on Idirhalla, and this realm is only one of many that the Father created for his warriors."

I glance sidelong at Odessa for confirmation, but she's smiling and waving at the people passing, absorbed in her queenly duties.

"Oh, I didn't know that," I mumble.

The embarrassment of my lack of knowledge floods my cheeks.

We continue making our way down the street, and we slow as we come upon a large white tent sprawling an entire alley. The people inside are speaking or arguing with vendors. Tables are full of fruits, vegetables, flowers, and spices. They pause their bartering as we pass, turning to us with smiles as they wave in our direction. Everyone seems so happy here.

Mathilda sidles up on the other side of Mina and leans over her to tell me, "That is where all the best fruits and vegetables are sold."

Odessa even points out a few stores to me in between her

waves to the people. "I know you're used to the human realm with its rigorous customs and laws, but here, there aren't so many rules and regulations. Some of the citizens and their families find fulfillment in opening up stores to sell clothes, books, and jewelry, or run bakeries and restaurants. But some are happy to only live off the land. The royal family provides the basics, but of course, for the extra things people desire, they will barter for with gold, livestock, weapons, handmade items, and the like." She waves at a passing family as she explains.

Mina points out a little girl from a family that's waving at us. "Her mother is from Egypt when Hatshepsut was the female king."

Her revelation stuns me; there is an abundance of history and different ways of life, and they all live harmoniously in this place. She waves to the girl's mother, but I continue gawking at her. Mina nudges my shoulder and points to the little girl who extends a tiny hand holding a red flower crown out to me.

I kneel in front of her, observing the flowers woven into a crown, similar to the ones my mother used to weave for me.

"Thank you so much; it's so beautiful."

I reach gently to take the crown from her. She beams, her warm dark eyes sparkling, and she dips her head, insinuating I should do the same. I smile broadly at her as I bow my head, the noise of the crowd ebbing away as she places the crown upon my brow.

"Our savior," she whispers, her little voice ringing in my ears. My smile fades as her words land a blow to my chest.

Meeting the people was not the best idea. How will I be able to walk away from this place now after seeing children like her who depend on me?

She looks up at her mother, her smile still dimpling her cheeks. I glance up to see her mother smiling down at her with pride and love. A lump forms in my throat as I work to swallow back my tears. When they both turn back to me, I smile through my longing.

"She's precious."

The woman bobs her head, whispering, "Thank you, Your Majesty."

Before I can correct her, Odessa is pulling me along. Mina and Mathilda are right on my heels. The moment still pulls on my heartstrings, and the little girl's words continue to ring in my head. Savior. But more than that, though, thoughts of my own mother weigh me down.

"Mina, is this an afterlife? Like, are the warriors dead?"

She shakes her head. "No, they're granted new bodies when they choose to come with us. They leave their human bodies behind and accept Odin's gift of a new life."

My mind whirls at the new information.

A caw from above has me swinging my head up. My eyes narrow on the raven perched atop one of the towering black street lanterns, the red banner attached waves slightly in the breeze, and the golden sword emblazoned with two large wings on either side of the banner. The bird clicks its beak at me, and a familiar sensation crawls across my skin.

That can't be the same bird from the human realm, can it?

Odessa notices my stare and whispers in my ear while she continues to wave, "It's one of our guards, Helena."

"That's not a bird?" I ask, my face pinched in confusion before she nudges me. I plaster on a smile and begin waving to a family we're passing.

She sighs, and I worry that my lack of knowledge is beginning to cause her some annoyance. "Shapeshifters, remember?"

"I thought that was just the wings to tattoos. I didn't know they could actually turn into birds!" My voice rises out of the whisper and into a shriek. Mina giggles at my surprise.

But Mathilda casually says, "It's a real challenge telling them apart in that form."

Odessa ignores me as she continues to smile and wave to the people that we're passing. I glance at Evander behind us. His wings absorb the light from above, but his smile glows brightly as he tilts his head in question. The movement is so familiar, like the raven that was once stuck in the chimney; the thought causes me to giggle.

Evander cocks his head even further, confusion marring his smile; he mouths, "What?"

I shake my head with a grin and turn back around.

Odessa nudges me and points to one of the buildings that's painted a bright red. "This is one of our schools. We have two. One is on this side of the city, and the other one is on Scota, the next island over. The classes are divided by age groups and are taught by volunteers with a curriculum approved by the crown."

The bright red building is lined with children out front, some smiling, some with perplexed expressions at the crowd.

"What is their curriculum like?" I ask, curious if the school in Idirhalla is anything like the schooling my parents gave me in the human realm.

"Our material is a bit dated." She wrinkles her nose in disgust. "We haven't been able to travel back to the human realm, or any other realm, to catch up on new theories, and we've restricted our history lessons, so mainly they learn languages, sciences, and math."

"You haven't let us teach our history," Mina grumbles under her breath. Her comment breaks through my thoughts.

Odessa whips her head in Mina's direction, anger radiating from her posture.

Then she sighs, her anger melting into exasperation.

"There's no need; there's not a war coming. We shouldn't frighten the young ones into thinking their purpose is to battle mythical monsters in a multi-realm war." My mouth parts, clear disagreement on the tip of my tongue. History is important; history repeats itself if you don't learn from it.

But Mina shakes her head. "Not now," she whispers.

I don't heed her warning.

"So you used to travel to the human realm a lot before?"

I hope it's a subject she's willing to talk about.

"Yes, of course, for centuries, we would retrieve the fallen that Odin had chosen. But as time went on, we received fewer and fewer directives. Then, we would often venture back and forth to learn the latest theories or technology we thought would be suitable for Idirhalla, but then that too ceased. We marvel at the human's new inventions, but most are not anything we would like to introduce here," she adds.

My curiosity grows.

Such a delicate balance of the old world meeting the new world. There are people here who lived in the human realm thousands of years ago. I wonder how much they marveled when the Valkyries brought them modern toilets.

The street begins to curve as we continue along, and the buildings grow closer together. We're approaching the peaceful river and the large arched bridge that crosses it.

Mina whispers in my ear, "This is the mighty Ayele River." She walks closer to the bridge. The waters are a crystal clear blue, and several warriors float by on carved long boats. Odessa leans back to hear something Julius whispers in her ear, and she nods in agreement before the ground starts to vibrate lightly. Mina stands a few paces in front of us, her wings appearing and flaring slightly. Her head tilts back, and she scans the surrounding rooftops.

Mathilda positions herself between me and the group of people that followed us from the Great Hall. Her wings also reappear and flare slightly, as if she's about to spring into the air. There are fewer citizens gathered on this end of the street, and some were downright glowering at us before the vibrations began.

A stark difference from the smiling and waving citizens we passed at the beginning of the parade.

The ground shakes more violently. The small vibrations turn into an earthquake. Odessa grabs my arms as the ground shudders beneath us. It's not enough to knock us off balance, but the citizens on the street clutch each other and duck into doorways. Our gathered group moves in closer together, panic flashing on many faces.

But then, all of a sudden, it stops.

I breathe a sigh of relief and check our surroundings. There is no damage, not even a knocked-over flower pot.

Odessa plasters on a smile before turning to me. "Julius was just telling me that because we started so late, we're now cutting into your training time."

My eyes shift to Julius, and I find him sneering at me.

Are we going to ignore the earthquake? And what is his problem with me?

Odessa doesn't notice his sneer as she continues, "So we'll have to end the tour prematurely and turn back now."

Evander slips in behind us to Mina's side, and Odessa turns us around and back towards the Great Hall. Mina and Mathilda turn together as one. But the tone of the group is disgruntled and slightly alarmed. This apparently was not the plan. Julius takes up Odessa's other side and flashes me his usual look of smug arrogance.

Maybe he wants Odessa to stay the Queen, and I threaten that future for him?

I lean in to whisper to Odessa, "I'm so sorry, I didn't realize we were on a tight schedule."

She simply waves me off.

"Don't fret. There will be another time to explore the Capital and the other islands."

Grasping my arm, she resumes our stroll up the street.

"Are earthquakes normal here?" I whisper.

There are still some people lingering to wave at us, but most have left either because of the earthquake or because they were not expecting us to come back this way. The people still on the street seem surprised to see us return.

"No, they started a few months ago. What magic we have left is struggling to keep our world balanced." She winces.

Their world has literally been falling apart since my mother left.

"Why doesn't Odin replenish the magic?"

"The magic is too far gone, and we haven't been able to reach him. But that doesn't matter anymore. You're here, and with you, in your rightful place, all will be restored."

A commotion behind us halts our group, and Evander raises his wings out wide, blocking our view. His wings are massive, and the light is completely gobbled up by the long black feathers. Mathilda and Mina spread their wings out on either side of him, effectively cutting us off from whatever is on the other side of them.

If Evander's wings are the night, theirs is the moon. The white feathers reflect the light back sharply enough that I have to shield my eyes from the rays.

A raven from atop a lantern flies down to the direction of the shouting, and a grunt can be heard before it cuts off.

Odessa curls her lip. "Well, this is a city of warriors. There are plenty of drunken fools roaming about," she says sharply. "Nothing to worry about."

Evander, Mina, and Mathilda hold their stance between us and the disturbance, but Odessa resumes the parade route, pushing us further away from them.

There are whispers around us as the people in our group murmur about the commotion. I can only make out a single word repeated several times, *rebels.*

However, Odessa seems decided to continue our earlier conversations.

"Did you have any questions for me so far?" She smiles and this time it reaches her eyes. Not wanting to wreck her current cheerful mood, I opt for a question about the realm, and not what we witnessed.

"Yes. Why did Odin return to his realm?" I ask, hoping to capitalize on her sudden willingness to answer questions.

But that seems like the wrong question.

Her shoulders tense. "The day after your mom left, Odin met with me to give me ruling authority over the Valkyrie covenant. He provided instructions that I was to hold the title until the rightful heir returned." She smiles at me. "And that he would be returning to the God's Kingdom because there would no longer be a Great War."

Something about her tone seems smug, but if I had the realm bequeathed to me by the God who created it, I would probably be a bit smug, too.

"Oh…." I trail off. "How did my family become the royal family?"

Surprise lights her eyes. "That's a great question. Odin had always favored your ancestor, Brynhildr; she was one of the very first Valkyries he created. Your mother looked exactly like her, and much of the gossip around here claims that she was the reincarnation of her soul." Confusion mars my face, but she continues. "Even though we seem fairly immortal, we can die with the right injuries at the right time; several of the accidents that have happened recently have taken the lives of many of the older ones."

There's a strange gleam in her eyes, but she quickly cuts off when Julius nudges her.

We continue back through the city and up the stairs to the Great Hall.

Odessa turns to me once we've reached the throne room. "Have a bite to eat, then change into your leathers. Julius will meet you on the training grounds in an hour."

In a surprising move, she hugs me, the embrace a comfort I hadn't realized I needed.

TEN

The comfort does not last.

My new tight training leathers squeak faintly with each movement as I pace back and forth, waiting for Julius. My stomach growls loudly and I groan. My nerves got the best of me, so I only managed to pick at my lunch.

But before my anxiety can grow even larger, Mathilda walks through the archway, and relief lightens my mood. I'm elated that I won't have to be out here alone with Julius. Something about him makes me uncomfortable.

"Hi!" I call across the grounds as she heads my way.

She grins widely at me. "I overheard you had your first training today and came to give you moral support."

"I could kiss you right now. You have no idea how relieved I am that you're here."

She giggles and ties up her long honey hair. During the parade, she wore it down and the voluptuous curls bounced as we walked, making her appear more feminine. But now, with her tight, high pony, there's an edge to her features, a warrior's face.

"What, you're not a fan of Julius?" she asks, rolling her eyes.

Her voice is laced with sarcasm, the tone instantly reminding me of Lachlan.

"Oh my Gods," I squeak. "I thought it was just me! But he's off-putting, right?"

The relief of hearing like-minded thoughts untangles the knot growing in my stomach. I thought he'd been rude to me because I was a threat to Odessa's title, but maybe he's rude in general, and I'm not a target.

"He's an acquired taste for sure. He's the only son of a Roman Legate and was born here in Idirhalla," she replies.

"The only child thing makes total sense," I murmur. "My parents were terrified I would have only child syndrome." She laughs at my joke, and it emblazons me to press on. "It's weird he's mated to Odessa because she seems so—nice," I finish slowly, trying to speak delicately.

"She hasn't been the same since they've become mates; she's…" Mathilda hesitates, searching for the words. "Distant and very easily irritated."

My shoulders drop. "I thought I just annoyed her with all my questions."

Mathilda chuckles. "No, it's not you; we all used to be close before," she trails off.

My eyes widen as Tane sneaks up behind her, his arms outstretched, aiming to put her in a headlock. But before he can, she whirls, dropping into a crouch. In one swift motion, she kicks out with her leg meant to sweep his legs. But at the last second, he moves, and she only gets one of his legs. He wobbles, trying to maintain his balance, and then he stands upright.

Tane grumbles, "I thought I'd get you that time. What tipped you off?"

Mathilda giggles. "I saw your reflection in Lena's eyes, you oaf."

Tane slings an arm over her shoulder, and her wings twitch as she adjusts to his weight. He eyes me up and down, his brow is severely shadowing his dark brown eyes. He's very intimidating, and I struggle to meet his eyes.

Instead, I study the elaborate tattoos lining his arms. The swirls and lines are unique to the Maori people. I remember reading somewhere that their tattoos have something to do with their ancestry, skill, and social rank. By the looks of his, he must've been very important, judging by the amount of work and lines that accentuate his brawny arms; he's a mass of corded muscles.

"Why do you look like that?" he asks me.

Mathilda bumps him with her hip. "We've gone over this. You're a big guy with a grumpy brow. You have to smile or something when you talk."

Tane grimaces in an attempt at a smile. "Like this?" he speaks through his clenched teeth.

Mathilda giggles. "No. Now you'll frighten children."

"Oi, sorry, I mean you seem different from yesterday?" he says to me, but fake whispers to Mathilda, "Better?"

Mathilda and I share a look before we both laugh. Tane grumbles something about ridiculous women.

"It's fine. You are right; I am a bit different now. Odessa said it's because the realm has something to do with it, but whatever it is, I feel amazing."

I'm about to change the subject and ask them how long they've been together when Julius walks up. His presence ends our conversation. "This doesn't look like training to me?" he jests, but it comes out harsh. Tane's face shifts into something more glowering, and I realize the face I was getting from him was pretty pleasant compared to this.

Mathilda shifts slightly in front of Tane and his arm slips from her shoulders. "Sorry that's our fault," she says to him before adding, "We'll take the east sparring ring."

"Then it looks like we're left with the west end." He frowns. "In the shade."

As if I didn't like her enough already, I realized that Mathilda picked the sunny portion of the training grounds and had left the shaded side with the refreshments table for me. Gods bless her.

Tane keeps glancing over his shoulder at us as Mathilda drags him to their side of the grounds. I might be mistaken, but a glimmer of worry flickers in his eyes before they are back on her.

"Alright, since I gather, you know absolutely nothing about training." He smirks. "Let's just focus on getting a baseline today to see how much work this is going to take." Julius' lack of confidence isn't surprising, and if anything, his typical rudeness is kind of boring at this point, so I don't engage. I only nod.

He frowns at my lack of rebuttal. "Let's start with some sprints. I'll mark six lines in the dirt. Sprint to a line and then back to the fence, to the next line and back, until you've done each line."

Julius points to the training ground fence behind me, and I walk towards it, deeper into the shade. He begins drawing lines with his foot in the dirt.

Behind the fence stands a large maple tree. Its trunk is so large a single person couldn't wrap their arms around it. A weapon is lodged in the trunk of the tree. It looks to be an axe, but the blade is buried nearly to the hilt into the tree and it has started to grow around it. The shaft of the axe is a work of art, the carved wood depicting an elaborate scene of ravens in various stages of flight. Julius approaches behind me, having finished marking the lines.

"What's this?" I ask, pointing at the axe in the tree.

He widens his stance and crosses his arms over his chest, a very defensive stance. "Odin's axe." His reply is curt, obviously not wanting to elaborate, but it doesn't deter me from asking more questions.

"Why is it here?"

The feathers carved on each raven's wing are so detailed you can see the vanes and barbs.

"Because no one has been honorable enough to pull it from the tree." His words are laced with exasperation. The urge to grab the hilt and try myself burns through me. But before I can even try, Julius walks to the axe and slaps the hilt. The action is so crude and disrespectful, a taunt to the God who created this realm. I reel back in shock.

But he barks, "Now run!"

I force a neutral expression on my face while breaking into a sprint, racing to the first line and dropping low to tap the line with my hand before running back to the fence. My breath comes easy, and my muscles seem to vibrate, itching to go faster. I've never been a quick runner, having always enjoyed longer distances instead, so this is a surprise. This new body revels in the challenge, and I finish the task much quicker than Julius seemed to expect. I come to a stop in front of him, my breath still steady after hitting all six lines.

Surprise lights his eyes, but he glowers and yells, "Again!"

The sounds of sparring drift to us from where Mathilda and Tane are working together, slower than they were yesterday. My eyes meet Mathilda's several times during my sprints, and she throws me an encouraging smile each time. Tane catches my attention on my last line and even gives me a thumbs-up. Why couldn't they train me? They seem much more encouraging, and I feel immensely more comfortable with them than I am with Julius.

When I finish that set, I decide to feign exhaustion and pant slightly. Testing a theory that Julius will relish in my struggle.

Unsurprisingly, it works.

A satisfied smirk tugs the corners of his lips up, but not enough. "Again," he growls.

That continues ten more times before the exhaustion becomes real, and he's finally satisfied with my discomfort.

"Now that I've got a baseline for your endurance, let's see where your strength is. Pushups!" he orders.

He's getting pleasure from ordering me around. If he had wings, his feathers would be puffed up by the ego trip he's exhibiting.

Tane and Mathilda are taking a break beside the water table on our side of the training ground. Tane chimes in, "Hey man, you might want to let her grab a drink first." He raises a water cup in our direction, the glass dripping with condensation. Water sounds amazing right now.

My throat burns from my sawing breath, and my tongue is thick as I work hard to swallow.

Julius waves him off. "On the ground. Now."

I sink to my knees, and the dirt clings to my pants. My arms glisten with sweat, and my face burns. I can only imagine it is bright red from the exertion. A bead of sweat rolls down my cheek before dropping onto the dirt below me. Tane sets down his cup and crosses his arms as he leans against the table. Mathilda assumes the same position, aggravation radiating off both of them in waves.

Once I'm in the pushup position, I raise myself. But a heavy boot slams into my back, shoving me face down into the dirt.

A cry slips from my lips, but not in pain, in shock.

My arms collapse under the weight, and my face strikes hard against the ground. Dirt coats my forearms, exposed midriff, and cheek that slammed into the ground.

I look up from my sprawled position and through the cloud of dust.

Mathilda shoves off the table, but Tane wraps a hand around her arm and tugs her back to him.

Tane calls out to Julius, "That was uncalled for."

Mathilda is glaring daggers at Julius but doesn't fight off Tane's hold.

Julius leans toward me but says loud enough for everyone to hear, "I didn't say up yet."

A metallic copper taste fills my mouth as I bite down on my tongue, struggling to keep my temper in check. But my blood is boiling at the lack of respect.

I wouldn't last one second fighting this man, *not yet*.

But I curl my hands into fists, violence surging through me. I struggle to keep a level head and focus on my surroundings and not Julius.

A raven caw sounds from the tree behind us, and he quickly rightens himself. "Up."

I push myself up and hold the position. I lift my head up to meet his eyes when he doesn't immediately say down.

"At least you're a quick learner." He sneers. "Down."

Tane and Mathilda do not move from the water table, their sparring indefinitely on pause as they keep an eye on me. Their eyes gleam, never taking them off of Julius for the fifty reps he makes me do.

My arms are starting to wobble, my strength fading, when he finally says, "That's enough, let's check your balance."

He makes me stand with my feet shoulder-width apart. My arms outstretched at my sides before he begins shoving at my shoulders and swiping at my legs. Untrained and exhausted, I do my best to keep my feet planted and square my shoulders to weather his abuse. But he manages to knock me on my backside several times.

My eyes begin burning, not full of tears of pain, but of rage. My father had trained me in hand-to-hand combat and sword-play. Not once had he ever treated me this way. Even when I would be arrogant or challenging, he was always kind and patient. What Julius is doing is retaliation for me threatening his place in power. Despite his towering frame and lifetime here, he's just a small, weak-minded little boy with too much power.

He shoves me to the ground again, but this time, I struggle to rise.

Mathilda shoves past him, having seen enough of this abuse, and pulls me up. Julius takes offense to her help and squares up to her. She angles me behind her while Tane takes up a position right behind Julius. Tane's eyes blaze with barely contained wrath. He's absolutely terrifying. Julius realizes he's trapped between the two of them, and his smirk fades.

Mathilda speaks with lethal quiet. "That is not the way we train Valkyries, especially not our future queen."

Julius doesn't balk at her tone, even though her voice sends shivers down my spine.

He crosses his arms. "Interesting that you think you deserve an opinion. When the *current queen* saw me fit to be in charge of her training."

Mathilda continues to stare him down. "She's done for the day. We will escort her back to the Great Hall."

She reaches back, wrapping an arm around my waist, and keeps herself between me and Julius as she leads us past him. Tane glares at Julius a beat longer and then falls into step with us. Taking up the position on my other side.

Needing to have the last word, Julius shouts, "See you tomorrow, *Helena*!"

The raven perched on the tree flies above us, soaring towards the Great Hall. Mathilda follows it with her eyes, a slow grin softening her feral expression.

Once we've reached the Great Hall, Mathilda mutters to Tane, "Go check."

He nods and begins jogging back outside. Mathilda finally lets go of my waist and turns to me.

"Are you ok?" Worry creases her brow as she checks me over for any injuries. I'm covered in dust and my cheek throbs from where it smacked against the ground. But thankfully, my necklace remained tucked under my leathers, the shining gold remaining dust-free.

"Yeah. I'm fine." I dust the dirt off my leathers. "Thank you for sticking up for me back there; I didn't want to upset Odessa," I mutter my excuse.

I don't imagine my only family member on this island would take too kindly to me punching her mate in his arrogant face. But I'm beyond relieved to see that Mathilda and Tane will have my back no matter the opponent.

Mathilda rolls her eyes. "Julius is a wanker. I get into it with him at least a dozen times a day. No worries at all."

Her concern dulls the anxiety that had begun dampening my palms. "Thanks again."

She smiles at me before turning on her heel and leaving in the direction that Tane left in. The smell of an impending storm floats in from the direction she left. Memories of Lachlan bubble up, and I follow it to the terrace.

It's stronger here than it was inside, and I inhale deeply, allowing the familiar scent to dull the bitterness of my anger. I scan the horizon for storms, but there's not a cloud in the sky now.

I know he's not really here either, but if I ever want to see him again, I have to get this magic thing figured out quickly. With that thought, I decide I need to do some research on this place and its training customs or history to speed this along. I march off in search of the library.

My chest hurts as I take in the pitiful remains of what was once a grand library. Rows of empty shelves line the colossal bookcases. There should be thousands of books here, but there are only a few.

What has happened?

My footsteps echo through the empty chamber. Light spills in from the windows high above and the hole in the ceiling. Torches line the wall, casting light into the shadows between the shelves. This is a tomb; the emptiness gnaws on my soul. I stroke the spines of several books I pass, but none of them pique my interest. I need to read something about the history or customs here to better understand their ways. But all that lines the shelves are math books, philosophy texts, biographies on the different gods, and a few plant books.

There's nothing about the realm itself. No genealogy texts, religious customs, training guides, or history books.

How strange.

I know Odessa said they don't observe the old ways anymore, but shouldn't there still be evidence of their past?

I find a shelf of what looks like children's fables. Picking one, I carry it over to one of the small reading tables. Pages ruffle as I flip through them and my eyes widen. Stories my parents told me are beautifully portrayed on its pages.

Pookas, giants, selkies, witches, dragons, and the fae. Their stories are all combined within the many pages. I flip through to the end and pause. There on the last page is a picture of a man with hair black as night, emerging from the sea to battle a dragon. The words above the picture read: Sigurd and the Dragon.

I smile fondly at the picture, remembering the story my father once told me.

Sigurd battles the dragon that guards the Valkyrie, who was sent to the human realm as punishment and turned into a swan. Once Sigurd slays the dragon, he rescues the Valkyrie and removes her cloak so she turns back into a maiden, and they fall in love. He would always kiss my mom at the part, and a younger me would make retching noises.

They were so in love, so happy.

Slamming the book shut, anger stings my eyes. How could they keep all this from me?

My grief and anger have me pushing away from the reading table. I stalk over to the bookshelf and gently slide the book back in its spot. It's not the book's fault my parents lied to me my whole life about my entire existence. I don't even have anyone here that I can complain about this to, at least not anyone who understands me or them.

I wish Lachlan was here.

My mind conjures him up, the scent of cedar lingering in the air; he's always been my safe space. I plop back down at the reading table, allowing his memory to soothe my frazzled nerves. I wish he was actually here with me. I close my eyes, imagining his arms wrapping around me in comfort. My head tips back to the sun streaming in through the roof.

I whisper his words, "Tomorrow will be better."

CHAPTER

ELEVEN

Tomorrow was not better. My body feels like I've been hit by a truck. Every single muscle aches and throbs. Even after a large meal, a long soak in the tub sprinkled with salts and floating petals, and a good night's rest, I still wake feeling like death.

I rise earlier than I had the day before. The sun is starting to peek above the mountains in the distance that are visible from my windows. The brief stabbing pain between my shoulder blades has become constant. The pain increased suddenly and dragged me from bed bright and early.

On my walk toward the dining hall, I think through ways to bring up Julius' abuse towards me to Odessa without seeming weak or stirring up too much trouble. My fingers tug on my lilac skirt as I worry over what to say. My eyes are on my feet as my mind works through different scenarios, each one ending disastrously.

As I turn the corner, my eyes fleetingly rise and I catch a glimpse of Evander. He's walking beside someone, his body and wings blocking most of the stranger. His longer dark hair is a sharp contrast to Evander's copper, as it gleams in the sunlight. I'm assuming it's a male since he, too, has raven-colored wings like Evander's. But this man is a whole head taller, though, and his wings are enormous. Their feathers ruffle as they briskly exit the throne room and onto the terrace.

They're gone in an instant, but a desire to follow to see the stranger's face causes me to halt. But when my stomach growls, its hollowness threatening, I shove away the urge and keep trudging to the dining hall.

Odessa is already seated and biting into her breakfast, a thick slab of rye bread smothered in lingonberry jam, when I plop down in the chair next to her.

"Good morning darling, how're you feeling today?" She takes a sip from her tea and looks at me expectantly.

Darling? She certainly is in a great mood this morning; maybe now would be the perfect time to voice my concerns.

"Um, alright, but I need to—" I roll my shoulders back, trying to work out the words, but I flinch. The movement sends shooting pain down my spine and up my neck.

"What is it?" she asks, reaching a hand towards me; her face is full of concern.

"I woke up with a sharp pain in my back," I reply.

I tilt my neck from side to side, trying to ease the aching muscles. I need to tell her about Julius, but the pain is crippling.

"Do you mind if I take a look?" She stands abruptly.

"Not at all," I reply. Worry immediately replaces my hunger.

Odessa pulls at a strand of my leather top, moving the weaves of leather across my back to take a peek at my skin.

A small gasp escapes her, and my muscles lock into place, fear slicing through me. But she happily squeals, "Your wings are budding!"

"You're joking?" I accuse, whipping around to face her, sending more sparks of pain throughout my back. I ignore the pain as my mouth parts in surprise or shock. I'm not really sure which one. Perhaps I really do belong here. With that thought, a small smile begins to bloom across my face.

Odessa claps her hands together and shakes her head. "Oh, how exciting! I had hoped you would grow wings, but I didn't know if it was possible since you had been with the humans for so long. Then I thought, even if you did grow them, it would take ages. But my goodness, how exciting!"

Her words come out in a rush, and her smile is genuine. But there's something off about her eyes; they seem darker than yesterday, the gray fully eclipsing the blue.

She notices my lack of enthusiasm. "Are you not thrilled?" Her excitement sputters out as she sits back down.

I'm beyond excited; it has been a dream of mine since I was a child to be able to fly. But the pain of a dream coming true and then having to leave it behind when I return to Gran causes guilt to crash upon me like waves.

"Yes! I am; it's just another shock, I guess," I mumble, trying to work through the guilt.

Her eyes darken further. Is it the light in here? The candles are lit along the walls, and light streams through the ceiling opening. It's the same light as yesterday, and I don't remember her eyes looking so dark. Could it be the periwinkle dress that leans toward gray, bringing out the darker hues in her eyes?

She gently squeezes my arm, and I glance down to where her hand is gripping me before meeting her gaze. Exhaustion suddenly weighs heavily on me.

"You'll love this, though; I promise it's not a responsibility, but a gift."

Before I can respond, a servant places my food in front of me with a small bow. "Thank you," I reply, and a tentative smile blooms on the girl's face.

Odessa notices the exchange and looks down her nose at it. "You know you don't have to thank them every time, right? It's a highly coveted position to serve in the Great Hall."

I shrug, but her words have me bristling. "It's just polite; they're doing something nice for me. The least I can do is acknowledge it."

Odessa's brows raise at my response, clearly assuming I would agree.

She clears her throat and swirls the juice in her glass. "Helena, before your training today, you are to join me for a council meeting."

That certainly sounds like something I have no business partaking in, but I nod while I begin devouring my breakfast. The edge of hunger ebbs away.

When Julius joins us for breakfast, my window for bringing up his abuse slams shut. He slumps into his usual carved fox chair and leans over to place a kiss on Odessa's temple.

My stomach roils at the gesture. I couldn't stand having him that close to me, but he is her mate. Julius doesn't acknowledge my presence, and I don't say a word to him either. A servant quickly deposits his plate and scurries away, leaving us alone.

"Where is everyone else?" I ask. There are rows and rows of empty tables.

Odessa's brow lowers. "Usually, the other Valkyries have breakfast elsewhere; their schedules are quite full with their continued training, checking on their districts for complaints, meetings, and various other activities."

"Oh," I murmur. I miss breakfast at the Hall.

Odessa interrupts my thoughts. "Speaking of training, I've changed the schedule for the use of the grounds. Julius said they were a bit crowded yesterday, and that he was worried you'd be embarrassed by your lack of skill in front of the others," she adds, looking over at him adoringly.

I purse my lips and study the food on my plate. I weigh the merits of correcting that statement. But I have no rapport with her; yes, she's my aunt, but we've only recently met, and this is her mate. Unfortunately, I don't think she would ever believe me over him.

I mumble, "That's so considerate of him."

My tone is not as convincing as I would have liked it to be, and she studies my profile for a moment. I meet her eyes and plaster on my best smile.

Odessa and Julius spend the rest of our breakfast chatting between themselves, and I do my best to ignore them. My thoughts flipping between new wings and home. Such a strange set of events, and if it wasn't for the pain I was subjected to yesterday and its aftermath today, I'd think it was still a dream.

After breakfast is finished, I dutifully follow behind them to the council room.

It's exactly what I expected after touring the rest of the Great Hall. White marble constructs the walls and floor, the marble shimmering from the light streaming in from the skylight above the room. The marble floor is covered by several large, rectangular rugs, each one hand-woven patterns.

One entire wall is painted as a map of the realm. Idirhalla is an archipelago spanning four islands: the Capital Island, Ishtar, Olundy, and Scota.

Another wall is covered in several oil paintings. Gorgeous paintings of battles and colorful lakes, with elegant swans and Valkyries in flight. But the one in the middle, the largest, immediately demands my attention.

The painting is a depiction of a story my mother used to tell me as we snuggled around a campfire in the winter: *The Wild Hunt*.

I study the painting, noting how the artist perfectly captured the tumultuous procession of Odin astride Sleipnir, his eight-legged stallion with glowing eyes. They fly along the storm winds and through the lands with his wolves, Geri and Freki. Her words echo in my mind: *"The hunt begins with a howl cleaving the silence of the land."*

I examine the rest of the hunting party: spectral hunters, warriors, Valkyries, and many other mythical creatures. All so vividly rendered, it makes my skin pebble in goosebumps as if I can hear the howl now.

My mom's tale plays through my mind, and the meaning behind the folklore is a reminder of the cycles of life and death. Her final words of the story ring in my mind. *"To see the Wild Hunt is a harbinger of war."*

I shake off the sense of dread and turn away from the painting.

In the center of the spacious stone room, a massive, round table that takes up a good portion of the room. It's large enough for at least twenty people, the top lined with black rings swirling around and around. Admiring it closer, I realize the entire table top is made up of a single disc cut from the trunk of an enormous tree.

Odessa pulls up a chair, the red velvet cushion harsh against the white background that makes up most of the room. She gestures for me to take the chair on her right. Once we're seated in our chairs, the rest of the council members take their seats.

Every chair is the same, not a single one indicating a place of power.

I smile, realizing this is a reign based on a partnership between the royal family and the councilors. The council consists of a few Valkyries, but the rest are citizens that I haven't been formally introduced to. It's an eclectic mix of men and women. Some of them give me kind smiles or polite nods, but the others eye me, *an outsider*, it seems to say.

Odessa makes a show of introducing me to the council. "This is my niece, daughter of our former queen, the rightful heir to the throne, Helena."

There's a brief pause and I glance down at my hands folded in my lap to avoid all the eyes that are now turned on me.

Odessa begins introducing the council members seated

around the table, starting with the man on her left, and I look back up. "This is Ashur of the Mesopotamian District."

She gestures to an olive-complexioned man. His thick, dark, curly hair bobs as he nods to me. His jet-black eyes appear friendly as they meet my own. His long beard is neatly trimmed and braided down to his chest. The robe he's wearing is very regal, and the dark red of the fabric adds an air of superiority. I suddenly feel underdressed in my simple lilac skirt and leather training top.

Odessa explains, "The Mesopotamian District is located on our next closest island, Ishtar."

"After the Goddess?" I ask.

Ashur's eyes blaze with delight and something else, but he nods. His voice is like thunder as he asks, "You know our history?"

I have to hold myself back from nodding to excitedly. "I do. I've always been fascinated by history and cultures."

His smile is kind, his eyes warming instantly. "That will serve you well here."

"This is Satiah, the elected councilor from the Egyptian District."

Odessa gestures to the woman beside Ashur. My eyes meet hers, and I have to stifle a gasp. She is breathtaking. Her warm, brown eyes are lined with kohl, and she studies me in return. Her short black hair is sleek and shiny, the length reaching right above her thin shoulders. She places a hand on her chest and gives me a seated bow, the white robe she's wearing slipping down her forearm and her gold bracelets twinkling with the movement.

"Boudicca, from the Celt District." Odessa points to the woman seated beside Satiah. This woman is a queen in her own way; her keen green eyes crudely analyze me. I lock my muscles into place so I don't squirm under her gaze. But then, as if she's satisfied with what she sees, she smiles. The change in her appearance is like the sun breaking through clouds.

She also bobs her head in greeting, the rioted mass of oxblood curls bouncing with the movement. "Our district makes up half of Scota Island."

Her voice is lilting, and her accent is comforting in a way that Lachlan's often was.

It's becoming difficult trying to keep track of the names and districts of each person. My palms become clammy, and I rub them together under the table. My necklace is tucked under the neckline of my top, and I focus on its familiar weight to work past my rising panic.

Breathe, focus, *I got this*.

"Joan, of the South District." Odessa gestures towards a petite woman with very short, espresso-brown hair. "That district is a collection of multiple groups," Odessa explains.

Joan does not bow or even move, but her large dark eyes briefly scan over me before she stares straight ahead again. It's not a dismissal, and for some reason, I don't even take it as a slight. It seems as if the girl, or woman, is very untrusting. She's dressed much differently than the other women, too, in a black tunic and pants. I admire her choice and smile at her. A twitch of her lips was the only sign she noticed.

Odessa is already introducing the man seated next to Joan. "Leif, of the North District."

The broad-shouldered man stands, his dark blue eyes locked onto mine. He thumps his brown tunic-clad chest with a large fist. His sandy blonde hair is shorn to his scalp on the sides, leaving a single braid that stretches down the middle of his head. I smile at him in response, his greeting impressive compared to the others. His severe expression remains in place as he resumes seating.

"What a fine greeting, Leif." Odessa eyes him, a single brow arching.

He meets her stare head-on before flicking his eyes to me. "She is our savior, is she not?" His words drop like a stone in my gut.

That word again, savior.

She ignores him and waves to the four Valkyries seated together. "These four, you know," she murmurs.

I smile at Mathilda, Mina, Luna, and Elowen.

"Each Valkyrie is assigned a district or several to oversee with their elected councilors."

Odessa continues on, "This is Marcus, the councilor for the Roman District." Her voice is tinged with pride as she introduces the man, who bears a striking resemblance to Julius.

Marcus smiles kindly at me. "I'm also Julius's pater."

"Pater?" I ask, my brows creasing.

"It means father," Odessa replies.

So, I was correct.

But his smile throws me off kilter; there's a genuine kindness radiating from his face. He's not what I expected Julius' dad to be like. His green eyes are full of wisdom and not the arrogance that seeps from his son.

"It's nice to meet you, Marcus," I say to him, and I can't help the smile that grows in response.

There's an empty seat next to him, and Odessa frowns at it but then quickly moves on, introducing the next woman.

"Artemisia of the West District."

A statuesque woman with tanned olive skin and a strong brow turns towards me. Her smile is friendly, and there's a hint of mischief twinkling in her lightly up-tilted chocolate-brown eyes. There's something about her that makes me instantly like her. A sense of such vivaciousness shines from her.

"And last but not least, Cynane of the Pella district, which makes up the other half of Scota, the furthest island from us." Odessa points to the astonishingly beautiful woman next to me.

She shifts to face me, throwing her long platinum blonde

hair over a muscular shoulder. Her icy gray eyes study me as if she's mapping out each one of my weaknesses. There's such an air of power radiating from her I have to lock my muscles in place again to remain upright. The urge to bow at her feet courses through me. I struggle to keep my face neutral and not gape at her beauty. I settle on a dip of my chin towards her.

A fleeting expression passes across her face at the respect, the severity of her gaze lightening as she dips her chin in return.

Satisfied with the introductions, Odessa tilts her head towards me. "Do you have any questions before we begin?"

I bite my lip at the onslaught of attention from the councilors but forge through it. "Yes, you said Districts; how is that determined?"

Her smile is full of admiration. "That is another great question. When the Father established our realm, he did not only select the Norse warriors but any warriors that met his prerequisites; it didn't matter if they worshiped him or had even heard of him; they only had to be worthy."

My eyes widen with more questions, but she continues. "A worthy warrior has bravery, strength, and reasoning. They are not only brutes with strength but smart, cunning warriors. Male or female also did not matter. So we had warriors flocking in from all over the place, different races, cultures, religions, and languages." Her hands wave wildly as she recants the history. "As one usually does, birds of a feather flock together, so people of a similar background set up in certain areas. However, we were a realm united for a singular cause, to guard the realm from evil and fight in Odin's army." Julius scoffs from where he guards the door, annoyance creases his brow.

She blazes on, "So to stay united and keep the peace between us, a counselor was elected from each of the areas that were inhabited by that group of people so that we could meet like this and discuss any arising issues without waging wars amongst ourselves."

"That makes sense," I mutter. My mind files away all that information to study later. This is the history that she doesn't want to be taught in schools? That many people from that many places and periods all in one place united under one goal? I can't even begin to fathom why that would be a bad idea. The stories and the customs they must have.

"If you have any other questions, let me know at the end, and I can answer them for you." She grins at me. The kindness of it leaves me grateful for her guiding hand. She calls the meeting to order, and it begins with Boudicca, who is standing to list her current grievances for this week. She ticks off her fingers, her tone sharp. "With the training grounds closed, boredom has afflicted many of my citizens; the amount of ale we've gone through this week is astonishing; someone broke into our stores and decimated our supply, and there have been complaints that arrows are becoming nearly impossible to find."

Odessa nods and reaches a hand behind her, pointing towards Julius. "Can you make a note to check our stores for more ale and arrows?" He nods at her request. Boudicca sits, but she looks disgruntled still.

Leif stands next and glowers at the room before announcing, "A few of my citizens have decided to move from the Capital since their forges have been forced to close." His voice is laced with anger. "They wish to move to Olundy and open forges there. Do I need your approval to grant their request?"

Odessa, surprisingly, stares down her nose at him. "Of course, your citizens are free to live in any district or island they wish in this realm. But we have no need for any more forges." She bristles.

Leif's expression had been edging towards relief with each of her words, but with her ending remark, his glower returns. The name of the island, though, was Olundy; no one had mentioned that island yet. I eye the empty chair at the table; maybe that's why?

Ashur stands next and lists a few grievances: petty squabbles on property lines, overcharging at the market, and a problem I wasn't expecting to hear, teens sneaking out at night. Odessa addresses them easily, and Ashur sits, satisfied. I do my best to pay attention and learn, but my body is buzzing with energy, my mind fluttering from one thing to another but consistently going back to one thing, or rather one person, *Lachlan*. I begin daydreaming of his charismatic smile and how relieved he would be if he could see me now. I need to figure out how to travel back once I have power. But my chest begins to ache when I think of going back, knowing I'll be leaving this entire realm to its fate. The selfishness of that act presses down on me.

Odessa clears her throat in an attempt to recapture my attention, and I glance her way. She nods towards Artemisia. "I'm so sorry, I must've zoned out," I reply sheepishly.

Odessa gives me a chastising stare. "Artemisia," she says again, her cunning eyes scrutinizing me as I shift her way. "Has suggested that we reopen a few of the training grounds, but I've said there's no need. Whatever would we train for, don't you agree?"

"Oh, um, I don't know," I reply, my eyes focusing on Odessa, who gives me an inquisitive stare.

Across the table, I note that Mathilda shares a look with Mina while Elowen frowns slightly, her eyes becoming hazy. Surely my disagreement or agreement wouldn't negatively impact them? We have a training ground right here at the Great Hall. A few of the other councilors share a stunned expression, while Ashur and Marcus remain neutral. Cynane has an interesting reaction, though, and makes a fist with the hand she has resting on the table. However, no one speaks up about their disagreement or agreement vocally.

Odessa glares, her eyes wholly gray. "What do you mean?" I want to sink into my chair; the expression on her face has me thinking I've made a grave mistake.

I force a small smile before I forge on. "I mean, what would be the harm in opening up a few? It might help with the boredom and the teenagers sneaking out, right?" I gesture to Ashur and Boudicca, and they nod in agreement. I press on, "They'd be too tired from training to stay up late." I attempt a jest, but it falls flat. She looks away dismissively and addresses the rest of the council. "Before we adjourn, I would just like to add that I am so very glad, my niece"—she gestures towards me but doesn't meet my eyes—"has returned to us at last. I fully believe she was brought here, as fate intended to bring power back to our realm. It is my hope that she will soon take her place on the throne, as Odin decreed. These issues that we have been facing will most likely dissipate with her being in her rightful place, and there will be no need to further discuss the training grounds." She nods sharply to the room before swiftly exiting, Julius on her heels. Abandoning me to face the council. No one was prepared for that statement and the plans she laid out for us.

Most of them are still staring at me when I bolt from my chair. "Um, excuse me," I throw over my shoulder as I scurry after Odessa.

The hallway is full; at least a dozen guards line the walls. They lurch to attention when I briskly pass. The sound of their wings ruffling blends in with my echoing footsteps. Odessa is crossing the threshold to the throne room and I jog to catch up to her.

"Odessa!" I call. She keeps moving, her pace quick, and her wings hidden away. Julius hears my call and throws a smirk over his shoulder at me.

Finally, I catch up to her and throw my arm out to stop her. "What the hell was that about?"

Her pace halts at my obstructing arm, and she raises her brows at my tone. Julius passes us, thankfully, and marches through the passageway without her.

"What do you mean?" She feigns innocence but crosses her arms over her chest.

"I mean, that I've told you I need to get home to take care of Gran, that I planned to go home all along, but then you highly insinuated to the entire council that I would be taking over as queen and staying here to bring stability to the realm!" I shout, my panic rising with each word.

Odessa looks around the empty throne room before she drops the innocent act and gives me a reproachful look, disgust curling her lip. "So you mean to tell me after all that you have seen here that you would still choose the life of an elderly, ailing woman over the life of your people?"

Her question brings me up short. I hadn't compared the two quite like that before, and I don't have an adequate response. I look down at my feet, the guilt pressing down on me again. The anger I felt raging through my veins has vanished, leaving a chill in its wake.

She takes a deep breath, squaring her shoulders before saying, "Look, I know this has all been a whirlwind for you and that you feel an obligation to Skadi, but now that you know everything, don't you believe that this is your path? Skadi was once Queen; she understood her responsibilities and chose her own fate by living in the human realm. Now, I need you to choose yours here; at the very least, be a figurehead and don't disrupt my plans. But this is your birthright; there are lives at stake here. Many, many more than the one you left in the human realm." Her tone is still terse, but her countenance towards me has softened.

I'm left speechless, my plans crumbling around me. Odessa throws me a pitying look over her shoulder as she leaves me standing alone. My necklace pulses slightly, the gold warming against my skin as if it agrees with her.

Her wish all along was to get me to stay, so I don't know why I'm surprised, but still, it feels like she pulled the rug out from under me. The rest of the council members funnel out of the hallway.

Mathilda finds me right where Odessa left me, twirling my necklace between my fingers. "I take it her parting words weren't planned?"

My body trembles slightly, with the pressure now dropped on my shoulders, and I shake my head.

"Hey, you ok?" She rubs a soothing hand down my arm. "It can't be that bad, having to stay here, can it?" she asks, gesturing to the Great Hall.

"No, it's just there was"—I sigh, Lachlan's face flashes in my mind—"responsibilities to take care of back home." I finish with a shrug.

"That sounds stressful. How about we blow off some steam? You fell from one responsibility to an entirely new realm with even bigger responsibilities. You need some fun!" she says enthusiastically, but her smile has turned mischievous, a glint of trouble sparkling in her eyes.

I frown at her enthusiasm. "What did you have in mind?" Wariness floods my veins.

"After training, I'll meet you in your room. It'll be fun, I promise!" she throws it over her shoulder as she leaves.

TWELVE

The feeling of life constantly beating the shit out of me makes me want to soak in a hot bath, but I stand in the throne room, pondering the direction of my life. Then realization slams into me. Julius had walked out before Odessa; he's probably already down at the training ground. Which means I'm late. I sprint to my room to change out of my skirt and into my training pants, barely pausing a moment to throw my hair up before I race out of the Great Hall, across the terrace, and down to the training ground. Where I find Julius leaning against the archway, arms crossed. Shit.

"Well, well, late on our second day already?" His words are laced with venom.

"I apologize. It won't happen again." I try my best to keep my voice as steady as possible, but being down here, alone, with him is already making me queasy.

Julius pushes off the archway and takes a step onto the training grounds. "Let's see how knowledgeable you are with weapons today. I'm still trying to get a baseline for your skill level."

"Well, I can save you some time there. I've never used

anything but a child's sword and bow," I say, hoping my honesty will win me some points with him. But I should've known better; a cruel smile is his only response. We walk across the training ground and into the long timber building. The sloping roof nearly touches the ground on either side, and strange carvings line the door frame. My swallow is audible, fear pulsing in my veins as we cross the threshold; no one would be able to hear me from inside the building.

Hanging on the wall beside us are rows of shields, some plain metal, others intricately detailed. The rest of the walls are lined with rows upon rows of weapons: swords, axes, pikes, bows, maces, and clubs. A long, narrow table running the length of the room is covered in piles of armor, gloves, sparring pads, and silver helmets. Alone in this building full of weapons is not a place I feel comfortable being with him. He rips a sword and shield off the wall before thrusting them at me. "Hold these."

The metal of the sword gleams in the light; its blade is sharp, but the hilt is cracked wood, worn and abused, and held together with leather wrappings. The shield is smaller than the others and crudely made. The metal is scarred with several large dents, but it's sturdy enough to do the trick and light enough not to weigh me down. Julius grabs himself a beautiful sword, the hilt glinting with a ruby the size of a chicken egg, and the shield he grabs is painted with a golden serpent in a striking position. A bit ostentatious for a weapons lesson, but whatever.

He marches out the door, and I have to raise my knee quickly to keep it from slamming shut in my face before following behind him. Gods, he's insufferable. He leaves me in the sun on the east side of the grounds with a gruff, "Stay here."

Julius marches to the tree with Odin's axe buried into it. For a second, I think he's going to try to pull it from the tree, but he merely slaps the hilt again before stalking back towards me.

"This is how you hold a sword." He shows me his grip for a split second before expertly spinning the hilt over the top of his hand and back into his palm. "And this is how you hold a shield," he adds.

His voice is soaked in sarcasm while he hoists his shield up and down.

I reposition my sword in my hand, spinning it smoothly like he did without dropping it. His surprise mirrors my own and strokes my ego, giving me the confidence to hoist my shield up and down sarcastically. "Got it."

Years of my father's instructions flood my mind, and I pick through the memories, looking for the instructions on fighting a much larger opponent.

Julius' face grows eerily calm as he mutters quietly, "Now block."

He swings his sword abruptly down at me.

My panic is fleeting as self-preservation and muscle memory take over, and I surge my shield arm into position just before his sword can cleave through my skull.

The reverberation of his sword against my shield rattles my whole body. My teeth clack together loudly.

Son of a bitch.

I barely have time to adjust, my arms vibrating still as he's swinging his shield at my exposed chest. Twirling away at the last possible second, he misses my chest with his shield, but his booted foot lands square between my shoulder blades and has me flying face-first to the ground.

The impact knocks the wind out of my lungs, and I lay there gasping for air.

The pain sears down my spine, and I briefly wonder if you can break your wings before they even grow.

Julius squats in front of me, the pain and lack of air keeping me sprawled on the ground.

"I see why your parents didn't raise you here. You're too weak." He steps over me and kicks my sword out of my hand. "Get up," he barks.

Get up, get up.

My mind screams at me, but my body doesn't want to listen.

Slowly, I manage to pull myself up to find him sneering at me. When I reach for the sword, he kicks it further away and swings at me again.

I thrust my shield into place to block his blow.

Did he really attempt to attack me without a weapon?

My vision tinges red, and I use my shield again, but this time as a weapon, and I swing at him with it. The action catches him off guard, and he takes a step back, giving me time to dive for my sword.

The weapon is now firmly in my grasp, and I smile.

But that was a mistake.

"Do you think you actually did something with that little maneuver?"

The words are sharp, meant to cut me.

He races at me, and I barely dodge his attack.

I can't seem to take on any position but a defensive one, and I'm constantly several seconds too late. With my left arm outstretched with my shield to block his latest blow, my right arm sags to the ground with the weight of the sword I'm not accustomed to yet. Which leaves my midsection vulnerable to an attack.

Julius begins raining blows across my ribs with his knee. The air is ripped from my lungs, and I sag to the ground, my sword and blade forgotten on the dirt beside me as I keel over.

He squats down beside me and murmurs, "You're pathetic and weak. You don't stand a chance here."

I can't even tilt my head to the side and meet his eyes. His words hurt more deeply than the hits he landed. He rises and walks across the training ground to the weapons building, ending our training session. That was short and not sweet.

I roll over onto my back, the searing, burning pain lashing down my spine from the movement.

Get up.

But I can't; I lay there for a very long time.

The sun is sinking below the trees when I finally pull myself up off the ground. Julius is long gone. But his words spun around my head, ripping up every decent thought in its path.

My anger bubbled over until only one thing became very clear: I am staying.

I'm never going to be ok with allowing someone as vile as him to rule over these people. If he does this to me, who threatens his newfound power trip, I can't imagine what he'd be like decades into his reign.

Once I get enough power to stabilize Idirhalla, there's nothing to stop me from traveling back and forth freely as they once did; I could visit Gran or even bring her back with me. I wonder if I could convince Lachlan about the existence of this place.

We might be able to have a future here.

But I will not be forced out by someone like Julius. At the very least, I should stay for my parents. This was my mother's home, and she would not agree with me turning my back on these people if I could save them. I still don't know her reasons for leaving, but I know my mom, and I trust her; she would have never left them if she knew this was going to happen.

A low whistle sounds from the archway, and my muscles ache as I flinch.

"I was worried I'd have to call the Captain and tell him you died tragically on my watch," Evander says with a smile, approaching me before it immediately drops. My tear-streaked face causes him to freeze. "Lena, are you ok?" Worry creases his brow.

"Honestly," I breathe, trying to gather myself. "No, not at all." My lip quivers as my voice cracks.

"Are you injured?" he asks, scanning my body for injuries.

Evander's kindness lifts some of the burden off my chest.

"I'm fine, just a little worse for wear; Julius was not very mentor-like today." My shoulders rise and fall as I sigh.

"Why don't you train with me, Mathilda, and Tane?"

"I don't know when I would even have the time for that or when you guys would have the time." I don't want to intrude on their busy schedules, but it would be nice to learn something. The words 'learn our ways' to stabilize the realm whiz through my mind.

"For you, we would make time. No one else, more than me, would love to see you knock Julius on his ass. Let me talk to them tonight, and I'm sure there is a time each day one of us could help you out." He nods as if he's already working it all out in his head.

"If you think it'll help, I'll try."

Hope begins surging through me, battling back the discomfort of having to ask for help. There are people here willing to help me, kind people, who seem to always look to do the right thing. This is a place worth sticking around for, a place worth saving.

"Oh, it definitely will. Trust me, I've been there." Emotion shines in his eyes.

"What do you mean?"

Evander looks up at the sky before settling his attention back on me. "I wasn't always the man you see before you. I was born here to two warriors from very different times and cultures. It wasn't a love match, but a coupling born from fleeting desire." He shifts uncomfortably on his feet. "Needless to say, my childhood wasn't a happy one, and I never quite felt like I belonged anywhere."

My eyes burn from the story he's struggling to tell and the image of a small child with bright copper hair suffering from the loneliness that I'm very familiar with.

He pushes on. "As peaceful as this place seems now, it wasn't always, and there was a lot of bullying towards kids who didn't have friends. I was one of those kids. But when I was growing up, the royal guards were a brotherhood. A place where people of all cultures and periods could be chosen. I wanted that more than anything and started training as fiercely as I could, but it wasn't enough. Until Mathilda and Mina took me under their wings—pun intended—when they saw me struggling through the selection process five years in a row. They helped me achieve my dreams. They took a nobody kid off the streets and built me up into the person I am today."

Pride and gratitude surges across his face when he speaks of his friends, who were there for him. His story strikes a chord within me. His friendship with them reminds me, a great deal, of mine with Lachlan.

I grin at him. "Into the great person you are today."

Evander's eyes flash to mine, gratitude shining warmly in the hazel pools as he smiles broadly at me. He bumps his shoulder against mine as we walk back to the Great Hall. "You're going out with us tonight, right?"

"Yeah, Mathilda invited me. I hope that's ok?" My eyes are on the winding path in front of us so that I don't miss a step. My body is sore and sluggish from lying on the ground most of the day.

"Of course it is! We'll have a good time." He smiles. The setting sun brandishing the sky a deep burnt red mimics the strands of his hair.

Silence settles between us, and I have the urge to fill it.

"I thought you were the captain of the guard?"

Evander's eyes stay on the path. "What made you think that?"

My brow furrows. "You said you didn't want to have to call the captain if I was dead back there, and I thought that you were the captain because I've only ever seen you with Odessa, and you were our guard for the parade," I say slowly, thinking it through as I speak.

Evander chuckles. "I see why you would think that I was just the replacement while the actual captain was away. It's not my usual position." His shoulders slump marginally, and I get the feeling he wants that role.

I bump my shoulder against his. "I think you would make a great captain."

Evander's smile is as bright as the setting sun.

THIRTEEN

Mathilda has taken over my room, covering my bed with piles of dresses. A row of shoes lines the wall by my bed, and she's sitting cross-legged on the floor, still in her leathers, eating a bowl of fruit.

"It's about time! I thought you'd be here sooner?" She grins up at me, berries coating her teeth red.

"Julius introduced shields and swords today," I grumble.

"Ahh, I take it that it did not go well?" She scans my body for injuries.

"No, it did not. I swear he was really trying to hurt me." I throw it out there, trying to gauge her response.

She talks around a mouthful of fruit. "Nah, he's an ass, but he knows Odessa would have his ass if he did seriously hurt you. But I'm sorry we weren't there today; they changed the schedule."

Lifting a green dress with cutout sides, I ask Mathilda, "Would your offer to train me still be available?"

She swallows her mouthful, eyes bright with excitement. "Uh, yes! I would love to help!"

The anxiety I suffer from when asking for help, especially from strangers, dissipates. But she's not really a stranger anymore; she's a friend. My emotional range is quite large today, from hopelessness and acceptance to happiness. It reminds me of my days with Lachlan. He was always there to lift me up on Gran's hard days.

I reach for my necklace. The runes against my fingertips ease the pang. It seems that I've turned my heirloom into a security blanket.

"I'm gonna jump in the bath and then what should I wear?" I ask Mathilda.

She rises from the floor. "You just bathe and leave the rest to me!" Her grin is wicked.

While in the bath, I brood over the past couple of days. Endless questions starting with 'why' cycle through my mind constantly. Mixed together with Julius's emotional attack. Was he right? Did they not think I was strong enough to survive here?

I don't think that my mother would leave this place to ruin if she knew what was happening here. But now I think I must stay here and see these wrongs righted. I should have been given a choice in this matter from birth or at least told why I wouldn't be getting a choice and why they decided this path for me.

My anger begins to build, but in the end, it's futile. They won't be giving me an explanation any time soon. The bath soothes my aching muscles, and I sink lower into the tub. The water rises past my chest, my necklace shimmers and the light from the torches on the walls casts shadows all around the chamber. I close my eyes and lean my head back against the rim of the tub, the eucalyptus oil in the water revitalizing me with each inhale.

Accepting Mathilda's help was a good idea for 'learning their ways,' but I need to speak with Odessa if I'm going to stay here long-term; I need to be able to travel back and forth to make sure Gran is ok.

I rise from the tub, water running in rivulets down my body, and I marvel at my newfound strength. The sharp pain between my shoulder blades has dulled to an annoying ache.

Mathilda calls from my room, "You decent?"

I wrap myself up in a navy blue towel before answering. She pops her head in the door. "I had a chair brought up, and I figured I could set it in here to do your hair and makeup?"

My smile stretches wide across my face. "Great!"

I've never done this before, but my excitement is burning through my veins. I've dreamt of this moment, getting ready for a night out with friends.

Mathilda breezes through the door, a tall chair in her hands, and places it in front of the marble sink. I watch as she hauls bags of products from my room. Glass jars and vials clink against each other as she sets them on the counter before heading back for hair brushes and ribbons.

"Alright, I'll set everything up here, and you can get dressed. I think you should wear a red dress. It will set off your eyes and bronzed skin." She smiles and gestures to the bed, a red dress lying apart from the other swathes of fabric on my bed.

The dress she suggested is stunning but more modern than what I've seen other women wear here. It's strapless, with pleats of ruffles running horizontally down the bodice into an asymmetrical hemline that cuts back up over my knee. I step into it and pull up; the fabric like silk against my skin. It fit like a glove, accentuating my hips and showcasing my long, lean legs. But it seems extravagant.

"Mathilda...." I call out to her.

The bathroom door cracks open. "Gods. You look amazing!" she squeals as she jumps up and down, clapping her hands together. "Give us a spin!"

My smile is so big my nose scrunches, and I twirl in place. "That's the one!" she declares.

"Are you sure it isn't too much?" I bite my bottom lip. The dress is incredible, but it highlights my body in a way I'm not used to.

"No. I promise it's perfect. Just wait till you see what I'm wearing." She wiggles her eyebrows, and I giggle. I follow her back into my bathroom and plunk down on the chair.

She picks up a large brush and begins brushing my hair. While she works, she launches into her life story before I came. "I was born here; my mother was Gunnr, one of the original Valkyries. Our moms were best friends before my mom passed."

Her hands stall, and I see the familiar look of grief pass over her eyes in the reflection of the mirror. I turn and grasp her hand. "I know what that's like, and I'm so sorry," I say, sympathy coating my words.

Mathilda gazes at me. "It's rare for Valkyries to pass on. Our life spans are as close to immortal as possible, but it was weird. So sudden, both she and my younger sister were just gone."

I bob my head, a lump forming. She lost a mom and a sister. That kind of grief, the kind from being the one left behind, is not foreign to me.

I mumble, "It is weird. One day, they're there, and then the next, they're just gone, and it's hard to imagine a world without them in it."

"Exactly," she sighs before shaking her head. "But enough sadness. This is your first night out. We have to have fun!"

I face forward again and she resumes brushing. I feel such a connection with her and had I grown up here, I know we would've been best friends. The life I could have had if I had been raised here flits across my mind. No endless moving in search of the adventure my parents obviously missed from this place. I could have belonged here, to these people.

"So tell me about you and Tane." I watch her face closely in the mirror, looking for any reaction.

"Um, there's nothing to tell." She shrugs. "He's my best friend and was my first warrior to recover. We've been really close since that day. Tane was lost when he first came here." I know the feeling. "He only has a deep sense of loyalty to me because I brought him here. He thinks he owes me something. Even though it was his decision to join us." She's doing her best to remain impassive, but there's a longing in her eyes that I recognize in my own when I think of Lachlan.

"I thought you guys were mates when I first saw you together," I reply, cutting straight to the point.

Mathilda flicks the top of my head gently, and we both giggle. She begins braiding my hair into a coronet, leaving the front pieces out before braiding them too and tucking them back into the main braid.

"What was your life like before?" she asks.

I stare down at my hands folded into my lap. "Well, it was just me and my parents. We didn't really ever have a home. We traveled all over the States. Do you know where that is?" I ask.

She rolls her eyes and I smile. "Well then, you know it's very religious there. Not ideal for making friends. But it was fine. I had my parents, and we had great adventures."

"That sounds lonely," she murmurs.

"It was even more so now that they're gone, but enough sadness," I tease. I want to tell her about Lachlan, but if we're avoiding sad subjects, I definitely don't think I can bring him up without bringing down the mood.

The silence stretches on for a moment when Mathilda begins working on my makeup. She taps a red vial into her palm and dabs it onto my cheeks. The liquid smells strongly of roses and vanilla.

"What is that?" I assume it's blush, but the smell is nothing like the makeup I'm used to.

"This is raour; it's to color your cheeks," she replies.

My eyes flutter close as I savor the aroma. "Oh, it smells divine."

"All of these products are all made here on the island. We should get you some while you're here."

I shift uneasily in the chair. I want to tell her I plan to stay, but I need to discuss the details with Odessa first.

Mathilda notices my shift and says quietly, "I know you probably feel an obligation to go back, but this could be your home, too. You are wanted here if you decide to stay."

Wanted. I am wanted here.

Not 'please stay to save us,' just wanted.

Despite Julius' cruel attempts to break me and his blatant disdain, everyone else has been extremely welcoming. "

Thank you," I respond softly, my cheeks heating.

She ends her work with a light sweep of kohl around my eyes. "There. All done, look!"

I sit up to check my reflection, and I'm shocked by the woman staring back at me.

I'm ethereal; my eyes glow in the mirror set off by the subtle sweep of black.

"Woah," I breathe. I stare, barely recognizing myself. "You're good." I pat the thick braids and admire the gloss of my hair. "You're really good."

She laughs before patting some of the raour on her cheeks and sweeping on the kohl. "I've got to run to my room to change, but I'll meet you in the throne room, ok?" she asks as she packs up the products and brushes.

"Sure, no worries," I respond, still admiring the goddess staring back at me.

My confidence begins stirring under my skin, remnants of the girl I was before all this loss coming back to life before my eyes.

Mathilda walks out my door, calling over her shoulder, "Grab a pair of shoes, and I'll see you in two seconds!"

I pad over to the wall lined with shoes, so many different strappy sandals in black, nude, and metallic to choose from. I slip on a black pair that has minimal straps reaching right above my ankle. Satisfied with my choice, I smile, excitement bubbling up in my chest as I walk out my door.

FOURTEEN

Torches light the way as I follow the sound of laughter coming from down the hall. Tane, Evander, and Mina are already waiting in the throne room.

"Hey," Mina calls. "Are you coming with us?"

Her tight, strapless, emerald dress resembles mine, and I feel at ease about my choice now. Her short bobbed hair is curled and shows off her long, slender neck. The guys are dressed in black jackets and matching black pants. Their outfits are almost modern looking except for the shiny black thread embroidered on the sleeves in runes. The thread is so delicate you can barely see them until the light hits them just right.

"Yeah, Mathilda invited me. Is that ok?" My insecurities overtake the confidence I had felt walking down here. Mina grabs my hand and pulls me towards her.

Her smile is lethal. "Of course! Now we can show you some real fun."

"Oi, don't scare her off; it's only a bit of dancing," Tane throws my way.

"We're going dancing?" I ask, my eyes bulging.

"Drinks, dinner, and dancing," Evander answers.

My swallow is audible, and everyone chuckles.

Tane whispers to me, "It's not torture, just a night out."

It would be pretty pathetic of me to tell my new friends that I've never danced before, besides in the kitchen with my parents, so I nod and try to will calmness into my sweating palms.

Mathilda rounds the corner into the throne room and the group cheers. Mina is the loudest. "She's only a few minutes late!" I get the feeling they do this a lot and try to find my place in the group. I follow along, smiling and clapping for Mathilda. They are a tight-knit group, a family. Mathilda gives a mocking curtsy before throwing her arms over mine and Mina's shoulders. "Alright, let's go have some fun!"

We meander down the steps and head into the city instead of flying down. Tane and Mathilda bicker over which restaurant has the best 'welcoming' feel for my sake and ultimately lead us to the one Mathilda picked in the West district. The restaurant is a little cottage on the main road in the city. There are tables out front and lights strung from the building across the seating area and into the trees. It reminds me of the whimsical lights Lachlan set up for family dinner, our last dinner together.

I feel the faint stirrings of homesickness.

The sun has set, but the streets are teeming with life, full of people coming and going through the shops and restaurants. The smell of the food from the restaurant we chose makes my mouth water. A waiter, an older man with a kind face, approaches us, all smiles and welcome.

Evander calls, "The usual Carlo, plus one extra plate, please."

Carlo studies my face for a moment. I can see the realization dawn, and he places a hand on his heart, bowing lowly; with a slight Italian accent, he says, "Welcome."

My cheeks catch fire at the sentiment, and I bob my head in return. "Thank you."

While we wait for our food, I try to follow the conversation around me, but my mind wanders to Lachlan, wondering what he might be doing and if he misses me as much as I miss him. A waiter walks by with a plate of bread stuffed with meat, cheese, and arugula. Homesickness continues to make my chest ache, only now I'm left feeling lost all over again.

Mathilda must sense my discomfort and nudges my shoulder. "You ok?" she asks, frowning.

"Yeah, I just—just was thinking of my family back home," I say dejectedly.

Mathilda's smile is understanding, but she nods towards the table, where our group is discussing the merits of flying versus Luna's traveling. I refocus on the conversation at hand.

"Wait, what do you mean she disappears and then reappears somewhere else, like teleportation?"

My mind is completely blown that something like that is even possible.

Tane responds, "We call it traveling, but yeah, she just poofs and then she's somewhere else; it's wild."

The group agrees and I ask, "Does everyone have powers?"

Mina smiles and says, "The Valkyries do; I can move things with my mind, Elowen can see visions, Odessa can create shields out of thin air, and," she cuts off.

Mathilda jumps in. "And I'm very strong," she says nonchalantly.

Tane rolls his eyes. "That is an understatement."

Carlo drops off plates of pasta and bread.

My mouth waters from the smell of garlic, parmesan, and butter. Our conversation halts as we begin eating. The sounds of glasses clinking and forks scraping against the plates are the only sounds for several minutes while we inhale our food. Carlo comes back later with glasses of red wine that are promptly accepted and gulped down.

Mathilda offers me a glass with a warning, "This is really strong, so prepare yourself." She winks as she hands it to me.

The dry, fruity flavor is the perfect companion to the buttery garlic of the pasta, and I savor every sip and bite.

Tane is the first to break the silence. "I don't know how we're gonna dance after this; I want to lie down." He pats his stomach for emphasis.

Mathilda rolls her eyes. "Whatever. You say that every time and every time we have to drag you off the dance floor."

Evander tosses a few gold coins on the table when we leave, and we all wave goodbye to Carlo.

The night sky is now adorned with millions of sparkling stars, their brilliance outshining the flickering flames of the street lanterns. Music drifts from doors opening and closing, mingling with the sound of laughter that carries onto the street as we head out. The tavern we approach has its doors flung wide open, the music spills out onto the street in front of the blue building. The breeze causes the sign to sway, and "The Poppy," painted in bright red, greets us as we walk beneath it and step inside.

There's a band on stage playing lively tunes while people dance on the crowded dance floor. A bar runs the length of one of the sides, and the barstools are full of people drinking and talking.

"Let's grab a table at the back," Mina yells as she pulls me with her to the back table that's surprisingly vacant. Evander offers to grab us drinks, and Tane stays to help him while Mathilda follows us to the table. The tavern is loud, the music melding with the conversations and laughter. I can't help but absorb the happiness in the air on the way to the table, my grin stretching wide across my face.

The three of us pile into the corner booth in the back while we wait on the guys. The music slows to a halt, and the dancers flee the dance floor to find beverages to quench their thirst during the break.

The table next to us is full of hulking men in kilts, their

melodic accents hinting at Scottish ancestry; my mind instantly drifts to Lachlan again. Everywhere I go, I'm reminded of him. Homesickness churns like acid in my stomach, threatening to ruin my good mood. I overhear part of their hushed conversation.

"She closed all the training grounds and most of the black-smiths," the larger one in the middle complains; the others nod in agreement. The man who spoke makes eye contact with Mathilda. He freezes, but she gives him a slight nod, and he resumes his conversation.

I lean forward and whisper, "What was that about?" Mina shakes her head and scans the room.

But Mathilda leans closer to whisper back, "Do you remember the council meeting?" I nod. "Remember how Artemisia asked for the training grounds to be reopened, and Odessa said no?" she whispers, but there's a glimmer of malice in her eyes.

"Yes, is that what they're talking about?"

"Idirhalla is a realm of warriors. Our purpose here was to fight for the Father in the Great War; we need the training grounds," she replies, determination set in her jaw.

Odessa's request from after the council meeting echoes in my ears: "Don't undo all my plans."

"But there's not going to be a war. Why do you still have to train?"

"Is there not going to be a war?" She asks, her eyes beseeching mine.

"Odessa said that Odin left because there wasn't going to be one…" Mathilda's eyes begin blazing. "You think there is going to be war?"

"Have there not been signs that say war is coming?" she asks, studying me intently.

I realize I can't answer that either because I don't know. My necklace turns cold against my skin. A warning. What do the signs of war even look like? I stare back into her eyes.

She continues scanning my face, looking for something, before she sighs. "Ask yourself this instead: if the warriors want to continue to train, why even stop them?"

I had asked the same thing once and was met with a non-answer.

The band on stage picks up their instruments when a tall, lanky man with long, curly hair walks through the crowd and hops onto the stage. Cheers erupt, and even Mathilda's claps excitedly. "You're in for a real treat, Lena!" she squeals.

The man is unassuming, his skin fair, hinting towards Irish ancestry, and his eyes are a striking blue. But as he lifts his hand, a hush falls over the entire place. The guitarist hands him his guitar and the anticipation in the room pulses. Everyone is deathly quiet, straining to hear him. He clears his throat, and I scoot to the edge of the booth to get closer.

He begins singing, his voice so soulful and rich that my skin erupts in goosebumps. I'm swept away by the poetry of the lyrics as he croons about a swan trapped on a lake. The song evokes the emotional imagery of a familiar love story.

The ominous mood is swept away by the powerful music. I nod along to the lyre and drums, the music filling my heart with the urge to dance and sing. The song finishes, and the crowd erupts in applause; the man bows and steps off stage, taking his calm but commanding presence with him.

Evander and Tane bring our drinks to the table and slide into the booth with us. The band resumes with something cheery, the revelers revitalized, and back on the dance floor, Mathilda eyes Tane.

"No, I just sat down," he whines.

Mathilda begins pushing us out of the booth to drag Tane to the dance floor.

Giggles bubble out of me when I see Tane wiggling his hips

to the beat while Mathilda sways along to the rhythm. They paint such a portrait of happiness it's hard not to be a bit jealous. Evander and Mina are immersed in conversation, their heads bent towards each other, a smile gracing Mina's lips before she takes a sip of her wine.

It's fun being with them, but the loneliness of being the fifth wheel starts to creep in. I take a sip of my wine to fill the time. Unfortunately, it does nothing to diminish the burning between my shoulder blades that's ramping back up.

Several songs later, Tane and Mathilda haven't stepped a foot off the dance floor, and now Mina and Evander have joined them. All four of them dancing and jumping along to the band on stage. My delight grows watching them.

But a prickling sensation tickles the back of my head, like I'm being watched. I shift in my seat, scanning the tavern.

No one is blatantly staring at me, but the feeling remains. The band begins playing another cheery song; the music blends with the stomping of the dancer's feet. Evander pulls me from the booth and onto the dance floor. I fall into step between Mina and Mathilda, laughter flowing out of each of us as we stomp to the beat and twirl in place.

This is the most fun I've had in what seems like ages.

But it's only been two or three very long days since I was smiling across the North Sea with Lach. The realization ripples through me like a stone dropped in water.

After the song, Evander and Mina walk with me to our table, but as they settle into the booth, I pause.

"I think I'm gonna head back," I call to Evander and Mina over the music. "I've got an early training session in the morning with Julius, and I'm exhausted."

They both frown, but Mina asks, "Are you sure? We can walk you back."

"Nah, I'm ok. You guys have fun. Tell Mathilda and Tane I said bye," I reply over my shoulder. I shoulder my way through the crowd. Careful to avoid wings and spilled mead on the floor.

The sound of the music and laughter tumbles out of the door after me. Outside, the night air is crisp and I draw in a lungful. The coolness refreshes my balmy skin. Music from the tavern follows me up most of the street before it finally quiets.

There are still quite a few people outside enjoying the night on patios or strolling together down the street to different taverns. Lost in a daze, the flames of the lanterns flickering overhead, hushed conversations from the surrounding people begin to pierce through my thoughts.

Two male teens turn onto the street in front of me; their voices are agitated, and my ears strain to hear them. I wonder if they are part of the curfew-breaking teens Ashur complained about. I can only manage to pick up pieces of their conversation, something about the great tree and how it's an omen.

Great tree?

I've never heard anyone mention that yet. How could a tree be an omen?

They begin vibrating with outrage, the larger one exclaiming, "It's really dying, I'll show you!" The urge to follow them outweighs my exhaustion, and I trail behind them at a comfortable distance. They walk briskly towards the center of the capital, and I'm grateful they stick to the main streets so I don't attract their notice.

We take the second bridge that crosses over the Ayele River, the water still, and reflects the night sky above.

The city on this side of the river is different from the part of the city Odessa paraded me down. With each new street I turn down, the buildings become further apart; no longer are there flower pots or decorated store windows. Here, the buildings themselves look more medieval than decorative. The colorful, bright buildings shift into plain white stone with red-tiled roofs. It's not run down by any means, but it's not the picturesque street that I was led to believe encompassed the entire capital. The street lanterns get further apart, and before long, only the blazing light of the stars illuminates the path.

The teens turn off the main street and walk through a narrow gate, the wood creaking open their last sign before I lose sight of them. Beyond the gate is a footpath, with muted lights on either side lighting my way.

However, the lights aren't flames like the street lamps; they are glowing orbs resting on tall stones. The winding path leads to the top of a small hill, and at its peak is the base of the largest ash tree I've ever seen. The trunk rivaling that of the redwoods we would drive through in California.

The glowing orbs shine all around the tree in welcome, and a few more are sporadically placed high up into the tree itself. The orbs shine into its branches, highlighting its majesty even on a night as dark as this.

The tree is surrounded by a garden, a babbling brook sings in the distance, and several wooden benches are placed under the broad branches of the tree. I walk under an outstretched branch, leading me to the trunk. Leaves flutter above me, but they don't sound like normal leaves because they're not leaves at all but strips of fabric. There are thousands tied along the lower branches.

My mother used to cut strips like these during Yule, and we would tie them to the branches as wishes for the Father.

A strong wind rips through the garden, whipping fallen pieces of my hair across my eyes and making them water.

Leaves begin cascading down upon me as the mighty wind tears them from the tree. The iciness of the wind lifts the hair on my arms.

The sight of the leaves being thrown so forcefully makes my chest tighten. Something is very wrong here. I struggle to look up at the tree and shield my eyes from the wind; the orbs in the branches dim and resemble glowing eyes.

But as violently as it came, the wind suddenly stopped. The leaves now flutter peacefully to the ground. The staggering calm the wind left in its wake should have brought a sigh of relief, but high up in the tree, there are completely bare branches.

Sadness creeps over me. This great, majestic tree is withering away and slowly dying. Is this from magic fading or something more?

I plop down on a bench and tilt my head back to the sky. Fighting to keep the warring emotions at bay. A tree this old withering away is heartbreaking. Ribbons of greenish blue light begin to dance overheard setting ablaze the stars that dance between the branches of the mighty tree. The sight of them soothes a bit of the sadness permeating my mind.

It's so stunningly beautiful in this magical place. When the shadow of a large bird flies overhead, blotting out clusters of stars, I try to follow its flight to determine if it's an actual bird or a guard. But I lose sight of it through branches that still have a few leaves clinging to them, those branches looking healthy and full of life.

I'm disappointed I wasn't shown this on my brief tour of the city, but I'm even more surprised that it wasn't even mentioned.

Or was it? When I first arrived, Odessa said weird things were happening, and she had hoped when they heard the charm that it meant my mother was finally returning to restore things, but this seems more foreboding than that. More along the lines of what Mathilda said.

If I stay, will the tree begin to heal? The decision to stay and fulfill my duty begins to take root, with each falling leaf that flutters down. I watch as several more fall, but the sadness it brings pushes me off the bench and back to the Great Hall; I can't witness any more of it.

I have to do something to help, and quickly.

With each step away from the dying tree, my new path opens up before me. I begin planning what I can do to help. The first thing I need to do is tell Odessa about the abuse from Julius. Suffering through that will get me nowhere and if I want to help, I need to push myself so my powers will manifest. I also need to ask her to teach me how to travel back and forth so I can visit Gran.

My self-reflection is interrupted, though, when a wiry man with bright white hair is thrown from a pub.

"War is COMING, and we should all get ready, you fools!"

The doors swing shut. Luna materializes from the shadows beside the pub, the moonlight bathing her in its glow.

She looks serene, her feet gliding over the ground with each step as she approaches him. She pauses a foot away, holds one slender finger to her lips, and whispers something, but I'm not close enough to hear her words. The yelling man goes rigid and silent. I've only seen her twice now, but something about her makes me want to avoid her at all costs. A sense of foreboding rises in the air. Dread has my knees trembling. I scurry my way to my room, nausea roiling in my stomach from uneasiness or exhaustion; I can't tell.

Before I get ready for bed, I take one last look at my appearance. My cheeks are flushed, and my eyes still glow brightly. I barely recognize myself, and my parents probably wouldn't recognize me either. I tip my medallion up to study it closer, running my fingertips over the poppy engraved in the center of the swirling runes.

"Am I where I'm supposed to be now, Mom?" I whisper, before letting it rest on my chest again.

Warmth blooms when the cool metal nestles against my skin, like a sign convincing me to stay here, see this through, and try to help in any way that I can.

FIFTEEN

The scent of cedar and rain jolts me awake. The sunlight seeping through the windows and thin curtains gives me a pounding headache. I tumble out of bed and to my feet. My entire body throbs and aches as if I'm one giant bruise. I have no idea how they continue to train every day. But I suck it up and head to my training with Julius.

It goes the same as it has the last couple of times, some kind of emotional abuse, followed by slight physical abuse, and then abandonment.

Today was pretty bad.

He wanted to see if I could shoot a bow, and when I struggled to pull the bowstring, he not only had a marvelous time telling me what a disappointment I was, but he also pulled the string for me and let it slice my cheek when he abruptly let it go. I'm really glad I agreed to Evander's suggestion for additional training because I would never learn anything at this rate.

After the complete waste of time, my morning training was. I find myself in the dining hall for lunch, and for once, it is not empty.

"Hey! I missed you leaving last night. Were you ok?"

Mathilda asks, worry creasing her brows. Her opalescent wings are out on full display today, and I realize the backs of the chairs are thoughtfully designed for people with wings.

"I'm sorry I just left. I got really tired and knew I had double training today," I reply, taking a bite of my apple. The juice spills over my lips and down my chin, and I wipe it away with the back of my hand.

"Oh yeah, you're with me today after lunch." She winks. "I won't take it easy on you, but you will definitely learn something, I promise," she adds. I'm looking forward to it. I can't wait to see her in action again today. The brief time I saw her sparring against Tane, I've held onto as an example of what I could be—what I hope to be.

"Thanks, I feel like a punching bag for Julius," I grumble. The abuse he gave my ribs the other day is still tender to the touch, and I wince.

"You're drinking your healing tonic at night, right?" She stares at the blackish-blue bruises on my ribs that peek through the gaps in my leathers.

"What healing tonic?" My food is forgotten on my plate as I stare at her.

"Gods, you haven't been healing at night?" She practically yells the words, her wings ruffling with her agitated movements.

"Uh, no. No one told me?" I wince again, not just from her anger, but from the pain spearing through my ribs and the burning of my wing buds down my spine.

Mathilda's wings vanish as she launches from the table and hurtles out of the dining hall; she yells over her shoulder, "Don't move!"

I'm left staring at the door, but I only have time to blink before she swiftly returns with a gold vial.

"Here, drink this. Now." She shoves the bottle in my face.

"What is it?" I uncork it. The smell of honey wafts from the vial.

"It's what you're supposed to drink every night. It's a healing tonic and heals any damage you sustained during training. Since magic is fading, we aren't healing as fast as we should be, and the healers created this to help speed up the process. I cannot believe Julius, *or even Odessa*, didn't give you a supply. You could've been really hurt. I'm so sorry." Her eyes are tinged with sorrow as she presses her lips into a tight line.

"I'm sure it was just an oversight," I mumble.

But her eyes continue blazing, not wanting her to focus that rage towards me. I throw the vial back in one gulp. It does taste like honey, but something more, something citrusy.

Instantly, my body begins to tingle. The bruises on my rib begin fading away before my eyes, and the throbbing diminishes. The burning and itching from my wing buds lessen to a more tolerable annoyance as well. Small cuts on my exposed arms stitch together the pink, fading away to a soft white.

"Woah, that's incredible. What is that made from?" I ask, eyeing the vial.

"It's made from the leaves of the Idir tree." Sadness dims the rage in her eyes.

"What's that?"

"It's a tree on the island, in the middle of the city," she answers.

I feel a pang in my chest.

"The sick tree," I mumble. Mathilda's head cocks to the side, a question on the tip of her tongue, but she pauses as Odessa breezes into the dining hall. Her cornflower blue robes trailing behind her. She approaches our table and Mathilda glares at her. "Is there a problem, Mathilda?" Odessa asks, staring down her nose at us.

"Yes," Mathilda grits out between her clenched teeth. "Lena

has gone to several training sessions without being given a supply of healing tonic."

Odessa's eyes widen slightly but that is the only emotion that she emits before she turns her cold face to mine. "Apologies, Helena. Julius was instructed to explain the intricacies of that after your first training."

I smile up at my aunt, wanting the tension in the room to abate. "No worries. Mathilda got me squared away." I hold the vial up in my hand. "I didn't know anything like this could exist. Mathilda says it's made here on the island from a tree?"

Odessa purses her lips and looks at the floor. The movement is unusual for her; I've never seen her look anything but composed and confident.

"Yes." The word comes out in a hiss. "It's made from the leaves of the Idir tree."

"Oh, I thought I heard something last night about it being sick?" I force a frown, feigning cluelessness, but only Odessa buys it. Mathilda's foot nudges mine underneath the table.

"Again, yes," Odessa grits out.

"Is that the magic fading or some kind of omen?" I ask, looking between them.

Mathilda smirks, looking up at Odessa. She eyes the wall behind me and sighs before glancing back at me. I'm getting the feeling she does not want me to know anything about what that particular omen could mean.

"It could be an omen that the Fomorians are gathering an army and that a leave falls for every soldier they possess," she grumbles. "Nonsensical old tales, though. It is directly tied to magic fading."

Mathilda's eyes burn onto the side of Odessa's face. "And how would we know if they were old tales if every book in the library about it was taken away?"

My breathing halts as I stare intently at my aunt, desperately waiting for her denial.

That is why the library was so empty.

No denial comes from Odessa, and I swallow forcibly. "You've taken away books?"

Something about this just doesn't feel right. Hiding books is never a good sign, and what could you possibly gain from hindering the enlightenment of your people?

Odessa's eyes flick to mine. "To begin anew, we had to build a foundation; those books were a reminder of our past. A past that is better off forgotten."

Her eyes darken in challenge, but mine burn brightly to meet hers. "You shouldn't ever erase the past; even if you want to forge a new path, you can always learn from it." I grit my teeth. "And destroying books is an atrocity." I throw it out there to see if she'll rebuke my insinuation.

Odessa merely shrugs before turning on her heel and leaving. *She didn't deny it.* I said destroy, and she didn't rebuke it.

Oh my Gods, she actually destroyed the books. My eyes burn from the thought of all that knowledge, all that history, just gone.

My muscles itch for action, craving the physical challenge to dissipate the growing unease from that encounter. The destruction, the hindering of study, it should be illegal.

I would make it illegal.

I shove away from the table, and Mathilda follows. Rage burns in my veins as we walk down the hall.

Mathilda breaks the silence. "What do you know about the other realms?"

Her question makes me bristle. "Next to nothing. What about you?"

"From what I remember reading, the Fomorians," she begins, "are a race of beings from a realm called Toraigh, a place much like the ocean. Long ago, they sought to conquer the human realm and enslave humanity. The Father battled them back with the help of the Fae, another race of beings from

Tuadanaan, and some of our other allies I can't remember. But the Fomorians weren't defeated. They only fled back to their realm. Legend claims they will join other malevolent beings in the other realms—like the giants from Jotnar, the dragons from Sutr, and the demons of Helheim, to battle us again in The Great War. They seek to destroy every realm that stands in their way, and enslave the humans or any beings they deem less."

"And you think there are omens happening, like the leaves falling are about the Fomorians?"

Mathilda nods. "The signs could very well be that magic is fading, but we wouldn't know because the books that detailed the omens of the Great War have vanished." The tree could be the first bad sign of many and we wouldn't even know.

"So what's been happening around here might not be tied to my mom leaving, but omens of the Great War?" The question slips from my lips, and Mathilda quickly pulls me to a stop.

She looks up and down the hall before whispering to me, "Yes, but to say such a thing is to question Odessa, and she hasn't treated the people who question her too kindly. Just last night, a rebel sympathizer wound up floating face down in the Ayele."

I nod, catching her meaning, but none of this makes any sense.

How long do I have to be here before Odessa realizes maybe I'm not the savior after all, and would that mean I'll never get to go home if I won't be able to restore the magic here?

If there is a war coming, who will protect the humans?

The answers to my questions lie just out of my reach as we make our way to the training grounds.

Tane is already there when we arrive. His back is to us, and he has one foot pushed against the fence. He struggles with all his might to pull the axe from the tree. Mathilda snickers as we walk towards him, his grunting becoming louder.

"Tane, you fool, every time?" She giggles, but her eyes are locked onto his corded arms as he continues pulling on the hilt.

In between each pull, he grunts out, "I am worthy, dammit!" Before he lets go of the handle and slumps against the fence. He sighs heavily before looking up at us. "You give it a try."

Mathilda glances sidelong at me before tilting her head. "Fine, I will." She places one hand on the handle and tugs gently. "There, I tried."

Tane grumbles, "You didn't even give it a real tug."

She places her hands on her hips. "Because I am not destined to pull it out, and neither are you." She stretches out her hand to help pull him to his feet, and they both look at me. "You try it, Lena."

Something about looking like a fool in front of them makes me shake my head violently back and forth. "No, thank you. I'm definitely not worthy."

They both scoff at my reluctance, but don't push me further on the matter. Tane shrugs and says to Mathilda, "Let's show her the warm-up first, and then I figured we'd start with the basics?"

She nods and looks at me excitedly. "Let's start stretching!"

Their enthusiasm and positive support are opposite from anything I've encountered from Julius thus far. Mathilda plops on the ground and begins stretching her legs and back. She's surprisingly limber to be so muscular. Tane leans over and touches his toes before standing upright and stretching out each thigh.

"Just stretch until you feel limber," he instructs while balancing on one leg. After we're loose, Tane leads us around the ring in a brisk jog to warm us up. Mathilda and I continue around several times while he ducks into the timber building and comes out with a roll of linen and some padded gloves.

"What're those for?" I ask as we halt at the water table for a quick sip.

Mathilda glances over to Tane. "The linen is to protect your knuckles and align your wrists, and the gloves are what you're going to punch."

I gulp down the water quickly and begin bouncing on my toes with excitement.

Tane chuckles at my eager expression. "We're not scary enough, Mathilda; she's still excited."

Mathilda rolls her eyes and catches the roll of linen he tosses to her. "Hold out your hands," she instructs.

I do just that, and she wraps my knuckles and wrists with the linen. It's not too tight; I can still ball my fists, but it is tight enough that I can't tilt them.

"This will keep you from breaking anything if you throw a sloppy punch," she replies, as I struggle to roll my wrist.

We stand in the middle of the shade on the west end of the grounds as Mathilda throws a staccato of punches into Tane's gloves. The beat floods my senses, and my eyes flare with excitement.

They are both so freaking cool.

Tane grins fiendishly at Mathilda as she effortlessly throws punches into his alternating hands. He absorbs each of her punches easily, and then he swipes out at her. After their demonstration, Mathilda moves me into position, commenting on my stance and making adjustments.

"You need your feet balanced beneath you, not too close together; it'll put you off balance, and not too far apart where you can use the power from your legs."

She nudges my feet gently to get them in the exact place she wants them, and I'm grateful that she took the time to explain the reasoning, much like my dad used to.

Mathilda holds her fists up in front of her face, and I mimic her placement. "You want to throw your punches from here. If you drop your hands, your opponent will drop you."

I nod; my father's voice resurfaces from my memories, and

the many instructions he gave me on throwing punches click into my muscles. Tane holds his left glove out further than his right, indicating where I should strike first. I throw a punch, twisting slightly from the hips as I shift my weight.

"Good," Mathilda praises, and Tane holds out his left glove. I bring my left fist back to my face before throwing a punch with my right hand. My punches don't land as loudly as Mathilda's, but my muscle memory is just beginning to come back to life.

Mathilda corrects my arm position gently, and Tane nods. "Again."

I move slowly at first, jabbing with my left, then my right, and then two lefts before Tane extends an arm and I duck under it.

"Good Lena, remember to shift your weight slightly with each punch, but not too much or you'll be off balance."

Tane switches the tempo in the opposite direction this time and we move together quicker.

"Again," he orders, and we go faster and faster each time.

My muscles burn, but my fists slamming against the pads ring out louder and louder each time, spurring me on. Mathilda's voice calls out over the thumping. "Control your breathing, in through your nose, out through your mouth. Make sure you pay attention to everything around you, your surroundings, your position, even the direction of the wind."

Tane swipes out with a hand, and I duck quickly, but this time, he shoves his left-padded glove out right after, and my instincts take over as I let my body move freely. My right fist connects with the pad so forcefully Tane stumbles back a step.

Surprise flashes in his eyes and he grins broadly at me, shaking his hand out. "That was incredible, Lena."

Mathilda claps beside us. "Natural footwork and you didn't drop your hands once; good job."

Their words fill my heart as much as my head, and I grin broadly back at them.

"You guys are great teachers," I say in between gulps of air.

Time has passed quickly. The sun is beginning to set.

My arms hang limply at my sides from throwing so many punches, and my skin glistens with sweat. I stumble over to the water table, and my arms twitch, trying to pick up the glass. Gods, I am out of shape. Mathilda and Tane follow behind me and laugh at my shaky arms.

"Next time, we'll start with some hand-to-hand sparring, and then we can go over the various weapons and their grips," Mathilda offers.

Tane shakes his head. "No, we need to work more on sparring and footwork before we introduce weapons."

They argue the merits of both plans, but my body begins to sag. My stamina is running on fumes.

"You guys figure it out and let me know. I need a bath," I murmur.

They nod, and I begin trudging back to the Great Hall. My body is exhausted, but my mind is sharp. The elation from a successful training session is filling me with joy.

The sound of a crowd spills through the passageway and onto the terrace. I try not to grumble at having to meet anyone new; my body is covered in sweat and dust. But I square my shoulders and enter the throne room. This is a realm of warriors. Surely, my appearance, which was caused by hard work, would be appreciated.

Odessa leads a large group of warriors across the throne room and, as luck would have it, in my direction. But my eyes lock on to the familiar tall, dark-headed man at her side.

It's Lachlan, *my Lachlan.*

My breath catches in my throat, and I let out a small cry before hurtling myself across the throne room. He's actually here. All this time, I've been constantly wishing he was here, and now he is.

Thank the Gods.

My footfalls echo across the hall with each slap upon the marble, my necklace bouncing in time with my steps, and my heart races alongside them.

Surprise widens his eyes a moment before I'm catapulting myself into his arms. His scent smells stronger somehow, the cedar scent reminding me of the evergreens lining the Ayele. It wraps around me before settling into my bones.

He smells like home, *this home*, and this is real; he's really here. I pull back to look into his green eyes, my own eyes burning with tears. I blink furiously to keep them from spilling over. But his eyes are vacant; no happiness or relief is displayed on his features; it's just blank. He doesn't seem nearly as happy to see me as I am to see him.

"How are you here?" I whisper, not caring about anything else, just so relieved to see him here.

His jaw ticks as he clenches it, a familiar perturbed gesture like when he's put on the spot. My arms are the only thing keeping me up, and I realize he's not embracing me back. The ruffle of wings over his shoulder draws my attention from his distant green eyes.

The feel of leather against my body causes my mind to stall before it begins rapidly spinning. Those are wings peeking out above his shoulders; Lachlan has wings; he's in Idirihalla, and he has glossy, iridescent black wings that the guards have.

My mind finally puts the pieces together.

Lachlan is a royal guard.

He gently places me on my feet before taking a step back and dropping into a low bow. "Your Majesty," he murmurs.

My mouth drops open, and I take in the man before me, *the stranger in front of me.* Odessa places a hand on his arm.

"Helena, I'd like to introduce the captain of the guard, Lachlan Freysson."

My eyes bounce between hers and Lachlan's before taking in

the group of warriors and guards around them. Realization hits me right in the face, and I stumble back a step.

He knew.

All along, he knew who I was and what the necklace meant. The necklace that now hangs like a deadweight from my neck.

I trusted him. I imagined a future with him. My heart shreds in my chest, tears well in my eyes, and I fight with every ounce of my being to hold it together in front of all these warriors.

This is Idirhalla. And I am the future queen. All respect to my title would be lost if I crumble like a small child in front of them now. Several warriors begin eyeing me, my step back a sign of weakness.

Odessa analyzes me as well, a slight glimmer of something in her eyes. Lachlan grinds his teeth together, the movement the only flicker of emotion he's shown this entire time.

I dip my chin. "Nice to meet you, Captain. I'm sorry for that display. I mistakenly thought you were a friend of mine."

The words come out cool, but the fire in my eyes cannot be mistaken. His eyes meet mine, widening a fraction. I nod to my aunt and the warriors before squaring my shoulders and walking away as steadily as I can back to my room.

The door clicks shut, and with it safely between me and the outside world, my breath saws out of my chest as my heart shatters. I collapse to the floor, sobs wracking my entire body.

Tears fall in a race down my cheeks and splatter onto my lap. The evidence of my heartbreak and embarrassment pours out of me. He tricked me into coming here. My entire life, everything I knew was a lie. And he was a part of it. He was my first friend, my only friend, and it was only a facade.

He knew who I was.

For several long moments, I allow the flood of emotions to rise to the surface, a dam breaking.

CHAPTER
SIXTEEN

his can not be happening.

As if I haven't already suffered enough. He did not just spend our entire lives lying to me?

My despair begins to dim as rage burns through my veins. Brick by brick, I build the dam back, pulling myself together until I'm slowly standing and walking to the bathroom to splash water on my face.

My eyes are swollen and bloodshot. I glance at the necklace that shimmers in my reflection. The necklace he gifted me. Did he orchestrate this whole thing? He knew this whole time? My breath comes out in hiccups. I want to scream, but with the open windows, I know someone will hear and come running.

I take deep, slow breaths, hoping to dissolve some of the fury building inside of me. But I need answers, and I want them right now.

Slinging my door open, it crashes loudly against the adjacent wall. Spiderwebs stretch across the cracked marble. I hadn't realized I was that strong, but I don't even pause to consider the damage as I storm down the hall. He's not in the council room, dining hall, or any of the other meeting rooms.

My fury grows with each empty room.

The sound of metal on metal reverberates all the way up to the terrace and I turn my rage towards the training ground.

The breeze whips the loose strands of my hair around my face, and dirt kicks up around each of my thundering steps. Crossing under the archway, I see Lachlan sparring with Tane while Mathilda sips water by the refreshment table.

"Back so soon, Lena?" she calls.

Her smile is bright as she waves excitedly in my direction. Lachlan freezes at her voice, causing Tane to stumble to keep from slicing him in half with his sword.

"Hey, what's the —" Tane cuts off as I round on them, fury radiating off me in waves.

"Oh shit," Mathilda mutters, and she lurches off the table, heading in our direction.

"You fucking lied to me?" I scream at him, shoving past Tane. I stand toe to toe with Lachlan. He drops his weapons to raise both hands in surrender.

"Lena, I am so sorry. I dinna ha' a choice."

The misery reflected in his eyes is almost enough to make me pause. His accent becoming thicker than it usually is. At least now he is finally showing some emotion, but it's too late. My rage has burnt all other emotions away.

"You didn't have a choice? Where was my choice?!"

How many people were implicated in this scheme? And why didn't anyone ever tell me?

But it's hard to focus on the intricacies; all I see is red.

Mathilda comes to my side. "Wait, how long have you two known each other?" she asks, her eyes bouncing between us.

Tane crosses his arms. "Good observation," he whispers to her.

She rolls her eyes at him. "Let's give them a minute." Tane nods towards the water table.

My chest heaves. The anger continues to course through me as we stand facing each other.

I barely even register Tane and Mathilda slipping away as I study the stranger I thought was my closest friend. I thought I knew him, but the Lachlan I knew could have never done something like this to me.

"Lena," he begs. "I never wanted to hurt ye or lie to ye in any way, but you had to come here, and I dinna think there was any way I could convince ye otherwise."

"You never meant to hurt me? This whole time, you knew, you knew EVERYTHING, and you lied to me," I shriek at him, tears begin cascading down my cheeks. "You knew what you meant to me, what I felt for you, and you led me on and into this." I gesture around us. "I trusted you more than anyone. How could you do this to me?" My voice cracks under the weight of the emotion, quickly rising to the surface.

My fury has finally given way to the crippling grief it had held back. But it's now plainly written on my face.

"Key, please, ye ha' to believe me; I dinna want this to happen." His eyes gutter at my last words, and he clutches his chest with both hands, *pleading.*

Deep down, I know that he means every word.

The man before me, the man that I've grown up with, is nothing but honorable and kind, but I can't see past the utter betrayal, looking me dead in the eye. I muster up my last dregs of dignity, willing myself not to break down any further in front of him.

"Does Gran know where I am? Does Torin?"

His head hangs between his shoulders for a moment, and my stomach ties into knots. His eyes sparkle, silver lining the green. "They ken, and she wanted me to tell you"—he pauses, taking a deep breath—"not to come back."

My mind empties.

The rage, fear, and crippling grief slipping away into utter silence. Blood pounds in my ears. My bottom lip quivers, and I do my best to hold the rest of me together.

"She doesn't want me to come home?"

His jaw flexes, and he scrubs a hand down his face. "Nae, she wants ye to stay here; this is where you were always meant to be."

The dejection I feel outweighs everything else. I spin around and stalk toward the archway, leaving him behind.

He calls after me.

But I don't look back.

CHAPTER

SEVENTEEN

My body is numb, the morning sun trying its best to warm me out of the anguish I'm trapped in. The birds chatter in the trees, their happiness annoying as I wait for the abuse Julius is sure to bring. I arrive earlier than usual, having not been able to sleep last night or eat this morning.

I'm angry, but beyond that, I grieve for the life I thought I had. The life I was so desperate to return to. It's gone.

Julius' low whistle has me turning around as he stalks through the archway.

"Being early isn't going to score you any points with me, Helena." He stalks over to the maple tree and slaps the hilt of the axe.

I hate him.

"Lena," I murmur under my breath.

He doesn't hear me, but I guess he caught my lips moving.

"What was that?" He sneers.

Not being able to bite back a retort, I snap, "It's Lena. You keep calling me Helena, and I prefer to be called Lena."

He rolls his eyes and crosses his arms over his chest. "Somebody is in a mood this morning."

When I don't respond, he smiles maliciously at me. "Oh, did you finally meet our handsome captain at last? A heartbreaker, that one is."

There's an evil glint in his eyes. Did this asshole know, too?

I clench my jaw, trying my hardest to keep from exploding on him. He stares me down, waiting for the eruption. When nothing comes from me, he sighs.

"Go get your sword; let's do some sparring."

I turn my back on him and walk towards the weapons building. My muscles ache to be used, and I'm ready to swing a sword at Julius's head. But when I return, Julius is still where I left him without a sword or shield.

I stare at him quizzically, and he gives me a flat look.

"Run sprints with your sword and shield."

My brow furrows; he can't be serious. "I thought we were—" I begin, but he cuts me off.

"Now!" he snarls.

I spend the entire morning running with my shield and sword.

At lunch, I stumble into the dining hall and see Mathilda and Lachlan glaring at each other. Mathilda's eyes soften when she spies me, and she waves me over.

But I freeze when Lachlan slowly turns my way.

My breath stalls.

I haven't seen him so crestfallen since we were kids. His eyes are hollow. The vibrant green is muted and murky with misery. Mathilda mumbles something to him I can't hear, and he hangs his head, dropping something onto the table, before stalking out. I slowly approach, and she stretches her arms out wide, enveloping me in a hug.

"Lena, I am so sorry. I promise we had no idea you guys knew or didn't know each other like that."

She smells of sunshine and poppies, and I sigh in her warm embrace. She steps back to stare into my eyes. There's a sharpness to her gaze.

"I swear on my mother's burial mound that I had no idea who he was to you."

I believe her.

Nodding my head, I take a seat at the table. A small white flower, like a clematis flower, sits alone at the end of the table where Lachlan had stood. My chest aches.

Mathilda attempts to make small talk with me throughout our lunch, but my thoughts are muddled. I force myself to eat my lunch to prepare for my session with Mina. Mathilda walks with me down to the training grounds, and I get the feeling that she will not be leaving my side until my mood improves. There's a warmth blooming in my veins at her kindness; she truly is a wonderful friend.

Mina sits cross-legged in the shade, her eyes closed, and her palms face up in her lap. I share a look with Mathilda, and she grins at me, mouthing *'have fun'* before turning back.

Quietly, I approach Mina. Her hair begins to float around her, and the small pebbles floating up from the ground begin to circle her. The shock has me stumbling, and her eyes flash open. Her hair and the pebbles drop instantly. She looks up at me with a small smile.

"Hi," she says softly. I give a small wave and plop down on the ground beside her. She pats my leg gently, her eyes studying my face. "You okay?"

My braid whips back and forth as I shake my head and heave a sigh. "I'm dealing with a lot right now."

She smiles sadly and nods. "Today we're going to work on some strength and conditioning. Not just for our bodies." She taps the side of her head. "But our minds too."

I grimace; my mind is not the place I want to be in right now. She stands quickly and stretches out a hand to me. She's so small compared to my taller frame, but there's a fierceness glimmering in her eyes. I take her outstretched hand, and she pulls me to my feet but doesn't let go of my hand.

"Close your eyes," she murmurs to me. I follow her instructions and close them. "Listen to your heart and just breathe."

My muscles tense as my pulse begins racing, anticipating all the emotions that have been warring under the surface to break through. My parents, Gran and Lachlan, circle around and around in my mind. I'm furious with my parents for hiding my birthright from me. I'm shattered that Lachlan, *of all people*, was a part of the scheme and kept all of this from me. I'm devastated that Gran doesn't want me to come back.

I'm lost.

I take a deep breath, trying to push my distressing thoughts away.

"Don't push your thoughts away," Mina murmurs, and I crack an eye open before quickly closing it when she begins speaking again.

"Change your mindset; you're not a victim here but a survivor. You have survived so much that would have broken other people. Yes, bad things have happened to you. But you control how you react to them. If you don't like how you feel, then change it."

Her words stun me as they strike a chord.

She's right.

Everyone else made their choices, and now I can make my own. If I know anything about my parents, Gran and Lachlan, it's that they wouldn't ever maliciously hurt me. They would try their best to make the right decision at the time. I let that thought settle into my very bones. That's right. They did the best they could, and they had their reasons. I can not dwell on things I cannot change.

Mina squeezes my hand gently. "Come back to your body

and your surroundings." I take another deep breath and open my eyes. My chest is lighter, and my head is clearer.

"Better?" she asks, smiling at me.

I nod, and a smile begins spreading across my face. "It is. It's not gone, but much more manageable."

She places her hands on her hips and her hair whips side to side as she looks around the training grounds.

"Let's do some warmups and then some core work; it'll help with all your training going forward if you have a strong core."

"Sounds good," I reply and follow her as she begins a slow jog around the training room.

"I'm glad the mind work helped," she says. We jog slowly, following the perimeter of the fence around the grounds.

"Me too; how did you know I needed that?" I ask.

She jogs so gracefully, that her feet barely make a sound against the dirt. "You've dealt with a lot in the past couple of days, and from what you said, you weren't even aware this place actually existed. I assumed you'd be struggling with thoughts of betrayal."

I grimace. She called that perfectly. "I am. Well, was. It was just hard to conceive a world where my parents kept something this big from me. It was only ever us three, and we were so happy; I just don't understand why they wouldn't tell me, ya know?"

She bobs her head and bites her bottom lip. "You must miss them a lot."

I swallow hard and try to focus on my pace so that I don't start crying. "I do very much, but in a way, I'm relieved they went together. They couldn't survive without each other."

Mina slows as we approach the large maple tree that holds Odin's axe. "I wouldn't understand what that's like," she murmurs. Sadness dims her usually bright eyes.

I struggle with the right words. "I'm so sorry, I—I didn't know."

She shakes her head. "No, it's okay. I had a decent childhood compared to other Valkyries. But my parents never mated, and their relationship was rocky at best." She reaches her arms up over her head and begins stretching. She's so lithe and graceful with each of her movements, and I do my best to follow suit.

"That's got to be rough, though, and I'm still sorry you had to deal with that growing up."

She sits back down and straightens her legs out in front of her. "It definitely showed me what I did not want. It was always like our house was on fire; there was so much discord, and they wielded me as a weapon against each other, even though I never seemed to be good enough. I refuse to settle for a relationship like that. But it has been lonely."

Understanding fills my eyes. "I had the opposite experience, but the same feeling." I chuckle. "I don't think I'll ever have a relationship as great as my parents; love like that is rare."

Mina nods and grins. "Team no mate."

We high-five.

She lays down flat and pats the ground beside her. "Okay, you're about to hate me, but I promise it'll be worth it."

My stomach hurts so badly by the time we finish our core workout that it hurts to breathe. Mina cracks jokes on the way back to the Great Hall, and I glower at her.

"I swear to the Gods, if you make me laugh right now, I'll punch you."

She sticks her tongue out at me and flits away quickly when I struggle to reach out to push her.

"Take a bath with the blue oil when you get to your room. It helps with the muscle soreness, and don't forget your healing tonic," she calls to me as we go our separate ways, her into the city, and me, straight for a bath before getting some dinner.

My leathers are coated in dirt and I push the loose hairs back from my forehead as I trudge across the throne room. Lachlan materializes from the greenish shadow beside the throne and stalks towards me. *I am not in the mood for this right now.* I clutch my sore stomach and make a beeline for the hallway.

"Lena," his voice echoes across the empty throne room, and I halt but don't turn towards him. I miss him desperately, but I don't think I'm ready to face this yet.

"Lena, please, may I speak with ye?"

My head hangs, and I struggle to control my rising fury. We are stuck here together until the magic returns from my presence or war erupts. I need to figure out how to make peace with his presence. Lachlan's hand grazes under my elbow, and I slowly turn to face him. His eyes are swimming with misery. The tattoos on his arms ripple when he flexes his hands into fists. I realize now that when we were in the human realm, he never wore anything but long sleeves.

My brow furrows, and I study him closely for anything else I hadn't noticed before.

I don't understand how I ever assumed he was human, his size, strength, and unnaturally good looks. It was all so blatantly obvious.

"I am so sorry. I was ordered not to tell ye. But ye have to believe me; I wanted to more than anything."

I purse my lips as my eyes narrow. Anger is rearing its ugly head again.

"I'm not ready to have this conversation with you," I grit out.

He nods quickly. "I understand; I just needed to tell ye that I am so sorry, Key. I never wanted to hurt ye."

The use of my nickname makes me snap my mouth shut. I ball my hands into fists at my side. The urge to punch his stupidly perfect face surges through me.

"*Again.*" I glare at him. "I am not ready to speak to you, and don't fucking call me that."

I turn on my heel and stalk from the throne room.

The sight of my door causes me to sigh deeply, my room, *my sanctuary.* I shut the door quietly behind me this time and take deep breaths, working to change my mindset as Mina taught me. But I also pick through my emotions like Torin showed me.

I am angry, but I don't have to be.

I can accept this and move on. He will not disrupt my peace right now. Slipping into the bathroom, I strip my boots off before turning on the tub. The blue vial that Mina suggested is sitting on the marble ledge by the window, and I dump the entire thing into the bath. The room immediately smells heavenly and I inhale the chamomile scent.

A knock on my door startles me, and I lurch upright. I swear to the gods if Lachlan followed me here, I really will punch him in the face. I throw open the door.

"What?" But I'm surprised to find Odessa standing there. "Oh sorry, I thought you were someone else."

Her expression is a mix of irritation and disgust. "Ah, I see," she replies, a bit coldly tugging at the neckline of her silver blue gown. "I was hoping you and I could train together tomorrow and wanted to ask if that's something you would agree to?"

It's phrased as a question, but it's obvious she expects me to say yes. "Yeah, that would be great. Are you sure you're not too busy?" I ask.

She shakes her head. "No, I'm curious to observe the progress of your training. There are rumors circulating that you are training with others."

"Oh, umm, yes, a few people had offered, and I didn't think there was any harm in it if I'm going to stay here, ya know?" I reply.

I do not understand why she seems upset. Isn't that what she wanted from me? To stay here?

"So you have decided to stay with us even after magic restores?" She crosses her arms over her chest and her eyebrow arches.

"I have given it some thought, and you were right. My responsibilities and duties lie here, and if there's a chance I could bring stability to this realm, then I should honor my birthright," I reply, steel in my veins.

But her reaction to this conversation is not at all what I expected.

"I see," she replies curtly. "Well then, I will assess your training tomorrow, and from there, we can plan your official coronation."

She turns on her heel and leaves me standing there with my brow furrowing.

What the heck was that about?

She threw me to the wolves by formally announcing me as the savior of the realm, and now that I've agreed, she's offended? I didn't even get a chance to ask her if traveling back and forth would be a possibility for me once the magic returns and I accept my new title.

But even as I think about it, Gran's words to Lachlan circle through my mind: *"Don't come back."*

EIGHTEEN

Word has spread about my decision to stay and my training with Odessa. Clusters of people are gathered along the fence of the training grounds when I arrived this morning. They've all come to see how the future queen will measure up.

My palms grow slick at the eyes turning my way, and I clutch my necklace in my hands; it's cold to the touch, but the feeling of it brings peace to my nerves. My feet get tangled beneath me and I almost fall flat on my face when I spy Lachlan leaning on the fence next to Evander. His arms are crossed, and he studies me closely as I walk carefully across the grounds. There's an overwhelming sadness still rolling off him, and his jaw clenches when I pass without addressing him.

Great.

That's not who I wanted to see down here. Especially since I've never sparred in front of him before. He's managed to become the captain of the royal guard, and I'm only a novice. The last thing I want to do is embarrass myself.

Metal clashes, startling me out of my thoughts as I take in Julius and Odessa warming up together. Their new training leathers repel the abundance of sunlight around us. The sight of them is causing whispers and even a few glares from the people gathered. Their color is so unusual compared to the dark brown ones that the rest of us wear. The onyx black gives off a sinister vibe.

Usually, gossiping about someone's clothes is not an activity I condone, but this time, I actually agree with them; they look wrong. It's not just the color. The weave pattern of the leather itself resembles snakeskin, and the dark red buckles like drops of blood.

They halt their warm-up as I approach.

Odessa gives me a long look, from the top of my head to the boots on my feet. "I want you to spar with Julius for your warm-up, then we'll begin."

Her tone brooks no argument, but sparring isn't a warm-up activity for me. "Usually, I begin with some stretching and jogging to get loose first…" I trail off at her scathing glare.

"I don't have all day, so you'll spar now," she reiterates.

She turns on her heel, walking to the fence with the other spectators. On my end of the grounds, I spy Artemisia standing with Boudicca. Her eyes linger on Odessa and then narrow in suspicion. Boudicca gives me a small smile of encouragement, her crude green eyes radiating warmth, and I nod in return, grateful for her support. Julius scoffs at the sentiment between us and sneers at me.

My nerves vanish; I cannot wait to remove that look from his smug, stupid face.

I draw my blade and get into a ready position. We're on the shady side of the training grounds, but Julius's blade reflects a ray of sunlight right into my eyes, blinding me, and he quickly slashes out.

I manage to dodge at the last second while furiously blinking my eyes to clear the dazzling spots blotting my vision. Grunts of disapproval ring out at his unsavory tactics, the loudest I recognize coming from Leif. He's standing right behind Julius and in my direct line of sight. I see him cross his arms and spit on the ground in pure disgust.

I do my best to stay focused on Julius and his movements, while also utilizing Mathilda's instructions and staying alert to everything else happening around us.

When we begin to circle each other, I notice Evander and Lachlan making their way closer to us.

Julius chuckles, and I decide to take an offensive approach. I begin attacking Julius with upward slashes and strikes.

My sword is firm in my grip, but its weight is light, like an extension of my arm.

He blocks each one of my attacks, but my offensive tactic has caught him off guard, and he's only able to take a defensive approach. Whenever he trains me, I've always been on the defensive, so he hasn't had the time to memorize any of my moves.

My footwork is impeccable, thanks to Mathilda and Tane, and my balance never wavers, thanks to Mina.

Overall, my breathing stays relaxed, and my core is strong. I work him into the corner with ease. I've been clever at hiding my newfound abilities from him during our mornings, afraid of a moment like this, where he would try to embarrass me in front of others.

Cries ring out as spectators clear the fence. I push him into an undesirable position against the railing, and I catch a glimpse of Satiah, her black hair glinting in the sun. An approving smirk graces her mouth.

But I underestimated the lows Julius would stoop to if he became cornered.

With an evil grin, he kicks dirt directly into my eyes. The gritty sand stings and scratches painfully. I scrub my eyes with my free hand and try to force them to remain open.

But his booted foot connects with my stomach. My abs flex

too late to absorb the impact, and the force sends me flying through the air.

The ground is unforgiving as my back makes contact and my breath is ripped from my lungs. My head collides with the ground.

A muted thud rings out at the collision.

Lachlan is immediately at my side. "Lena, are ye ok?"

He pats my body for injuries, and I try to push his hands away. The ability to speak is gone, along with my breathing still. But through my watery and spotted vision, his face radiates pure wrath as he glares at Julius.

"What the fuck was that? That's not how we spar!" He roars with rage, the veins in his neck push against his tanned skin.

I shove away from Lachlan. Rolling onto my stomach, I brace myself on my hands and knees. Air inflates my lungs and I groan as I force myself to stand.

Odessa's voice rings out from her vigil at the fence. "Captain, are you interfering?" Her words sound bitter, and she stares at Lachlan with contempt.

His eyes lower in submission, but then he gathers himself, meeting her stare with his own.

"No, Your Majesty, merely questioning the tactics being used." He gestures to where I'm still wiping the dirt from my eyes. "This is not how we do things."

Blinking the dirt completely from my eyes, I can now see he was positioned in front of me, placing himself squarely in front of Julius.

Odessa scans Julius before turning her gaze back to Lachlan. "You're dismissed, Captain."

Lachlan's jaw clenches, and his eyes narrow with barely controlled rage before his nostrils flare with a sharp inhale.

He turns to me, worry shining in his eyes. But he'll find no agreement here.

"Follow your orders, Captain," I hiss.

Lachlan's shoulders stiffen slightly, and he takes a step but pauses, leaning in close so no one else can hear. "He fights with the arrogance of someone who's never seen true battle; use his ego against him, and you can beat him. Ye have natural ability like I've never even seen before, Key. You are better than he is. Believe in yourself," he whispers.

The use of my nickname and the support he displays dulls some of the anger I feel towards him. When he stalks off to the guard quarters, my eyes trail after him.

Taking a controlled breath, I reposition myself, readying for Julius to take the offensive approach that is common for him. Odessa claps once, signaling for us to begin. Julius attacks.

Big surprise, but this time I'm prepared. I thrust my knee up and into his gut as I feint a dodge around his unguarded attack. He grunts, shock written across his twisted features. I can barely contain my smile at the sound of his pain.

He has no idea what I'm capable of.

Evander nods, his copper hair bobbing with the movement, and pride blazes across his smile. But I quickly bring my attention back to Julius, who is now fuming that I played him. We circle each other. My steps are slow and calculated. But his movements are stilted as he vibrates with fury.

His next attack is sloppy, his rage corroding his movements, and I dodge, bringing my sword down on his. The resounding clash ripples around us. Whispers begin swelling, and there are even a few cheers.

Julius scowls deeper. His brow obscures his vision as he strikes out again. He expected it to overpower me, but his feet were not completely underneath him, and I push him back with minimal effort.

He's too unsteady, and my push sends him careening onto his back. He curses, and a cloud of dust billows around him.

Before he can even push up onto his elbows, I level my sword to his throat.

My victory comes as a surprise to us all. Silence settles around us; the only sound is the heaving of his breath through his bared teeth.

But the silence ruptures as cheers erupt. Evander claps, Boudicca nods, and Artemisia howls with laughter. Even Joan, in men's training leathers over her usual black tunic, is giving an approving nod next to Satiah, whose smile is broad as she claps enthusiastically. I withdraw my sword, reaching out a hand to help Julius to his feet.

His face is twisted with disgust and he glares at me from his sprawled position on the ground before roughly grasping my hand.

I tug hard to heave him up, but he pulls violently against me. The action jerks me forward and right within reach of the quick jab he flings at my face. My balance is off, and my hand is held firmly in his grasp, leaving me with no way or time to block.

His fist connects.

The crack of my bone echoes through the training ground. Blood sprays and my eyes immediately begin to flood, the tears flow down my face. I'm so stunned it takes a moment for the pain to register. The tears and dirt from his fist begin mixing with the blood pouring from my nose.

The cheering cuts off and yelling begins.

Evander and several other warriors are upon me in an instant. Their bodies creating a defensive wall. Other warriors surge around Julius. He tries to fight off their hold.

Spit flies from his mouth and his face turns a blotchy shade of violet as he screams, "You fucking bitch!"

They drag him from the training ground. Odessa follows silently behind them, not once even glancing in my direction.

Evander cups my face between his hands and checks me over. "Someone go get me the healing tonic!"

Footsteps pound against dirt as someone races to follow his orders.

The sound of fabric being torn slices through the pain, and Joan hands Evander a piece of fabric torn from her own tunic. He uses it to staunch the flow of blood streaming from my nose. I try to look anywhere but at the puddle of blood, at my feet. The warriors surrounding us are all showing signs of rage or shock at the shameless attack. Artemisia spews something in Greek, and Boudicca's green eyes are ablaze with fury as she assesses my nose from Evander's other side.

"Are you okay?" Worry creases Evander's brow as he holds the fabric scrap to my still-gushing nose.

"Am I gonna be ugly now?" I whine.

Everyone freezes before laughter rings out; even Joan's face breaks into a small smile. "You took down the queen's mate, took a punch to the face, and you're worried if you're going to be ugly?" he mutters, shaking his head as he tries to hold back his laughter.

I smile at him and warm blood trickles over my lips.

Satiah returns with the tonic and throws it at Evander. She turns towards me and bows gracefully. "It was an honor to watch you, Lena." With her liquid black hair and fiery expression, she looks every bit like a bronze statue of a long-ago queen. Her eyes pierce me. "You will be a formidable queen."

The ability to speak leaves me at her declaration, and I can only manage a dip of my chin as she turns to leave. The bleeding is a trickle now, and I gulp down the vial of healing tonic Evander hands me. The coppery tang of blood mixes with the honey flavor. I continue to breathe through my mouth.

As my bone starts to stitch together, the bleeding ceases. Evander removes the soaked fabric scrap, and the warriors depart. Rough hands patting me on my shoulders or back as they leave, in congratulations.

The sentiment is not lost on me, and my eyes water for a completely different reason.

Evander and I are the only ones left on the training ground before long.

"Are you sure you're okay?" he asks again.

He eyes me speculatively, and I get the feeling that many emotions flit across my face.

"Yeah, just shocked, I guess. That wasn't normal, was it?" I work through the last few moments in my head. The rage on Julius' face as he was pulled away is etched into my mind.

"No, it definitely wasn't. I don't think you should go back to the Hall for a while; let him calm down," he replies.

I stare down at my blood-splattered leathers and the small puddle on the ground as it absorbs slowly into the dirt to create burgundy mud.

"I don't really have anywhere else to go," I mumble.

He looks at me with pity before slinging an arm over my shoulder. "Let's go for a ride, then."

Evander leads me down the path between the training grounds and the armory.

"I've never been on this side of the grounds before," I say to him as we pass by the wood building full of weapons and training gear.

The path is more worn here, and the cobblestones have crumbled away into dust in some areas.

"I can't imagine you would need to. The only things down here are the stables and the guard's quarters." He nods at the two-story, long building peeking out from the trees in front of us. "That's the guard's quarters; see that green door on the bottom, right?" I nod in confirmation. "That's my room, and the blue door above it on the second floor—that's Lachlan's."

Heat crawls up my neck.

But he continues on. "And on the other side, right there." He points to a wooden stable. "Is where we keep all the guards' horses."

Excitement has me bouncing with each step. I haven't even

thought about riding since I was back home with Sleipnir. I hope Torin is continuing to keep him in shape. Thoughts of home quell my excitement and guilt takes its place. I'm leaving all of that behind.

Evander hesitantly asks, "You know how to ride, right?"

I nod excitedly and a bright smile spreads across his face. "Alright good. We'll take a trail up through the mountains. You haven't seen any of the mountain farms yet."

NINETEEN

My smile is wide as I sit astride a white mare with the longest mane and tail I've ever seen. We follow Evander, on his dappled gray horse, up the path that leads into the mountains behind the Great Hall.

"It's just a two-hour ride up to the nearest farm. We'll stop there and rest a bit before we head back. Hopefully, everyone will be cooled off by then," he calls over his shoulder.

The trail is narrow and barely large enough for our horses. It also isn't very worn down, which makes it difficult to see from atop the horse.

"Is this a common path?" I ask, trying my best to follow where it leads through the tall grasses.

"Not really," he replies with a shake of his head. "The farmers take the main roads to town to sell their goods. This isn't used as much anymore."

My eyes strain to see where the trail leads, but I lose it when it enters the forest in front of us. The forest covers the foot of the mountain we're about to climb and hides most of it from view.

"Do you know where you're going?" I ask, wariness flooding through my veins.

"Yeah, this leads past an ancient temple; from there, it's a straight shot to the closest farm."

The ease of his answers soothes some of my nerves.

"A temple?" I scrunch my face in confusion and instantly regret it as my freshly healed nose throbs.

Evander slows so that we're side by side; his posture is that of someone as comfortable on a horse as they are on their own two feet.

He cocks his head as he asks, "What do you know about the Mother?"

"Ummm, a little, I guess. We practiced what my mother called 'the olde ways,' so we would worship many gods. She taught me that Danu was the Mother goddess associated with nature and fertility," I reply.

Before the deaths of my parents and during our many travels, we would often leave offerings of wildflowers or ripe fruit at streams.

"Your mother had this place in her mind when she taught you those ways."

His smile is tinged with sadness. My smile mirrors his. I see my mother in every bit of this place. It's bittersweet.

We cross into the forest and it smells of evergreens and rich soil.

"Danu, or the Mother, is connected to fertility, abundance, and the natural world. The temple on this path was erected so that people could pray and honor her. We'll stop at it so you can offer her prayers if you wish. The mountains we're trekking towards are the Badb Mountains, she's another goddess. The ones to the west are the Edda mountains, again, named after a goddess. We used to recognize a lot of the gods and goddesses, but we don't anymore." His shoulders seem to slump with each word.

"Yeah, Odessa mentioned something about that," I murmur as I watch the sunlight filter through the branches of trees.

"When Odin left, the rest of our gods and goddesses went with him. So there isn't a need to worship them anymore. They won't hear us." His voice is carefully neutral, and his face is cautiously blank.

"Do you really believe that?"

There's a tree directly in our path and we separate, leading our horses around it.

Evander sighs as he shakes his head. "No. Which is why I offered to let you pay your respects to Danu."

He glances sidelong at me, gauging my reaction to his words.

My lips kick up into a smile and he smiles back at me nervously. I turn my attention to the surrounding land that is teeming with stunning giant emerald evergreens. Ruby red poppies and cascading white flowers, their petals shaped like stars, weave through feathery ferns. The towering trees block most of the sunlight, so the journey is cool, with the constant soft breeze rustling the branches. Birds chatter, and a few small creatures scurry across our path.

It's a balm to my frazzled nerves. The fight with Julius, anger towards Lachlan, and homesickness slowly ease away to nothingness as the peace this land brings me.

"How're you dealing with all of this so far?" he asks, interrupting my wandering mind.

"It's been difficult, but I think I'll be okay." I don't necessarily mean the words, but I hope if I tell myself that enough, it will become true.

He purses his lips. "There's something I need to tell you about Lachlan."

"I'm not ready to talk about him." My stomach clenches, and I shake my head.

I dreaded this moment. When their friendship would bleed over into our outing.

Evander gives me a sheepish look. "Then can I tell you something about me?"

His words are not at all what I was expecting, but his face is leeched of color and now I'm more curious than cautious.

"Uh, sure."

He fidgets with the reins in his grip before he blurts out, "We've met before."

"We have?" My brows raise in surprise and I nearly jerk the reins.

I relax my grip, waiting for his response.

He swallows deeply, his throat bobbing with the effort. "I was stuck in your chimney."

A laugh erupts out of my belly, a deep, full-body laugh. Evander's face relaxes, turning into a hesitant smile. "You're not mad?"

Tears spill over and I wipe them from my cheeks. "No, I'm not mad."

"But you're mad at Lachlan?" he asks, tilting his head.

The movement is the exact same as when he's in his raven form.

"That's different. Lachlan knew me long before and kept all of this from me." The betrayal still stings.

All that time we spent together, all that time I pined for him, *and he knew.*

It's silent again, and I focus on the path before us. Branches sway in the breeze and my horse whips her tail side to side.

"But what if it wasn't his choice to keep it from you?" he asks suddenly.

A sigh works its way out of my chest. "I hope that was the case," I mumble.

Realizing just how much I do miss him.

The path isn't a harsh incline, more of a gradual slope, so I don't realize how high we've climbed until we come to a small outcropping of level stone protruding from the side of the mountain. Evander leads us around the wall of stone and onto the ledge; the land opens up, revealing looming ancient columns that support a domed roof, creating a pavilion.

The columns and roof are overgrown with heart-shaped, broad-leafed ivy. Crumbling urns, overspilling with lilac flowers, are rooted on either side of the arched entry.

Evander frowns in displeasure at the neglected temple. "As you can see, no one comes up here anymore."

I dismount from my mare, handing off my reins to him as I climb the four wide steps into the pavilion. I grasp a single violet from one of the urns and pluck it as an offering before walking inside.

There's a stillness inside this place, like a bated breath. A dull ringing begins in my ears, and I grasp my necklace at the familiar sound. It's warm in my hands. *Approval*, it seems to say. I spin in place, looking for anything remotely questionable, but there's nothing here.

Light spills in from the doorway, and dust motes sparkle in their glow. The stone walls are covered in faded frescos of wild animals and flowers. Only a few decaying petals skitter around the marble floor in the breeze.

But a single red petal among the mix of lilac ones draws and holds my attention. My eyes follow its glide across the stone. The sight of it begins to blur, and a sinking sensation overcomes my body, numbing me. The violet in my hand drops to the ground as I sink further and further away.

At a distance, I can hear Evander calling my name, but the sound is muffled as if I'm underwater. I struggle to tear my eyes from the red petal. I'm paralyzed, my muscles locked into place. Muffled voices begin whispering around me.

A woman's lilting voice sings over the rest. "*Come find us.*" It repeats, over and over.

Rocks tumble down the mountain. The thundering sound

rips me from the trance. My muscles flinch as the numbness subsides.

Evander shouts, fear lacing his tone. "Lena! Are you okay?"

I hear him walk the horses closer. Their hooves on the stone echo through the temple. But I'm already fleeing for the entrance.

"Yes, sorry! I got distracted," I reply, while throwing glances over my shoulder as I retreat from the temple.

His eyes narrow, and his mouth pops open to question me, but two large shadows streak along the ground between us.

Our heads swivel towards the sky. Two masses of white and black wings break from the sky and descend towards us.

Mathilda and Lachlan slam onto the ground behind our horses, causing them to cry out in fear. Evander reins in his horse while I try to soothe mine.

"Gods!" Evander yells. "Was that necessary?"

They straighten from their crouched position, their massive wings flaring at their defensive stance. My pulse races at the sight of Lachlan with his wings out. They're larger than Evander's, the black color hinting at more of a purple undertone than a blue one like the other guard's wings I've seen before.

Lachlan answers Evander first. "We ha' to get her back right now."

My eyes flare slightly at his voice.

It rumbles like thunder as he stares right at the blood still splattered on my leathers. It is nothing like the voice I know. It rings with power and command. His expression is grave, and even though I'm still furious with him, I long to see the familiar sparkle in his eyes.

Evander and I share a cautious look before he replies, "What's happened?"

They both hesitate.

Mathilda finally answers, "Someone has destroyed your room, Lena; it looks like they were looking for something." Her expression is apologetic as her eyes jump between me and Lachlan.

My mind whirls; I don't have any belongings of significance here. Other than my necklace, I suppose, but I never take that off.

What could they have been searching for?

Unless they weren't searching at all. This is retaliation from a certain someone I defeated earlier today.

Evander seemingly reads my mind and rolls his eyes. "Are we sure it wasn't Julius retaliating?"

I smirk at his question. Julius raging through my room is not an image I was expecting in my time here.

Mathilda shakes her head. "Odessa said he was with her the whole time."

"Lena, may I have a moment alone to speak with ye?" Lachlan asks and his face is so full of anguish I nod my agreement before I can even register his words. He brushes past me and into the temple.

I make eye contact with Mathilda before I follow after him and she asks, "Are you sure?"

I nod and make my way back up the temple steps.

Lachlan's back is to me and his head is tilted up towards the dome ceiling when I approach. His wings are now tattooed upon his golden skin and he sighs deeply before turning toward me.

"I am so sorry I wasn't there to protect ye today."

My eyes flash to his. "I don't need you to protect me. I *needed* you to be honest with me."

My words land their blow and his eyes widen slightly. "I deserved that."

"Anything else?" I cross my arms over my chest and glare at him.

He takes a deep breath. "Ye ha' every right to be mad and if you're still not ready to ha' this conversation or hear my reasonings I willna push ye on it. But it is absolutely my duty to protect ye and I will be doing that, gladly, for the rest of my life." His eyes narrow onto the blood on my leathers and his jaw clenches tightly as he grinds out, "From here on out no one is allowed to lay a hand on ye and if I find out they ha' I will personally remove it from their body. I don't give a fuck who they are." His words echo through the temple and my blood heats in response. His eyes soften a shade as they meet mine again. "Be angry with me all ye like, but I will always be here for you."

I swallow audibly at the emotion rising in my throat. Every moment before this, he has always been there when I needed him.

But before I can respond, a howl rents the air, and a stiff wind rips through the temple. Lachlan's eyes grow wide at the sound, and I take an unguarded step in his direction. The sound of the wind's howl sends goosebumps down my arms and the hair on the back of my neck stands on end. Dread pools in my belly. We rush from the temple and halt as we take in the capital down below us.

My eyes widen with horror, and my jaw slackens as I take in the horrifying spectacle occurring.

A massive, dark thunderhead is ripping through the blue sky and building quickly right over the city. Lightning flashes and thunder rumbles loudly. That sound wasn't rocks tumbling earlier. It was thunder.

We all share similar looks of horror.

"It's just a storm, right?" I question. It looks similar to a storm but feels like something much, much worse. The black mass of heavy, rain-leaden clouds roils over itself as it builds at an unnatural rate.

Mathilda swallows. "There has *never* been a storm in Idirhalla." She flinches with a crack of thunder. "Rain, yes, but never a storm."

Evander pales. "It's one of the signs, isn't it?" he whispers.

Mathilda and Lachlan nod as a gust of wind surges through the trees and pushes us all off balance.

"Another sign?" I yell over the howling wind, but no one replies.

The pressure around us changes, and my ears pop painfully. The bottom is falling out of the storm.

Mathilda races to Evander with her arm outstretched as he swings her up and over his mount. She settles into the saddle behind him. Lachlan grabs me around my waist and throws me up over my horse.

As he settles in behind me, my mouth drops open. Lachlan nods to Evander. Lachlan wraps his arms around me, grabs the reins, and takes off like a shot down the mountain. I brace myself against his broad chest and grip the saddle horn with all my might as we hurtle down the mountain. We're both bent forward at the waist, adjusting to the speed of the horse. My body bounces against his.

Above the sound of the howling wind, Lachlan murmurs, "Hold on and do not fall. I would hate for us to ha' a lackluster death."

The sound of his voice, so close to my ear, unintentionally sends shivers down my spine. If I wasn't so terrified of our breakneck speed down the mountain, or the fact that I am still furious with him, I would relish having him so close.

But anger wins out over fear, and I lean further forward, trying to put some distance between us. Lachlan takes one hand off the reins and wraps it around my chest, pulling me back towards him. My stomach tightens from his possessive touch.

"Stop touching me," I grate out between clenched teeth, fighting against his hold.

"I focus better when I can feel ye," he chuckles, his usual charismatic self familiar and comforting, but I continue to pull against his hold.

"Unless ye want us to fall off this mountain, then be my guest." He loosens his grip on me immediately.

Our horse launches over a fallen limb, and the motion causes me to wobble in the saddle. A gust of wind kicks up dirt that whips past me. The shape of it is eerily similar to a wolf. Another specter races by us and looks similar to a man.

My stomach clenches with fear before I right myself, and I heave a sigh, irritated that I'm stuck in this position, before leaning back against him.

"Can't you just fly home?" I spit out.

It's grating on my willpower, the want of needing him battling the bitterness of his betrayal. His scent is enrapturing, and his arms embracing me give me the security I've desperately been craving. Thunder crashes, causing me to flinch, and the wind whips heavy tree branches into our faces. We duck to keep from being clotheslined off the horse.

"The wind says otherwise," he loudly yells over the storm.

We continue our breakneck speed down the side of the mountain, weaving in between the trees, and our bodies jostle against each other in a steady rhythm.

My cheeks heat at our thumping bodies, and I clear my throat. Lachlan merely sighs in my ear. He's not the least bit frightened or uncomfortable, and I clench my thighs tightly against the horse's sides.

We're clearing the forest and onto the narrow footpath behind the guard's quarters when the torrential downpour starts. It's as if the entire ocean was held aloft over the city and was dropped.

Rain soaks us as we make our way into the stables, our breaths heaving as hard as the horses as we dismount.

Evander leads both of our horses into their stalls and I whisper to Mathilda, "Is this because magic is fading?"

Something passes between Mathilda and Lachlan before she sighs and answers me. "No, that was the Wild Hunt."

The image of the painting flashes in my mind: the storm, the howl, and the specters.

It is an omen of the Great War.

I press my lips into a thin line. "But Odin is supposed to ride with the Wild Hunt and—" I stop myself from retorting as I glance at Lachlan and Evander.

They are guards, *royal guards*, sworn to Odessa.

Mathilda murmurs, "They think the same as me."

I nod before asking, "I just don't understand. Magic is still obviously fading, but you guys think it's a sign of an impending war?" The silence stretches between us.

Lachlan studies me cautiously. "Why couldn't it be both? Why couldn't magic be fading and signs that the Great War is approaching?"

"Is that what you guys think?"

Evander peeks out the stable doors before answering, "We know that magic is fading, but these disasters are coming more frequently and have been increasing in intensity. It's best to err on the side of caution, which is why we want the training grounds open, among other things."

When it's phrased that way, it does make sense. Coupled with the tale about the Fomorians and the Idir tree, why shouldn't we prepare just in case?

"What can I do?" I ask. There's a weighted pause; their faces vary in degrees of shock.

"Wait," Mathilda responds, "You will help us? *Just like that?*"

I get the feeling I'm missing something. "Yes—I mean, I'm here, and the disasters are still happening and now more rapidly. I know Odessa believes my presence should put an end to all of that, but it's not, and the problems are progressing for the worst, especially if that was the Wild Hunt. I definitely think you are all right, and it's an omen of war. My mother told me the stories."

Lachlan shakes his head, his gaze grim. "I dinna think ye ken.

What ye just said goes against everything Odessa and Julius are trying to establish with the council; this would make ye a rebel."

The sound of that word should make me afraid or, at the very least, guilty for turning my back on my only family member here, but it doesn't. Something about following this path spurs me on further.

"I can understand how they would initially think these disasters are related to magic fading, but this,"—I point to the storm like Mathilda did earlier—"is a really bad sign if it is the Wild Hunt."

The rain stops instantly, as do the roaring winds, as if they, too, agree with my words. The sun bathes the land, the clouds dissipating rapidly. It's still and quiet, almost as if there wasn't ever a storm to begin with. The only evidence is the soaked grass and mud.

"Lena," Mathilda starts, "You can't tell anyone what we think, not even Odessa."

There's something cautious about her words.

"Why not?" I ask, trying to understand. If I was wrong, I would want to know so that I could fix it.

"Let's just wait and see what they say when you get back. Feel them out, okay? This is dangerous," she replies.

My head tilts in confusion. "Dangerous, how?"

Lachlan's face turns grave. "There ha' been accidents, unexplainable *deadly* accidents that seem to take out anyone who disagrees with them. Nothing obvious enough to point a finger directly at anyone. But people who dinna share their opinions on this wind up dead."

Mathilda's eyes shine with sorrow.

I swallow loudly before asking, "Is that why you guys haven't done anything yet?"

They all share a look before Lachlan answers, "We dinna ha' the support before, with most being happy to live in peace. But with ye becoming queen, ye could save us in more ways than one. Ye can change things without the bloodshed we would cause if we tried to stage a coup."

I nod quickly. "I can do that."

Evander peeks out of the stable doors, checking both ways before he motions for us to head back. "Let's just keep our theories to ourselves for now," he mumbles.

The path is muddy and dotted with puddles as we trek back to the Great Hall. The fields of poppies have been shredded, their petals strewn about on the path. The scene is heartbreaking, and my eyes burn, taking in the desecration of the once resplendent land as we continue to slip and slide our way up the path.

My boots are caked in mud, making the trek even more treacherous as I try to stay upright. Water rushes down the steps out of the throne room, down through the terrace, and creates a waterfall on the gardens below. The water cascading over the edge violently drowns the flowers.

"Woah," I breathe as we carefully make our way across the rushing stream and into the throne room. People are still huddled together under the covered portions of the roof.

They stare up into the open air in the middle, a mix of fear and relief swirls around the room.

Odessa's eyes pin me the moment I enter the throne room, and she walks to the center of the room, her arms outstretched before her.

"Our heir has returned, and the storm has subsided; *there is nothing to fear.*" Her voice resonates around the throne room.

If I hadn't witnessed the howling and spectral wolves myself, I would almost believe the authority ringing in her voice. But now I fear that she might be delusional. *How would the decline of magic cause something so large and powerful?* I school my features and head to her side.

"Come, my dear, let us speak in private," she whispers. She locks our arms together and leads us from the hall. "If you could give us a moment," she throws over her shoulder as Lachlan and Evander move to follow us.

They halt, their eyes flicking to me in question, but I subtly nod my head. We don't want to seem like we're undermining her authority already.

We make our way from the throne room to the council room, and I whisper to Odessa, "Was that normal?"

She shrugs, not looking at me. "The Gods must have been angry that your blood was spilled, but I have rectified the situation," she responds, leading me into the council chamber and shutting the door behind us.

Odessa thinks all of this was because Julius punched me?

I study her as she rests her forehead on the door briefly before spinning to face me. She seems like she's struggling under the weight of her position, and I suddenly find myself feeling sorry for her.

"There was an incident after you fled the grounds," she begins, but I cut her off, her words making my hackles rise, and my sympathy vanishes.

"I did not *flee*," I reply, crossing my arms over my chest. Her mate threw a sucker punch at me, and she's trying to twist the story in her favor? She rolls her eyes but sighs as she continues, "Someone ransacked your room, but it was obvious they were looking for something." She walks around the table, her eyes on the paintings behind me. "I'd like to take precautions and establish a hand-selected private guard."

There's something about her demeanor, the maneuvering, that puts me on edge. I want to turn and point at the painting of the Wild Hunt, but I refrain. But her words have my stomach sinking; she wants to have me followed.

A guard would hinder any future movements or conversations about an upcoming war I would need to have, and *'hand-selected'*, undoubtedly by her hand, would mean the guards would report to her.

I feign confusion. "Surely the culprit realized I have nothing of importance here, and that's the end of that. I don't think a guard would be necessary."

Odessa looks shocked at my refusal. "Are you saying you don't see a need for a guard?"

I shrug my shoulders as I walk to stand in front of her. "I am safe here, Aunt, so no. I don't need a guard."

I force a smile. *I'll play this game.* She returns the smile, accepting my submissive attitude quickly and seemingly enjoying it.

"Well then, that settles that," she replies, gently stroking my cheek. "I'm relieved to see your nose has healed nicely."

My eyes hold hers. "Ack, no big deal. Accidents happen, right?" I shrug.

"More than you realize," she murmurs softly as she heads to the door. "Shall we?" she says a bit louder, leading us out of the room.

Something between us has shifted. I've just entered a game I don't know the rules to.

Even though she is my blood, I think I've finally realized that maybe we aren't actually family.

Mathilda's arms flex as she heaves the armoire upright, and Mina crouches to pick up the splinters of wood from the door.

"What're you guys doing?" I ask, taking in the disarray.

"You didn't expect to clean all of this up by yourself, did you?" Mina asks, twirling a particularly long splinter of wood between her fingers.

"Honestly, I didn't think it would be this bad."

I look around at the shambles that was once such a grand room. The duvet is in ribbons on the floor, and the clothes and shoes are strewn about everywhere. Entire drawers from the bedside tables have been thrown against the walls.

Evander whistles from the doorway behind me. "This certainly sends a message."

The girls nod their agreement as I pull Evander inside the room and shut the door behind him. I eye Mina, but Mathilda reads my mind.

"She agrees with us." Mina looks up at Mathilda, then knowingly nods at me.

"I didn't say anything to Odessa, but I get the idea that they still think I'm here to stop these things from happening," I say to the group.

Evander slumps on the bed, his wings transforming into tattoos down his arms.

"Did she say anything about the incident with Julius?" He squeezes his hands into fists, and the action is more menacing than I've ever seen him.

I huff. "She said she was relieved that it healed, but that was it; she didn't seem to care too much."

Mathilda and Evander nod, but Mina speaks up, "I'm sorry I wasn't there. But I heard it's like he's out to get you or something."

"It's beginning to feel that way. Maybe he doesn't want me to take Odessa's place?" I pick up a strip of fabric that was ripped from the curtains. "But she seems more than happy to relinquish the title, so I don't know." We're all quiet for a beat, trying to think it through. "She said she wanted me to have a guard, but I was worried about someone tracking my movements and conversations, so I declined," I tell them.

"That was probably for the best, but a guard wouldn't be a horrible idea," Evander trails off. His jaw ticks. The smooth skin visibly ripples with the movement. "I'll ask Lachlan to divide shifts with me."

The idea of Lachlan following me around or standing guard outside my room, especially after his comments in the temple, has me completely on edge.

"Absolutely not," I say quickly.

Evander raises his hands in surrender. His eyes grow large.

Mathilda whispers, "You know she's mad at him, you idiot."

I roll my eyes. Evander pales, and his lips press together.

A knock on the door halts my response. "Your Highness, we've been sent to clean your room and bring up new furniture." A male voice calls from the hallway outside my shut door. I shoot a glance at Evander, and he strides over to the door and swings it open. Two massive warriors in black leathers are standing there, baskets in hand.

I move to stand at Evander's side. They stare at us, their expressions cautiously blank, but there's something *off* about them.

"Thank you," I say to them, flashing my best smile. "We'll just step out so you two can get to work."

The men don't seem surprised to see our group, but they don't appear happy about it either, as we file into the hallway. The guards continue staring at us and make no movement to enter my room. But when booted footsteps echo from down the hall, courtesy of Lachlan stalking our way, the men scurry inside.

His face is twisted with rage and his large wings flare wide, taking up most of the hallway. He intercepts us and stops in our path, crossing his arms.

"How bad is it?"

Evander shakes his head. "It's not terrible, but it's definitely a message."

Waves of anger roll off Lachlan, and there's something so menacing about him that it sends shivers down my spine. I'm starting to get a better idea of the warrior he actually is.

Before, it was difficult to picture him as anything but my happy-go-lucky best friend, but now, with the way he looks like a wrathful god, I see how he climbed the ranks to become captain. But it's when his eyes flick to mine, and softness enters his gaze, that warmth pools low in my belly.

"Are ye alright?" he murmurs.

Our friends find anywhere else to look than us, and I stare down at my feet before bringing my eyes to his concerned gaze.

"I'm okay," I whisper.

He reaches out a hand as if to stroke my cheek, but then quickly drops it before nodding and stalking past us.

We spend the remainder of the day walking around the

grounds and assessing the damage from the storm before Mina and Mathilda have to check on their districts.

Evander and I are left standing on the path between the training grounds and the terrace.

"I need to fill Lachlan in on the rest of the damage. Are you okay to head back by yourself?" he asks, eyeing the Great Hall behind me.

I know he's hesitant to leave me alone, but I am not going with him to track down Lachlan. The sky is dark blue, and the puffy clouds are a buttery shade of pink from the setting sun.

"Yeah, I'll be fine; I'll see you later." I wave over my shoulder and turn on my heel.

My stomach growls, so I head for the dining hall. I missed lunch during our ride up the mountain, and I'm starting to suffer the effects.

Odessa and Julius are seated together at the high table. I almost turn around, but Odessa's eyes stab me from across the dining hall.

"Helena, darling, come and eat with us," she calls out to me. Her mood swings are starting to grate on my nerves.

I make my way to their table and see Julius give her a scathing look.

"I don't want to intrude," I offer, as he aims his glare my way.

"Nonsense," she says, smiling at us both. "We're family."

As I sit, she snaps her fingers, and a servant I don't recognize races my way with a plate of food. The smell of the food usually makes my mouth water, but for some reason, my appetite vanishes.

It could be that the fish on my plate still has eyes or that the berries have an iridescent sheen. Instead of grabbing my fork and digging in, out of instinct, I grab my medallion. It's cold. The frigid temperature almost burns my fingertips and I drop it quickly. I'm beginning to wonder what magic my necklace still possesses.

It's as if it's been guiding me.

Odessa notices my hesitation. "Do you not like fish?" She watches me intently.

"Not really," I reply sheepishly, biting my lip.

"Well, that's all there is to eat tonight, *princess.*" Julius sneers.

He's baiting me. Odessa doesn't even throw a glance his way, but pouts at me.

"No worries." I push away from the table. "I'll just grab something in town. Have a good night." I walk swiftly away from the table.

My pulse slows with each step I put between them.

But then Odessa calls, "Helena, dear." I halt, turning back towards them. "I'll be joining you again for training; we never had an opportunity to spar."

I turn and wave nonchalantly over my shoulder. "See you tomorrow then!"

I've got to get out of here.

I can't seem to find any of my friends after I leave the dining hall to go with me into the city, so I settle on retiring for the night. But my stomach protests with a loud growl. I turn on my heel and decide to check the kitchen for myself.

The sweet-faced young girl who usually serves me is slicing up some bread when I enter the stifling hot kitchen. Her knife clatters to the woodwork top as she sees me and drops into a curtsy.

"Your majesty," she squeaks out.

"Oh, I'm so sorry! I didn't mean to interrupt; please continue."

She stands and moves back to the work table, but her eyes linger on me awkwardly as I stand in the doorway.

"Actually, do you mind if I have a slice of that?" I motion to the bread.

"Not at all, Your Majesty. Would you like some cheese and grapes as well?" she asks, wiping her hands on her apron.

Julius' comment about no other food flashes in my mind. So he lied; *big surprise there.*

"That would be amazing," I reply. She grabs some grapes from a basket and some cheese from a large medieval-looking ice box before placing it all on a copper plate and handing it to me.

"Thank you so much," I say around the mouthful of bread I crammed into my mouth. She stands there, shifting from foot to foot, watching me. "I'll, uh, just eat this in my room," I mutter.

Her face relaxes, and she nods before heading back to work. I munch on my pilfered snacks, thankful that my good manners won over at least one of the staff.

I nudge my bedroom door open with my elbow and peer around the doorframe. Perhaps I'm being a bit paranoid. I don't think Odessa or Julius would kill me, but it's becoming apparent that Julius, at least, does not want me here.

Birthright or not.

My room has lost some of its sparkle and isn't quite the sanctuary it was before.

The new armoire isn't as large, so all my clothes are squeezed tightly together on the racks. I dig through it, trying to find my sleep clothes, which are shoved into the far back corner. The duvet is no longer a soft white either, but a sickly beige color. It looks ancient and smells musty.

After bathing and getting ready for bed, I slip under the sheets.

I want to scream at the feel of the scratchy linens against my bare skin. Exhaustion slides over me, and a shiver wracks my body. I roll on my side to get comfortable, but it's a difficult task.

They've replaced my mattress, too, and the new one is riddled with lumps. I sigh to myself, trying to think of an appropriate way to bring this up with Odessa without seeming ungrateful, but sleep drags me under, finally.

CHAPTER

TWENTY-ONE

My stomach clenches as I make my way to the training grounds, anxiety churns in my gut and my arms are heavy at my sides. I focus on my surroundings: there isn't a cloud in sight, the sun's warmth kisses my skin, and the ever-present breeze soothes the burn. Poppies are already sprouting up to replace the ones damaged by the storm. Their petals dance in the wind.

Today is beautiful and calm.

A bitter contrast to the storm raging inside of me, full of anxiety and chaos. My breath quickens into sharp pants, my fight-or-flight reflexes kicking in, but the source of my panic remains unknown.

When cold begins pulsing from my necklace, it puts me even more on edge. But it's quiet; not a soul around, and even the birds have ceased chattering.

The birds have stopped singing.

Realization has me stopping in the middle of the path and scrutinizing my surroundings. There's nothing out of the ordinary. The breeze through the tall grass is the only sound.

Sighing to myself, I resume walking. The mud squelches beneath my boots as I dodge the last few remaining puddles.

Odessa and Julius are the only people on the training grounds when I arrive. No spectators today. They're bedecked in their foreboding black leathers, and they stand close together, heads bent in conversation.

I cross under the archway, and my heart begins pumping erratically in my chest, blood pounds in my ears, and my vision narrows. Something inside me is screaming that this is a bad idea, but I brush the voice aside and continue on. One foot in front of the other, I force my body to push past the unease.

Odessa turns away from Julius and steps towards me.

"Hello, darling," she croons.

Her voice has the hair on the back of my neck standing on end. I give a small, awkward wave as I continue toward them.

Julius turns and saunters to the fence, where he has several weapons propped up against the railing. He grabs his ostentatious sword with one hand and rises to slap the hilt of Odin's axe buried into the tree.

It's a maneuver he has done before each of our training sessions, but the brazenness of the action still causes a flicker of disgust. He stoops again to pick up my practice sword before hurtling it at my feet. It slides against the dirt, dust clings to the handle, and floats up into the breeze.

Odessa glares at him with annoyance, and the action causes my anxiety to ease a bit. It looks like she won't be condoning his abuse today, after all.

"Today, I thought we could work on how to battle when you're outnumbered." She hoists her sword up.

Under his breath, Julius mutters, *"And outmatched."*

I nod, realizing they intend to give me no time to warm up, and it will be straight to action again. I take a breath to steady myself before separating my feet to get into my fighting stance.

My eyes narrow on Odessa as I prepare for her to go on the offensive. She glances at Julius, and they square up.

Odessa leaps towards me, sword out, jabbing quickly at my stomach.

"Good," she utters as I deflect her sword and bring mine back in front of me, readying for Julius's attack.

My skin tingles like a gentle current running all over my body, and I see the move he plans to make before it happens and dodge out of the way. They share a look. Confusion twists Odessa's face.

They didn't expect me to be ready.

The bottom half of my sight becomes hazy, a faint glow radiating up from my arms as they hold my sword out in front of me. Risking vulnerability, I quickly glance down.

I am, in fact, glowing; a light golden hue gleams from my skin. Odessa's eyes widen, and she gasps.

Julius takes a step back.

"You're using power," she whispers.

Odessa looks over at Julius fearfully.

"What are you doing?"

"I don't know, it just started happening," I insist, shock coursing through me. "My skin began tingling, and I could see in my mind what you were about to do before you did it."

I lower my sword and twist my arms, studying the light as it shimmers from my skin.

Julius frowns, turning to face Odessa, who's still staring at me, her mouth agape. "We can't allow this," he murmurs quietly to her.

My ears prick at the insinuation, and I glance up at them.

"What do you mean?" Wariness floods through my veins.

They share a long look. Something deadly passes between them before Odessa nods.

My necklace begins pulsing, its icy chill becoming painful.

Odessa swallows, turns back to me, and raises her sword. Pure hatred coats her features.

"What are you doing?" I retreat a step, my stomach bottoming out at her challenging stare. "What's going on?" I demand, but my voice shakes lightly with fear.

Julius launches himself at me, not pulling his strength at all. He swings his sword down in an arc meant to decapitate me.

Luckily, I see it happen a moment before he's actually launching himself at me, and I manage to dive out of the way. Fear pulses through me, causing my hands to tremble, and I grip my sword tightly.

A new vision flashes of Odessa skirting around me, and I struggle to discern what's about to happen and what's *actually* happening.

She tries to ease around me as I battle against Julius, and she sneaks a punch to my face as I block his latest swing. Spots erupt in my vision from the force of her blow. But I turn to the side, keeping them both in my line of sight, as they work me back towards the fence.

The clang of metal upon metal echoes around us, the pace becoming more frenzied. It's an effort to control my breathing; I don't want to gas out from the exertion it's taking to battle them both. My muscles ache with the effort it takes to continue to move quickly while deflecting their oncoming blows.

They continue slashing and jabbing at me, working in unison to break me. Constant flashes of what's coming followed by what happens vie for priority.

I misinterpret a few attacks, and it costs me a punch to the face and a burning sensation ripping across my ribs. I stumble back in shock. My blood boils; it's not fair; I want to scream to the Gods; they're both highly trained, and I'm still a novice. But my father's voice resonates in my head. *"Excuses are the timber that builds a house of failure."* The comforting mantra eases the disorienting flicker of visions.

I slowly adjust, beginning to grasp the timing of my blessed power. I smile to myself, triumph stirring when the visions become sharper and I can move accordingly.

I see, in my mind, Julius resorting to his unsavory tactics and kicking dirt in my eyes. So I use my free arm to shield my eyes right as he kicks. But it blinds me to Odessa's split-second decision to kick out with her foot into my loosened grip.

My sword flies from my hand.

I'm trapped between them and the fence, weaponless. Odessa's smug grin makes my skin crawl, but it's Julius's words that have my stomach plummeting.

"Just as defenseless as your parents were," he jeers.

The world cracks.

"A completely avoidable accident," he claims, sharing a grin with Odessa. My attention shifts to her for confirmation of this ground-shuddering revelation.

She merely shrugs. "Had they just brought you to us, none of this would've happened. We just wanted to make sure you wouldn't undo all of our carefully laid plans," she tuts. "But now you've grown too powerful to let live. We needed a puppet, a figurehead, but you just had to manifest your powers." She sneers.

The ground drops out beneath me, and the world grinds to a stop.

My body trembles, desolation creeping over me.

They murdered my parents to get to me?

The thought stops the grief, and anger rushes through my veins, cauterizing it in its path. It replaces the infection of fear with something razor-sharp and powerful.

Vengeance.

If I'm destined to die now, it will be on my feet, vindicating my parents, not on my knees like a coward. They will pay for what they took from me. But I need a weapon. I chance a glance in the direction of my sword, lying in the dirt too far away.

Julius follows my eyeline and scoffs. "Do you really think you would be quicker than me?"

Odessa chuckles. Her tongue darts out and licks her bottom lip.

The taste of copper fills my mouth as I bite down on my split lip. I spit the blood on the ground, stalling for time and trying to think up a plan.

Every training I've ever had spins through my mind. I could scream for help, but would anybody be near enough to hear me? How effective would my fists be against two swords?

My necklace begins to warm. I'm startled at the change in temperature. Mathilda's words bubble up from the recesses of my memory.

Pay attention to everything around you, *even the wind.*

The breeze shifts into a stiff wind, blowing my hair out of my face and whipping my braid behind me. *Behind me,* where a weapon is embedded into the trunk of a tree. I don't envision myself as 'worthy,' but maybe, just maybe, Odin would think my plight for vengeance is enough to draw his axe from the tree.

I fake a lunge towards my sword, effectively drawing them away and towards it.

Time slows to a crawl.

I spin around, bracing one foot on the fence and wrapping both hands around the worn hilt. It's smooth in places, from hundreds, if not thousands, of warriors attempting this very feat. I send up a silent prayer to Odin.

My muscles heave with all my might, straining against the pull of my arms and the push of my foot against the fence. The fence groans underneath the pressure of my boot, and my calloused palms give a small amount of traction against the ancient wood of the hilt.

Time continues to crawl, and I can hardly believe my eyes as the trunk begins to give way, the axe slowly easing out of its wooden tomb.

The metal of the blade whines as it finally releases from the tree, the blade glimmering as it reflects the sunlight while in my hands.

My astonishing moment of victory is short-lived, and I whirl back to face my two enemies. They are frozen in place, a mix of horror and shock marring their features. Odessa takes one tiny step in retreat, but Julius throws his hand out to her, causing her to halt.

"Go get the others," he orders her.

She flees the grounds, racing towards the Great Hall. My hope of coming out of this unscathed grows infinitesimally now that the odds are more evenly matched with the axe in my hand and only a single opponent to face.

"You will die here, girl," Julius declares as he stares me down.

My necklace is almost scorching, the heat a match to the tinder of my growing confidence, and a flicker of fear crosses his eyes. The light coming from me swells, reflecting off the blade of the axe.

"The Gods have other plans for me."

There's a brief pause as my words settle, and then Julius swings.

I pray the ancient hilt of the axe holds as I use it to block. My breath whooshes from my chest, *the hilt holds*, and Julius' sword ricochets off with more power than I expected. It throws him onto his back, and he crumples to the ground.

His eyes are wide and filled with terror as he realizes Odin's axe isn't a useless ancient relic but a powerful weapon, just as mighty now as when it was wielded by the Father himself.

Julius heaves himself up and takes one look at me, my skin shimmering and the axe in my hands. And like the coward he is, he sprints for the archway.

My relief is fleeting when I realize his return will be swift and with more people than I can face on my own. I take off running in the opposite direction, heading towards the one

person who will hopefully hide me from the shitstorm I created
—*Lachlan.*

The Gods seem to agree with my choice as the wind pushes me along, urging me down the path. My feet fly as I race to the guard's quarters.

My necklace pounds against my chest, with each stride seemingly pushing me to run faster. I grip the axe tighter as the faded blue door on the second floor comes into view.

I slow into a jog before taking the steps two at a time. Fear crawls its way up my spine at the possibility he might not even be here, and I'll have nowhere else to go. But as I bring my fist to the door, he swings it wide open.

I can only imagine what a sight I must be with my lip busted, a bruise beginning to throb on my cheek, and a small slice to the ribs. I didn't realize the extent of that last one, though.

The thud of my axe against the wooden floor draws our attention to the blood dripping next to it. Lachlan looks back up at me; the wrath marring his features is an expression I'm still not accustomed to.

He looks dangerous, savage.

"What happened?" He grates out between clenched teeth. His jaw is flexed so tightly that I'm amazed his teeth are not cracking.

The adrenaline begins fading at the sight of his face. My head is light and my vision doubles. I grasp the doorframe to steady myself. Tears begin pouring down my cheeks.

"I didn't have anywhere else to go." I sob. "They killed my parents."

He reels back in shock, his lips part as he sucks in a sharp breath. "Who did?" He reaches out towards my bleeding side and presses his large hand on the gash; the blood seeps through his fingers as he tries to apply pressure.

It runs down my hip and thigh before splattering the ground

and my boots. A shrill bell begins ringing in my ears, my head spins faster, and my knees threaten to buckle.

Lachlan bellows, "Lena! Who did this?!"

My vision dims, but his face comes closer to mine; his eyes are full of terror. The veins on his neck bulge as he continues to yell my name.

Fear like I've never known before is etched into every line on his perfectly handsome face. I feel both his arms wrap tighter around me in an attempt to hold my side together and keep me upright. The pain burns through me, darkness dims my sight.

But I have to warn him; he has to know what's coming for me. My throat is dry and scratchy, the blood a dark red now pooling below me, zapping all my strength and willpower.

I swallow forcefully, barely managing to rasp out, "Julius and Odessa."

He begins roaring, his words not permeating the darkness as it consumes me. I collapse into his arms.

TWENTY-TWO

I'm vaguely aware of the sound of voices and rumbling thunder, but the pain consumes me.

I black out again.

When I finally come around, I blink hard; my eyes leaden, and they struggle to stay open. My head pounds, but I'm not as weak as one should be from the amount of blood I lost. My ribs are wrapped in linen, and I've sunken down into a very soft bed covered in thick pelts. I don't recognize this room. I sit up quickly and hiss at the tug of skin on my injured side.

The room is cozy, with wood-paneled walls and ceiling. Thick blue velvet curtains are drawn closed, obscuring my ability to tell what time of day it is. The crackle of wood in the stone fireplace draws my attention to the wall on my right, and that's when I see Lachlan sprawled in a high-back, cushioned chair.

His neck is tilted at an uncomfortable angle, and his face is scrunched deeply in worry even while he sleeps. My eyes sting, and I swallow hard to push past the lump forming down my throat.

My audible attempts at swallowing rouse him from sleep.

His eyes find mine, and his face radiates pure, unadulterated relief at seeing me alive.

My heart stutters at his unexpected joy.

He must've put in an astonishing amount of work to keep me on this side of the ground.

"How long was I out?" I croak.

My mouth is dry, and my throat burns when I try to push out the words. He stands abruptly, crossing the room to the water ewer in the corner, pouring me a glass before sitting on the side of the bed and handing it to me.

"Just a day." He sighs, staring at me like a blind man, seeing for the first time.

The elation in his gaze causes my heart to gallop in my chest. I gulp down the water; the coldness soothes the burning in my throat and the warmth blooming in my chest.

"Where are we?" I glance around the room.

"Someplace safe." His hand rests atop mine, and he absently traces circles on the back of my hand. The tattooed wings stretch down from his neck to his wrist, rippling around his forearm at the movement.

I nod, relief coursing through me as I ease back onto the pillows. Lachlan takes the glass from my hand, sets it on the side table, and then begins fluffing the pillows behind my back. I try to smother the smirk that blooms at the gesture, mother hen.

He takes a moment before looking back at me. "Can ye tell me what happened? Do ye remember anything?"

Images of Odessa and Julius as they decide to attack me flicker through my mind. But it's not fear that taints my memories with an unnatural shade of crimson; it's rage.

I swallow down the venom bubbling up. "I was supposed to practice two-on-one maneuvers with Julius and Odessa; it was going fine until I started seeing things before they happened. My body started shimmering with golden light, and Odessa said it was my power manifesting and asked what I could do."

Lachlan goes rigid. "Julius said something about how they can't let that happen, and then they started attacking me." I shudder at the memories. "They were going to kill me. Odessa managed to get me disarmed, and they bragged—" My voice cracks.

"They bragged that they killed my parents." Anger collides with my sorrow to create an unholy storm of emotions threatening to spill over. "I was disarmed and enraged. I had no other options, so I reached for the—" I stop speaking abruptly and began urgently looking around the room.

Lachlan stands and pulls the axe from behind the chair.

"Ye pulled the axe," he says softly, wonder and pride in his gaze as he looks at me.

I sink back onto the bed. "I prayed to Odin to help me avenge my parents and pulled the axe from the tree. Odessa fled for reinforcements, and then Julius attacked. I used the axe to block his blow, and it rebounded from the hilt so forcefully it knocked him to the ground, and then he fled." I finish telling him, leaving out the part where I chose to run to him.

But he reads my mind.

"Then ye ran to me," he finishes, grinning broadly at me.

I pout, crossing my arms over my chest before mumbling, "I didn't really have any other options."

He snorts, but the fabric underneath my crossed arms catches my attention. I pull at the cropped cotton tank that exposes my midriff and the wrapped linen around my torso that's holding my wound together.

"Who changed me?" I ask, looking up at Lachlan.

His ears redden, and he rubs a hand on the back of his neck. "We, uh, couldn't get to your wound with your leathers on."

"We?" I shriek.

He raises his palms in a placating gesture. "Mathilda and I!" he quickly responds. "Look, I said we should get your consent first," he begins, but the door swings open, and Mathilda walks in.

"But I told him you were actively bleeding out and unconscious, so we weren't getting you to wake up before your body pieced itself back together," she says as she crosses her arms over her chest and levels him with an annoyed look.

"What're you doing here?" My voice cracks at seeing her here, alive and well. She huffs before sitting on the bed at my side and stroking her hand down my unbound hair.

"I couldn't stay behind with those murderers while my future queen was fighting for her life with this tosser," she says, as she jerks her thumb towards Lachlan. He rolls his eyes, but a smile quirks his lips.

Commotion outside the open door draws our attention. "Who else is here?"

Mathilda chuckles. "The usual suspects." She ticks off her fingers. "Tane is in the kitchen, Evander is guarding the front, Mina the back, oh and Elowen is on the roof. She showed up late since she had to grab a pack full of supplies that hero over here forgot to grab."

She sticks her tongue out at Lachlan.

Amusement swells at the affection between them; I have friends. Amazing friends who are willing to risk their lives for me.

Tane shoulders his way into the room with a plate of food. "Oi, glad to see you're alive," he says. "Hungry?"

My smile stretches the split on my lip, and it burns, but it doesn't deter me the slightest bit as I smile even wider, "You're my new favorite person," I tell him and reach out gently for the plate. It's piled with cold meat, cheeses, and lingonberries.

Tane waggles his brows at Mathilda as he passes. "See, someone likes me." She huffs at him but doesn't respond. I begin stuffing my face with food, and the three of them watch me intently.

I pause with a portion of cheese in my mouth. "Uh, what's up?"

Lachlan clears his throat. "You're the queen; ye give the orders." I glance around at them, realizing they are, in fact, waiting for me to tell them what to do. I swallow the piece of cheese before sitting up straighter. "I'm gonna need all of you to help with that, because I didn't really know what was happening until they tried to kill me."

Mathilda raises her hand. "I'll go first!" I giggle but nod for her to go ahead.

"They've been actively trying to keep us from preparing for the Great War by shutting down the training grounds, closing weapon shops, and not allowing the citizens and children to be taught the signs of the approaching war."

Tane interjects, "And they've been blatantly ignoring the warning signs that have happened." We all nod in agreement.

Mathilda continues, "So I think our first course of action is to start preparing for war and trying to find a way to get you back on your throne." I take a breath, knowing that was the obvious direction she was heading in, but for some reason, I did not want to admit it to myself.

"To prepare for war and take the throne, we're going to need a lot more people," I voice aloud.

The three of them share a look before Lachlan steps up. "About that." He pauses as if he's not sure how to continue. "There have been quite a few people who have disagreed with the way Odessa had started doing things." He grimaces a bit. "Most have relocated to Olundy to continue training there." The name of the island tugs at me.

"That's a good thing, isn't it?" I ask, to understand his reluctance.

"Aye, it is." He nods with the words. "But they don't really, uh, like ye," he finishes before holding his breath and waiting for my reaction.

"They don't like me?" I screech. The wound on my ribs pulls.

"It's not that they don't like you." Mathilda glares at Lachlan.

"They just don't know you," she offers. "You weren't raised here, and they kinda didn't know you even existed."

"Yeah, once they'll meet you, they'll see that you're not so bad," Tane adds.

Mathilda whips her head to him and mouths, "Not so bad." But he only shrugs, a look of innocence on his face.

"Great, I guess I'll deal with that when we get there, but first, we need someone to stay here and recruit more people to our side," I order. Lachlan recoils in surprise, but pride radiates from Mathilda, and Tane dips his chin.

"More people?" Lachlan asks. "Ye don't even ken how many people we already ha' there."

I bite my lip and wince at the pain. "Yes, but if my memory serves correctly, only one council member has been absent from meetings; we need to get more of the councilors on our side to recruit from their districts if we really want to change public opinion so I can take back my throne without too much bloodshed." I look around at the three of them. "So, who would be the most inconspicuous?"

Without skipping a beat, they answer in unison, "Elowen."

Chuckling, I say, "Ok, we get Elowen to stay here and recruit warriors to our side and help them get to Olundy, which is where, by the way?"

Tane replies, "It's two islands over. We could fly there, but with your wounds and even with the healing tonic, we run the risk of your side opening up again mid-flight; it'd be safer to take a boat." Mathilda bobs her head in agreement, her eyes darkening as she gazes at him.

"Fine. When do we leave?"

"Now," they agree again in unison.

They file out with orders to pack our stuff up and locate a boat. Left alone as they ready for our departure, I slide out of the bed and head for the window. My body aches all over, but the wrap on my side holds, and luckily, I don't feel my skin tear as I slowly reach out to pull back the curtains. It's nighttime and the stars flicker brightly in the sky.

My room faces the back of the street; there are no street lanterns, so darkness covers the view. I crack the window open, craving fresh air, and I groan as the motion causes my wound to sting.

The smell of the sea floats in through the cracked window and eases away my pain. I've always felt a sense of peace by the sea.

My father used to tease that I had a saltwater battery that needed to be charged by regular dips in the ocean. I hadn't realized just how right he was until the salt air washed over me, and I reluctantly breathe deeply.

I'm pleasantly surprised I've managed to do so without any pain. But when I think of Julius's claim that he was behind their murder, my body temples. They had sacrificed themselves to keep me out of harm's way and then I ended up here anyway because of—Lachlan. He brought me here, probably under Odessa's orders.

As if my thoughts conjure him, he slips through the door. "We need to ha' that conversation now," he mutters softly.

I spin around to face him; my anger at its full height. When he glimpses my face, his jaw clenches.

"Let me explain," he grits out.

I shake my head. "My parents died trying to protect me from this place, and you tricked me into coming here; you better have a really good reason if you expect me to trust you," I reply.

My hands squeeze into fists, and I have to hold myself back from rushing across the room to pummel his face.

He sighs but doesn't break our stare. "I brought ye here to save our lives."

I don't—can't respond to his words.

"It wasn't until I was a teen that Torin sent me to Idirhalla for my training, and I found out the truth of my existence. But five years ago, I became captain and was sent back to the human realm and ordered to find ye and keep an eye on ye. They dinna want ye here. Ye were and still are a threat to whatever their plans are. But after your parents died, the necklace appeared on my doorstep in Orkney. Your mum sent it. She attached a note to the necklace because she realized only ye could stop them."

His words pelt me like stones.

He draws out a folded piece of paper from a hidden pocket in his leathers and holds out the note. In my mom's scrawling script are the words: Take Lena home, it's time.

In a last-ditch effort, my mom orchestrated my coming here to save her people. My necklace warms on my chest, and I lift it up, studying the runes that are glowing faintly.

"Mom," I whisper, and the runes flare. A tear slips down my cheek; she was with me all along.

But then that means. "You were the raven at the cairn…." I trail off, looking up to meet Lachlan's heartbroken eyes.

"Ye were our only shot back home. I dinna ken how else to get ye here. With magic fading, I wasnae strong enough to travel us both back. There was barely enough to travel back and forth in my raven form, and it's nae like I could ha' just asked ye to come. Ye would ha' thought I was insane." The words tumble out.

"But I never meant for ye to get hurt in all of this, and I was with ye the whole time, keeping an eye on ye and making sure ye were safe. Ye were my salvation, Lena, and I couldn't." His voice cracks and his eyes beseech mine. "Wouldn't come home without ye." His words ripple around me, swallowing me whole. Sorrow and hope are etched into his soft smile. "Ye are not only my salvation, but ye are quite literally the Key to solving all of this," he whispers.

The use of my nickname makes my chest tighten.

I do understand his motives, and he's right; had he told me all of this, I wouldn't have believed him for a second. I'm also relieved that he wasn't ever part of Odessa's plans. Actually, quite the opposite. But it doesn't completely staunch the bitter burn of betrayal.

Lachlan slowly approaches, reading my face for any signs of reluctance, and drops to a knee before me. His hands are warm as he takes mine in his, stroking a thumb over the top of my knuckles.

"I know my words canna undo this, but let my actions speak for my remorse and allow me to swear my fealty to ye." He looks at me expectantly, and I barely manage to dip my chin.

The sight of him on his knees before me wreaks havoc on my already chaotic mind.

"I, Lachlan Freysson, swear my fealty to ye and only ye, Lena, rightful queen of Idirhalla, to serve ye and this realm for all of my days until my last breath."

His words echo in my ears, the sound ringing loudly.

Time crawls to a stop.

The impact of this moment waits, like the pressure of a needle just before it pierces the fabric. My heart leans towards forgiveness for the man I've known my whole life, but my mind cautions me about the man who used me as collateral to reach his own goal. Even if that goal was for the betterment of the realm, my realm.

I clear my throat. "I accept."

The needle pushes through the fabric. His answering smile is bright enough to stop my heart, but I continue, "On one condition." His brows raise. "If you ever keep something like that from me again, I'll kill you." His eyes widen at my vow, but amusement crosses his lips; he quickly rises and wraps me in his arms.

"If I ever betray ye, I will gladly kill myself and save ye the trouble."

I smile into his embrace, and he places a kiss on my forehead. A piece of my soul finally returned to me at last. Not just a piece, but what feels like half my soul. His familiar scent fills my nose and burrows into my bones. I've really missed this, missed him.

A knock on the door has me flinching away, but he releases me reluctantly. Elowen slips into the room.

But Lachlan cups my cheek, pulling my attention back to him. "I'm going to make sure the boat is ready. I'll be back shortly to escort ye."

He saunters from the room and I feel a pang in my chest. His absence already plaguing me. But I turn towards Elowen, who is deathly silent.

Her eyes are steely, and her jaw is set in stiff disapproval.

"I am so sorry for the deaths of your parents."

"Thank you," I whisper. The pain of their deaths and the split to my side warring inside of me. Elowen extends her arms, handing me a new set of training leathers.

"I never would've thought Odessa capable of something like that, and I'm sorry I didn't see it," she mutters. Her eyes shift into a hazy blue, as if she's studying the cosmos for any hint of something she's missed. I take the offered clothes.

"It's not your fault the power is fading here, Elowen. Don't beat yourself up," I reply.

She nods, but looks down at her boot-clad feet before her sharp gaze meets mine. "I need to explain my reluctance to accept you." My wary eyes meet hers. "I'm sure most people have a sob story about their childhood that explains away their moral failings as an adult, so I'm not going to wield mine as an excuse. But I do want you to know the facts and why I kept my loyalty to her and ignored the signs." Her tone sharpens, and I sit on the edge of the bed.

"Go on."

She crosses over to the window and peers out. "I was locked away since I could speak. Seeing visions is not normal for a child and can be construed as dangerous. My parents believed in the latter, so I was locked away." Her admission has my heart stalling in my chest. "No one even knew of my existence for a long time until Odessa. I was alone almost every day of my existence before she found me. She liked to hike in the Edda mountains when she was younger. Lucky for me, she came across the cave my parents kept me in. She fought for me when no one else did, and that's why I have believed her for so long." Sorrow washes across her face. "The Odessa I knew would never have killed your parents. She loved your mother as a sister, but with their deaths, she killed my allegiance to her. I cannot look past the obvious truth anymore; something is coming, and I will be on the right side of it, on your side."

Her words silence me, and for a moment, I can only stare at the woman before me, the woman who has already suffered so much in her lifetime and is still trying to do the right thing.

"Thank you for telling me your story. I understand completely how your loyalty to Odessa kept you blind, and I appreciate your sacrifice in choosing me over her. I can't even begin to imagine the pain you must have experienced. But you're not alone anymore and you never will be. I will not let you down."

Elowen's eyes fill with relief and she nods. "I'm supposed to stay here and recruit help?"

"Yes, the others seemed to think you would be the best person for the job, but now that I know your story, I don't want you to feel like we're leaving you behind. This job is very vital to our success, but I do not want to put you in a position that makes you uncomfortable," I reply.

Something about her facial expression is warning me of her reluctance.

"You're trusting me with this when I just told you that my blind obedience has prolonged the suffering of this realm?"

"We all make mistakes, Elowen; it's okay."

Her eyes widen at my response. "I haven't ever been allowed to make mistakes before."

My shoulders slump at her honesty, and I reach out to her, grasping her hand in mine. "I am so sorry."

She eyes me warily. "I would rather stay by your side, but if it means helping you more in the long run, I'll stay."

Gone is the distant, aloof woman I've briefly known. In her place is a woman of hardened steel, rage, and retribution. I feel the exact same. The girl I was can no longer survive; I must be the woman this realm needs. My soft edges begin to sharpen in anticipation of the future before me. Reading my grave expression, Elowen asks, "You will make them pay?"

I grin back at her, violence dancing in my eyes. "We all will."

WE MAKE our way to the boat under the cover of darkness; officially rebels on the run. The darkness is like a tangible cloak hiding us from sight. I gulp down the salt air as it keeps me calm, grounded, even.

Lachlan slips a healing tonic into my hand. "You're gonna need another one of these to get through the journey," he cautions.

I throw the vial back, and the warmth seeps into my veins, dulling most of the pain.

As fugitives, we don't risk boarding one of the larger vessels in the port, but we opt for a smaller, sleeker, long boat that is the perfect size for the four of us.

Mina and Evander have agreed to fly to Olundy the following day to make sure we aren't followed.

Our boat has been tied off just beyond the shore, on the outskirts of the city. The perfect hiding spot for secretly leaving the capital. Our boots tromp across the black sand, and we wade quietly into the frigid water to the boat. The bow and stern rise sharply, straight up, and curl in on themselves, reminding me of a sea dragon.

I grin to myself as I graze my hand along the smooth wood. Mathilda reaches a hand out to help me aboard, and I grip my ribs tightly with one arm. I let her help pull me up and over the side onto the boat. Tane and Lachlan begin pushing the boat further into the tide.

Waves crash violently against the boat, causing me to hold tightly to the side with one hand and my wound with the other. My skin stays together, but the pain lashes across my midsection. Lachlan splashes up and over the side, spraying us with saltwater before giving us a wicked grin. He helps Tane onto the boat, and his large body swings over the side so gracefully. It makes me jealous.

"It's gonna be a long journey. Let's set a slow pace," Tane calls to Lachlan.

They pick up the wooden oars and begin rowing. Pulling us away from the city. My back to the sea, I watch the city slowly vanish before my eyes, darkness swallowing it up as we row toward Olundy.

This is my home now; these are my people, and I will do whatever it takes to keep them safe.

A single tear spills down my cheek. I just pray we're not too late.

The steady rocking of the sea and the rowing, coupled with the healing tonic, lull me to sleep.

I awake sometime later, my head in Mathilda's lap as she soothingly strokes my hair while she looks out at the sea. Her hair is braided back, and the plait is draped over her shoulder. It reminds me of how my mother would braid her hair back on long journeys. I slowly rise from her lap, stretching my arms up over my head and yawning before quickly dropping my arms to keep the pain from lancing across my side.

But there's no pain.

I pull the linen down to check my wound, but I'm startled by the light pink scar in its place.

"It's healed," I whisper.

Mathilda chuckles. "Morning, sleepy head," she teases. "Of course, it's healed; you were able to rest and let the tonic and magic do their jobs." Her eyebrow raises. "You do realize that you're basically immortal now," she says it so casually, as if she's commenting on the color of the sky. But I was just a human a mere month ago.

The realization is unsettling.

The sun peeks over the horizon. The dark blue of the sea embraces the golden ball that leaches light into the sky. Salty air invigorates me with each inhale, and I smile at the sea, a true, broad smile, as happiness envelops me.

A curse rings out as Lachlan fumbles with the oar and tries to get in sync with Tane again.

"You woke just in time. We're nearly there," Tane calls from his seat and tilts his head behind him.

Piercing the surface of the sea is a sheer cliff steadily climbing higher with each row. As we get closer, I have to crane my neck back to see to the very top of it. I'm too busy looking up. I don't see the small crack in the cliff that we're squeezing our boat through until the sound of the wind over the sea cuts off, replaced by the lapping of gentle waves.

It's too tight a squeeze for our oars, and the guys heft them onto the boat as the tide pushes us along the channel between the rocks. I can touch the rock on either side of us from my seat as we cruise along, and my fear of small spaces squeezes the air from my lungs.

Tane shivers as the rock presses in and closes his eyes. "I hate this part," he grumbles, and I smile, relieved I'm not the only one.

Lachlan's wooden seat creaks as he reaches under it to pull out a horn. It's a glossy black with runes carved into the side, their geometric shapes glittering gold. A strap of leather wraps around the middle and the end of the horn, connected with a long, thin piece like a handle. Noticing my stare, he winks at me, bringing the horn up to his partially parted lips; he inhales a large breath, his broad tattooed shoulders moving with the effort, and then he blows the horn.

The loud blast makes me quickly cover my ears as he blows the horn again in two shorter blasts. The last sound of the horn echoes through the narrow pass before ebbing away. I release my ears, my mouth open in shock, and I stare at him in utter bewilderment.

He merely shrugs, his eyebrow arching.

"We ha' to signal so they ken who is coming."

CHAPTER

TWENTY-THREE

The boat continues to be gently propelled along the channel for a while before the walls start to drift further apart, and the tide spits us out into a small bay. The beach around the bay is glittering black sand and surprisingly flat compared to the towering cliffs we traveled through.

The levelness of the land stretches out a fair distance, turning a deep, rich green as it transforms into rolling hills enclosed by a large silver cliff. Dark green against the bright silver reminds me of moss growing on river stones.

There are long wooden houses with thatched roofs dotted all around the bay, and I barely make out the looming stone walls of a castle atop one of the hills further out.

A small congregation of people are gathering along the shore as our boat runs aground. Tane hops out to help Mathilda out of the boat, and Lachlan and I mirror their actions. Several men and women dressed in normal brown training leathers are a few paces away. The familiar color of their leathers and not the ominous black brings me solace.

My necklace is warm against my chest, easing some of my anxiety.

This is a safe place, it seems to whisper.

An older woman with long, wavy, silver hair and a single braid down the center stands in the middle of the group. Her face radiates kindness, and wisdom gleams in her eyes. Lachlan steps forward, and her familiar honey-brown eyes crinkle as she smiles at him.

"Auntie A," he calls to her. As she steps forward to meet him, they clasp each other's forearms. She gives a slight nod of her head, as does Lachlan.

"Lachie," she greets him. There's a familiarity to her that I can't quite place.

Lachlan turns to me. "Auntie A, this is Lena."

Auntie?

She brushes past him to embrace me tightly. "Lena, my sweet girl." She squeezes me tightly once more before she lets go and steps back, her arms still clasped to mine. "I'm Agatha, Torin's sister; it's so nice to finally meet you."

My mouth drops open as she lets go of me. "Torin's sister?" I stutter before glaring over her shoulder at Lachlan.

"Whoops," he mouths. "Surprise!"

Agatha grasps my hand and pulls me closer to the group of people gathered on shore. "Come! Come! I don't expect ye to remember everyone's name, but just a brief introduction," she tuts, before turning to face the people gathered on the beach. "This is the Affric Clan." She waves her hand to a group of simi-lar-looking men. The five of them are barrel-chested, and broad-shouldered, all with long dark hair and wild, untamed beards. They're dressed in green, yellow, and red tartan kilts.

They clap a hand over their chests, and Agatha continues, "Clan Campbell."

She points to a group of at least ten men, all wearing green, navy, and black tartan kilts, as they nod. Their looks are more varying, with different hairstyles and facial hair, but all have similar light green eyes.

"And these are the Fairhair's." She points to a group of men and women with light-colored complexions and white-blonde hair. They don't nod or give any sign of acknowledgment, but stare inquisitively at me.

"This," she loudly announces to the group gathered, "is the Heir to the Throne, the wonderful Helena." I tense slightly at my full name. "But I hear she only likes to be called Lena." She winks at me.

I heave a sigh of relief, not having to address that again. Tane, Mathilda, and Lachlan have all gathered beside me. Their presence exhibits support, and it spurs me to address the assembled crowd like a queen would.

I force myself to look each person in the eye before loudly speaking. "I understand that not many of you know me or *that I even existed*." I glance sidelong at Lachlan, and he smiles encouragingly at me. "And I'm sure there is a lot of anger towards my mother for leaving." Several grunts ring out. "To be honest, I'm unsure of her exact reasons for leaving, but if I had to guess, it probably had to do with keeping me safe, and for that very reason, she was murdered." There are a few shocked expressions, and heads turn towards each other with words murmured in languages I don't understand yet.

I place my hand on my chest and continue, "But this was my mother's home; she died to protect it and all of you, and though I didn't realize it at the time, with her dying breath, she sent out a message, to make it possible for me to travel here and save us."

Emotion stirs at the thought of my mom doing everything she could. I swallow past the feelings. "This is my home, and I, too, will die to protect it, just as fiercely as she did."

It's not the ground-shaking speech I would have liked to give, but it's honest and to the point. The crowd seems to approve, and I get several more grunts of approval and nods before they begin dispersing back to their homes.

Agatha looks at me with admiration, her eyebrow arching. "Excellent, my queen."

Several men in brown leathers with silver chain-mail vests begin approaching with three horses; Agatha looks back at us apologetically. "I wasn't expecting so many of you."

Lachlan chuckles and says, "Lena and I can share." He throws an arm around my shoulder.

Mathilda's wings reappear, and she stretches them out, the iridescent white feathers throwing rainbows in the sunlight.

"I need to stretch my wings out, anyway; I'll meet you guys there." She shoots into the sky, her wings beating so thunderously that I can only stare up at her in awe. I cannot wait for my wings to be fully grown so I can fly with her. The stumps have pierced the skin and have begun to itch.

Agatha leads a large black stallion up to Tane and chucks him the reins. "You're large enough. You'll definitely need your own now, won't ye?"

"Yes, Auntie." He grins down at her before wrapping her up in a huge hug, lifting her off her feet. Her arms are stuck to her sides, and she looks so small and helpless, trapped in his embrace.

"Tane! You put me down right this instant!" she shrieks, but there's no bite in her words. Tane swings her small frame side to side before gently placing her on her feet.

She glowers up at him before a small smile graces her thin lips. But then she waves Lachlan and me to the white mare beside her chestnut one. My stomach clenches in anticipation of being so close to him. Lachlan gracefully swings himself up in the saddle before reaching out a large hand for me to do the same.

Tingles dance down my arm when our hands connect, and I try not to flinch at the unexpected sensation. I settle in behind him, inhaling his familiar scent, and a small weight is lifted from my shoulders. My thighs graze against his thick muscular ones, and warmth pools low in my belly.

It's a battle of mind versus heart. The betrayal of him keeping my identity from me still stings, but nowhere near as bad as the day I found out. We follow Agatha up a path that leads to the massive stone castle.

The land here has a charming character, more subdued than it is in the capital; the greens of the grasses are a bit softer on the eyes. Even the breeze is more subtle here. Huge fluffy clouds are scattered in the sky overhead, casting large shadows across the land.

The tranquil quality of the island extends to the wildflowers that are light blue and purple. They remind me of fluffy hydrangeas and feathery foxgloves with oversized petals. A few trees dot the landscape, towering cedars with bluish berries tinting their needles.

Colossal boulders are also strewn about, their robust size large enough to hide a horse behind. The dark gray of the stone is blanketed with dark green moss.

Lachlan points to various timber houses along the way, all with sloping rooflines that nearly touch the ground, mentioning which families live there.

As we ride closer to the castle, soft pulsing crawls along my skin. Goosebumps erupt, and I squeeze him just a bit tighter. His abs tighten underneath my embrace, like steel beneath my touch. He rubs a calloused palm along my arms.

"Cold?" he murmurs, turning his head towards me.

His profile is strong and chiseled. I can't help but take a moment to appreciate his rugged beauty that mirrors the surrounding landscape.

"Not really, I think I just had an anxiety shiver," I reply, going with bleak honesty. Lach throws his head back and laughs, the rich timber of his laughter causing me to grin and hide my smile against his back.

"Lena, ye literally faced death, pulled a mythical axe from a tree without any trouble in an entirely new realm, but became nervous just now on the way to that castle."

He points ahead to the looming stone castle. I release my arms from around him and jab my fingers into his side, a spot I know he's ticklish in. He grunts, trying to pull out of my reach.

"Thanks a lot for your support, Lach." I roll my eyes.

"Key, you've handled all of this remarkably well. There's nae need to get anxious now; we're already in the thick of it," he shrugs.

But he's right.

I am here; I'm doing it; there's no need to dwell on it all now; we just have to keep moving forward. We reach the stone wall around the castle and the portcullis begins lifting. A sharp whine from the ancient metal reverberates around us.

The horses whinny, stomping their feet in protest before we continue through the gate into the courtyard in front of the castle. It's very reminiscent of Balmoral Castle, with its Scottish baronial architecture and the ivy climbing its walls.

Its charm reminds me of the Hall. It's breathtaking, and I promptly fall in love with it. Where the Great Hall was more modern with straight lines, symmetry, wide open spaces, and stark white marble, this castle is like something out of a storybook with hand-cut gray stones, soaring peaks, elaborate rooflines, and formidable battlements.

Agatha dismounts and hands her reins to an appearing stable boy before patting his head and turning to us. "Shall we?"

Lachlan dismounts first and reaches up to grab my waist before hefting me off in one swift movement.

"I'm perfectly capable of getting off this horse on my own."

"Oh, I'm aware." He grins down at me, but leans in close to whisper in my ear, "I just wanted an excuse to touch ye."

My cheeks heat immediately, but I'm saved from a retort as Agatha walks by and gently whacks him upside the back of his head. He whirls, his eyes dancing with mischief.

"That's enough of that. She is the queen, and you are her guard," she admonishes him.

It's strange; for so long, I had wanted more out of our relationship, and now it suddenly feels like that might be coming true.

We follow her through the massive, arched wooden door clad in iron. Lachlan does not heed her warning very well as he clasps our hands together. The action brings a swarm of butterflies to my stomach, chasing away any lingering anxiety and replacing it with a newfound, bubbling excitement.

Chaos ensues, however, as we step into the foyer.

Servants briskly attend their tasks, some holding stacks of firewood or carrying trays of food, and warriors stride down halls and into various rooms. By the looks of it, some are coming and going from training, their weapons gleaming and leathers coated in dirt.

The Great Hall had always felt empty, but this place is abuzz with activity and an undercurrent of excitement. People smile and nod to us as we continue to follow Agatha, who points out various halls, rooms, and art adorning the walls. My mind flits from one thing to the next as we walk quickly to keep pace behind her, winding our way through the halls and out the back of the castle.

"These are our training grounds." She turns towards us, pride emanating from her.

The grounds are a mirror image of the training grounds from the Great Hall but twice the size and packed with people.

There are groups sparring, running through an elaborate obstacle course, and several target stations with warriors practicing knife throwing, archery, and spear throwing. My jaw drops as I take it all in. This is what training should look like.

They are all ferocious and shockingly organized as they flit from station to station, managing to work on several techniques in the same session without encroaching on each other's space.

A similar archway stretches across the opening of the grounds, connecting the fence. Lachlan leans close, pointing to the words carved into the wood.

"Train with honor, and you will not die with shame." His voice tickles my ear.

My muscles itch to join them and blow off the building steam. I take a few steps closer to the grounds, feeling drawn to it before a gentle tug on my hand halts me.

Concern lights Lachlan's eyes and he, not too subtly, looks towards my injured side. "Maybe give it one more day, Key," he says gently.

I know he would support my choice either way, but his concern is still comforting. My body craves a physical challenge to dull the edge of anxiety, but if I accidentally stumble on my first day in the ring, it would be catastrophic to my already precarious reputation. Slowly nodding my agreement to Lachlan, I turn to face Agatha.

"Do you mind showing me to my room? I think I'll need some rest after our journey."

She smiles kindly at me, not a hint of displeasure in my decision to rest instead of immediately training, "Of course, my dear, right this way." She turns and heads back to the castle.

Agatha leads me to my room, which is located on the third floor of the south wing, and overlooks the grounds. She swings open the door with a knowing smile and ushers me inside.

"This was your mother's room," she says with a nod to the fireplace. Just above the mantel hangs a large oil painting of my mother with the wings I never knew she had.

"My mother's room?" I question, my brows furrowing.

Agatha nods. "This is your ancestral home, from the first of your line down all the way down to you."

I turn back and take in the room with the new understanding. The door clicks shut behind me, leaving me all alone. I spend a few moments memorizing the painting of my mother and giving myself time to grieve this new version of her I never got to know, but lost all the same.

Tears spill down my cheeks when I think about all the things she's missed so far. It hurts knowing she'll never see me here. That she'll never walk these islands with me or see me fly.

She's the reason I'm here, and now she's gone.

I wish more than anything that she could be here. I wish she had told me about all of this. But above all, I wish she were here to give me advice.

I know in my bones what she would say, "You have to keep going, keep fighting, and listen to your heart. See this through." But there's a difference between knowing what she would say and actually hearing the words come from her lips. Seeing her mean the words with her expression and her making me believe them, too.

The clashes and thuds of the warriors training outside break through my grief, and my chest rises and falls with elation, chasing away the sadness. This is the right path; I can feel it deep down in my heart that this is what we're supposed to be doing. I have finally found my purpose.

I take a look around at the high-ceilinged room decorated with rich mahogany furniture. Dark burgundy curtains frame the bay windows, and an elaborate rug takes up much of the floor space between my bed and the sitting area surrounding the fireplace.

It smells of cinnamon and vanilla, the scent reminding me of my mom.

A small knock on the door draws my attention away, and I open it to find Lachlan leaning on the doorframe. His smile drops as he takes in my tear-streaked face.

"Are ye okay?" he asks, assessing the room behind me for any threats.

I step out of the way and point to the painting. Relief washes over his rigid posture and he comes to stand in front of me, cupping my face in his hands.

"She would ha' been so proud of ye," he whispers.

I force a smile onto my face. I'm so sick of always crying in front of him. He takes another step closer and brushes a quick kiss on my forehead.

My eyes flutter close, savoring the tenderness, before anger sparks, and I jerk out of his grip.

"Why do you always do that?"

Lachlan's brow wrinkles in confusion. "Do what?"

I glare at him. "The forehead kisses."

He hangs his head briefly, clenching his hands into fists. He's battling with himself, and I wonder if he'll give me an honest answer.

But then his eyes flick up, meeting my own.

"Before,"—he begins but sighs deeply—"I thought it would be easy to keep my distance from ye, to separate our friendship from my duty and just guard ye until I could come back here for good and leave ye behind." He swallows. "But then I started to ha' feelings for ye. Watching ye struggle to find your way after your parents' death forced me to realize how I want to protect ye from every possible thing that could ever hurt ye. Seeing ye come out the other side of your grief reminded me of your strength and that ye don't need me to lead you through it. Ye just need someone to stand at your side, and I wanted to be that person. I wanted to walk this path with ye. Ye are strong and capable and breathtaking. I wanted ye immensely. But had it become more between us before ye found everything out, ye would never—*I would never* be able to forgive myself for deceiving ye in that way, too. So the brief forehead kisses were, selfishly, all I would allow myself."

His revelation floors me.

He did have feelings for me, too? My face must not reveal my feelings on this matter for once, or he misreads me because sorrow weighs heavily in his gaze.

"I ken I was the villain in part of your story, but let me be the hero now."

His honesty is refreshing, and his last words are a shock to my system.

I take a moment to collect myself and mull over his words before replying, "So, you did want to kiss me the whole time?"

His smile is broad and unrestrained. "Since we've been adults, aye." He nods. "But when we were younger, nae. I dinna think ye remember what a wild, precocious thing you were, do ye?"

Feeling a little too vulnerable at his admission and not at all ready to forgive him completely. "But you lied to me?"

I cock my head to the side, narrowing my eyes.

He freezes, his smile turning into something deadly serious as he adjusts to my change in attitude.

"I canna go back and undo what I did. The choice that I made in trying to keep ye safe by hiding the truth, and then the poor tactic I used to get ye here, *it was a mistake*." He takes a step closer to me, his hand reaching out to cup my face. "And I am sorry more than you'll ever ken. The look of hurt on your face when ye saw me in the throne room has haunted me every day since. I will always regret that. But I need ye to believe I would never do anything to intentionally hurt ye."

I remain quiet, trying to grapple with my feelings of betrayal and the feelings of longing that I've had since the moment I met him.

"If this is the end for us, that has to be your choice. Ye will ha' to decide that there won't ever be anything more between us because I canna." He swallows before whispering, "I will be stuck here in this moment, forever, telling ye that I'm not giving up."

Us.

My breathing halts before coming out in quick, rapid pants. My eyes water and my throat burns. I forgive him, and I do understand. But I can't find the right words to portray that. Tears begin flowing as I gaze into the depths of his green eyes, which are flooded with emotion as he holds his breath, awaiting my response.

I gently hold his hand to my face, barely managing to whisper, "This is not our end."

He leans his forehead against mine, our breaths mingling together as we savor this moment. I angle my head up towards him, our lips just a hair's breadth apart. I hunger for the touch of his lips on mine. To soothe the burning that has begun in my soul.

A loud knock echoes through the room, the moment crumbling around us.

"Lena! Did you want to get some lunch?" Mathilda's voice calls through the closed door.

Lachlan rolls his eyes, and I chuckle. The tension between us melts away completely.

"Yes, I'm starving!" I call back loudly.

I look back at him. "I think it'll take more than apologies to grant you kisses now, anyway. I need to see some actions, not just words," I throw over my shoulder as I walk to the door.

He sighs before mockingly placing both hands on his heart. "I will absolutely endeavor to please ye, Your Majesty," he bows low.

His breathy laugh causes a shiver to walk its way down my spine; he throws a wink at me as I leave my room. He follows behind but doesn't go too far, just to his room across the hall. I pause and follow him with my eyes the entire way, drinking in the saunter of his walk. I turn to face Mathilda, who's a few steps ahead; her eyes are ablaze with mischief.

"And what the hell was that about?"

CHAPTER

TWENTY-FOUR

The bustle of this place is exciting. Everywhere I look, there's a person coming and going. The exact opposite of the hollowness that was the Great Hall. This place seems to effuse so much more *life*. We pass portraits of my ancestors as we walk down the candlelit hallway and to the dining hall.

Long, colorful rugs line the walkways, softening our thudding footsteps on the wooden floors. Carved oak tables boasting poppies, ravens, and Viking runes are sporadically placed along the perimeter of the halls. It's like I'm walking through a museum or a time capsule of ancient history. The decor of this place is so similar to the Hall that I wonder if Gran had brought things from here.

Mathilda nudges me with her shoulder. "Are you going to tell me what that was about?" Her eyebrow arches and my smile grows, but I shake my head. "Seriously, you're not going to share the details?"

I laugh loudly, shaking my head. "There's nothing to share. He just apologized—again." But my smile is giving me away, hinting obviously at something more.

"Oh, there's definitely something you're not sharing," she mutters, frowning.

A large painting of my mom and dad hung at the end of the hall, stops me in my tracks. Mathilda stops alongside me.

"Are you okay?" she asks softly, tracking my sight to the life-size painting in front of me.

My parents smile softly at me, the artist perfectly capturing an exact likeness of them in royal garb in the throne room of the Great Hall. My mom is seated on the throne, but not the one Odessa sits on now. This one is a white marble that matches the construction of the Great Hall. The timeless arching seat is a much better fit than the ostentatious one that sits there now. My father stands just beside her, on her right.

For once, my chest doesn't ache as I gaze at them.

"Yeah, it's just weird. There's so much about them I never knew anything about."

Mathilda takes a step closer to the painting. "I never realized how similar you look to them."

My eyes crinkle a bit as I study the portrait. But there's something a bit different about my dad that the artist managed to capture. I can't quite put my finger on it.

"Does my dad look human to you?" I ask Mathilda, my brows furrowing in concentration.

"Not really." She shrugs, and her stomach growls.

The sound breaks through my concentration, and I giggle. "Let's go eat."

She grins sheepishly at me. "Sorry, I didn't want to rush you, but I am starving."

We continue our way to the dining hall, but the painting tugs at me.

The dining hall is boisterous, and the food smells divine. Long tables are set up in even rows, their seats actually occupied by many of the warriors and the servants that live here.

Light streams in from the long leaded windows showcasing their views of the stunning landscape, and a roaring fireplace makes up the entire wall by the kitchen door. Young women and even a few men stream in and out of the doorway, taking platters full of food or bringing back empty plates to the kitchen.

Tane has already beat us here and has a table all to himself with several full plates. He waves us over, and I don't miss the way Mathilda's eyes sparkle when she spies him. I nearly have to jog to keep up with her as she marches across the room and to the chair next to him.

"I didn't know what you would want, so I grabbed a few things," he mumbles while chewing on what looks to be a turkey leg.

Mathilda plops down right next to him and grins timidly. "Thank you for thinking of me." A slight blush creeps up Tane's neck, but Mathilda doesn't notice it as she pulls a plate of pasta to herself.

"Uh, I'll just help myself, I guess?" I mutter, but I don't think they've even heard me.

I walk over to the long buffet table that has a large spread of different types of food all laid out. Seafood, roasted meats, vibrant fruit, and vegetables are all mouthwatering. I'm busy loading up a copper plate when Lachlan hops in line behind me.

I briefly look him up and down, appreciating how his wet hair gleams in the sunlight. He must've freshened up before following us down here.

"Are ye sitting with the love birds? *Who aren't love birds*," he jokes.

My lips kick up into a smirk. "Why is it that it's obvious to everyone but them?"

Lachlan shrugs and loads his plate with various meats. "They've been that way for as long as I've known them."

I glance at Tane and Mathilda before turning back to Lachlan. "And how long have you known them?"

Lachlan's face scrunches up adorably as he thinks back. "Well, I was fifteen when Torin first brought me here, so ten years now."

I do the math in my head. "Wow, so you were only twenty when you made captain?" How on earth did he manage to climb the ranks so quickly?

Lachlan smirks and steers us back towards the table. "Superior genetics, I guess," he mutters.

The table is unusually quiet when we approach and take our seats. Mathilda blushes when I glance her way, but I don't bring up their obvious attraction to each other as I begin digging into my food.

"So, what's the plan now?" She asks, not taking her eyes off the pasta she's wrapping around her fork.

Years of my father's battle strategies flood my mind, and I sift through all the information. Every practice, every lecture from history to politics, and every book they forced me to read was in preparation for this place. Reading Sun Tzu at seventeen hardly seems silly now.

"We need to have a system in place for the new recruits that Elowen sends to the island. A way to make sure they're not spies, and then another system in place for setting them up with a place to stay and a job. If we just allow anyone in, we'll open ourselves up for an attack, and if we let too many people in at once, we'll be too disorganized and chaotic."

Lachlan's mouth drops open as he stares at me in shock.

Tane and Mathilda share equal looks of surprise with each other before looking back at me.

"What?" I ask, glancing around at everyone.

"You sounded so official," Tane replies.

I roll my eyes and continue on, "I'd like to delegate roles to each of you to help with incoming rebels while also making sure we all work together as a team. If you get overwhelmed, I want us to be able to communicate that with each other. Help pick up the slack."

Lachlan's face shifts into something akin to pride. "I can help with whatever ye need and move between multiple jobs."

I nod while thinking it through. "I would like that, thank you."

As he is the captain of the guard and my only link to all my new friends, it would be beneficial for him to be my go-between.

Mathilda pipes up next. "I would like to set up a school here for the children of the warriors who join our cause."

I smile gratefully. "That would be excellent; if we keep with a routine for the young ones, it would lessen the stress on their parents. Great idea Mathilda."

She is the most maternal of the group, so it only makes sense that she would think of the children first. She smiles in response and continues eating.

Tane eyes Mathilda before looking my way. "Well, new recruits will mean more houses or, at the very least, tents; I have experience with both."

"Perfect, thank you. I know very little about either. That just leaves Mina and Evander. When they get here tomorrow, I'll ask what roles they feel comfortable stepping into. But at least now we have something figured out."

Having just a few things marked off a to-do list I hadn't even officially planned out yet settles the growing tension in my stomach.

"So now we just need to figure out how to take control of this realm, how to prevent the Great War from happening, and how to restore magic. This is doable, right?" I ask, looking around the table at my friends.

Lachlan smiles warmly. "Sure, Key."

Mathilda gives me an unwavering smile and two thumbs up. "Very doable."

Tane looks around at us like we're crazy before Mathilda elbows him in the ribs. "It's doable," he grumbles, rubbing his side.

CHAPTER

TWENTY-FIVE

Sunlight shines through the open window in my bedroom and warms my face. My first night in our rebel hideout felt like the first night of restorative sleep I've received since coming to Idirhalla. Birds chirp merrily outside and my mom's smiling face gazes down at me from above the mantle. It feels like at any moment she could sweep through the door and tell me breakfast is ready.

Every square inch of this place sings of my mother. My body feels whole, my mind feels quiet, contented even, and I'm excited about today's challenge. I slowly ease myself up, propping against a pillow, when Mina barges in.

"I'm here!" she squeals, hurtling across the room. Her wings vanish a split second before she throws herself on my bed. I giggle as she flops herself on her side. "It was a race, and I beat Evander," she snickers.

"Did he even stand a chance?" I ask, admiring the flush of her cheeks.

"Not even a little bit." She smirks.

There's a knock on the open door, and Mathilda peeks her head in. "I thought I heard you two in here."

I pat the empty side of the bed, smiling up at her. "There's room for you too."

Mathilda waltzes across the room, already dressed for the day in her leathers, but her wings are nowhere in sight as she snuggles down onto the bed with us. "Any trouble on the way here?" she asks Mina.

"None at all, but the rumor is that Lena has fled the capital after attacking Odessa's mate in a fit of jealousy." She rolls her eyes.

I gawk at them both. "Are you serious?"

They laugh loudly, but Mathilda speaks up, "I don't understand why you're surprised. Of course, they would spin something in their favor."

I cross my arms over my chest. "I know, but still,"—look between both of them—"gross." Mina throws her head back and laughs, quickly followed by me and Mathilda.

There's another knock on my door, and we all share a look. "Come in!" I call.

Lachlan pushes his way through the door, a tray full of food balanced in one hand. He pauses as he takes all of us in, sprawled across my bed.

"Uh, ladies,"—he nods—"Key, I brought ye breakfast, actions and all that." He smirks.

The sight of him, all muscular lines clad in leather with breakfast in hand, has me fighting the urge to jump up and wrap my arms around him.

Mathilda looks at me and my budding smile before glaring at Lachlan. "Just leave it on the table."

He purses his lips, annoyance flashes across his face, but he does as she instructs. He halts at the threshold before leaving. "Agatha wants to meet with ye in the throne room, so I'll be right outside when you're ready."

"Thank you," I call to him, but the door is already shut.

Mathilda frowns at the smile still on my face. "You can't be serious," she huffs.

Mina glances between us. "What's going on? What did I miss?"

Mathilda stares me down, prompting me to fill Mina in like I did for her last night. I twirl a lock of hair around my finger, avoiding her eyes.

She groans with annoyance. "Lena here has had a crush on Lachlan her entire life, her whole life that she didn't know about the existence of this place, but Lachlan did." She gives me a look again before glancing back at Mina. "Then he basically tricks her into coming here, and essentially betrays her." I open my mouth to interject, but she cuts me off. "Yeah, yeah, he brought you here for the betterment of the realm and to protect you, but still, he knew, and he didn't tell you."

I stare down at my fingers, gently pulling at the threads of the burgundy duvet, and to my surprise, Mina pipes up. "So he didn't handle it as he should have, but did he apologize?"

"Yes."

"And did he mean it?"

"And then some," I grumble, glaring at Mathilda.

"Then forgive him."

My eyes flick to hers, but her eyes bounce between mine and Mathilda's.

She sits up, clearing her throat. "Once is a mistake, twice is a choice, and three times, well, that's just who they are at that point."

I nod, agreeing, and even Mathilda sighs. "Fine."

They clamber out of my bed. "Eat some breakfast and get dressed; we'll see you after your meeting," Mina calls over her shoulder before they leave my room.

Dressed in my new, unscathed leathers, my stomach full of delicious eggs and toast, I smile to myself before stepping out into the hall. Lachlan is standing beside the door. His magnificent wings are out; they take my breath away. I've only ever seen them twice before, and besides the first time, never this close-up.

The raven black feathers remind me of oil as they shimmer in the soft sunlight flooding in from the windows down the hall. My fingers itch to stroke a feather, but his knowing smile catches my eye.

"Impressive, huh?"

I roll my eyes at his arrogance. "You're ridiculous," I mutter.

"Right this way, my queen." He grabs my hand and tugs me down the hallway.

Agatha is waiting for us in the throne room of the castle; my feet echo against the stone floors as sunlight lights my path, streaming in from the second-story windows high above. The shafts of sunlight spear through the room every few feet.

Light, dark, light marks the walkway to the large wooden throne at the far end of the room.

Her back is turned to us, her head bowed in supplication to the throne before our echoing steps reach her, and she rises. We come to a halt a few steps behind her, and a ghost of a smile lingers on her face when she takes in our conjoined hands.

"Today will be the first of many of your, hopefully, long rule, Lena; let's set a precedence, shall we?" Her voice reverberates all around us, scattering the dust motes floating in the shaft of sunlight between us. I look at Lachlan for support, but he's already gazing at me. His lips kick up into a small smile, giving me the support I desperately need. I look back at Agatha, who is studying us closely.

"Let's do this," I say.

Her smile is broad and contagious. "Let's get you in the ring, my queen."

There must be something in the air here, in Olundy. My muscles are twitching with untapped energy as I bounce from foot to foot and shake out my shoulders. My hair is braided back in one single plait down my back, and the ends of my hair tickle my exposed lower back. My new leathers are the same woven leather as my old ones, but the color is a richer chocolate brown.

Fit for a queen, Agatha had said on our walk here.

The training grounds are not as packed as they were yesterday, but at least a dozen warriors are doing various activities.

I hope once they see me in action, it will help build their confidence in me. No one has been outright rude, but I don't have a firm reputation here, and I still need to earn their loyalty. That will probably take months of hard work, but I understand that it's not something that can be rushed. If I'm going to lead them in the upcoming war or, at the very least, into this rebellion, I need their support.

Armed with my axe and a shield, I stare down Lachlan as he draws his sword and spins it from one hand to the other hand, show off. Tane, Mathilda, Evander, and Mina are present, leaning on the wooden fence rails or, in Mina's case, perched on top of them. Their expressions are a mix of bemusement and delight as they watch us circle each other.

Tane murmurs loudly to Evander, "I bet you a dozen cakes she kicks his ass."

"I bet you a dozen he drops her in 2 minutes." Evander scoffs, and his feathers ruffle.

I'm not offended; Evander hadn't been able to train with me before we left the capital. Tane has a vested interest in my sparring capabilities, so he just smirks, stretching out his hand to shake on the bet.

"Let's go, Lena!" Mathilda calls.

Mina raises a fist over her head and howls her best war cry. I shake my head, trying to ignore them, but a smile breaks across my face from their support.

Lachlan's eyes narrow slightly, and like before, I see his moves play out like a movie in my mind before he's side-stepping in my direction, his sword slashing in line with his footwork.

I parry two of his blows with my axe hilt before using my shield on a glancing blow. His face gives nothing away; his expression remains neutral. But I can't help but smile as I think of how far my training has come in such a short amount of time.

His next maneuvers play out in my mind a split second before I have to dodge his swing. I recenter myself and struggle to clear my mind so the visions can come across sooner, but the cheers from our friends are making that difficult.

Taking a chance, I opt to go on the offensive when Lachlan pauses a beat, adjusting his stance, and I catch him off balance. He shuffles his feet to rebalance and block my blows, but the reverberation from the axe was something he was not prepared for.

My skin begins shimmering, and I force myself to use more of my power; a tingling begins across my chest and into my limbs. I prepare for his next moves, but no visions come. The sight of my glittering skin is a distraction for him, and he lowers his sword.

His mouth drops open, and his eyes are full of wonder.

"Ho-ly Gods," Mina mutters, and our friends shield their eyes from my growing light.

A hush falls over the training ground, and I spin in place. The light wasn't this bright last time, and a warmness spears from my chest. My necklace pulses more rapidly than it ever has before. The dozen warriors on the grounds cease their activities. The Affric Clan, with their yellow kilts, drop to one knee and bow their heads.

Other warriors can only manage to stand and gawk. I hear the clatter of Lachlan's sword on the ground and turn back to him. His eyes are even wider, the wonder edging on complete shock, before he, too, sinks to one knee and bows while covering his heart with a fist.

"What's happening?" I whisper to him.

He looks back up at me, smiling wildly. "It's a blessing from Odin, Key; you're God's blessed."

"What does that mean?" My voice raises, but the light is beginning to dim, back to the normal shimmer.

My necklace ceases its pulsing, settling into a gentle warmth. Our friends are still stuck in varying states of shock.

"It means," Agatha's voice carries across the grounds. "That Odin does recognize ye as the rightful heir to the throne and your unequivocal worth to carry his axe."

Lachlan stands and grasps my hand. His touch grounds me in a way I desperately needed after just feeling untethered. "It means he sees ye and that you're on the right path."

THE LIBRARY SMELLS of old parchment and mint. A fire crackles in the fireplace of a large sitting area. Comfortable couches and deep cushioned armchairs are placed around a navy handwoven rug.

Light flickers from torches anchored to the walls beside rows of bookshelves. Lancet windows are alight with sunlight cascading through the leaves of the giant trees beside the castle. The sizable space is already crammed full of people, and servants carry even more chairs from the surrounding rooms.

My small group of friends take seats at a long table in front of where the other warriors begin gathering. Everyone waiting for me. But as they get settled, I walk around the library, trying to settle my nerves and wrap my head around Odin's blessing. There's something unsettling about it.

To distract myself, I study the paintings that are hung all around the library and attempt several rounds of mindfulness. I pass by a painting of a large tree with several names carved onto the branches. A very large painting of a Valkyrie astride a white stallion holding Odin's axe snares my attention.

The beauty of the Valkyrie and her white wings reminds me of the Winged Victory statue in the Louvre. An unusual shimmer of light radiates from the painting and I step closer to scrutinize it before I notice the candles placed at the sides.

My eyes scan over the surrounding paintings before falling on another sizable painting further along the wall. Stepping closer, I admire the celebration on the canvas. It's very festive and merry as the artist depicts people dancing and singing. Cedar boughs line the banquet hall and a large tree is decorated with scraps of fabric. This must be a painting of Yule.

That's another item on my agenda to fix, the traditions. We need to celebrate all the old ways.

Resolves settles me and I square my shoulder. Much more prepared to address the room, I take my seat in the middle of my friends and stare out at the warriors in front of me. Mostly stoic faces stare back at me, but a few offer me comforting smiles.

I look at those faces when I address the room. "As many of you are aware, the omens of the Great War have been increasing. In addition to restoring our war preparations, we also need to know what we're up against. My knowledge is very limited, so if any of you have insight, we would love to hear it." I gesture to my friends seated around me.

A warrior seated directly in front of us glances sidelong at Agatha, who is standing beside our table, and she subtly nods. The warrior, a Fairhair, if I remember correctly, with white hair and a long white beard, stands rigidly.

"My queen." He addresses me and thumps a fist on his chest, his distinctive Scandinavian accent thickening the words. "I don't know much about what we're up against, but I do know we have allies."

A frown tugs the corner of my lips down. "Go on," I command.

Mathilda had only briefly mentioned something about our allies. But the bulk of that conversation was centered around what we're up against.

"Our allies are the Tuadanaan Fae, the Valkyries of Valhalla, and Freya's realm of Vanaheim. But without being able to travel to our allies, they won't be of any use to us. Our first course of action needs to be restoring magic in our realm to open the gateways."

Mathilda's earlier wisdom comes back to my mind: counting us that makes four realms against our enemies. We'd be up against the giants, dragons, and demons alone if we can't manage to reach our allies.

"Thank you…." I trail off, not knowing the man's name.

"Bjorn," he finishes for me, nodding his head in respect.

"Bjorn." I smile down at him. "Does anyone have anything else to add? Or any questions?" I ask, looking around the room.

A petite red-headed woman with fiery blue eyes shoots a hand up. "Aye, my queen." I nod at her. "The name's Merida, I'm with Clan Campbell. Is it true you're going to try and take the throne?"

The quiet chatter that had begun building ceases at her question.

Lachlan clears his throat next to me and raps his knuckles on the table, irritation simmering in his eyes.

But I stand and smile serenely at the room. "We're all here for the same thing. We see the signs, we're worried about our future, and we want to do something about it. Obviously, my knowledge of what we'd be facing is murky at best. Mathilda" —I gesture in her direction—"has briefly explained to me that our enemies in this war would be monsters. Giants, demons, and dragons who see lesser beings as nothing but food or animals to be slaughtered." I clear my throat and stand up straighter while gesturing with both hands to my friends beside me. "Our goal here is to protect this realm and all realms from the threat of destruction. If I have to take back my throne to do that, then so be it." I shrug, violence glowing in my eyes. "But I will not sit idly by any further, allowing neglect to destroy our home."

The meeting adjourns a little while later, with no additional useful information coming to light. So we're right back where we started—with no answers.

We have allies, but do not know how to reach them; we see the signs but don't know how soon it means war is coming; magic is still not regenerating and we do not know how to solve it.

My frustration begins rising, and the stress of what this means for our future weighs down my shoulders. How can I stop any of this if I don't know where to go from here? I turn to my friends, and a divot forms between my brows.

"While we're all here, Mina and Evander, I'd like to assign you guys new roles. Tane is in charge of housing and Mathilda volunteered to set up a school. So I was wondering if I could put you in charge of our food storage, Mina?"

Mina's eyes sparkle and she grins broadly at me. "Of course."

"Thank you," I breathe. "Evander, do you think you could scout out places for training grounds? It might be a bit presumptuous of me, but I'd like to think we'll eventually need more spaces for training."

Evander nods enthusiastically. "I can do that."

I exhale fully. "Well, with that settled, then, let's go through some of these books and see if we can find anything about our allies, magic, or enemies."

We split up and begin scouring the shelves. I trail a hand along the rows of books, marveling at how better-stocked this library is compared to the one in the Great Hall. But it still seems limited in areas I would expect it to flourish.

Why are there no genealogy texts on the Valkyrie's lineage? And how many books on worship practices does one need?

The last thought, coupled with my earlier thoughts on the holidays, causes me to pause.

"Lachlan," I call between the stacks.

"Over here!" he answers. I follow the sound of his voice to the west end of the library. He's surrounded by tomes of battle strategies.

"What do you think about observing the holidays again?" I ask, my brow furrowing.

His head tilts to the side. "Can ye be more specific?"

"It's June, and I haven't heard anyone talk about Midsommar preparations," I reply. Traditions were such a huge part of my life with my parents. Giving thanks and recognizing the gods was a way to connect to the world around you. "We have to celebrate Midsommar this year."

"Okay…why?" he asks, staring at me like I've grown two heads.

"Observing holidays is a perfect way to connect to the magic and the world around you. Traditions are very important and can help create a lasting foundation. I want my reign to be peaceful and fruitful. We need to observe all the olde ways, not just the training, and we will start with Midsommar."

"I will tell Agatha to begin making preparations then, but ye realize Midsommar is next week; that's not a lot of time," he mutters and slides a book from the shelf. I clear my throat when he begins reading the book.

"Do ye mean right now?" he asks.

I nod, giving him my best smile. "Yes, please."

Lachlan leaves to track down Agatha, and I continue browsing the stacks. As luck would have it, there are a few tomes about the other realms, Helheim and Jotnar. It's not bene-ficial for restoring our magic, but I know next to nothing about the other realms, so this will still be helpful.

Grabbing the books, I make my way to the leather couch by the fireplace and flip through the first one, Helheim. Located the furthest from the God's Realm, it's ruled by Hela and swarmed with various terrifying creatures. Images of the different types of demons stare up at me from the pages and I shudder.

A particularly grotesque rendering of a foot soldier causes me to pause and study its mottled gray skin and black hollow pits for eyes.

"That's not terrifying," I say under my breath.

But Mina leans over the back of my couch and points at the picture. "They look scary, but they're only bad in numbers."

I stare up at my friend with my mouth open. "You've fought these things?" I gape.

Mina shakes her head. "No, but my mother did." Her eyes are empty and I realize it's not a good memory she's drug up for my benefit. Quietly closing the book, I set it down.

Mina shivers before muttering, "I didn't realize I might have some useful information. It's not something I tend to think about." Apologies bloom in her eyes.

But I shake my head. "It's okay, I'm sure there are plenty of things I haven't been able to tell you guys yet."

Mina smiles gratefully before plunking down beside me and continuing, "They don't use weapons and have no thoughts other than to kill what's in front of them. They can't even work together or use any kind of battle strategy. Your powers wouldn't work against them because they don't have any foresight for you to see. They always go for the easy kill. The trick is to not panic and just keep slashing away."

I grimace. "Good to know."

She grabs the book about Jotnar and flips to the back, where it lists the species that live there. "The giants are obviously much harder to fight because of their size, but they're not very quick and rely heavily on their brute strength." I nod along to her lecture, trying to absorb as much as I can. "The asphidra's are an easy kill too, but just steer clear of their venom and their blood. It's black, so it's easy to see, but it's essentially acid and will melt anything in its path. The venom is green, and it's worse than their blood. It can paralyze you and subdue all magic."

My brow furrows. "What's an asphidra?" Mina tilts the book my way and shows me a picture of a creature with greenish-gray scaled skin, long fangs, and elongated limbs. "Yikes! It's like a snake person," I mutter, leaning away from the picture.

"You should see what the dragons look like or the shapeshifters in Sutr." She shudders.

"And we're supposed to battle all of these creatures in the Great War?" I ask, my mind whirling.

Mina shrugs. "Between us and our allies, we're the only beings that stand in between these monsters and total annihilation for the rest of the universe."

With no way to know how our allies are doing, or even our gods, we might actually be the last thing standing in the way, too. I close my eyes and breathe through the range of emotions that begin bubbling up at that thought.

Footsteps scuff against the stone floor as Lachlan strolls through the stacks and heads towards us, a smile gracing his lips. "Agatha said it was a marvelous plan and will make the preparations immediately."

Happiness shines in my eyes. "Thank you."

"Of course," he murmurs, kissing the top of my head before heading back through the stacks, no doubt in search of the book I made him put down.

"I'm gonna put these back and see if I can find anything magic-related," I mutter to Mina before hopping up from my seat.

"Uh huh, good luck with that." She chuckles before reclining on the couch.

Hours later, with no new knowledge gained, we call it quits. There's nothing here about magic or how to contact the other realms, and my frustration grows again.

To stave off the feeling of hopelessness, I tell Mina and Mathilda, "We're going to celebrate Midsommar this year."

"Really?" Mina gushes. "We haven't celebrated a holiday in ages."

Mathilda shakes her head. "I can't even remember the last holiday we celebrated."

"Well, we are now. It's going to be great! Cured meats, flower crowns, dancing, Bløtkakes!"

A round portrait of my parents catches my eye as we walk by, and once again, I wish they were here, or at the very least, could give me a sign, just a direction in which to go for the answers we need.

I know I'm on the right path thanks to my blessing earlier today, but where do I go from here? The last holiday I had with them, Samhain, flutters about my mind, bringing gloom with it.

TWENTY-SIX

I'm engulfed in my father's strong arms as he tucks me tightly to his chest. A warmth settles through me as my mom gently caresses my hair. Her body pressed against my back. I'm sandwiched between them.

They whisper how much they miss me and how proud they are of me. I absorb their words and inhale my mom's familiar cinnamon and vanilla scent. I can feel the stubble of my father's beard against the top of my head.

This is exactly how I remember them.

I want to stay like this forever.

A feeling of complete and utter safety, which I had taken for granted, wraps around me, squeezing me tightly.

But all too soon, their edges begin to fade into nothing, and I struggle to hold on to them. My father's deep voice calls out to me to forgive them as he fades away, the words echoing in the space between us.

Right before he vanishes, he whispers, *Find your family.* My mom begins to fade away next, and she reaches out, her eyes beseeching me as she whispers, *The throne.* She trails off and I can't make out the rest of what she's saying.

She vanishes in a puff of eerie black and green smoke. Their words are forgotten as my heart cracks wide open in my chest. I scream, begging them to stay with me. To not leave me again. Tears stream down my cheeks, and I bellow with rage at having them torn from me all over again. Screaming echoes in the void that devours me.

The sound of a hundred of people suffering the same fate as I am.

"Key!" Lachlan's voice breaks through the dream, and the screaming abruptly cuts off as my eyes blink open.

It was me; I was the one screaming.

I flutter my eyes open and shut, trying to focus on the dark room around me. Moonlight floods in, illuminating Lachlan's face. His eyes are lined with silver as he rubs a hand down the side of my face.

"It's alright, Key, it was only a dream."

I hiccup, my breath coming out unsteadily. He wipes the tears from my face and pulls me into his arms. All this time spent around my parent's memories must have conjured them up tonight. Their faces and voices fade quickly from my memory.

My tears begin trickling down my face again as I struggle and fail to recall the entirety of the dream. Only the wound of their absence remains. Lachlan holds me tightly as I sob, feeling as if they were ripped from me all over again. He rocks us back and forth.

"I've got ye; you're safe," he whispers.

"I miss them so much," I choke out between sobs.

Lachlan nods. The stubble of his beard grazes my forehead as he presses his lips to it.

"I know, Key, I'm so sorry."

He holds me tightly to his chest until my tears dry up and my breathing steadies. Lachlan eases back against the headboard and sighs heavily as I snuggle into his side.

"Do ye remember when we were kids, and we used to pick wildflowers by the fairy tree?"

His words have me pulling away from his chest so that I can look into his eyes.

"Yes, why?"

"I used to plant more flower seeds after ye had gone back to the States to replenish the ones we had taken. Even after ye stopped coming back every summer, I would still tend the flowers. Making sure the birds hadn't eaten the seeds, and that they were still sprouting. It was my way of passing the time and holding ye close during the year until ye would return the next summer." His face glows in the moonlight, hard planes and long lashes casting shadows across his skin.

We had stopped going to Gran's every summer after my 18th birthday. Four years had passed and still he had gone out every year and tended to the flowers.

"I thought I was wild and precocious," I mumble.

"Oh, you were." He chuckles. "But you were my wild and precocious. I guess I just dinna realize it at the time."

My fingers have a mind of their own as I absentmindedly trace his naked skin with a fingertip, starting at his ribs and making my way to his chest.

"How do you do that?" I whisper.

He cocks his head to the side, his unkempt hair brushing against his collarbone. "Do what?"

"Help me breathe, even though I was just drowning."

Lachlan shivers under my touch. "Because I can and ye need me to."

He angles his head down and towards mine, his eyes locked onto my lips. Courage surges through me.

I grasp the back of his neck, pulling him down towards me.

Our lips touch and fire erupts through me, burning away every bad feeling I've ever had. My body heats, my cheeks flush, and my heart stutters to a stop before it explodes in my chest. It's everything I ever dreamed it would be.

His hands tangle in my unbound hair, pulling me deeper into his embrace. When my mouth parts with a sigh, our kiss deepens. The taste of him is electrifying.

This is it.

This is the home I've been searching for.

My lungs begin burning and we break apart, both gasping for air. His hands slide out of my hair and glide down my arms. Our breaths mingle in the air between us before his gaze darkens and we dive back in. If our first kiss was madness, our second kiss is like wading into a warm pool. My hands find their way up the sides of his neck and into his hair while his tongue plunges into my mouth, eliciting a moan from me. My heart begins stitching itself back together.

The pieces of myself click into place and leave me whole once more.

CHAPTER

TWENTY-SEVEN

I awaken the next morning, tangled in the sheets. The nightmare a million miles away as I look out the window full of the early morning light upon the rollings hills beyond the castle. I grin sleepily while stretching out my limbs, thinking of the kisses and stories shared last night.

We both agree it would be best if we didn't move too fast.

A budding romance and an impending war on the horizon are a lot for me to juggle at once. I barely have my current role figured out. I don't want to add too much to my already full plate. But that doesn't stop me from nuzzling into my sheets and inhaling his cedar and rain scent from the night before.

Today is going to be a good day.

Word of Odin's blessing from yesterday has spread like wildfire through the tiny island. Throughout the day, from my training to lunch, and even now, while Lachlan and I head to meet the others in our newly appointed council room, warriors from all over greet me and shake my hand. Odin's spectacle solidified me as the queen in their mind. My fledgling support, which was evident yesterday, has now evolved into complete and utter loyalty that garners the respect of the rebels we've amassed so far.

The months I was expecting to need to gain their trust took only a second with Odin's blessing. I'm relieved but also apprehensive that their trust was so easy to gain; what little will it take to lose it? Thoughts of Odin circle my mind when I think about the blessing. The unsettled feeling creeps back into my stomach.

There's something we're missing.

The surrounding land is peaceful and serene. I allow my mind time to wander as I stare off into the distance to the cliff that rises up and over the ocean. Lachlan and I walked out here together after lunch for some fresh air.

The land and stolen kisses were needed to reinvigorate my senses. I stare at Lachlan, his hair ruffling in the breeze, his strong jaw shadowed in the stubble that's grown since we landed on the shores of Olundy. If Odin had the ability to bestow a blessing, why couldn't he just come back? Tell the realm there is a war, after all?

My nose scrunches, and Lachlan studies my face. "Where'd ye go, Key?"

My mind whirls through all the bits of information that Odessa has dropped during my time here. I inhale slowly and steadily, pushing my mind to put the pieces together.

Wasn't Odessa the last to see Odin?

Shouldn't He have ridden in the Wild Hunt? And they kept mentioning plans. What plans? "The blessing from yesterday. Something is strange about it. What if Odin had to bestow a blessing on me because he couldn't come back?"

"What do ye mean?" he asks, his face reflecting his obvious confusion as he tilts his head to the side.

"I mean…Odessa was the last one to meet with Odin before he left to go back to his realm, and she said that his reason was because there wasn't going to be a Great War, right?"

"Aye," he replies hesitantly.

"Well, what if she lied?" He reels back at my words, squinting in confusion. "She was willing to kill my mother, her own sister, to keep me from coming here to thwart her plans; what plans? And wouldn't she want to make sure an actual God couldn't stop her either? What's the end game here?"

My questions ramble together as I quickly work to get all my thoughts out. Lachlan's eyes narrow and his mouth is set in a grim line.

"Ye think she did something to Odin so she could control the realm?"

I nod profusely. "It makes sense. We think the omens are happening because war is coming, but wouldn't He have shown up by now to confirm that? We know he sees us because he can bestow blessings. And Odessa and Julius literally said they wanted me as a figurehead because they thought I'd be easy to control, but when that proved otherwise, they tried to kill me."

My mind keeps spinning, grasping at the pieces and trying to fit them together.

"Maybe the omens are actually Odin trying to get our attention the only way he can from wherever he is?" My voice trails off.

Lachlan shifts on his feet, his brow furrowing even further, and he inhales sharply. "I canna believe I dinna think about it before," he mutters. "I was so caught up in just seeing the omens as signs of war I dinna even stop to think about the fact that He should ha' come back when they started."

"Odessa also said that the power was fading because my family wasn't here, but I don't think that's true because the magic is still limited. What if it's fading because Odin isn't here?"

Lachlan's eyes blaze. The brilliant green catching the sun. "So ye think he's gone, and that's why there are omens and the magic is fading?"

"I don't know. I mean, it could be a possibility. I'm not saying the omens aren't a sign of war, it could be both, but I'm saying magic might be gone because He is."

"We need to tell the others, and now." He scoops me up and launches us into the sky.

His wings beat fiercely, and my heart drops into my stomach at our rapid ascent. My arms cling to him in a death grip as the ground drops away.

Lachlan chuckles at my terrified expression, and I glare daggers at him.

"Some warning would have been nice," I say loudly over the wind.

"Oh, come on, Key, don't tell me ye dinna want to fly."

The land is majestic from this high up, and I do actually get a thrill out of the flight. My hair tears free from my braid, and the waving mass of golden brown hair behind me reminds me of flying in the saddle on Sleipnir.

My grin stretches across my face, and Lachlan whispers into my ear, "There's my girl."

I snuggle further into his arms, enjoying the short flight back to the castle. Our rapid descent has my stomach falling again, but only from the motion, not from fear; it's exhilarating, a pure adrenaline rush. We race up the steps and into the council room ahead of the others.

My feet wear a path in the woven rug in front of the red marble fireplace in our newly appointed council chambers. Another one of my mom's portraits hangs above the mantle. Her eyes seemingly follow my every step.

The power wasn't fading because the heir wasn't here; it was fading because Odessa must've trapped Odin somewhere. The door creaks open, halting my steps, but I still pull at my fingers. Our friends waltz in, all looking slightly harassed by Lachlan as he herds them inside.

"Easy man, we're all here," Tane grumbles as they sprawl onto the chairs and couches surrounding the room.

Mina's eyes miss nothing as she studies my discomfort. "What's going on?"

Lachlan comes to my side, surveying them all, as he folds his arms across his leather-clad chest. "Lena had a terrifying thought."

All eyes flick to me as I take a steadying breath. "I think Odessa and, probably, Julius have something to do with the magic fading. They possibly trapped Odin somewhere."

There's a collective gasp, and Mathilda murmurs, "Merciful Gods."

My heart beats loudly in my ears. "Think about it, guys. She murdered my parents to keep me from coming here, which, thanks to Lach, that plan was thwarted." I gesture towards him, and he grins. "She wanted me only as a figurehead to puppeteer until my powers manifested and then they decided killing me was easier, and she was supposedly the last and only person to see Odin in this realm? Really?"

Evander shakes his head from side to side. "There's no way,"—he looks around at the group—"this is just a ploy to keep her in power." He looks from me to Lachlan, whose face is set in a mask of frozen fury. "You guys really think it goes much deeper than that?"

Lachlan and I share a look, and I shift on my feet. "Yes. If Odin can send omens of war or blessings but can't come here himself to set the realm straight when we're obviously very divided, it might be because he can't."

Mathilda shudders. "It would also explain the power fading. Lena's here, and the magic isn't restoring."

Tane's eyes don't shift around the room; he keeps them locked onto the fireplace before us.

Mina wrings her hands in her lap. "This is really bad, isn't it?"

I nod. "We need to prepare for the worst and fill in the recruits we have here now, including each one who comes from Elowen's efforts."

"No," Tane replies, his voice breaking him out of his trance. "That could spark an entire wave of panic if people begin to realize we won't have Odin fighting on our side; we need to keep this to ourselves."

Lachlan nods. "I agree. The only people who should know are in this room. We need to keep preparing for war, regardless."

I glance at Evander, Mathilda, and Mina. "And what do you guys think?"

They all share a look before Mina pipes up. "You're giving us a vote?"

My nose scrunches up at her response. "Of course I am; everyone should have a voice."

Mathilda's eyes swim with an emotion I can't quite place. "I say we keep quiet about it until we know for sure." Mina and Evander nod in agreement.

"Ok then, let's keep this buttoned up and keep training for the war until we know for sure." My voice rings with an authority I hadn't realized I possessed, and the power of it sends a thrill down my spine.

That could be dangerous.

The quote 'absolute power corrupts absolutely' rings in my mind and I make a mental note to always put everything to a vote in the future.

As they file out of the room with farewells, Lachlan lingers close to where I stand.

"Ye did amazing today, Key," he says quietly.

My stomach fills with butterflies as his voice deepens, his accent becoming thick. Heat blooms in my chest. He's standing close to me, his back resting on the fireplace mantle. Both of my hands are outstretched in front of me, gripping the wood of the mantle. I bend down, using my arms to support me, and stretch my lower back.

"I just feel like I can't catch a break," I mutter.

He moves to stand behind me, his deft fingers working the knots out of my lower back that my stretch wasn't releasing. His knuckles push down into me and send waves of goosebumps down my arms and legs. My blood thrums in my veins, and my pulse accelerates. His touch does wonders, not only for my sore muscles but also for the lingering anxiety in my chest. I bite my lip to stifle a moan as his hands travel up my spine, carefully avoiding my wing buds that have pierced my skin and the gaps of my leather top, but still working the soreness out of each muscle.

"Geez, your back is like a gravel path with all these knots," he mutters, pushing on a particularly sore spot.

"Ouch," I cry out, as it sends a sharp pain down my back.

His hands release their assault on my back immediately, but then he grabs my hand and drags me out of the room and up the stairs. He leaves me standing on the threshold of my room while he walks into my bathroom.

"I'm running ye a bath," he calls over his shoulder.

The sound of the water turning on and splashing into the copper bathtub fills the space, and the aroma of lavender floats out the open door. I follow the smell to the bathroom and find him measuring out vials and pouring them into the bathtub.

"Mathilda says the Valkyries like this stuff in their baths," he says over the sound of the tub filling.

I lean against the doorway, taking in the spectacle that is Lachlan Freysson drawing my bath. Since my stubs of wings have protruded even further from my skin, the itch has become unbearable.

Lachlan grabs a handful of pink salt and sprinkles it into the steaming water. "This is what they use for the children who are growing wings; it helps with the itch," he says before looking back at me.

It's like he can read my mind sometimes. Satisfied with his handiwork, he places his hands on his hips, watching the tub fill up more before turning the water off. Steam floats up from the tub, fogging the mirrors above the white marble sink.

Lachlan saunters towards me and pauses beside me. "Enjoy your bath and get some rest." His voice tickles my neck from his proximity, and I want more than anything to finish our moment from last night.

But the pain from my wings is still there, writhing under the surface. I bite my lip and stare up into his eyes. There is so much longing reflecting in them, I freeze. He leans towards me just the tiniest amount before he kisses my temple, murmuring, "Good night, Key." Then he's strolling out of my room.

The suspense bursts with the door closing, and I hang my head. I have an entire realm to save, a war to stop, a throne to take back, and yet, here I am holding my breath, wondering if some man is going to kiss me again.

Pathetic.

I strip down and ease into the bath, the aroma and heat unknotting each of my wound-up muscles. The itch from my wings subsides, and the water washes away the grime from the day. Peace and relaxation quiet my nerves, and I close my eyes, resting my head on the lip of the copper tub. It's not too often that I'm granted these moments of quiet reflection, and I do my best to enjoy every second of it.

It isn't long before the sun drops out of the sky, dimming the bathroom. As I rise from the tub, water sloshes up and almost over the side. I shiver lightly before wrapping myself in a fluffy, warm towel.

The lit candles in the bathroom and my bedroom cast soft light in the growing darkness. I relish the coziness but tread carefully with wet feet to the attached closet to locate some night clothes. Dressed in a light linen set and my wet hair wrapped in the towel, I walk to the window by my bed.

The smell of food drifts from the tray that has been left on my nightstand, and I roll my eyes; he thinks of everything.

The sun has been replaced with a bright full moon, lighting the grounds completely, rendering the blazing torches useless. A few warriors are still lingering on the training grounds, using the night as a training technique. I smile to myself, hope flickering my chest as I reflect on the positives in my life.

Odin picked me, showed me I was on the right path, and blessed me not only with powers, but with an amazing support system that I have found in my new friends.

My whole life, I had wanted friends such as these, and I finally found them, or rather, they found me.

CHAPTER

TWENTY-EIGHT

A few days later, the sound of a horn blasting, followed by two short bursts, pierces the still air. The first of Elowen's recruits have made it to our shores. I'm not the least bit surprised to see Artemisia walking along the beach and towards our waiting party. Her wild, curly black mass of hair frames her lovely face. I am surprised to see Julius's father, Marcus, walking alongside her.

My eyes narrow into slits, and I shift from foot to foot.

The movement has me leaning forward ever so lightly to counterbalance the weight of the wings I'm still growing accustomed too. The buds have begun sprouting feathers and if I thought the itch was unbearable before, nothing could have prepared me for this. Lachlan shares my concern and crosses his arms, his muscles rippling with the movement, and his wings flare slightly, the threat easily readable. I relax my pinched stare and smile at Artemisia.

"Welcome to the rebellion," I greet her, grasping her outstretched hand.

Lachlan glares at Marcus, and he holds his hands up in front

286

of him. "I'm aware my presence probably wasn't what you were expecting, but I came to pledge my allegiance to your cause."

Artemisia smiles warmly at him, her head tilting in his direction. "He has my support. I vouch for his claims of allegiance."

A look of love passes between them, and my mouth parts.

They love each other?

Lachlan is unconvinced, however, and doesn't relax his position by my side.

Shrugging, Marcus slips a book out from beneath his white robes. "I knew you'd probably need more convincing; I managed to sneak this from the royal library before Odessa destroyed all the books. I hope it will help secure me a position here."

He offers the book to Lachlan, who roughly grabs it from him before flipping the cover face up, 'Runic Pathways: Ancient Travel Symbols' Lachlan's head whips up to me.

I purse my lips, fighting a gasp. Lachlan nods and hands the book to Evander, who places it in his saddlebags.

If our assumption is correct, that will come in handy to reach our allies and Odin. That book might very well hold the key to a few answers.

"Thank you," I murmur to Marcus, who bows his head.

"I managed to sneak out more and have brought them with us." He gestures to their boats. "I am not aware of the extent of my son's plans, but I do know that I will not agree with them, he was a troubled boy, and I had hoped my position on the council could undo a lot of the damage he caused." His eyes turn grave. "I was wrong, and for that, I am sorry. I will do whatever you need to help right this wrong."

I nod my head, dismissing him, and reach for Artemisia. "Walk with me?"

She takes my offered hand, and we walk alone down the beach, leaving our gathered party.

"What's happening in the capital?" I ask, curious but also afraid to know what has taken place in our absence.

"Absolutely nothing," she mutters, her eyes turning glassy. "It's as if you were never there. She's doing all she can to cover it up, but there are whispers. I fear she's growing agitated."

We stop a few paces away from the group, out of earshot, and I heave a sigh.

"She had my parents killed," I murmur.

I feel at ease opening up to her. There's something about her presence that calls to me. Like we've been friends a long time and not just the acquaintances we actually are. Her eyes sharpen as she watches the slow, receding waves in front of us. "I know our rebellion is outmatched in numbers, but I will do everything in my power to seek justice for my parent's death."

"I am so sorry for the loss of your parents, Your Majesty," she breathes while turning to look at me. "But do not fret about being out-manned. I advised Xerxes on the willpower of the few, and he did not listen, resulting in our defeat from the smaller Greek fleet. Mighty is your cause; you will not fail."

I grin, her confidence soothing my unease, and look back at the other people on the beach. "Are you sure you trust Marcus?" I ask, studying her face.

"With my life," she confirms. "We should not have found each other, and we should not have fallen in love, but fate prevailed." Her oath is enough to sway my judgment, and my necklace warms on my chest in agreement.

"The plan so far is to gain as much support as I can to take back my throne. I'm hoping to do it as peacefully as possible. But we'll need as many people on our side as possible to make that happen. I'm reinstating old traditions, starting with Midsommar in a few days and mandatory training for the Great War."

Artemisia opens her arms, palms facing up towards the sky.

"That's why we are here. War is coming, and too long have we ignored the signs."

We walk back arm in arm, and I nod to Lachlan, who whistles to bring the horses around. He orders Evander to show Marcus, Artemisia, and their companions to their rooms in the castle. A handful of Greek and Roman men and women unload belongings from the boat tied up offshore and begin trampling through the waves.

Lachlan stands at my side.

"It's beginning," he says calmly.

But my heart races as more waves crash against the shore.

WHEN WE RETURN to the castle, Lachlan pulls me to the council chambers where Agatha is waiting.

"Mina is going to meet with our newest arrivals to assess the food they ha' brought with them and allocate land for more farming," he addresses us both.

We are going to need a lot more food to feed everyone if Elowen's recruitment keeps going this well.

Agatha pipes in, "I can asses our current food stores and begin a rationing schedule with her."

"That's good. I'd also like to have trusted guards stationed at the bay to vet the incoming citizens and receive their pledges, too." I murmur.

My thoughts flit through the next couple of steps to ensure our success.

"Oh, and Lachlan, can you go with Evander to locate the new areas to establish as training grounds? We need them to begin training in units as soon as possible and assign leadership roles to the ones who show the most promise."

Lachlan's face breaks into a wide smile, and he nods. "Of course."

Agatha looks between us, a smile lighting her face, before addressing Lachlan, "She was made for this role, wasn't she?"

A deep, heated blush creeps up my cheeks at her remark, and I bite my lip, waiting for Lachlan's response.

"She was," he agrees.

His eyes glow as they land on my face. A gentle tug pulls on my heart, and I unknowingly take a step towards him. Agatha's eyes widen in response, but Lachlan merely bows deeply before setting off to do his tasks.

The wood in the fireplace cracks loudly. The sound breaks me out of staring after him.

Agatha clears her throat. "Is there anything else you need, dearie?"

I ponder her request for a moment before quietly asking, "Did you know my mother well?"

"I did." Agatha's smile turns sad.

A lump forms in my throat at the thought of my mom. "Do you know why she left this place?"

She shakes her head and looks down at her booted feet. "Unfortunately, I do not. But if I ken your mother like, I think I do. She dinna make the decision lightly, and it was probably based on her love for ye or your father."

Her words dull the sharp edge of my grief.

"She would have been very proud of the queen you are becoming, Lena."

TWENTY-NINE

Gulls cry overhead and waves crash against the rocks. I open my eyes, looking out at the vast sea that stretches before us. This should be the perfect place to quiet my mind as I usually am calmer near the sea.

But the whitecaps on the water mimic the turbulence swirling within me.

My thoughts continue to ebb and swell over the events of yesterday as I sit cross-legged under a cedar tree with Mina. Agatha's words are still fighting to give me a small amount of peace over the frustrations I felt after going through a few of the books Marcus brought. Without magic, they're useless, but there's still more I need to go through.

"Breathe in through your nose," Mina whispers as I hold my breath while my thoughts continue spiraling.

I work to inhale deeply through my nose, but I shift uncomfortably.

"Lena, are you okay?" Mina asks, her eyes still closed, but her lips are kicked up into a smile.

"I can't seem to quiet my mind today."

She chuckles and stretches her legs out in front of her. I roll my shoulders, trying to itch my wings against the leather.

Everything is bothering me today.

My brain hurts from the stress of my duties, my heart still aches from the loss of my parents, and my body aches with the changes brought upon by my wings and the skills I practice every day in training.

Mina studies me briefly and grins. "All right, let's start with what you're feeling physically."

I hang my head and sigh through my nose. "I don't mean to be whiney," I mutter.

She pats my thigh. "It's not whiney; just tell me what you're feeling."

I tilt my head up to the sky, watching the light filter through the green leaves. "My wings itch and throb every second of every day. I can feel each feather as it pierces my flesh. My muscles are always sore from training or stress, and my heart aches."

"I have a solution for most of that." Mina nods thoughtfully.

My eyes flick to hers. "Really?"

She nods. "But we need to calm your mind first." She pokes me in the forehead. "What's going on up there?"

I lean back on my hands and stare out at the sea. "Too much. I'm lost again. I don't know where I should be leading us; I know I'm doing the right thing by restoring our old ways, but what's next? And I'm angry. *So angry.* They killed my parents, and I'm just sitting here, doing absolutely nothing."

The words tumble out of me.

I hadn't realized I had kept them bottled up.

I am furious, and the rage is consuming me more than I had realized. I was used, lied to, and betrayed.

Mina dips her chin, sadness lining her features. "I was wondering when you would realize that."

I take a breath, and it finally fills my entire chest.

"Close your eyes," she whispers. "Hold on to that anger, and with each exhale, I want you to let it go."

We take long, slow breaths together, and I work to let it all go.

"Anger can be a good thing she whispers; when you sharpen it into a weapon you can wield, but you have used it to hinder yourself from your full potential, *it's holding you back*. So you must let it go."

Her words, coupled with my controlled breathing, lull me into a state of peace, and I begin to feel lighter.

It's a long while before I realize she hasn't spoken in some time, and my breathing is slow and steady. I'm not quite asleep, but not fully awake either; I'm relaxed in a place in between.

Slowly, I float back to the surface of my body, my pain gone, the itching of my new wings easily ignorable. Mina twirls a cedar needle between her fingers. The wings I rarely see on her are out on full display.

"I think your wings are big enough now. I can teach you to vanish them so they won't bother you so much."

I nod and study her wings closely. A few scars mar the tops of them where the feathers are attached.

She notices my scrutiny and smiles sadly. "I might have lied a bit about my childhood," she murmurs. My stomach sinks. "My parents did use me as a weapon against each other, but first, they had to hone me into one. Weapons aren't allowed to have weaknesses and wings are sensitive things."

Her eyes darken with the weight of her memories, and I swallow hard.

My eyes burn with unshed tears. "Oh, Mina, I am so sorry," I whisper.

"I learned very quickly how to hide the things that were important to me, but you'll have plenty of time to learn." I nod quickly, but my chest begins throbbing for the kind soul that is my friend.

All the horror she must've suffered to have scars like that but still remains as kind as she is, astounds me.

Mina is a rare soul.

She turns so that she's sitting cross-legged in front of me, and I mirror her actions. She clasps my hands and stares into my eyes. The breeze floats between us, bringing with it the salty air of the sea.

The tightness of my chest eases slightly, and Mina talks softly.

"I want you to focus on where your wings protrude from your skin for a moment." I shift my focus to the area she's talking about. "Focus intently, but don't get discouraged. Magic is still less here, so this will take even more concentration than it should normally take," she whispers. I focus on her words, my attention locked onto her face. "Now I want you to visualize the empty space between your wings, the very air itself, and *will* your wings into nothing."

I focus with all my might, my abs tighten, and my eyes strain as I focus on everything from the silvery-white of my feathers to the air between them.

Mina smiles. "Remember to breathe."

My breath whooshes out of my chest, and I work to inhale slowly.

We try for an hour before I'm mentally and physically exhausted.

"Let's call it a day; we have plenty of time for you to learn." She rises and stretches out a hand to me.

As she pulls me up, the temperature plummets. We look at each other in alarm.

"Do you feel that?" I ask, looking around for any cause of the temperature drop.

My words come out in puffs of steam.

Frost grows on the ground beneath us. Mina looks up into the sky as her teeth begin to clatter together.

"Lena, look," she stutters out between shivers.

Snowflakes float down from the sky. I look from the sea to the castle as snow begins to fall. We share a look before we turn and sprint down the path that takes us back to the castle. The snow falls harder, and flowers freeze over in our wake, their petals shriveling up and dropping.

Warriors on the training ground pause their training to stare up at the sky.

Snowflakes clumping to their beards and sticking to their eyelashes.

Lachlan and Evander are on the edge of the grounds, racing towards us when we finally cross paths.

"What is happening?" I ask, looking around.

Lachlan shakes his head. "It never snows this far south," he says in between pants.

"Or this out of the blue," Evander mutters, his hands on his knees.

"So, this is another sign?" I ask, my teeth chattering as I work to catch my breath.

Mina nods. "This isn't good."

"We need to finish going through the books Marcus brought with him." I stutter out between shivers. I hold my palm up to catch a snowflake.

"It's worth trying." Lachlan nods.

Snow begins melting before it hits the ground, the temperature rising rapidly. Heat caresses my skin and my teeth stop chattering. I brush off the snow that had begun piling up in my hand against my pants. The wetness darkening the brown of the leather.

"If we can just solve our magic problem, then everything else should fall into place."

⚭

THE CASTLE IS a thrum of energy as the final preparations for Midsommar are in full swing. Flowers are placed on every flat surface and the smell of sugary goodness wafts from the kitchen.

But a dark cloud hangs in the hall as we run into Elowen standing alone, waiting for us.

Her face looks paler than usual, and her mouth is pressed in a grim line.

"What's happened?" I ask, scanning her for injuries. Immediately, Lachlan goes on high alert, scanning the halls and entrances for a threat.

"I had a vision," she rasps out.

It's only then I notice that her eyes are completely white. A noise echoes from down the hall, and I glance behind us to see servants walking with firewood and trays of flowers.

"Let's speak inside," I whisper and nod to the council room door behind us. "Mina, Evander, can you guys grab Tane and Mathilda and meet us in the library?"

They both nod and continue on as Lachlan ushers Elowen inside; I square my shoulders and master my emotions as best as I can before crossing the threshold and entering the room.

We take seats in front of the roaring fireplace, the warmth of the flames chasing away the last of the chill from the freak snowstorm.

Elowen hugs her body tightly.

"Are you okay?" I ask her. She looks frightened.

"Before I tell you what I saw," she whispers. "You need to know that my visions aren't as clear as they used to be." I nod in understanding; with magic fading, it only makes sense it would impact her gift, too. "I used to be able to give more details or specific things that would come to light; now, it's only vague glimmers or feelings."

She grimaces, her eyes never leaving the flames.

"Whatever you can tell us is appreciated."

I do my best to smile encouragingly at her, but my stomach is tied in knots.

Her eyes flicker with darkness before she mumbles, "I saw a wolf devouring our realm whole; there was no more sky, no more sun, only darkness, and then I saw grey and fire before a blue light speared through and huge giants began ripping branches from a tree while a dragon was breathing fire at it."

She shudders and grips herself tighter.

"Do either of you know what any of that could mean?" I ask, looking from her to Lachlan.

She shakes her head before hanging it and staring at her lap. Lachlan stands and begins pacing in front of the fireplace. After a few turns, he stops and leans a hand against the mantle, his back to us.

"Well, the giants and dragons are enemies of ours," he grumbles.

"They're foretold to battle us in the Great War," I add, thinking back to the brief lesson Mathilda gave me back in the capital.

I scan Elowen as she shivers, her strawberry blonde hair ruffling with the movement. "Do you have any idea when this could take place?"

Her eyes flick up and are more hollow than before.

"Soon."

CHAPTER

THIRTY

"What was her vision again?" Mathilda asks, her eyes widening in horror.

Anxiety curls in my belly as I look around at my friends.

War is approaching, and I'm no closer to restoring magic, contacting our allies, or finding Odin.

"She thinks it means war will happen soon," Lachlan answers for me. He gives my hand a comforting squeeze.

The action dulls the edge of my anxiety.

I sigh loudly. "I know we discussed the omens meaning Odin was trying to get our attention but with Elowen's vision I think we need to really focus on training for war, so I've asked you guys to meet us here to help look around the books Marcus brought for anything that might help. Same thing as last time. We need to figure out a way to contact our allies, restore magic, or a way to reach Odin. Ideally, it would be all three, but I'll settle for just one; we need magic back. Marcus brought a few books about runic pathways, but without magic being restored, they are useless. I've gone through about a third of what he brought with him, but I need help to go through the rest. Look for anything about magic."

The pile of books Marcus brought is stacked neatly in front of the fireplace, and they each grab a few books and haul them back to chairs or couches.

Elowen reluctantly left to head back to the capital to finish recruiting, but I wish she could have stayed longer. Maybe we could have tried to get her to see something else. I need to ask her how the visions work.

Do they just happen randomly or can she focus on something?

Sighing to myself, I get back to the task at hand and walk to the large stack of books. A book about crystals shimmers in the firelight and I pluck it from the top of the stack and amble back to the couch Lachlan's already sprawled on.

He pats the cushion next to him and I settle comfortably into his side, gently opening the book to protect its spine.

I inhale deeply, absorbing the smell of the pages, and happiness flutters in my chest. Books have always brought me serenity.

The beginning chapters outline the history of crystals and how they were used in many cultures. Egyptians, Greeks, and Romans all used them for their healing and protective properties. The rest of the book dedicates a few pages per crystal.

Quartz has the ability to amplify. Amethyst can protect and ground you. Selenite can inhibit dark magic. And black tourmaline can absorb negative energies. All great qualities, tied to magic, but all useless without magic.

If I could somehow manage to bring back magic, quartz would be helpful in amplifying it, but still doesn't help me restore it.

Pages rustle in the quiet library and I focus on the sound to settle my temper. But my rising frustration has me snapping the book shut and leaning away from Lachlan.

"Nothing?" he asks, peering at me from over the top of his book.

"Nothing," I grumble. I rub my fingertips in circles on my temples, trying to relieve some of the pressure building behind my eyes.

Mina whispers from beside me. "I know there is a lot outside of your control right now, but try shifting your attention to something that is."

My eyes blink open to find her staring at me from perched on the arm of the couch. "Like what?"

She smiles softly and gazes at my wings, "Try vanishing your wings."

I frown. "I didn't feel like I was getting anywhere earlier."

Mina shakes her head. Her short hair swings back and forth. "You can't just give up because it doesn't come easy to you the first time. Try again."

I pout, but close my eyes again.

I focus on the fire crackling in the fireplace, the smell of all the books, and the pages turning before refocusing on my breathing. Once I take a few slow breaths, I turn my mind to the feeling of my wings protruding between my shoulder blades. The feel of the tendons attaching them to my body and the very air between them. I focus even harder on the air between them before I feel a tiny pop, like a knuckle cracking, and then nothing.

I peek one eye open to see Mina's face radiating pure joy.

"I knew you could do it." She smiles broadly.

I turn my head to see and sure enough, there are no longer wings in my periphery vision.

"Okay, but how do I bring them back?" I ask, my eyes growing wide.

Lachlan and Mina chuckle before she quietly says, "Close your eyes again, and just imagine them unfurling from your back. It's much easier to bring them out than put them away, I promise."

Again, I focus on the fire before bringing my attention to my breathing and imagine the silvery white of my feathers unfurling from my back. There's a feeling of release before I can feel my wings graze against the back of the couch.

"It's like working out a muscle. The more ye do it, the stronger you will be and the easier it will become," Lachlan murmurs, returning to his book.

I smile gratefully at Mina. "Thank you."

"Of course, you needed a win today."

I don't have to focus nearly as hard before my wings are vanishing again. "I did. And this will make it easier to dance at the party tomorrow."

Mina slips from her perch on the couch and heads towards the fireplace. "Don't even think about jumping the bonfire with your wings out tomorrow."

My laughter rings through the quiet library.

CHAPTER

THIRTY-ONE

Drums beat slowly at first before gradually building.

I hop and twirl around the large bonfire erected on the black sand of the bay. Mathilda is holding my right hand while Mina is grasping my left. We laugh at my lack of rhythm, and the happiness of this moment is seared into my mind.

I am blissfully happy.

My lilac gown flows out around me with my movements, and the salty breeze of the bay soothes the heat away from the close flames.

Like Mina suggested, my wings are vanished away.

The drums come to a stop and we walk back to the table where Tane, Evander, and Lachlan are sitting. The men have been drinking most of the afternoon already and give us lazy grins when we approach. Tane pulls Mathilda onto his lap when she gets within reach, and I swear her eyes become as bright as the flames of the bonfire.

Lachlan grasps my hand and pulls me into the chair next to him. His familiar scent envelops me, and thoughts of my own future with him begin swirling in my mind.

"I got ye a slice of cake." He grins at me, scooting a slice of the spongy, fruit-filled cake my way. "I even remembered to put lots of whipped cream on it," he adds, scooping a dollop of the whipped cream onto his finger before plunking it lightly onto my nose.

My mouth drops open in surprise.

Mina and Evander share a quiet laugh at my expense. But Mathilda and Tane are too wrapped up in their own conversation to even realize what happened.

"Very funny; you know I can remove you from your position for such atrocious behavior, correct?"

Lachlan grins fiendishly at me. "But then you'd miss me too much."

He's not wrong.

With the whipped cream still on my nose and the wine I consumed simmering in my veins, I have an even better idea. I rub my nose onto his neck, smearing all the sugary goodness onto his skin. Lachlan freezes; his nostrils flare before a low groan sounds at the back of his throat.

I quietly whisper in his ear, "I'm saving it for later."

I hop up and dash out of his reach.

I walk past the large table full of food and to the smaller table that is filled with goblets of wine and pluck one from the table. There are smaller tables set up throughout the bay for people to gather and eat. Women pass out flower crowns, and the men gulp down their mead.

It's a true celebration of the power of light over darkness.

The longest day of the year.

My chest feels light, and my breathing comes easy. Men jump over the bonfire for good luck and the maypole gleams brightly in the light of the flames.

A small child with light blonde pigtails toddles up to me with a flower crown in her hands.

"My queen," she whispers shyly, holding the crown up to me.

A moment weeks ago, a very similar instance flashes in my mind, but no feelings of dread haunt me this time.

I smile broadly at the little girl and kneel in front of her. She places the crown upon my brow and runs away, darting back into the crowd.

I stand and realize the celebration has gone quiet, no drums beat, no people speak and all heads are turned, looking at me.

Lachlan chuckles wickedly behind me, and I whirl around to find him smiling down at me. "Ye just accepted the maiden crown, Key."

My brow creases. "What does that mean?"

His eyes slide up and down my body, and heat pools low in my belly. "It means that ye opened yourself up for suitors."

I swallow, my eyes going wide. I stammer out, "But—but I don't want any suitors."

He tips his drinking horn back and takes long gulps of the mead inside. His throat bobs with the movement, and I watch a single drop slide down his chin before he wipes it away with the back of his hand.

"I should think not. Because you're mine."

My whole body catches on fire. His words reverberate through me and the drums beat. Lachlan pulls me into a dance, our bodies flowing along together perfectly.

There's no hesitancy, no misstep, just the perfect gliding movement of two people who belong together. With my arms around his neck and his hands on my waist, I feel the heat of his body against mine.

His lips brush against mine and I allow myself to get swept away, knowing this moment won't last forever, but I will covet it for however long I can.

THIRTY-TWO

Weeks later, thoughts of Midsommar still dance around in my mind. But not right now, as my arms tremble at the force necessary to block Tane's strike.

Sweat drips down the side of his face and drops onto my outstretched arm.

"Gross," I mutter.

A flash of humor lights across his eyes before his face cracks into a wide smile.

"Lena"—he shakes his head—"you need to stay focused, *no distractions*, or it will cost you." His voice is light, but I heed the warning, anyway.

We break apart and walk together to the water table. I sheath my axe on my back. The past few weeks have passed in a flurry of meetings, training, and introductions. The only time I feel relaxed is when I'm on this training ground. It seems like every day a new family arrives, and a tent is erected.

"Thank you for all your instructions and the new houses look great," I say after throwing back an entire glass of water.

Tane has been a tremendous help not only with keeping me

on a rigid training schedule but also with housing logistics. Several of the new timber homes were built by his very hands. Thatched roofs and sturdy timber constructions, are the perfect fit for some of the warriors with smaller children. The rest of our population has had to make do with the tents.

"It's what the rebellion needed. I'm more than happy to help." He shrugs.

But something glimmered in his eyes with the word 'rebellion.'

"Have you ever been a part of a rebellion before?" I ask hesitantly.

Tane turns to look at me, but his eyes are a million miles away. The breeze that floats between us does nothing to cool off the intensity of his gaze.

"I'm sorry. I shouldn't pry," I say apologetically.

But Tane just shakes his head before gruffly clearing his throat.

"I was a part of a rebellion once, and I died there protecting my people and our land."

His words are heavy.

"Mathilda said she was the Valkyrie who brought you here."

At my words, Tane's face relaxes, and he tips his head to the sky, closing his eyes and embracing the sun.

He sighs deeply before continuing. "I thought there had been a mistake. My soul was supposed to journey to Hawaiki. But when she broke through the clouds, I held my last breath. It was like looking into the sun. Her face, it was light and warmth, and every good feeling I'd ever felt before. I didn't know pain in the end; I had died a warrior's death, and she was my reward. She took my hand, asking if I wanted to join her, and then brought me here. She explained to me what my duty now was. But none of it mattered; I would have gone anywhere or done anything she'd ever ask."

His revelation has me gasping for air; *he loves her.*

Tane shakes his head lightly. "But it doesn't matter; I'll never be worthy of her."

My brow furrows, and disagreement is on the tip of my tongue when Lachlan walks through the archway.

"I thought I'd find ye guys here," he calls out to us.

I wave but glance over my shoulder at Tane. "You're wrong, you know? *You are worthy.*"

He smiles sadly at me.

"You guys finished already?" Lachlan asks us.

"Aye, I think she's had enough of me," Tane jokes.

But his words still weigh heavily on my thoughts. It's not my place to tell Mathilda, but I *desperately* want to. I know she feels the same way about him, and in the chaos of our world, more love couldn't hurt.

Lachlan stares quizzically at me and my own feelings towards him bubble to the surface.

"I could do some more sparring if you're game?" I ask him.

His grin is wicked. "I've just finished meeting the blacksmiths, and the new arrows have me itching to fire some. Want to do some target practice?"

I bite my lip, knowing I've outshot him every time we've practiced so far.

"Of course," I reply. From checking on our weapons supply, population logistics, and even tents for the healers, Lachlan has been a godsend. I don't know if I would have gotten anything done without him.

"How're the councilors settling in? Do you have any new information?" Tane asks.

The information we've gathered from the new arrivals has been troubling. Odessa and Julius spin more lies, claiming that the ill omens are, in fact, signs that I will bring about the destruction of our realm.

Cynane, Boudicca, Leif, and Satiah have officially joined our ranks. Joan was one of the last to arrive, and with even worse news. The Idir tree in the middle of the old square is rapidly dropping leaves, and limbs have begun crashing down onto the surrounding garden.

If the tales are correct, that means the Fomorians have gathered a rather impressive army. Flocks of birds have also been spotted dropping dead in mid-flight, freak storms pop up over the capital, and skirmishes between clans are occurring more frequently.

The civil unrest has been one of the angles we have worked in our favor to bring warriors here. Offering them an outlet for rising tensions and a variety of training grounds was exactly what they needed.

"No news, and everyone seems to be getting along well. It's amazing what people can do when they're united under a similar cause," Lachlan replies.

His gaze is heavy on my fledgling wings. Initially, we had assumed the silvery hue was just because they were new, but they're only getting darker.

They aren't the iridescent white of the other Valkyrie's; but a unique silver.

The color resembles the sun reflecting off the North Sea we once crossed together. We walk towards the archery area at the far end of the training grounds, but our steps falter when two large shadows spear across our path.

Elowen and Mina dive from the sky, slamming into the ground just mere feet from us. The look of sheer anger blazing from their eyes sets my teeth on edge.

Before I can even ask, Elowen speaks first. "I have news from Odessa," she begins.

Mina cuts her off, agitation bristling from her, and her wings flare. "Not news, *a summons*. She requests your presence at the Great Hall."

Lachlan snorts while rolling his eyes. "She can summon all

she wants, but Lena is the queen, so she can decide not to answer if she wants."

He crosses his arms as if that solves the matter, and my lips twitch at his support.

Elowen sighs, impatience flickering across her eyes. "She found out I'm behind the mass exodus of citizens who fled from the capital. I can't go back."

Shit.

"Well, that was bound to happen. It's fine. Those who haven't left probably made up their minds, anyway. But I'm not going back, not yet. We're not ready." Elowen's face is filled with relief at my response. "Actually, this is perfect. Now that you're here, we can begin training as a unit," I reply, looking from Elowen to Tane and Lachlan.

"That's a great idea. Let me round up Mathilda and Evander," Tane replies and jogs from the grounds back towards the castle.

THE SEVEN OF us are standing as a group on the training grounds. The sun filters through large fluffy clouds and dirt kicks up in the wind. A huge part of my job has centered around my ability to delegate to those who have the best ability for the task, and knowing next to nothing about battling as a group, I look at Lachlan.

"Captain, this is your area of expertise. Lead the way."

Lachlan steps forward, clasping his hands behind his back as he walks back and forth in front of us. His broad tan shoulders gleam in the sunlight that shines through a gap in the clouds and I stifle a sigh. Seeing him as he is now makes me question why I ever thought he was human.

This man is a warrior, a highly trained and skilled one at that.

"The first step is going to be placing ye next to someone ye already work well with. For instance, Evander and I ha' years of training together under our belts, so we work well side by side. We ken each other's rhythms, strengths, and weaknesses. Partner up with who ye think ye'd work the best next to," Lachlan orders.

Tane and Mathilda take a step closer to each other, while Evander and Mina do the same.

"So we need to ken where to place Lena and Elowen," Lachlan mutters, gazing at me before his eyes shift to Elowen.

Lachlan has her spar with Mina first.

Where Mina is sharp and fast, Elowen is intentional and severe. They both work like opposite sides of the same coin.

"Ye two naturally reflect one another," Lachlan says as Elowen blocks one of Mina's blows.

I smile next to Mathilda as I watch them spar.

"They're so fast," I whisper to her as their swords clash.

But Mathilda's eyes are haunted. "They both have faced terrible things, different, but terrible. It makes sense that their fighting styles would reflect that."

I swallow her words and begin seeing their styles for what they really are.

Mina survived torture and had to think on her toes to get through it. So now her fighting style is built on speed.

Whereas Elowen suffered alone and had time to think out each plan to survive. Each of her maneuvers now are intentional and thought out.

Lachlan calls them to a stop.

"I think ye two would be best together, coupled with Evander's strength, which leaves Lena," he says, turning to look at me.

His eyes rake up and down my body and my blood heats before I can get a grip on myself. "Lena spar with Mathilda, I want to check something out," he orders.

Mathilda and I step forward and into the place that Elowen

and Mina just vacated. My muscles are still loose from my training with Tane, but I retie my hair back into a pony while Mathilda stretches her arms and bends down to touch her toes.

"Ready?" she asks, after she finishes stretching out.

"Ready," I reply, pulling my axe from the sheath on my back and bracing my feet.

We've spent the last few weeks training together, so I know that she favors attacking first and then sinking into a defensive position so that I'll eventually tire myself out before she comes in at the end, having rationed her strength to finish me off.

It doesn't matter how many times we work together or if I see her moves before she does them, I always manage to fall into the habit of attacking and running out of steam. We slowly circle each other before the sight of her slashing out at me blasts through my mind, but almost instantaneously it's happening and I barely manage to bat her advance away.

Mathilda smiles fiendishly. "Come on Lena, you know you want to play," she teases.

I roll my eyes, sucking in a breath. "Not today."

"Let's go, ladies," Lachlan barks as we continue circling each other.

The stern command in his voice has my body trembling. Mathilda attacks while I'm mid-tremble, the vision happening a split second before. The blade of her sword glances off the blade of my axe and then I'm swinging it around back at her.

Mathilda is not only powerful but lightning-quick, so I have to center my thoughts to use more of my power. Unfortunately, my capabilities are still not as powerful as I need them to be. She swings out while I'm still fully extended and off balance, knocking the axe from my hands.

If I had another weapon, I might have stayed balanced and been more of a challenge for her.

She grins wickedly at me but picks up my axe and hands it to me hilt first. "You're getting better."

As I take my axe from her, I grin in return. "I have great teachers."

"That you do!" Tane calls from his vigil by the fence.

Lachlan studies us as he crosses his arms. "I think you two would be great paired together. But Mathilda and Tane have history together."

Mathilda's cheeks heat and I cough loudly while staring Lachlan down. But he ignores me. "Alright, here's how we should line up Tane, Mathilda, Lena, me, Mina, Evander, and Elowen," he calls. We get in position. "Let's take a few laps around the ring in this position. I want ye to get comfortable with the person next to you. Their movements and breathing."

At first, the sounds of our feet are a jumble of out of rhythm and trampling footfalls as we circle the ring. But soon our footsteps begin to thud in line and we run together, as a team. We make several passes before Lachlan calls for us to stop and we pause to rest.

"Let me get a group of warriors together for us to practice against," he calls over his shoulder before heading off to the other side of the grounds.

THIRTY-THREE

It takes a few days for us to get the hang of working together. At first, we struggled with staying in line together. Mathilda and Tane would blast through their opponents too quickly, leaving a gap in our right side and the rest of us would quickly become besieged.

Then Lachlan and I struggled with our timing. I faltered from the visions slowing me down, or getting used to using my sword and axe. He'd already be too far ahead to give aid and then the rest of our line would fall.

By the third day, we finally got our timing down.

Mathilda and Tane became in sync with Evander and Mina on the opposite side, while Lachlan, Elowen, and I would spearhead the enemies in the center. We worked in one swift, fluid motion.

As a team.

Today is a test, a big one.

As we face off against the leading unit of warriors. They've been training together since before the rebellion was established. A combination of the Affric Clan and the Fairhairs.

They're an eclectic mix of different-sized warriors and fighting styles, our most difficult challenge yet.

For once, my mind is still and the task at hand centers me in a way that is foreign, yet familiar. As if I was born to do this. I focus on my wings and vanish them as we line up facing each other. I'm still not accustomed to their weight when fighting and we'll need every advantage we can get today.

The lithe Fairhairs are situated on their flanks while the robust Affric warriors are to be the battering ram at their center. The grounds are quiet and still, even the breeze has halted.

Leif's voice booms. "The winner is whoever can push their opponent past the 'defeat lines' drawn on either side in the dirt. Ready?"

Battle cries ring out and Lachlan bangs his swords against his shield. Lief grunts and then loudly blows on the horn.

The Fairhairs immediately begin attacking our flanks. Unfortunately, they have sorely underestimated Tane and Mathilda.

They incorrectly assume that because of their size, they would be slow. And they are immediately caught off guard by the speed and efficiency of which they are met. Mina and Evander also match the Fairhairs on their side in quickness and agility.

A vision sparks in my mind's eye a beat before the battering ram of the Affric Clan begins their assault on our middle.

"Shield!" I order.

Maces and clubs thunder against the shields as Elowen and Lachlan hoist into place, protecting the three of us from the blows.

As the reverberation dwindles away, they remove our shields and we meet them blow for blow. When I stumbled from a vision coming too slowly, Lachlan and Elowen are there to pick up the slack and so forth.

All of us moving as extensions of each other.

The sounds of weapons clashing and heavy breathing are the only sounds for long moments as the battle rages on and we push our opponents back. My strength not faltering as I attack with both my sword and axe. Slowly we begin gaining ground and with each step, force them across the line of defeat.

The battle is officially ended by three short horn blasts from Leif.

My breath saws out of my lungs and my entire body aches with the effort that training demanded, but I smile broadly. Pride pulses strength into my sore limbs.

"We did it." I smile.

Lachlan throws a slick arm around me and returns my grin. "We did."

"Thank you all so much!" I yell to the Affric and Fairhairs warriors who trudge from the ground. I was met with a few waves, but mostly grunts.

"That was our best training yet," I say to the group as we gulp our waters by the refreshments table. "How are the other units faring?" I scan the warriors as they leave.

"They still ha' a ways to go," Lachlan answers. "I've been working on partnering the Northmen with the Roman legions Marcus brought, but it's been a challenge. There's bad blood between a few of them that span centuries," he mutters.

Why Odin saw fit to bring enemies to a single realm and expect peace is beyond me.

I chuckle. "Yeah, I expected that. Any skirmishes, though?"

Lachlan shakes his head, but it's Evander who answers. "Not really. There's a growing feeling of time running out, so the consensus is we need to work together and quickly."

It has been too quiet.

There's been no news about Odessa and Julius, or how they feel about the fact that most of the capital now resides here.

My anger towards them has also shifted into something else, something quieter.

"And how do you all feel?"

"It does feel like something is coming," Elowen mutters.

Mina sweeps her hair out of her face. "Well, I'm ready to take back your throne whenever you are ready."

I smile at my friend, so eager for retribution.

"Elowen's right," Tane replies. His braid sways slightly as he shakes his head. "I do feel like something is coming, but I'm not sure we should be storming the capital any time soon."

"Why is that?" I ask, my face reflects my confusion.

"We've only recently solidified our ranks and have begun working together as units. We need more time to make sure we have all the kinks out."

"That is correct. Most of our guards had trained together for years before they began working efficiently as a team," Lachlan answers.

"But we don't have years. We might not even have months."

Mina jumps in. "How long do we continue building our ranks and strengthening our rebellion before we attempt to take back Lena's throne, then?"

"Ideally before war breaks out," Mathilda grumbles, but freezes.

"I think she'll want to storm the capital now," Elowen whispers.

"And why is that?" Lachlan asks.

Mathilda and Elowen share a look, a flicker of fear passing between them before pointing at the sky, and that is when we see it.

The sky that is rapidly darkening.

The clear blue becomes an eerie silvery gray. I stare up at the sun but shield my eyes just enough to see a circle of blackness beginning to devour its golden light.

"It's an eclipse," I whisper.

I shoot a concerned look at Lachlan, whose face mirrors my own. My wings pop back out as I need their familiar weight centering me.

"Has there ever been an eclipse here before?"

But no one answers as the moon continues its orbit over the sun.

Through quick breaths, Elowen says, "Tell me I'm imagining things." Her voice pitched a bit higher than usual. Fear, *genuine fear*, shines in her eyes.

I shake my head, the movement ruffling the feathers on my fledgling wings.

The moon fully eclipses the sun, and the surrounding land is pitched into darkness. Only light blazing from the torches around the training ground illuminates our faces.

"The wolf will devour the sun, plunging the realm into darkness; the stars will vanish from the sky, and the war will begin," Elowen whispers.

Her voice is hauntingly beautiful as it casts a chill in the air. Tane swears colorfully under his breath. Lachlan's hand finds mine, and we interlace our fingers. His callouses scrape against mine as we watch Elowen's vision come to life before our very eyes.

Her words ring in my ears: *'War will begin.'*

If war is beginning right now, we're not even close to being ready. We're still divided as a realm, seeing as I've taken more than half our people for the rebellion. I've made us weak by dividing us.

Guilt drops into my stomach.

"We're not ready," I mutter. "We need to unify our realm," I say louder. "I need to take back my throne. *Now.*"

Lachlan gently squeezes my hand. "Key, they tried to kill ye." He shakes his head. "We just discussed our ranks not being ready. And even if they were, we canna launch a full-scale invasion that quickly. Are ye just gonna waltz in there alone?"

Mathilda hums her agreement. Emotion sticks in the back of my throat, and I swallow forcefully.

"But now our realm is divided at a time where we very much need to be unified," I answer. "We'll have to go with just the seven of us."

THIRTY-FOUR

The sound of many booted feet thud along the grounds heading in our direction. Agatha appears with several warriors, each one carrying a torch.

Her voice carries out across the grounds to our group. "I figured I'd find you and your court here." She hands out torches to Evander and Tane. "If you're insistent on returning to that snake hole, you'll need to be dressed for battle, my queen; follow me."

The land is as black as night, but there's not a star in sight. Night-blooming jasmine floats along the breeze. The darkness blankets us as we follow Agatha and her troop back to the castle. Shadows slither along the path as the wind picks up, whipping the torch flames around.

Eclipses are a normal celestial occurrence in the human realm, but here, it certainly feels like one of the more sinister omens. Lachlan's expression is grim from the slight glimpses I catch in the flickering light.

The weight of my gaze has him turning to face me, pulling us to a stop.

"I dinna think ye realize the weight of this decision."

His posture is rigid, and his grip on my hand is strong. I flex my fingers, and he loosens his hold immediately, shooting me an apologetic look.

"I don't want to go back there either, but I have to try." His jaw flexes at my words, but I continue. "We could very well be wrong about Odin being trapped somewhere, and he's just busy gathering the rest of his forces from the other realms. But Elowen said her vision meant *soon*, and now it's happening. Just like she said." I try to make my voice light, joking even but fail miserably.

"I canna lose you," he announces. His eyes glitter in the fading torchlight.

I cup his face with my palm, the stubble of his beard grazing my fingers. "And you won't," I breathe.

He dips his head lower and rests his forehead against mine. I tilt my chin up until our lips touch. Our kiss is light, gentle in a way that eases the burn.

The world around us disappears until it's only just him and I.

There's no war, no impending battle for my throne.

Just us two and the serenity of this moment.

Someone politely clears their throat. The sound plunging us back into the present. Lachlan wraps his hand around mine and we walk side by side towards the castle.

Our friends stand just outside the door, having not gone too far without us. That small gesture of loyalty has some of the tension leaving my shoulders. I've surrounded myself with an entire group of friends. A group who became my advisors, too, and I seek out their wisdom with each new challenge we face together.

In the face of so much chaos, it's kind of funny that my journey led me to something I had wanted all my life, *friends*.

Darkness gives way.

Losing its battle with the light as the sun slips out from behind the moon's shadow.

The land is now an ashen gray as we enter the back doors of the castle. The silence that greets us is unsettling, in contrast to the usual liveliness of these halls.

A shiver walks its way down my spine. The castle is entirely hushed; people are lined up at the windows. Mouths firmly shut in mute horror as they observed the eclipse slowly fading away. It has never not been a flurry of activity in this place since the moment we arrived, but right now, time has stopped. Our boots thudding across the floor are louder than any beating drum.

A looming sense of dread hangs over my head like the proverbial sword about to fall, and I breathe through the rising sense of panic.

I can do this.

I can face Odessa and Julius and convince them to see the reality of this situation. *Or I will defeat them.* Hopefully, the eclipse will help them see reason and that their intentions are not as insidious as we had begun to suspect.

Agatha makes a right at the top of the second-floor landing and enters the library. Silver light spills in from the lancet windows and we make our way to the back of the room, pausing in front of a painting I've admired before—of a Valkyrie.

A golden crown of feathers resting upon her brow, her copper hair flowing out around her, as she sits astride a soaring white stallion. Her muscular arm is out raised as she clutches a golden spear in one hand, and an axe, identical to mine, in the other. The hilt of flying ravens held firmly by her chest. The first time I saw it, her wings reminded me of the *Winged Victory* statue in the Louvre.

Agatha gazes at the painting, her eyes sparkling. "This is the Goddess Victoria, the mother of Valkyries."

She strokes the golden frame of the painting, and a click sounds before the painting springs forward on a hidden hinge. The warriors beside Agatha fan out on either side of the hidden pathway, guarding our backs as we duck under the sparkling amethyst archway and inside.

"What is this place?" I whisper, following close on her heels.

The air in the hallway isn't damp or musty like one would expect from a hidden tunnel, but light and floral. The air shimmers. Breaks of light pierce across the dark path and fresh air wafts through the open grates on either side.

"We had to hide your family jewels somewhere, dinna we?" She chuckles at my startled expression.

Family jewels? *My family?*

Torches spring to life as we pass, lighting our way as our footfalls reverberate on the stone floor and walls around us.

"How is this possible?" I ask, as another torch springs to life. "I thought magic was waning in our realm? I've never seen anything like this before."

I definitely would've recalled magically lit torches instead of the memories of seeing servants carry torches to light the candles around the castle. "This place has always had a certain way about it." She grins. "I've noticed it becoming more awake since the Midsommar festival, but I figured it had something to do with you finally being home."

I marvel at each torch we pass, and Lachlan chuckles at my obvious amusement. I glance back to see Tane also looking bewildered, while Mathilda rolls her eyes at his childlike wonder.

Agatha stops at the end of the hall, where it opens up into a circular room, and I almost slam into her, still gawking at the large iron chandelier with at least a hundred candles flaring to life above us.

Candlelight is reflected in tiny rainbows from the cases all around us. Lined up all around the stone chamber are at least twenty glass cases, all bursting with millions of jewels. My gasp is echoed between the women while the men let out low whistles.

"This"—Agatha whirls in place—"is all yours."

My jaw drops.

Lachlan chuckles and presses a kiss to my temple before murmuring, "Whoops, another surprise."

I close my eyes briefly, savoring the feel of his lips against my skin before I'm brought back to the present.

Turning in place and taking in the spectacle of my family's wealth, my eyes bulge. How is this possible? There must be thousands of jewels in this room. Where did it all come from?

My eyes spin around, landing at the back of the room, tucked away in a small corner on the wrought iron stand supporting dazzling, webbed chain-mail armor attached to a silver chest plate and shoulder guards, the silhouette obviously designed for a woman. A silver helmet crowned with golden wings is perched on top of the stand, and a shield emblazoned with poppies is propped up next to it.

My mother is the reason I'm here, the reason any of this is here. My eyes begin to water as I realize Agatha's intentions by bringing me here.

She gestures to the stand. "This was your mother's,"—she pauses, looking back at me—"and I know she would be honored for you to wear them." I feel a pang in my chest at yet another moment my parents will not get to see.

But the emotionally tense moment is abruptly shattered by Tane loudly asking, "Oi"—his accent heavy—"did you even see the swords?"

Followed by what I swear is him prancing in front of a glass case wedged full of swords, daggers, throwing knives, and even a broad sword. I chuckle while walking over to the glass case full of weapons that he's still pointing at.

All of them are works of art, with engravings and jewels on their intricate hilts. Evander mirrors Tane's excitement with a whistle, his eyes growing wide while pointing out a particularly stunning dagger that has black jewels encrusted on the hilt.

But a small dagger encrusted with sapphires set into carved waves draws my attention. The waves are extremely detailed and remind me of the waves I surfed with my dad in California. I close my eyes, wishing for just one more afternoon in the ocean with him.

Mathilda peruses the jewelry and gasps when she sees a necklace that has a ruby the size of her fist surrounded by diamonds. "I can't believe I didn't even know about this place."

She shoots a look at Lachlan, who holds up his hands with an innocent gesture.

"Hey, I'm just a guard."

His blatant lie garners eye rolls and chuckles from the group. Studying the amour in front of me, I run my hand the length of the shield.

I'm flooded with memories of my mom. It's not unfathomable to imagine her carrying this shield now that I know what a force of nature she was here in this place. Pieces of my memory stitch together with who I knew her as in the human realm and with who she was here, creating a complete picture of the woman she was. It makes sense; she was always otherworldly to me; it's nice to know my assumptions were correct all along.

My necklace pulses slightly, the warmth chasing away the chill in the room.

But Lachlan breaks my train of thought. "I hate to rush ye, but we need to hurry back. It's going to take a while to get the group ready to leave, and I assume ye want to have this confrontation with your aunt sooner rather than later?"

I nod.

Agatha begins dismantling the stand and handing me the armor. Once in my hand, I marvel at how light it actually is, and up close, I can see that there's a pattern engraved into the chest and shoulder plates, poppies, of course. I look up at Agatha. Her face is serious yet kind, and she places the helmet crown on my head.

Time slows to a stop.

I hold my breath, and everyone freezes in place.

The weight of the crown is heavy on my brow, not just from the metal, but the weight of my new responsibilities. It's as if they're tangible in the metal. It's not unbearable, but it definitely makes itself the foremost priority in reorienting my balance.

I can feel the ripples of this moment race outward, and despite myself, I wonder if Odessa can feel the impact all the way in the capital.

Agatha clears her throat. "There's one more thing." She walks up to a case that is hidden in the shadows. "This was your father's."

She pulls a single item from the darkness, a sword that mirrors the sapphire dagger. It is long but lean, and the weight is comparable to the sword I've been using alongside the axe.

The blade is made up of layered steel, distinct markings ripple along its surface. I meet Agatha's eyes and her mouth parts as if there's more she's about to say, but she shuts it quickly, nodding before turning on her heel and leading us from the vault.

THIRTY-FIVE

Mathilda, Mina, and Elowen helped me carry the armor up to my room. My bed is strewn with armor and our weapons. The moment feels bleak compared to my time getting ready to go out with Mathilda, but similar all the same. The candles lit around the room cast shadows, but the sparse light is a warm glow.

There's a comfortable silence as we're each lost in our own thoughts, mentally preparing for the battle ahead. The only sound in the room is that of clothes being shed and armor being donned.

The metal of the chain-mail clinks together lightly as Mathilda hoists it up over my head and waits patiently for me to concentrate on vanishing my fledgling wings. They're just as long as my unbound hair and the silver feathers have begun growing in length.

I sigh as they vanish and I immediately miss their weight. I wish my parents had been here to see them. I smile sadly to myself while imagining a younger me flying with her mother. My wings are not quite strong enough for flight yet, and I have to be very careful that a wayward draft doesn't buckle my fragile tendons.

According to Mina, that pain is excruciating.

Mathilda settles the chain-mail over my torso and straps the chest and shoulder plates into place. Her armor glints in the sunlight that streams in through the windows again. The brightness of the sun's rays is ironic given the shadows darkening each of our eyes. We stand there silently together.

Mathilda is the first to break the silence as she tightens the straps holding my armor into place. "How does that feel? Can you still raise your arms?" she asks.

I raise my arms up above my head and then back down to my sides with a quick nod. "We should have had you practice in your armor to get used to it. I'm sorry." She grimaces.

But I smile sadly in return. "We didn't have enough time."

Mina tightens the straps on Elowen's armor and then they switch places. Their movements are sure, as if they've done this a million times.

I suddenly feel very out of place.

Mathilda stalks to the bathroom and comes back with a vial of black kohl. "War paint?" she asks, looking around the room at us.

"Of course," I agree and move to stand in front of her. She smears a good amount around each of my eyes.

"May your blade be as fierce as Freya," she declares. The words settle into my bones. Mina is the next to have her war paint applied, followed by Elowen.

I grab the vial of kohl from Mathilda. "Your turn."

Mathilda's eyes narrow. "Make me fierce," she demands.

My smile grows. "You already are."

After I finish making her look like a warrior from a nightmare, we begin retrieving our weapons from the pile on my bed. My axe slides into the straps on my back while I sheath my father's sword at my side.

The responsibility of morale falls on my shoulders and I clear my throat.

"I would just like to say—" I take a breath looking around the room at my friends. "That it's been the honor of my life to be here and get to know you all." Tears begin glistening in Mathilda and Mina's eyes while Elowen looks down at her feet. I push on. "Before I came here, I didn't have very many friends and had always dreamed of having just one, and now here I am blessed to have you three." Mathilda sniffles. "I won't say I'll never make a mistake, but I vow to always strive to be the queen you all deserve."

Elowen quickly raises her head, her eyes meeting mine.

The usual striking blue color has turned a milky blue. *She's seeing something.*

"There's something wrong," she whispers. "We need to hurry."

She squeezes her eyes shut. Panic weighs my arms down, but I force it aside and square my shoulders. Elowen's eyes shoot open, and she looks between all of us. But there's a wildness to her gaze.

"Are you ok?" I ask.

She shakes her head, her strawberry blonde hair whipping back and forth. "Talons and fire."

The three of us share a look as Elowen covers her face with her hands.

"What does that mean?" Mathilda asks as she moves closer, placing a hand on Elowen's shoulder.

"One is not the same," Elowen whispers through her fingers.

Mina shivers lightly. "That is not ominous at all." Mathilda pats Elowen's shoulder gently.

"Elowen?" I whisper. "Is there anything more concrete you can tell us?"

But she shakes her head, shoulders slumping in defeat. Blood pulses quickly in my veins and my head pounds with her words.

But I take a deep breath, knowing the only way through this is forward. There's no going back now. War is on the horizon, and we are divided. If I can't pull the realm together, we will be defeated, and the human realm will be at risk.

My thoughts circle around Gran, Torin, Maggie, and Lizzie.

If I fail, how long would they survive against an invasion?

"That's ok, Elowen. We will face this together," I reply, my small bit of hope fizzling.

There's something still lingering in Elowen's eyes, but before I can ask, she pulls away from me. The confidence we had all felt with the application of our war paint, dissipates.

We're walking into a battle severely outnumbered. If Odessa has rallied the remaining warriors in the capital, we could be facing this battle with no hope of winning.

As we file out of the room, I push aside the negativity. I will not face this afraid. I will face this with my head held high and my friends at my side. We quietly make our way back downstairs. The only sounds are that of our armor clinking and our boots thudding against the wooden floor.

Tane, Evander, and Lachlan are waiting for us in the castle foyer. Their faces all show varying degrees of resolve; *they're ready.* I glance around for anyone to say farewell to, but it seems only our circle is in the castle.

A stillness seeps down the empty halls. I glance around at the stone walls decorated in tapestries of ravens, wolves, and longships. This is my home. I finally found my ancestral home, and now I have to leave it.

No. I'm not a victim; I'm a survivor.

I can choose how I react to this.

But my chest tightens at the thought of never returning. I push it aside and follow the others out the door. The silence follows me through the threshold and then pops as I enter the courtyard. It's completely filled with every person on the island, and my heart stutters to a stop.

The enormous crowd gathered in front of the castle fractures the silence with loud cheers and the beating of drums. I glance sidelong at Lachlan.

"What is this about?" I ask over the loud cheering; his smile burns away all my doubt and dread. He leans in to whisper into my ear, rain and cedar clearing my head.

"They've come to wish their queen farewell."

The realization squashes my doubt and fills me with hope.

"They truly support our cause," I whisper back to Lachlan.

He grins. "They truly support ye, Key." My eyes burn with tears as I take in the cheering people. Their faces reflecting their happiness and faith in me.

My heart pumps fiercely at the sentiment.

As we walk through the crowd, they throw blue and purple wildflowers at our feet. Shouts of well wishes for our safety reach my ears and I smile gratefully. Several warriors beat axes or swords against shields in a steady, comforting beat in line with war drums and our footsteps.

I wave to the crowd. Children squeal and wave while clambering onto their parent's shoulders for a better look at our court as we pass.

My people, these are truly my people. My mind flashes back to the parade when I first came here. Those cheers now seem forced compared to the ones now.

The support and loyalty that I've earned burn wildly through the crowd.

We weave our way through the cheering and to the horses that Agatha has saddled and ready to go for us. Evander, Mina, and Elowen opt to fly back to the capital, so the rest of us mount our horses a few feet from the portcullis. My armor is not the hindrance I assumed it would be as I grow accustomed to moving around under its weight.

Our hoof beats are thunderous as we gallop towards the beach. It was nothing but rolling green land and a few timber houses when we first landed here, but now the land is teeming with tents and newly built houses.

With each gallop away from my home, my anxiety rears its ugly head, but after a few rounds of mindfulness, I have successfully pushed it back. I send a silent thanks to Torin for not only growing my confidence on a horse but for teaching me how to still my mind in the face of so much chaos.

If I ever make it back to the human realm, I'll wrap him up in the strongest hug possible.

If I ever make it back, my mind repeats, but I battle the thought away.

I made my choice to stay here and serve this realm because serving this realm protects the humans. I release the lingering guilt and focus on the battle before us.

The sun is just beginning to set, a second darkness spearing for the land from behind the cliffs as we finally reach the bay. The glittering black sand kicks up around the horses before we dismount. Lachlan gathers our horses to lead them back to Agatha. She stays mounted on her horse.

A somber expression graces her face as she stares down at me.

"Listen to the Gods, Lena. *They will guide ye*. And above all, stay safe, my queen."

I nod my farewell and turn towards the boats before I think better of it and turn back to her.

"Thank you, Agatha, for supporting me." I cross a hand over my chest; the sign I've learned is the utmost respect between warriors here.

Her somber expression is replaced by a grateful smile. "I would ha' followed your mother anywhere. I will follow ye just the same. She would ha' been so proud of ye."

Her words fill my soul and lighten my chest.

"Thank you," I breathe. The emotion flows freely through me and I embrace it.

Agatha smiles broadly at me and takes the reins from Lachlan. She leads the horses back to the castle, leaving us alone on the bay; my eyes follow her before falling on my friends around me.

Lachlan interlaces my hand with his as he leads us to the long boat tied up offshore. He holds out a hand to help me onboard.

I stop and turn, looking back at this island that has become my sanctuary for the past several weeks. Tane helps Mathilda on board, subtly giving us a moment of privacy. We haven't even left yet, and the familiar pains of homesickness begin to stir low in my gut.

Lachlan's gaze is heavy on the side of my face and he gently squeezes my hand, sensing the turmoil swirling inside of me. "We'll be back home soon." I gaze up at him, soaking in the last few seconds of peace, and admiring the surety of his gaze.

He strokes his palm across my cheek. "I promise."

THIRTY-SIX

Idirhalla is an island of ghosts.

Silence lurks, and even the shadows seem to cower.

The capital island is a mass of darkness, except for a few blazing fires shining into the blackness when we breach the shores. Smoke overpowers the crisp sea air. Evander, Elowen, and Mina slink out of the shadows and help drag our boat onto land. The only sound is our boots sinking into the thick sand.

"Okay, so we need to make it from here." I mark an X on the sand as we crouch down on the shore. "To the Great Hall." I drag my finger in a winding motion. "Once we get there, we need to be prepared for a few different scenarios." Mathilda, Tane, and Lachlan nod along, already having heard my plan in the boat. "Hopefully, it will be a swift takeover, and they will just relinquish the throne; if that's the case, any guards that you trust need to set up a perimeter around the palace in case there is pushback from the citizens who have decided to stay." Evander's eyes flash to mine, the moon shining on his stern face. "But more than likely, this will be the first battle of many. Mina, Evander, Tane, and Mathilda divide the hallways amongst yourselves to guard against the reinforcements they will call in. Leave Odessa to me. Got it?"

In the dim light, Lachlan's eyes burn with rage. "Julius is mine."

Tane and Mathilda share a subtle smile. Mina grins wildly, the moonlight reflecting off her dark hair as she nods.

Evander stares up at me, pride lining his face before he slowly smiles. "Got it, Your Majesty."

Surprisingly, my nerves have yet to reappear, but the air around us seems to crackle with anticipation.

"Alright, let's stick together and follow the main road up. We'll work as a unit, but if it gets chaotic, we might need to split up and meet at the Great Hall by the training grounds."

As quietly as possible, we stalk from the shore and onto the road, using the buildings as cover. As we sneak up the main road, we come to some buildings that are partially ablaze or are already in smoldering cinders. I share a look with Lachlan. What happened here? Whole streets are pitch black, and where lanterns should have been lit, there's nothing but darkness. The destruction grows as we continue on.

"What the hell is going on here?" I whisper to our group.

Mina responds, "The eclipse must've brought the civil unrest to a head."

"But where are the guards?" Elowen asks, her brow furrowing. Wood cracks loudly from the devouring flames not too far from our hideout. The unexpected sound has me flinching. But that's the only sound. There are no other sounds, no screaming, no yelling of 'fire.'

There are no people at all.

Evander and Lachlan both wear masks of fury as they take in the ruins dotting the streets.

"Where are the people?" Mathilda whispers.

"I don't know—this is all wrong," I reply, looking around. "There's nobody here at all."

Lachlan shakes his head. "The guards should ha' been ordered to patrol." He pauses. "It should ha' never gotten this bad. I'm going to shift and fly ahead to check our path. Stay here," he orders. But nothing happens. His wings stay tattoos and his brow creases in concentration.

"What's happening?" I whisper.

He puffs his cheeks out with the effort before grunting. "I can't shift. There's something blocking my power." His breath comes out in a long whoosh.

"Has that ever happened before?" I reply quietly.

"Nae, I've never had issues performing before," he says, rolling his eyes.

I snort loudly at his obvious joke and then freeze, clapping my hands over my mouth before shooting a glare at him.

"This is not the time."

But Lachlan winks at me. "You needed a second to breathe."

He is right, and his joke eases some of the tension that had begun tightening my shoulders.

Growling rumbles from up the street and my stomach bottoms out. As the tallest, Tane has the vantage point we need to see over the building debris. "It's—holy gods," Tane swears. His skin goes a sickly pale color and his eyes widen with fear before narrowing into slits. "We're under attack."

My blood stills in my veins as I make eye contact with Lachlan.

"It's demons," Tane breathes, his face frozen in horror.

"Change of plans," I order. "We stick together and we work as a team. Mathilda and Tane, you guys take the right side of the street, Elowen, Evander, and Mina will take the left, and Lachlan and I will take the middle."

I've never faced anything remotely this terrifying in my life, but I force myself to stay calm and rely on my training.

Slipping out of our cover, we fan out on the street.

One heartbeat.

We're trampling through debris.

Another heartbeat.

We're hurtling towards the demons that have spotted us.

I want to scream. On the page they were scary, but in real life, nothing compares to the horror right in front of us. Their skin is the mottled gray of corpses with blackened veins visible beneath the lifeless flesh.

Their lipless mouths are stretched grotesquely wide and their pointed teeth gleam in the firelight as they hurdle over the flames. But their most petrifying feature by far is the hollow black pits of their eyes. No light reflects back from the depths of hellish darkness.

Like a wave crashing on the tide, our forces collide.

With a mighty scream, I slice my axe through the neck of the first demon I encounter. It's black blood sprays my face as it collapses to my feet. The warmth and odor are enough to make me gag, but the next demon is already racing towards me.

It manages to slash at me with its elongated claws. The sharpened talons screech across my metal breastplate, gouging deep scars into the metal before my sword thrusts through its belly. Its death scream pierces my ears and has me grinding my teeth as I push harder through its muscles and bones before withdrawing my sword.

The metal of my blade makes a grisly sound as it comes free. Its body crumbles to the ground before me and I whirl around, ready for the next, but there is none.

With a final savage swing, Lachlan decapitates the last demon of the pack. Its head squelches against the cobblestones. The smell is so putrid I resort to inhaling through my teeth to avoid the stench. I scan my friends to make sure we've all remained unscathed.

Mathilda kicks at the lifeless demon in front of her. Her face twisted with disgust. Tane's eyes are on her. Relief coats his features when he's satisfied she's uninjured and he steps over a corpse and towards her. There are three demon corpses littered around him. Mina wipes her throwing blades off on her leathers, smearing the black blood against her leather-clad legs.

Elowen stares ahead, her face set in a mixture of wrath and disgust. Evander is monitoring the street behind us, his blade still out in front of him.

"What the fuck was that?" I seethe.

Lachlan counts the lifeless corpses at our feet. "There are thirteen demons here."

Tane shakes his head. "How did they even get here?"

Mina pipes in. "And are there more?"

Silence pulses down the street, the only sound comes from the fire still consuming buildings.

"Let's push on," I order. As the others move forward, Lachlan pulls me to a stop, his eyes still shining with adrenaline from the battle. "Are ye okay?" His words are soft.

"I'm fine," I breathe out. My first real battle is now behind me.

"We got more incoming!" Mathilda yells.

We sprint to our positions in line with our friends. Creatures claw towards us as they cling to the walls of buildings that are still standing. Some are on all fours as they run. It's like there's a beacon on our position as they swarm us.

We're severely outnumbered. There are too many.

I glance to my right to see Mathilda, her knuckles turning white, as she grips her sword tightly in front of her. Tane is angled slightly ahead of her, his brow set in fierce determination. Lachlan's jaw clenches as he counts the horde heading towards us.

I look to my left. Evander has both swords out in front of him, ready. While his bow remains strapped to his back, waiting. Mina takes a deep, steadying breath, readying herself for battle. Elowen twirls her sword in her hand, a feral grin grows on her face.

They're upon us in seconds. We hack through the incoming horde. Bodies of the demon foot soldiers begin piling up at our feet as we push our way forward. But just as soon as we cut one down, two more take its place.

"They're coming from the Great Hall," Mina yells over the chaos.

I can't even chance a glance in that direction as a demon grazes its talon across my cheek. The ripping of my skin sharpens my senses as I force my blade through its neck.

"We need to get Lena and Lachlan to the throne room!" Mathilda shouts, and her blade cuts through the demon's skull in front of her.

"Evander, get to the roof and cover us!" Lachlan orders.

My eyes follow Evander as he slips out of the fray and towards the building to our right. An arrow knocked and ready.

A shove forces me roughly to the side and almost off my feet.

Elowen screams, the sound slicing over the sound of the surrounding chaos. I watch as her body disappears beneath trampling talons.

Mina and I converge over the gap Elowen and Evander's absence has caused. I hack and slash towards where I saw her body last.

She's fine, she has to be fine.

My breathing comes out choppy as I fight through the exhaustion rapidly slowing my movements. I'm too slow and a demon lunges for me before it stops in midair. Fletching from Evander's arrow pokes from between its eyes.

Blood rains across my face and the creature falls to the ground in front of me. On top of Elowen. My vision blurs. Blood gurgles from between her lips. Her gaze on the night sky above us. Lachlan yells my name as he runs my way, avoiding the dead bodies now piling up between us. I fall to my knees.

The impact of my bone against the stone shoots through me.

"Elowen," I cry.

We did it, we killed the horde. But at what cost?

I tug at her arm, pulling her from beneath the pile of monsters. She coughs and blood dribbles from the side of her mouth. I tug her to my chest. The metal of armor clangs. I inhale deeply and gag. The smell is horrendous.

A metallic stench that mixes with the mottled gray corpses around us. There's movement around us and fear lances through me before I realize it's just Tane, Lachlan, Mina, and Mathilda. Evander guards our position from the rooftop.

"Do something!" I shriek. Looking up into the grave and somber faces of our friends.

Tears stream down my face and Elowen squeezes my hand.

"There's nothing to be done," she rasps out.

My head slumps to my chest as I stare at her through my burning tears.

"Stay with me, please."

Blood pours from a slash across her throat. More seeping out when she tries to nod.

"It's an honor to die among friends." Her words come out gurgled and I have to strain to hear her past the cries of Mina and Mathilda. They hold each other tightly.

"You're not alone, Elowen. You will never be alone. We're all here."

My voice cracks as I force them out past the burning in my throat.

"You're not alone," I whisper.

She smiles faintly, her eyes turning glassy as her hand relaxes in my grip.

She's gone.

Tilting my head up to the sky, tears streak down my face, and I tighten my grip on her hand.

"You're not alone," I repeat.

Howls rent the air. They must scent her blood. A large hand settles upon my shoulder and I flinch.

Lachlan whispers in my ear, "I'm so sorry, Key, but we've got to go. We've got to move."

I stare down at her. She's so still. So small. Her eyes are still gazing at the night sky. The stars twinkling above us. The savage slash across her throat is the only evidence she's not sleeping peacefully.

"We can't just leave her here," I choke out.

"Let me take her." Lachlan's voice is only a whisper. It's like he's afraid to startle me. Afraid that I'll fall apart. But this isn't the first time I've seen death this closely.

I can barely manage to nod.

He sweeps her up off the ground. Holding her brutalized body close to his chest, and walks swiftly to the building on our right. I trail after them. My head held high as I whisper prayers for my departed friend. Tane swings the door open. His lips set in a grim line. Mina and Mathilda are on the other side, heads hanging, voices whispering prayers and goodbyes.

Clothes are hung on the walls of the shop. The smell of fresh leather and linen drifts around the room, cleansing my senses from the rancid scent of death on the street. Lachlan lays her gently on the rug in the middle of the room. I tug a cloak off a wooden hanger and drape it over her body before gently closing her eyes.

The growls outside are getting louder, closer. Footsteps thud against the wooden floor, heading back outside.

There's a gentle tug under my arm and I turn to look up into Lachlan's eyes. "We ha' to go. We—I need ye to push past this. We will grieve her together. After we finish this. Okay?"

My mind empties.

They did this. They killed her.

This woman whose only wish was to never be alone. Anger burns away my sorrow, sharpening my resolve. They will pay for this, for all of it. My parents, this realm, Elowen, all of it.

Lachlan gives an order to the rest of the group. "Lena and I are going to make a run for the capital. Kill as many as you can and meet us there."

And then we're off. Pushing my legs harder than I ever have before we sprint up the road. A creature shrieks in front of us before it's gurgling in its own blood, an arrow protruding from its neck. With each slash of my axe, Elowen's face burns in my mind.

With each demon we down, I get one step closer to making Odessa and Julius pay.

The whacking sounds of blades meeting flesh follow us up the road. A crack of a blade against bone makes my stomach lurch.

"We need to stick to the shadows," I breathe out in between pants.

My mind finally thinking past the pain. "We won't be able to face that many on our own if we run into another horde." Lachlan nods and we slow into a jog. We slink from shadow to shadow, the sounds of battle tapering off as we move further away from our friends. I send a silent prayer up to Odin to protect the rest of them.

Hopefully, he hears me.

We cross the second bridge over the Ayele and debris glide down the raging river. Clothes, building materials, and even crates of supplies, bob along the current. My teeth clack together. Working to control my breathing, fury rages through me.

"How could this happen?" I glare at the water below us.

The debris begins swirling when it meets the rapids by the rocks. Lachlan shakes his head, his movements jerky from rage. Where are the guards? Why are demons just running amok?

Fire crackles from the building beside the river and we finally reach the foot of the stairs.

The smoke grows dense as we hit step two hundred that it blots out the stars above us. My legs burn and I choke on a cough as we crest the last stair and I prepare myself for the sight of a massacre.

But there's nothing.

My feet echo loudly against the marble floor. If they didn't know we were here before, they do now.

"My dear, sweet niece." Odessa purrs across the hall. She lounges on the throne, my throne. I freeze at the sound and ball my hands into fists. "How fortunate that you timed your arrival just hours after the eclipse you undoubtedly caused."

Her voice is intrusive as it prods at my mind.

A shadow moves next to her and Julius materializes beside the crystal chair, a crown of what looks like black tentacles upon his brow. He cuts a very intimidating figure in his loathsome black leathers. Moonlight illuminates the perpetual sneer carved on his face.

I know the plan was for me to attempt diplomacy first, but Elowen's death, the destruction of my home, and the demons we just faced have me sliding my feet apart, readying for battle.

Odessa and Julius act casual, relaxed, even. Like there are not demons roaming our streets. Either they don't know about them, or they don't care.

"You called for me." My voice rings out and the authority of my words has her shifting in her seat. She must have expected the old me, the people-pleaser. Not the new Lena that was forged when she allowed her mate to attack me.

The woman standing before her now is the very person who claimed Odin's axe and was deemed worthy. The same person who just faced a demon horde and made it out the other side.

"Yes, I've called to send you home," she replies nonchalantly while shrugging her delicate shoulders.

I glance at Lachlan, and he crosses his arms over his blood-splattered chest, not at all believing anything that spills from her venomous lips.

"I thought it was impossible for me to go home until power was restored?"

I sheath my sword and begin walking towards the throne. Lachlan follows and we stop just a few feet shy of the throne, leaving blackened footprints in our wake.

Heavy footsteps and metal clinking sound from the doorway. Tane, Mathilda, Evander, and Mina breach the throne room.

They're all in one piece. Relief has my shoulders lifting.

Lachlan knocks a boot against mine, urging me to focus. I turn back to face my aunt.

We stand directly under a shaft of moonlight that pours through the open ceiling.

Odessa glares down at me, scrutinizing my new armor and the blackened blood that coats most of me. I stare her down. My lip curls as I take in her black dress that is sheer. Her naked body visible underneath the fabric that looks as if it were spun from cobwebs.

There's a glint in her onyx eyes as she scrutinizes the color of the blood on us and her face cracks into a satisfied smile. So she is aware of the demons, after all. The smell of festering rotten meat permeates this end of the throne room, and my stomach churns in response. The madness within her is now written across her wild eyes, pursed lips, and arched brow.

She looks insane. A matching crown of black tentacles rests upon her brow as well. Her wings are nowhere to be seen, and a green light shimmers from her skin.

"Well we,"—she gazes at Julius—"have decided that your presence here has become a nuisance. We're either sending you back to the human realm or...." She trails off, shrugging, and brings her hand up to study her long black nails.

"Are you threatening to murder me?" I chuckle at her obvious intimidation tactic. "Again?"

Lachlan murmurs, so only I can hear, "Focus on her movements, not her words. She's trying to goad you into making a mistake."

Odessa's eyes slide to Tane and Mathilda where they have taken up positions on one side of the throne room and then to Mina and Evander on the other side. Their heavy breathing can be heard from where we stand.

One more fight.

One last fight and then the throne is mine and we will have secured our home. We just need to win this last battle and then this nightmare will be over.

"I do not tolerate idle threats," I grit out between clenched teeth.

Anger races through me at her threat and the hell of what I have already faced to get here. The life that they have cost me.

"I think you've misunderstood my presence here, Aunt," I say louder. "I have no intention of leaving or being murdered; I've come to claim my throne and fix the problems you've so obviously left to fester." I gesture towards the mud-splattered floors of the Great Hall, the dead demons in the streets beyond. The ghost of those battles blazing in my eyes. "I had hoped you would agree and relinquish the throne willingly after seeing the eclipse for yourself."

I take a breath, my voice softening a shade, when I remember that she is my family, my only family in this realm. "Odessa, please see reason. This goes beyond holding onto the throne. Look around you; the war is here. There are demons in our streets."

Odessa leans forward on the throne, resting her chin on her palm; a wicked smile grotesquely marring her face.

"Is that what you believe, Helena? That I've ignored the signs of the war, that I mistook them for the realm needing you? *No one needs you.*" She sneers. "I knew all along what the signs indicated."

My eyes narrow on her traitorous face, and she nods to

Julius. She rises from the throne, pulling a sword from behind the crystal chair. Diplomacy is no longer an option, family or not.

My rage at her willful neglect by allowing the realm—my realm, to go to shit, sends tingles down my arms.

"It's Lena," I grit out. I jerk the axe from the straps on my back. "*Or, Your Majesty.*"

CHAPTER

THIRTY-SEVEN

Wind tears through the throne room and Odessa halts a step away from the bottom. My necklace chills slightly before plummeting into frigid iciness. The bitterly cold temperature burns my skin.

Julius takes a small step towards Lachlan and then quickly lunges at me to catch us off guard. But Lachlan jumps in front of his path, deflecting the blow that was clearly meant for me.

I'm confused that I didn't see the move before it happened.

But if the guys can't shift, power here must be blocked entirely. Lachlan begins to slash at Julius, forcing him away from me.

Their blades clash together and echo throughout the throne room. Odessa lets out a low whistle, and demons begin surging in from the hallways, their claws scraping against the floor. Evander, Mina, Tane, and Mathilda jump into action, battling them back.

Odessa smirks at me as she saunters down the last step. "It's a pity it had to come to this."

I glare while squaring my shoulders and tightening the grip on my axe.

"Yeah, it's a shame you murdered my parents and turned out to be a raging bitch."

She freezes, her mouth stretching grotesquely wide. "Helena, such language is unbecoming of a *wannabe queen*."

I snort. "Oh, and murder is perfectly acceptable?"

She throws herself at me after she reaches the last step, and I easily bat her sword away. Her movements seem sluggish, and I'm not sure if it's just a tactic to get me to underestimate her or if it has something to do with magic not working.

Fighting her is easier than the demons we just faced, even without my powers. Her black sandals slide along the marble. She's too weak to even pick her feet up.

"We don't have to do this. Wouldn't you rather just face up to your crimes? I'm sure we can construct a prison or something for you both."

She rolls her eyes at my suggestion and slashes wildly with her sword. Her effort increases marginally, but there's still little force behind her attack. She's like a child playing with a sword that is far too heavy.

Julius and Lachlan are locked into a tumultuous battle across the throne room. Their violently colliding swords send tiny sparks bouncing across the floor.

A grunt of pain causes me to flinch, fear slicing through my focus.

I flick my eyes to their battle to confirm that it wasn't coming from Lachlan. But my brief assurance costs me. Odessa manages to graze her sword along my bicep. It's only a shallow cut, and it's more than worth the relief I felt at seeing Lachlan still moving and on his feet. Julius, however, seems to be waning.

Small droplets of my blood splatter onto the white marble floor. Odessa grins wildly at the shallow cut.

"Did I ever tell you how easy it was to kill your mother?" she hisses.

My entire body halts at her words. My blood boils, and I swipe at her with my axe with more force than before. Her eyes widen in horror as my blade narrowly misses her.

"Say one more word about my parents, and I will cut off your fucking head," I grit out as I deflect her sluggish lunge.

"Julius killed your father first, after it was obvious they wouldn't agree to our demands."

My stomach hollows out.

"Your mother wept like a child over his body. Neither one of them had even attempted to fight us."

My sight turns red, and a high-pitched ringing builds in my ears as I hack at her. Odessa scarcely manages to dodge and duck out of the way of my axe. My frustration boils over, and when I realize she's in range, I kick out, slamming my foot into her chest and knocking her down.

Her skull cracks against the marble floor, dark blood creating a halo around her raven-colored hair. I unsheathe my father's sword, the blade glowing in the moonlight spilling through the open ceiling. Odessa begins cackling like a mad woman.

The world around me withers away until the only thing I can hear is the words slipping from my lips.

"Do you have anything else you'd like to spew before I end your life?" I hold the point of my blade just above her chest. My blood hammers through my veins, red still coating my vision as my knees threaten to buckle.

She lays there laughing and wipes a stray tear from her cheek that spills over.

"You really think you're going to kill me?" she croons. "Not even your mother would have attempted to kill her own sister, and she was an actual warrior, born and bred. You? You're just a weak, pathetic girl that your own parents didn't see fit to raise here."

Her words slice through me.

I tip over the edge, blacking out.

My arm rears back before thrusting my sword through her chest.

I didn't have to push as nearly as hard as I thought I would to cut through her ribcage or sternum and into her heart. The metal of my blade clinks as it makes contact with the marble of the floor. The blackness ebbs away. My sight returns. I see why it took so little effort as her body began to twitch.

Smoke streams for her sliced-open skin and tendrils of it twirl around my blade.

A black oil-like substance spews from her body.

"Lachlan!" I shriek.

The writhing mass of flesh twists into something from my darkest nightmares. Footfalls thunder towards me. Julius is face down on the ground, Evander, and Tane holding him in place while he screams with rage. The demons that had been pouring in from the hallways, are now corpses littering the floor.

Their black blood is in puddles.

Lachlan skids to a halt beside me and watches the creature that was once Odessa writhe around the ground. Her golden skin shifting into blackish-green scales. Her raven hair fades to a brittle white and crumbles to dust around her.

What was once her beautiful, youthful face ripples and contorts into a grotesque serpentine monster.

I take a step back. "Is that what I think it is?"

The writhing body stills on the cold marble floor.

"It's an asphidra," Lach mumbles. He turns his terrified expression my way. "From Jotnar."

"The giant's realm?" I ask, kicking at the corpse to confirm it's actually dead.

My stomach heaves as its flesh gives a squelching sound, and black blood continues to ooze from the gaping hole in its chest.

Lachlan's expression turns murderous. "It's been shifted."

He storms towards Tane and Evander, where they have Julius's hands bound and leaning against the wall. A crack echoes through the throne room as a fist connects with his face. Blood gushes from his nose, and Lachlan grasps the torch beside his head. He wipes the blood pouring from Julius's nose and rubs it between his fingers.

The blood looks normal, but there's an odd silver sheen to it that I didn't notice until Lachlan held his fingers closer to the flame.

"Shape-shifter," Lachlan grinds out, and Julius begins to chuckle. His iridescent blood dribbles over his lip and down his chin.

"It took you long enough," he taunts. Blood coats his teeth.

I push past Lachlan and come face to face with Julius.

"Who are you? And what did you do to my aunt?" I scream into his face, but he merely shrugs.

"No one even noticed that this place was crumbling before their very eyes until it was too late. It was almost too easy to infiltrate this realm and begin dismantling it. I honestly don't know which was easier: kidnapping your queen and locking away your God or killing your pathetic parents." His declaration echoes through the Great Hall.

"You—you kidnapped the real Odessa *and* locked away Odin?" I ask, bewildered.

He only nods his confirmation, his eyes more hollow than I've ever seen them. His face cracks into a smile as he turns his eyes up towards the open ceiling.

My necklace begins rapidly pulsing.

An icy wind blows through the opening in the ceiling, dousing the torches and plunging us all into darkness. The smell of smoke from the torches and something sour permeates the air. The moonlight streaming in is the only light left, piercing the thick darkness in the Great Hall.

But the faint white moonlight shifts to a greenish color, and Lachlan presses a blade against Julius's throat.

"Don't ye dare move."

My necklace is still rapidly pulsing, and the hair on the back of my neck stands on end. "Lachlan," I warn.

My palms prickle.

Lachlan glances over to Evander and Tane.

"Go check that out," he orders, not leaving my side as he places himself between me and Julius, who begins chuckling louder.

The sound is full of malice, and in the faint light, is eerily sinister.

A heartbeat later, an explosion rips through the terrace, sending us sprawling backward towards the throne.

Our bodies collide against the marble floor, and flames erupt through the terrace passageway.

The blast causes my ears to ring, and I gasp for air as the wind is ripped from me.

From my prone position on the floor, I see the sky change to a brighter, more vibrant green, and then a blue light materializes from the middle and plunges straight into the Great Hall mere feet from Julius.

He wasn't impacted by the blast at all and stands unharmed, shrugging off his restraints before walking towards the blue light. I look around for help, but Tane and Evander are knocked unconscious, Mathilda and Mina are slumped against the wall, and Lachlan is struggling to rise onto his side.

A groan slips from his lips. He clutches his head.

Blood trickles from a gash on his temple. The sight of him hurt has me surging to my feet, past the splitting pain in my head.

I look around for any weapon in reach.

But I'm too late.

"Helena," Julius's voice slices through the ringing in my ears.

"You can have your pitiful throne back and I'll give Odessa your regards. Oh, and Skadi too when we breach the human realm."

He winks before vanishing into the light.

ACKNOWLEDGMENTS

I'm not even sure where to begin. There are so many people that helped through each step of the way. I guess the best place to start is the beginning.

Justin, I could not have been blessed with a more supportive partner. Thank you so much for not laughing in my face when I first told you I wanted to do this, for kicking it with the kids in double overtime when I needed to finish just one more chapter, and for the Mac, of course.

Jordan, dude, you are a real one. Reading every single crappy sentence I sent your way, watching the kids during the day while working so I could have a few moments to type things out. You are the best, best friend a girl could ever have and I love you so very much.

T, I couldn't have made it through the darkest days of my writer's block without you. From you sending me character art, helping me with my cover, and blowing up Facebook groups for advice for me because I refuse to get on Facebook. You're incredible.

The fabulous Kira, you are the world's best beta reader and none of this would have been possible without you. Your very gentle criticism for what was the most info-dumpy and error riddled first draft inspired me to keep going instead of giving up. From the bottom of my heart, thank you.

To my family, thank you all so much. From asking me about my book, cheering me on, and bragging about me to everyone you know. I wouldn't be here without you guys, and I love you all so very much.

Lastly, my children. If you guys are reading this, you must be much older now and I hope you know that it's never too late to follow those silly little dreams. Even if nothing comes of it, just go for it. You guys are my driving force behind each decision I made, and I am so proud of you guys.

www.ingramcontent.com/pod-product-compliance
Lightning Source LLC
Chambersburg PA
CBHW022002310726
48972CB00006B/1481